Ivan Vladislavić

Flashback Hotel

Early Stories

archipelago books

First published by Umuzi, an imprint of Random House South Africa, 2010

Archipelago Books
232 3rd Street #A111
Brooklyn, NY 11215
www.archipelagobooks.org

Library of Congress Cataloging-in-Publication Data
Names: Vladislavić, Ivan, 1957- author.
Title: Flashback Hotel / by Ivan Vladislavić.
Description: First Archipelago Books edition. | Brooklyn, NY : Archipelago Books, 2019.
Identifiers: LCCN 2018058740| ISBN 9781939810113 (paperback) | ISBN 9781939810120 (ebook)
Subjects: LCSH: South Africa--Fiction. | Short stories, South African (English)--21st century.
Classification: LCC PR9369.3.V57 A6 2019 | DDC 823/.914--dc23
LC record available at https://lccn.loc.gov/2018058740

Distributed by Penguin Random House
www.penguinrandomhouse.com

Cover art: Willem Boshoff

Flashback Hotel is made possible by the New York State Council on the Arts
with the support of Governor Andrew M. Cuomo and the New York State Legislature.
This publication was made possible with support from Lannan Foundation,
the Carl Lesnor Foundation, the New York State Council on the Arts, a state agency,
and the New York City Department of Cultural Affairs.

PRINTED IN CANADA

Flashback Hotel

Contents

Missing Persons

For my parents, Peggy and Steve

The Prime Minister is Dead

The Day They Killed the Prime Minister

They killed the Prime Minister during the winter.

I was ten years old. That year my parents and I moved to a house in a new suburb. Granny moved with us. Grandfather said he was too old to move, so he stayed behind in the old house. He gave us a post box and two plastic numbers for the gate, and wished us everything of the best in our new home.

It was an ordinary place. Three bedrooms, a lounge, a dining-room. No gnomes. No crazy paving. A reasonable path of solid cement from the front gate to the verandah steps. Laying the path was the first major task my father and I undertook.

When we moved in, the house still smelt of raw wood, fresh paint, putty. There was much to be done: the floors would have to be sealed, the fingerprints cleaned off the windowpanes, splatters of paint scraped off the tiles in the bathroom and the kitchen.

The garden was veld. The builders had simply fenced off a rectangle and cleared a patch big enough to put the house down on. The way to get the grass out is to attack the roots. You can't skoffel with a spade – it grows back. You have to work a fork in around each tuft, loosen the earth, stick a hose-pipe in among the roots, turn it on full-blast, blow the soil away. Then you pull on the grass until it comes out, roots and all, like a plug. Knock out the remaining soil against the ground, pile all the grass in the wheelbarrow, push it around to the compost heap at the back.

That's what my father and I were doing on the day they killed the Prime Minister. I was loosening the soil and my father was pulling the grass out. He was wearing his old army uniform, as he always did when we waged war against the garden. Granny was in her rocker on the front verandah, crocheting one of an endless pile of woollen squares which would eventually be herded together into a lopsided blanket. She was listening to the radio, silently, through a small earphone.

I was pushing a wheelbarrow full of grass around to the back. As I passed Granny, the rocker lost momentum, stopped. A brightly coloured square dropped to the floor. She hefted her large body out of the chair and stood swaying solemnly, still joined to the radio by the coil of flex. Then she bellowed: "The Prime Minister is dead! Some madman chopped him up with a panga!"

I carried that thought with me, like a peach pip in my cheek, as I pushed the wheelbarrow round to the back and tipped the grass into the hole my father and I had dug the weekend before.

I see now that the death of a Prime Minister has many consequences.

When my grandfather died he left us a suitcase. There was something in it for each of us. My father got a suit that was too big for him, and a pair of pruning-shears. My mother got some newspaper clippings and some photographs, old and cracked like leather. I got a pair of lucky nail-clippers given to my grandfather by an Italian prisoner of war.

When the Prime Minister died he left us a compost heap, on which practically anything would grow. Mealies grew there once, all by themselves. Granny speculated that Lazarus, who sometimes worked in the garden, must have thrown away the sweetcorn that she'd given him for lunch.

Once the Prime Minister was dead they started renaming streets after him, and stations, and schools, even pleasure resorts. Then they renamed our suburb after him. They wanted us to live in a monument. It was a new suburb, and no one minded.

When I came back around to the front with the empty wheelbarrow my father was standing to attention and my mother was holding a glass of sugar water to Granny's lips. She had unplugged Granny from the radio and turned it up so that we could all hear.

Granny finished a blanket that evening, during the seven o'clock news.

The Day We Buried the Prime Minister

We buried the Prime Minister in the spring.

My father and I were planting the orchard on that day. There were thirty trees in all. Three rows, ten trees in each. A platoon of trees, my father called them. The holes we dug were deep and perfectly round. We marked them out with a compass made of two nails joined by a piece of sisal string eighteen inches long.

My father loosened the earth with a pick and I shovelled it out of the hole. The ground was very hard and we had to soak it with water from the hose-pipe. Soon my hands and feet were covered with mud. As the hole got deeper the colour of the earth would change.

My father said he had desert sand in the turn-ups of his khaki pants, left over from the war. "Come," he would say to me, "hold your dixie here." Then I would cup my hands next to his hairy calves, and he'd peel back the turn-ups so that a trickle of sand flowed into my hands. "Dyed with the blood of patriots," he said, if the sand was red, and "Bleached white as bone by the desert sun," if it was white.

Granny was sitting in her rocker, under a beach umbrella, with the radio on her knees. At three o'clock they were going to cross live to the funeral. We would have a running commentary of the whole procession from the church, through the streets of the city, to Heroes' Acre at the cemetery.

"Numero Uno!" Granny shouted. "Rotting in the soil. A piece of meat. Shame. He leaves a wife and six children."

"He leaves more than that," my father said. And then to me: "Get in the hole, Private."

The holes for the fruit trees had to be four feet deep. I was the measuring-stick: when I stood in the hole the ground had to be level with the top of my head. We put rocks in the bottom of the hole for drainage, then compost, then a layer of sand sieved through an old mesh gate. Then smaller stones. More compost and more sand. Each layer of sand had to be thoroughly watered. When the hole was almost full we chose one of the saplings that stood ready in the shade next to the house. We left the name tag on each tree so that we would know which was which until it bore fruit.

All the trees grew except for the fig-tree, third from the right, in the back row. It didn't die either. It just stayed exactly the way it was when we put it into the ground.

My grandfather came once a year after that to prune the trees. Each time he would stop before the stunted fig-tree and shake his head. But he said that it was good that one tree failed: the earth should never be too kind. It spoiled people.

After he died we let the trees grow wild. We were sick of peaches and plums, and chutney, and jam. We let the weight of the fruit snap the branches and we let the fallen fruit rot into the ground.

"I'm pleased the old man isn't here to see this," my mother would say.

At a quarter to three my mother brought out tea and a plate of biscuits.

"You know," she said when we were drinking the tea, "this funeral is a big occasion. We're not likely to see another like it in our lifetimes."

"Unless they kill the new Prime Minister," my father replied.

"Don't speak like that in front of the child," Granny said sternly.

"It won't harm him if it's true," my father said. "They're pulling out all the stops on this funeral. Massed bands, tanks, a fly-past of jets. Every citizen issued with a flag, every building draped in crêpe. A twenty-one-gun salute. Now if they kill the new Prime Minister, and I think this is not unlikely, they'll have to do the same, won't they? It wouldn't do if they gave the next Prime Minister a half-hearted send-off."

"That may well be so," my mother said, "but the point is that we shouldn't think that way. You can't go through life taking the great events of history for granted. When one comes along you've got to grab it with both hands."

My father put down his teacup, took the beret out of his epaulette and shuffled it back onto his head, catching up the hair that spilled forward over his forehead. "What are you getting at?"

"I think it's our duty to let the boy be part of today's ceremony. Look." She took a page of the newspaper from her apron pocket and spread it out on the ground. There was a map with a dotted path running through it, and she traced this route with her finger. "The procession's passing by just here in about thirty minutes. It's a short walk away. Why don't the two of you clean yourselves up and then you take the boy down to have a look."

Just then Granny let out a terrifying scream.

My father stood. "All right men," he said to me, "you've got thirty seconds to wash your hands and feet. Then I want you formed up and ready to move out."

"You should wash up decently and put on some proper clothes," my mother protested.

"Nonsense," my father said. "In times of war we dispense with formalities. We'll go as we are, stained with combat and proud of it."

I washed my hands and feet under the tap, then fell in. My father inspected me briefly. Then he ordered me to climb into the wheel-barrow, passed me the newspaper, took up position between the handles, and we set out. Just before we disappeared around the side of the house I looked back. My mother was packing the teacups onto the tray. Granny waved.

The metal wheel of the wheelbarrow clattered on the tar. The sound seemed very loud, because the streets were so quiet and empty. Sometimes as we passed a house I could hear the muted voice of a radio. But there was none of the usual Saturday bustle. No children playing, no one washing a car or working in the garden.

We did not speak for several blocks. When we came to Theo's cafe, the limit of my world, my father stopped. He took the map from me and studied it. Then he asked me to hold one corner and with his stubby fingers, the nails still caked with mud, he showed me the way. "We have to go south now for three blocks. Then we have to turn west for another four, and we're there." We went on.

Now there were fewer houses, more shops and office blocks. The streets began to fill with people, all walking in the same direction we were. They were dressed in suits and church dresses, and they walked along in silence. Some of the men wore black armbands. As we approached the older part of the city the buildings became greyer, gloomier. Here huge columns supported stone pediments. Old statues, the flesh blistered and corroded, stared down at us.

When the tar gave way to cobbles the clanking of the wheel grew even louder and now several people stopped to stare at us. I leaned back in the wheelbarrow so that I could look up at my father. His jaw was as set and craggy as a statue's. His eyes looked stonily ahead.

The hair that curved back from under the beret could have been cast in bronze. Then I too looked ahead and tried to mould his hard expression to my face.

We stopped soon at a kiosk where we each received a little flag. Then we rattled on, and at the end of the block I could see a jostling wall of black cloth, splashed with colour – the colours of the flag – and many pale profiles all facing to one side. Some of these faces looked back, annoyed, as we approached. We parked behind the wall of people and my father hoisted me onto his shoulders. Then he climbed carefully onto the barrow.

"We're right on time," he said.

The wall had absorbed all colour and sound, but now that we rose above it we could see the bright, gleaming procession, hardly a block away, and hear the music.

The procession drew slowly closer. In front was a phalanx of traffic officers, the sun flashing from the windshields of their motorcycles and their black leather boots and gloves. Then came the drum major, shrouded in leopard skin, and the band, all its pipes and tappets bristling. Behind that another machine, a company of soldiers, slow-marching. And then came a truck towing the Prime Minister, in a box covered with a ceremonial flag, on top of a gun carriage, as if he was a secret weapon captured from the enemy. Behind him another squad of soldiers, and behind them tanks, and behind them more soldiers as far as the eye could see.

This solemn movement, this stirring music, hemmed in on either side by the frozen waves of mourners.

When the first company of soldiers had almost passed us, my father raised his arm in a rigid salute. I waved my flag. The men around us swallowed and stared ahead. Some of the women dabbed at their eyes with the little flags. A child started crying.

Then, as the gun carriage drew level with us, the truck suddenly coughed, jerked, and came to a halt. A cloud of black smoke poured from the exhaust pipe. The soldiers behind faltered. The front ranks began to mark time. Those behind marched slowly and solemnly into those in front. A few of the men dived for cover under the gun carriage.

The band and the first soldiers marched on. Between them and the stalled truck a fascinating gap began to open.

The driver of the truck climbed hurriedly down and opened the bonnet, tinkered with the engine. Behind, the soldiers stumbled and coughed in the smoke. The gun carriage was now completely obscured.

My father snapped out of his salute, jumped down from the wheel-barrow and squatted so that I could climb from his shoulders.

"Private, we must do what must be done."

He took up the wheelbarrow and, as if they understood our mission, the people parted to let us through.

The box was heavy. The soldiers were already half a block ahead of us. We set off in pursuit, my father pushing the wheelbarrow while I held the box steady. The crowd waved us on. Once the flag got caught under the wheel, and the box was almost jerked from the barrow. My father was breathing heavily by the time we caught up with the soldiers, and adjusted our pace to the slow rhythm of the music.

I looked back and saw that the crowds that had lined the streets had surged together behind us and were following. On the dark surface of that wave the flotsam of the flags and their faces bobbed.

Outside the cemetery a man in white gloves waved the band and the soldiers off to one side into a parking-lot. He directed us straight ahead, through the wrought-iron gates, along the stone walkway that led to the grave. On either side the stone faces of the men in the history books looked down from their columns, unblinking, unmoved.

The grave. The black figures clustered together, the man with the book clutched under his arm, the brass railings. They stood as people do on the edge of a cliff.

My father's stride lengthened. I had to run to keep up with him. The box bucked violently. My father began to run. I stopped, panting, and stared after him. He ran towards the hole. The mouths of the people at the graveside opened. The man with the book held out his pale palm like a traffic officer.

My father ran on. At the last moment, on the very lip of the grave, he dug the metal prow of the barrow into the earth and heaved.

Flashback Hotel ★TYYY

Fetched my mail. The man behind the counter was my father. He didn't recognize me. There was a letter I had addressed to myself several years before. My handwriting was young. I slit it open. Inside were a SASE and a note on pale-blue paper with doggies in the corners.

RE: MYSTERIOUS DISAPPEARANCE

The note described me: height, weight, colour of hair, colour of eyes, scars, moles.

It listed aliases.

It described what I was wearing when I disappeared.

It requested information about my present whereabouts.

It offered a reward for information leading to my arrest.

The dining-room walls were mirrored. Fat people were fattening themselves at little tables whose legs curved under the weight of plates and paunches. Waiters dressed in rags and clotted furs distributed roughage. Their wounds were bound with dishcloths. There were fatty spots on the bandages where the pus had seeped.

Embroidery of Johnnie Walker, Sealy Posturepedic, Toyota Corolla, Eno, Southern Suns.

I ran through the dining-room (I had to go badly) but kept banging into mirrors.

My nose began to bleed and one of the waiters (Nedbank) offered me an ice bucket.

Night.

I went to the Stadium. I was alone on the bus. In the Stadium I was a crowd of one. I climbed up to the highest tier and found myself a seat. A spotlight like a snooker cue slid down from the darkness above me. It rested on the centre spot. In the light was my father dressed in a white suit.

There had been

BOMB BLAST IN CITY HOTEL

(★TYYY)

There was a crater in the foyer filled up with water from burst pipes and with pieces of piano. Some dead waiters had been piled in the hole like stepping-stones so that guests could cross over safely.

I went into the Ladies Bar. The television set was repeating itself: action replays of the explosion with subtitles in many languages.

The Manager was laid out on a bed of ice on the counter. The edges of his suit were frosted.

The Assistant Manager was consulting with the Chief of Police at a table in a corner. They were sipping Blanc de Noir and staring into one another's eyes across a candle flame.

The sound of ice splintering. The Manager raised his head and, without opening his eyes, told me to leave.

They sent the City Late up to my room on a silver salver, and sauce in a plastic tomato and a crêpe bandage folded into a carnation.

The pages smelt of lemon juice and new ink.

A note on Flashback Hotel stationery told me to turn to the Hatches, Matches and Dispatches.

I turned.

I saw that I had been born, married and buried.

I was a bonny baby.

I was married to Bride of the Month for January (at the Temple David, Morningside).

My ashes had been scattered outside Fontana.

I had also been seen at Rugantino's with Toyota Corolla Salesman of the Year celebrating my birthday. All sorts of celebrities had attended. There was a group photograph. Because it was my birthday they let me hold the pizza – a battleground just two centimetres in diameter.

I went back to the front page.

There was an identikit photograph of me. This man was seen hurrying away from the scene of today's atrocity.

I went into the bathroom and looked at myself in the mirror. There were splinters of glass in my hair.

Then I shaved my moustache.

A large crowd had gathered outside, trying to see the bodies.

I mingled. I pretended to be a reporter so that I could gauge public opinion. Sardonically, with a wry smile.

It seemed that most of them had come for the raffling of the maitre d's eyewitness account.

A fat man in a school uniform cornered me and tried to sell me a brown-leather satchel with a peace sign on it. He had a flick-knife.

I took the satchel. Just then a policeman carrying a stack of raffle forms appeared.

Hello hello hello. *Wat maak julle daar?*

I ran back into the hotel.

The fat man said to the policeman: If he's innocent why's he running away?

I was ticking like a bomb.

I looked at myself in the mirror. I saw that I had my father's mouth. Immediate recognition. Gruesome. I drew the curtains. There was shattered glass all over the show.

In the satchel I found the passport of a man who was almost familiar, some make-up and a chauffeur's uniform, including a splendid peaked cap with gold braid.

I made up my face. I painted the Passport Man's moustache on my lip. I memorized his name and address. I put on the uniform.

I put my own clothes into a suitcase. The suitcase didn't weigh enough. I practised walking with it over the broken glass, but it wouldn't do. I filled it up with ashtrays, directories, the Yellow Pages, a collection of Tonight! and Today!

Better.

I went down to the foyer.

The stepping-stones had been submerged. I had to take the back way out, through the kitchen. The Assistant Manager was frying an egg. The waiters were stringing paper decorations in the alley. They wanted me to blow up balloons but I shrugged as if I didn't understand.

A long tiled corridor called WHITES led to the urinals.

There was a sign that said 4U2P.

While I was P-ing, I remembered that it was my birthday and wished that I could throw a party.

My epaulettes looked good. I could easily pass for a general or a traffic cop or a train driver.

The Station was closed for repairs. I wanted to check my suitcase into a locker but there was no attendant. I went down to the platforms. Perhaps I could go for a joyride, or send my suitcase on a journey. On the steps the suitcase vomited its contents but I stuffed everything back in. I put the suitcase onto a trolley and pushed it along the platform. No trains. The place smelt of people. I left the suitcase next to a bench and walked away as if I would just be a minute.

Instead I went to the cafeteria, helped myself to a pie and gravy, watched the action replays as I ate.

They showed the explosion in slow motion and reverse.

I found the dignity with which the glass and the furniture and the victims pulled themselves together again very moving.

Back at the hotel the crowds had dispersed. The crater had been pumped dry. They were pouring cement over the bodies.

In the foyer I met the Manager. His suit was still damp where the frosting had melted.

He greeted me like a long-lost friend. He patted my back. He said he was really sorry I had missed all the action. I could stay as long as I liked.

I went up to my room to fix my face.

That night there was a fancy-dress party in the alley behind the kitchen. I went as a missing person.

Sightseeing

The Crack of Dawn

Here comes a man with equipment for violence: suitcase, tent, walking stick, boots, camera, pen. The means to cover vast distances and inflict metaphor and defend himself.

This man is in league with coincidence. He has only come to see the sights but he is capable of turning the sea into an exercise in Royal Jelly or Cold Water Omo.

He comes carrying his hard suitcase with exaggerated ease and wearing his blisters like badges. He comes along a jeep-track through a plantation, noting that here tiny pine-trees spangle the verges and there a mushroom sprouts out of a turd. He feels grateful for the mist that forces his attention to the finer details. He stops from time to time, where a cairn marks a look-out spot, to catch his breath and observe the mist where the scenery should be. Comes on again.

He discovers that he is not alone. On a slope below the track a group of labourers in oilskins huddle with axes and saws, waiting for the day's work to begin. They watch him pass, puzzled by his safety suitcase (with fluorescent chevrons and a combination lock) and his limp and his sense of purpose. He consults his maps and hurries behind the mist to eat his breakfast: an energy bar and a boiled egg. As he crunches he hears the chainsaw, and the first tree falls.

In the Bundu

Or rather in a rain forest of trunks, torsos, severed limbs, he is finally alone. He slips and skids in his skidproof boots along a path between building-block rocks, greened and damped, noodle vines, Chinese puzzles, fern-furry insect legs of roots.

In the green light near a waterfall he sits, rests his suitcase on his knees, and takes notes for metaphors as follows:

Fern leaves' soft swooped symmetry of pagodas, head-dresses – stalks balance leaves horizontal, ever-steadying, swirled by my passing – the way waiters balance trays – noodle vines, Chinese puzzles, pretzels of root and creeper – nervous hands of fern – mottled rock under suds – trees wrung like clothes by jungle hands – vines koeksister towards a spearmint vault –

He goes on in this manner for several pages. Then for a long time he looks at his plastic pen.

The Ambulance

The Mobile Clinic, its red light revolving, is parked under a tree next to the village store. The store is closed. A group of men unload sacks of flour and mealie-meal and tins of meat and fish from a truck and carry them in through a back entrance.

The sightseer sits on his suitcase in the shade of a hedge. Everyone watches him. No one speaks.

The women of the village pass their babies to the ambulance driver who weighs them in a canvas sling suspended from a branch of the tree. Then he passes them to the nurse who sits in the driver's seat of the ambulance. She makes notes on white cards which she rests on the steering-wheel. Perhaps she examines the babies in the rearview mirror. The accelerator pedal amplifies a whooping cough. Her hand is on baby's forehead and her eye on the temperature gauge. The red light revolves. Next baby.

The sightseer, pen fingers itching, but ashamed of literacy and clean white curiosity, takes mental notes:

Underdevelopment in the Rural Areas

(1) The ambulance driver weighs the babies in a canvas sling, like fish.

(2) One of the babies has a sore poured like hot porridge over its
back.

and so on.

After an hour the sightseer realizes that the store is not going to
open, and goes away hungry. From the footpath down to the beach
he hears the ambulance howling.

Beggars and Thieves

The sightseer sees a goatherd climbing down the cliff and has to run
knees-up out of the surf to secure his camera and his pen. Theft is a
problem. The natives are not bought off with beads and copper wire.
Foreigners come here in and out of season, hauling themselves over
mountains to work up a sweat and flinging themselves into the sea
to wash it off. The local children go barefoot over rock and dive for
crayfish, which they sell at the standard rates. When no one buys they
beg for precise amounts of money and food.

"I am travelling light," the sightseer says to them. "I mean that I
have paper money and travellers' cheques, an airmail pad and one
rand's worth of five-cent stamps. I also have things like soya beans
and ProNutro, but just enough."

A pregnant girl holds her belly in her hands, presents the hungry
foetus to him as evidence.

In the bottom of his suitcase, under his skants and socks, the sight-seer carries a kilogram of powdered milk like a Conscience.

In remote places he comes to litter like his own and knows that he is not a voortrekker.

Two Englishmen

He buries his suitcase under pine-needles and creeps up close.

A Combi emits two Englishmen with one beard between them and bacon and eggs for a party of eight hot off the Cadac.

Snap! and edging closer, disguised as a tree, the sightseer turns breakfast into Colonialism. Under cover of leaf rustling he laughs at fold-up Morris chairs, unbreakable mugs, telescopic table, 75 litres of spring-loaded water, all coming with the Combi at fifteen rand a day and unlimited mileage.

"The one with the beard (he will pass it on to his friend after breakfast so that he can do the washing up) pierces the belly of an egg and it runs sticky sunshine,"

the sightseer notes.

One German

The German finds the natives here more savage, hardly civilized.

He fetches a carving-knife, lops and spears sausage, then cucumber, then bread. Gouges mustard from a pot. He clips the sandwich from the blade with his teeth. He wipes the knife on his knee and spears seven pear halves one by one and eats them whole. Drinks the syrup in one long swig. And tells camp-fire tales of mozzies, potholes, bandits, women in St. Lucia, Port St. John's, Hamburg, Dubrovnik, Tokyo.

The sightseer, shrinking from the knife, ashamed of modest distances and dehydrated food, marvels at the fridge that keeps the beer cold (drinks one gratefully) and comes with the Combi at a cut-rate twelve rand a day and unlimited mileage.

The sightseer goes to his tent early. He lies in his sleeping-bag with his head out of the flap and watches the German build a bonfire to scare away the boys who come to beg.

Afraid again, he sleeps with his suitcase in his arms.

Local Colour

Here he comes, proudly unwashed (seven days now) and travel-stained, and prepared to wait for two hours for a bus.

When at last the bus comes it admits him with indifference. His suitcase is taken from his hands and piled with sacks of pumpkins, cardboard boxes, shopping-bags, and trays of beer (cushioned by the mailbags). He gets a seat on the stairs where metal plates turn hot above the engine. A gap below the doors billows dust and hot wind over him.

He finds that he is soapy fresh among these smells. Centuries of wood-smoke in the old men's clothes, the women's blankets. Old Mum for Men under young armpits. Sweat and beer. He imagines sour smells of mother's milk, sweet red from a bulge in a child's cheek, apple vapour. He tries to smell himself.

Among the battered baggage his suitcase is crisp and bright. It shames him, lying there like Privilege and Leisure.

He sees some characters demanding to be documented: a toothless old man sucking pilchards through a hole in the tin; a baby breast-fed (he averts his eyes); a child whose face is full of the newsfronts of the world.

But he takes no photographs. These people have kieries and sjam-boks to use against the poacher. And his notebook is in the bottom of the suitcase.

The Terminus

in the marketplace, in the capital.

He notes: the fruitsellers try to make their apples and oranges glow against the dust. Then he drags his suitcase to the tiled privacy of a Caltex Restroom to knock the dents out of the lid, dust it off and flush away his chocolate wrappers.

There goes a man whose camera has failed him but not his eyes. Hurrying through the streets of the capital – he wants to be out of it before dark – he keeps his face like the picture in his passport. Out of the corners of his eyes he sees the faces of the people. Here is a language he understands and he knows how to reply, with distance.

Postcards

He is on holiday at last. He takes a shower, calls room service for a Scotch. He walks on the promenade. In a beachfront cafe he licks an ice-cream cone and turns a tower of postcards.

He finds his memories captive and complete, in glorious colour, with captions. His sticky fingers make the tower spin.

He stops the tower dead. Buys a view of his hotel and next to the window of his room he writes in ink

ME

Journal of a Wall

31 May

I have a feeling that I am starting this too late.

It is hardly three weeks since he started the wall – but already he has laid the foundations. That is not too much to catch up, perhaps. But it would have been pleasantly symmetrical to have begun on the same day, to have taken up my pen as he took up his trowel.

I should have foreseen it all. I had a sense, when they delivered the bricks, that something in which I would have a part was beginning. If I had not been watching from behind the curtains in my lounge, like a spy, perhaps it would have been clear to me that I was meant to be more than an observer.

They brought the bricks almost three weeks ago. Saturday 11 May, as I look at my calendar. I was watching the cricket on television when I heard the truck stop across the road. The engine revved for several minutes – I suppose the driver had gone in to check whether he was at the right address – and that's why I went to investigate.

When I looked out through the curtains he was crossing the lawn with a man wearing blue overalls. His wife was watching from the veràndah.

The bricks were packed incongruously in huge plastic bags, very strong plastic, I suppose. He went straight up to the truck, put one foot on the rear wheel and hoisted himself up. He took out a pocket-knife and cut a slit in the plastic, put his finger in to touch the bricks. He held his hand there for a minute, as if he was taking a pulse. Then he put his eye to the slit. It took a long time before he was satisfied. I had an inkling then that something important was beginning. I should have fetched a pen and started recording immediately. I would have had the details now, those all-important beginning moments. Already the memories are fading: I can't remember when she went back inside, for instance, but I don't think that she watched the unloading.

He supervised that task himself. It didn't take long. I wished that the bricks weren't wrapped in plastic; then they could have been passed along a chain of sure hands from the back of the truck to a corner of the garden. Instead the driver of the truck operated a small crane mounted just behind the cab, and the man directed him to pile the bags of bricks one on top of the other on the pavement. I remember at least that there were nine bags. When that was over he went inside – it was probably then that I noticed she was gone – and returned with a pen to sign the delivery papers.

After the truck had gone he went straight back into the house. I was surprised. I expected him to examine the bricks again. But apparently he was satisfied.

I returned to the television set. The game was over. I watched for a while, hoping to get the final score. But I was restless. The news came on. It was Michael de Morgan. He told us there was unrest in the townships again. He showed us a funeral crowd being dispersed with tear gas. A bus burned in the background. Then a camera in a moving car tracking along the naked faces of houses, and children peeling away from the vehicle like buck in the game reserve. A cloud of black smoke from a supermarket. Soldiers. Some people hurling bricks into the burning bus.

The following scenes may upset some viewers, Michael de Morgan said gently.

I switched off the set. I was upset enough.

I went back to the window. It was almost dark outside, the house across the road a blue shadow. But the front door was open, and in the glow from the lounge I could see him reclining in an easy chair on the verandah, with his feet up on a table, drinking a beer.

The pile of bricks was another dark shape in the twilight. From the way in which he was sitting, with his legs swung to one side, I would say that he was watching over them. He looked as if he was going to stay there all night. Or perhaps he was trying to decide what to build. Or had already decided and could see the final product, with each brick in place.

I was restless that evening, and upset and depressed. I drank too much. The room wanted to spin. That impulse came to me through the bedsprings, just a gentle tremor at first, but the walls of the house held fast. I put one foot on the floor, trying to weigh it down. Then it came again, the room trying to twist itself free from the rest of the house, rip up its tap-root and ascend into the sky. Plaster powder rained down on me as cracks chased through the walls and ran themselves into corners. Then the rafters cracked like ribs and the room began to turn. The whole place rattled and groaned, spun faster and faster, and then rose slowly like an ancient flying-machine, ripping roof-tiles like fingernails, tearing the sinews of electrical wiring, bursting the veins of waterpipes, up into the night sky.

I went to look through the bedroom window. The city was spread out below me like a map, but I couldn't get my bearings. There was my house, with its gaping wound. I felt a wind on my neck, and when I looked up I saw the ceiling drift away. The night, effervescent with stars, poured in.

I sat down on the end of my bed. The bricks began to peel away from the walls in squadrons and they flew down to my neighbour's house and assembled themselves into barbecues and watchtowers and gazebos and rondawels and bomb shelters. When all the walls had unravelled completely I was left floating on the raft of the floor, dragged by the currents of the sky this way and that, until the boards all rotted away below me and I sank down into my bathroom and got sick.

I woke up very late on Sunday morning, feeling terrible. It was several hours before I could bring myself to get up and take a shower. The room had fitted itself back into the house imperfectly, with the doors and windows in the wrong places, and the floors were awash with books, broken glass, clockwork, clothing, kindling. I decided to put off tidying up until after breakfast – which was lunch, actually.

While I was eating I suddenly remembered my neighbour's bricks, and rushed to the lounge window. I was surprised and hurt to discover that he had already started work without me. He was digging a trench along the boundary of his property, where the fence used to be. The fence posts were still there, but the wire itself lay in a huge buckled roll on the front lawn. A wall! Of course.

After some minutes of watching him I hit on a plan for getting a closer view of the building operations. I strolled to the shop, bought the Sunday paper, and then took a slightly longer route which would take me past his house on my way home. It worked perfectly. I stopped to tie my shoelaces, which I had cunningly loosened before I rounded the corner, so that I could get a good look at the trench and, indeed, at him. Fortunately, he was working with his back to me.

The trench seemed to me inordinately deep – although I must say that I have never actually built a wall myself – eighteen inches or more. And at least two feet across. It was possible that he was planning to build an extremely thick, high wall of the kind that is fairly common in our suburb, in which case the foundations would have to be secure. But I was more inclined to think that he was simply an amateur. He didn't look as if he had built a wall before either.

Frankly, he was a disappointment to me. It was the first time I had really seen him from close range. Indeed, until the day before it would be true to say that I had never seen him. He was simply the driver of a car or the pusher of a lawnmower. My first real glimpse of him, swinging up onto the truck, had convinced me that he was strong, seasoned, capable. Now I saw how wrong I was. He had taken off his shirt (it hung limply on one of the fence posts) and his back was pale and flabby. His neck was burnt slightly red. He was wearing long pants, which looked clean and ironed, not at all like work pants. What bothered me most was the way in which he swung the pick; there was no conviction in it at all. I wished that I could get a look at his hands.

Of course, I probably didn't think all this in the time it takes to tie a shoelace: it is more likely that I simply observed and then thought about it all later, as I read my newspaper in a deckchair in the front garden.

I spent the better part of the afternoon watching him from behind the paper. He never looked my way once. He worked very slowly, but steadily, and by five o'clock, when it had become quite cool and almost time for me to go in, he had finished the trench. He put on his shirt and fetched her out of the house to review the day's achievements. He seemed very pleased with himself: he even sprang into the hole and did a little jig for her, and that made me like him more. And she put her arm around his shoulders when they went back in, and that made me proud of her too.

I waited for a few minutes, thinking that they would perhaps come out onto the verandah for sundowners, but the door remained closed, and eventually I also had to go in.

Nothing happened for a week. I had hoped that he would not do any more building while I was away at work. I noted with relief that he was waiting for the following weekend. The week dragged.

Once or twice during the week I saw him inspecting the trench after work, probably checking for subsidence; and once or twice when my evening strolls took me past the trench I too was able to make a quick examination. It seemed to be holding up well. On those occasions I also managed to get a closer look at the bricks. He seemed to have forgotten about them. I admired that in him – his patience, his faith. It is possible, of course, that he inspected the bricks late at night after I had gone to sleep, but I doubt it.

Their habits seemed to be fairly steady. He usually came in at about five thirty and put the car straight in the garage. They didn't go out much. They would watch television every night until about ten thirty and then retire to bed. The television was on from about six, and so I presumed that either they ate as soon as he came in from work or they took their meals in front of the set.

I speculated about the programmes they watched. Did the news upset them? I for one was finding the news depressing – full of death and destruction. Who would build amid these ruins? I used to stand behind my curtain and look across at their lounge window, flickering blue as a screen. What on earth were they shoring up?

On the following Saturday (this would have been the 18th of May) I was up early, early enough to see the building sand delivered. Would that I had been ready with pen and paper to describe how that mountain of fine white sand slid from the back of the tip-truck, and the great cloud of dust that boiled up and hung over the houses.

I knew when I saw that perfect dune, white as flour, spilling over the kerb and the pavement, that the foundations would be laid that day. He materialized out of the dust-storm, wearing a blue T-shirt this time but the same pants (fortunately starting to look a little grubby and crumpled) and carrying a spade and a bucket of water. He stood for a while staring into the dust as if waiting for instructions. Then he set to, separating a pile of the sand and shovelling it onto a sheet of corrugated iron. He seemed a little more lively this morning. I was pleased. There was quite a spring in his step as he went off to the garage.

The combined haze of the dust-cloud and the net curtain behind which I was standing was making it very difficult for me to see what was going on. By this time a sense was growing in me that it was very important to catch every detail, although I was still blind to the fact that I should have been writing it all down as it happened.

There he was returning with a bag of cement on his shoulder. I could see him quite clearly for a while but then he was back in the haze.

I paced my lounge, searching for an excuse to get closer to him. The one I finally found was a little obvious perhaps, but he generally seemed to take no notice of me, so I decided to chance it. I pulled my car out of the garage, fetched a bucket of water, and started to wash the windscreen. By now the dust had settled somewhat, and I was surprised to see her coming into view. She was sitting on a kitchen chair, and wearing a pale-pink dressing-gown. She was holding a book, and at first I thought she was reading. Then it seemed to me that she was reading out instructions. As I watched he measured out a quantity of cement in a tin and sprinkled it over the sand. He looked at her. She spoke again. He mixed the sand and the cement with the spade and shaped it into a dam.

Jesus! I said to myself, they're following a recipe.

Then I realized with a start that I was staring. I quickly dipped my sponge in the water and sloshed it over the roof of the car. Schooled my arm to keep rubbing as I watched.

When he had finished the mixing he put the cement in a wheelbarrow and carried it to the beginning of the trench. She walked with him, reading all the way, and watched over him as he tipped the cement into the trench and smoothed it with a length of wood.

And so it went. After the third trip she went inside – presumably he had memorized the procedure – and I did not see her again that day. When he broke for lunch so did I. When I heard the spade clattering on the corrugated iron again a half-hour later I went back to washing the car.

He worked as doggedly laying the foundations as he had done digging the trench, and I found my admiration for him growing. After a whole day of washing my car I was exhausted; he neither slackened nor speeded up as he approached the end of the trench, just worked on at the same relentlessly steady pace. He seemed to me to be a remarkable example of soldiering on. I needed to take a leaf out of his book. I thanked him silently as he set to cleaning the wheelbarrow and the spade with meticulous care.

I resolved to try and follow his example in the week ahead. It would be at least a week before the building proper could begin; the foundations would have to settle. He would be patient, and so would I.

On the Monday evening after he had laid the foundations I saw him come home from work. After he had put the car in the garage and closed the door I expected him to walk down to the building-site for some kind of inspection. But he went straight inside. It made me feel a little foolish, as if I was letting the side down. I put the whole thing out of my mind. Yet I was waiting for the weekend with a growing sense of anticipation.

So I was immediately uneasy when he parked the car in the driveway on Friday evening, instead of putting it in the garage as usual. He hurried inside. Surely they weren't planning to go out? I had specifically decided to get an early night so that I would be fresh for the next day's building, and I expected him to do the same.

I was alarmed when he came out just a few minutes later carrying a suitcase. He put it in the boot and went back inside. Could it be true? Would they go away on such an important weekend? It was inconceivable. I brought a bottle over to the window and poured myself a large Scotch. There he was, coming out again. He went to the car and started cleaning the windscreen. Then I knew it was true. I finished the drink, poured another one. Perhaps they were going to the drive-in? With a suitcase? No … He went back inside. The lights in the house went out one by one. Then they both came out of the front door. She was wearing a nightie and large pink slippers and carrying a suitcase, a smaller version of the one he had put in the boot. They left the hallway light burning. He took the case from her and they walked to the car. How could they do this to me!

I quickly opened the curtains, switched the light on, and stood in the centre of the window, one hand holding the bottle of Scotch and the other pressed against the glass. I stared hard at them, took a long swig from the bottle. The car still hadn't moved. Then she got out and went back inside. Going to check that the taps are off, I thought. The swines. She was back very quickly, carrying a book and something in a brown paper bag. She got in and he switched the interior light on. They both looked at the book. Now the car started, the tail-lights glowed red in the dusk, the car was reversing, they were driving away.

The inside of the car was a warm, light bubble. I saw his profile, and beyond it her face, as soft and ripe as a fruit. She was looking at him, or perhaps at me, and I wondered what she thought of me, weeping at my post, holding my pickled tongue in one cupped palm and the bloodied bayonet in the other.

I finished the Scotch and went for a walk. Oh, I walked all over the place, staring into the blank faces of walls, peering into the blind eyes of windows, shouting obscenities into the leafy ears of hedges. I made the dogs bark. I rattled gates and banged on doors. I put the fear of the devil into the whole suburb. Those sleeping houses, their gigantic gasping and snoring, their tossing and turning. I waded through drifts of dry leaves in the culverts. I left my footprints in flowerbeds. I beat their welcome mats against their front doors until their gardens choked on the dust of ten thousand five o'clock feet. The breeze smelt of formalin. Everything was covered in wax and powdered and pinned. I brought back a newspaper billboard that said THREE MORE DIE IN UNREST and it was easy to believe in unrest and death with the rattle of leaves in the throats of the drains, the letterboxes choked with pamphlets, the bottles of milk souring on the doorsteps.

I forgave them.

I went over just after midnight, in an overcoat, in a balaclava. I shone my torch along the length of the trench: it was looking good. In a few places the earth had subsided, and I cleared it with my hands, and swept up a few dry leaves.

I brought back with me a brick.

I put it on my desk, on an embroidered cloth, and turned the fluorescent lamp on it. It was an extraordinary brick. It looked so heavy, as if it had been hewn from solid rock in the quarries of some not yet discovered planet. It was reddish brown, with a cracked, cratered surface, and it was still warm to the touch. It looked as if it would plummet through the desk, the floor, sink down into the earth as if it were water.

Yet the more I looked at it, the more it looked like a familiar object. After a long time of watching it, it began to look like a loaf of bread, hot from the oven, steaming, fermenting inside.

I could hardly sleep that night with its hard presence in the house, its bubbling and hissing. But I eventually sank into the mottled depths of a dreamless sleep.

In the morning the brick had cooled. Its surface had hardened to a stiff crust.

I was tempted to keep it as some sort of memento. But by late afternoon I had begun to resent its stony silence, its impenetrable skin, and I resolved to return it to the pile as soon as it grew dark. I wanted to maintain some connection with it, however, so I marked each of its impassive faces with a small dot of white paint, and put it in the oven to dry.

When it was dark I took the brick over concealed in a folded newspaper which I carried under my arm. On the pavement I was suddenly tempted to explore the house and the back garden. The front lawn lay spread like a huge welcome mat, inviting me into the nooks and crannies of their private spaces. But I was afraid: someone could see me and mistake me for a burglar. So I returned the brick to its pile and carefully folded the plastic wrapper over it.

I was just turning back towards my own house when I spotted the letters, jutting like a tongue from the letterbox. I looked around quickly. There was no one in sight. I was bold enough to take the letters onto their verandah and skim through them in the light from behind the frosted panes of the front door. There were three letters. One was addressed to The Householder. The other two were addressed to Mr G.B. Groenewald. I returned the letters to the box and scurried home with my discovery.

Mr and Mrs Groenewald returned from their outing on Sunday evening. I was overjoyed to see them. I wanted them to know that I had taken good care of everything in their absence, so I flashed my lounge light in a cryptic morse of welcome and affection. No answering signal came. I suspect that they were tired from their journey and went straight to bed.

The week that followed was uneventful: we were all waiting for the weekend. Then today – yes, it is the 31st of May today – I finally realized what I had to do: I had to write it all down. I have laid my own foundations, and from now on it will be brick for word, word for brick. Tomorrow the building begins. I must have a good night's sleep.

1 June

7.15 a.m.
I have made my arrangements; I have pen and paper, I have a chair in front of the window. I set it all up last night. This morning I was up at six. Showered, shaved, put on my work clothes. Now I am waiting for us to begin.

8.30 a.m.
Here he comes. He is wearing the blue check and the trousers. He pauses on the top step of the verandah, looks out over his kingdom. Ah, if he knew that I was watching he wouldn't stretch in that bone-cracking way. He goes to the garage. He looks quite energetic,

although a shadow of sleep drags across the lawn behind him. He opens the garage door, goes into the twilight. Comes out pushing the wheelbarrow loaded with a bag of cement, a spade, a box of tools. Goes to the beginning of the trench. Drags the piece of corrugated iron over, shovels sand onto it.

Let me leave him to mix while I describe briefly the sky behind him: It is a flat sky, like faded blue canvas. It could be dangling from the top of my window frame. At the bottom the canvas is notched raggedly by the roofs of the houses. A slight breeze comes up and the canvas sways: a black edge opens up between it and the houses, closes again as the breeze drops.

He has mixed the cement. He leaves it to set, pushes the barrow to the pile of bricks. He slits the plastic with one long, sure pass of the pocket-knife. There are beads of moisture on the plastic and they run to rivers as he peels it back from the wound. His hand goes in. Comes out with a brick. He weighs it in his hand, turns it to look at it from all angles, puts it in the wheelbarrow. Reaches for another. If I had binoculars per-haps I would be able to tell, even at this distance, which brick is mine.

The wheelbarrow is full. He pushes it to the beginning of the trench. He takes a ball of string from the toolbox, stretches a length between the first fence post and the second, checks it with a spirit level. When he stands the string cuts him just below the knee. Surely that is too low? He kneads the cement with the back of the spade. He takes up his trowel. He goes down on his knees in the trench. He reaches for a brick. Weighs it. His hands go down into the earth. Damn! I can't see what he's doing. I've missed the laying of the first brick!

10.30 a.m.

He works incredibly slowly. As if there were only one place in the whole bloody wall where any particular brick will fit.

He has laid three courses so far, and has just started the fourth. This is the first course I can see clearly. He weighs each brick in his hand. Then he settles it on its dollop of cement, shuffles it in, taps it with the handle of the trowel, slices off the oozing cement, taps it again. Sometimes he starts over, scraping the surface clean, putting the brick aside and choosing another. I cannot see why. They look the same to me.

I wonder where she is? I expected her to be there for the first brick.

I should go over and speak to him. It would be simple. Perhaps he would welcome some discussion. I would suggest, for example, that he make the wall slightly higher: what good is a wall if one can see over it? I would also advise him to wear a hat – I could offer to lend him one of mine. He's not used to the sun.

I could tell him how interested I am in his project. That would surprise him. If I told him about my own plan to document the whole process and showed him the work I have done so far, perhaps he would let me bring a chair over and sit right there, where I could record smells, noises; perhaps he would answer a few questions about his motivations, and even listen to some constructive criticism.

On the other hand my interest could affect him badly. Perhaps I should let him carry on unhindered for a while, until we have a clearer picture of the road ahead.

12.30 p.m.
I am pleased to note that he has moved the string to shoulder height. But now he is going inside, probably for lunch.

2.45 p.m.
I don't know whether I will be able to keep this up. He loves this wall, every brick of it, but he loves it so passionlessly, with a love so methodical and disciplined, that it might as well be loathing.

He has loved his wall up to shoulder height, brick by careful brick, and now he fetches a step-ladder and the wall goes higher. He checks each course with the spirit level, and then stands back to look at his work.

It is very boring to watch.

5.00 p.m.

He has finished work for the day. The wall is about two metres high. He has filled in the panel between the first two fence posts. Unless he speeds up considerably, I estimate that it will be several months before the wall is completed.

They are sitting now on the verandah. She came out a few minutes ago and put two beers on the table. Came down to inspect the wall. I couldn't see her response, because she looked at it from the inside, as if that was the more important side. But she seemed to say something to him, because he spoke and listened and then smiled. Then she went back to the verandah and sat in the other chair. They raised their glasses to one another and I raised mine too and clinked it against the window-pane.

2 June

It is Sunday evening. He has finished another panel. This morning he uprooted the second fence post and strung the marker between the wall and the third post.

I think that I have caught up with him only to become bored.

He is a machine. His hands repeat themselves – brick after brick after brick they open and shut like pliers. His flabby muscles contract and relax in a predictable rhythm.

I think I dislike him. Why must he weigh each brick and toss it over in his hand? Why must he tap each brick with the handle of the trowel, twice on one side, three times on the other, and once solidly in the middle, before he is satisfied? The man has no imagination. I can see already that his wall will be just another wall. An ordinary coincidence of bricks and mortar, presentably imperfect. It won't fall down, but then it won't fly either. He'll probably put plaster over his careful bricks and paint it green and people will think it was bought in a shop.

29 June

Today the wall finally passed the halfway mark. For the first time I can no longer see them as they drink their customary beer. I have resolved to speak to them before they disappear entirely.

30 June

I am writing this from the Cafe Zurich. I simply had to get out. I had to get away from them. I have delayed recording the events of yesterday evening because I needed time to calm down. I was so angry – and it will become clear that I had every reason to be – that I was sure my observations would seem spiteful and unfair.

But I think that I now have sufficient emotional distance from the incident to put it down objectively, as it happened.

During the course of yesterday afternoon, watching another panel of bricks edging up into the air, obscuring the house, I had become worried about the Groenewalds. More specifically, I had become worried about our relationship. There they were, celebrating the crossing of the halfway line, but hidden behind their wall. Here I was, celebrating the same occasion, but hidden behind my curtain. And just fifty metres or so separating us.

I began to regret my reticence. They were nice people, I knew. He was solid and reliable and purposeful. She was quiet and sweet and sensitive. They were my kind of people. If only I had broken the ice earlier. Now there was so much ground to be made up. Yet, at the same time, even though they were unaware of it, we had so much in common. The wall. They knew it from one side, I knew it from the other. I began to see it not so much as a barrier between us, but as a meeting-point. It was the thin line between pieces in a puzzle, the frontier on which both pieces become intelligible. Or perhaps it was like those optical puzzles in which you see the profile of a beautiful young woman or an old hag, but never both at the same time. I tossed these analogies around in my head, hoping to arrive at one I could share with them, an opening line I could call to them as I emerged from around the wall and took my first real steps into their lives. Eventually I decided to take a cup instead and ask for some sugar.

They were on the verandah, as I thought, drinking beer. They looked up as I crossed the lawn, suspiciously perhaps, although I couldn't see their expressions clearly in the blue gleam that the TV set in the lounge threw on them.

"Good evening Mr Groenewald, Mrs Groenewald," I called, approaching them at a pace I thought they would appreciate, neither too fast nor too slow. "I wonder if you could help me?"

He rose from his chair, put the beer on the table, and took one step to the edge of the verandah. She sat back in her chair and crossed her legs.

I stopped just below him but I spoke to her. "I'm making a trifle and, you know how it is, I've run out of sugar for the custard. Could you spare me a bit, just until tomorrow?"

She rose quickly, took the cup from my hand, and went into the house. I took a few steps after her, drawn by the flickering blue of her retreating back, but he stepped towards the door, as if to block my path.

I was disappointed. I had hoped to gain access to the house, to measure their space against my imaginings. I heard the familiar fanfare announcing the six o'clock news. If only he would invite me in to watch the news with them: that would give us many opportunities to discuss the state of the country, the newest trouble spots, local and abroad, and get to know one another.

But he made no move. I realized quickly that the more important opportunity was right in my hands – to discuss the wall with its maker. She, after all, had as little to do with the wall as a trowel or a piece of string. It was just as well she had left us alone.

I turned slightly, so that my pose suggested that I was watching the wall.

"I've been following your progress with interest," I said. "Perhaps you have seen me? I live right across from you."

"No," he said.

"It's a fine wall," I went on undaunted. After all, hadn't they been invisible to me for months, even years (I couldn't remember whether they had moved in before or after me). "A very fine wall indeed. A little high perhaps. A little forbidding."

"I would make it higher," he said, "but there are municipal regulations."

I began to feel uneasy. He hadn't invited me to sit, so I perched on the edge of the verandah.

"Have you built a wall before?" I asked.

"Many times," he said. "More times than I care to remember."

That threw me. I was going to say that he was doing a good job, for a first attempt. But perhaps I would never have reached that line anyway, for it struck me then, with a sense of loss, that I couldn't see my house at all from this side. It had vanished completely. The sky above the wall was a blank, moronic space, as high as the stars. There was nothing in it that would provide comfort to a human heart, that would fill a human eye. The world beyond the wall was empty: there was not even a world there. Perhaps my house would be visible from the verandah? I stood, hoping to find a way up. But he had moved, while I was musing, to the top of the steps, and was looking back over his shoulder through the open window at the flickering television screen. The curtains were open. You could see right in. I moved towards the steps.

Just then she came out with the cup of sugar. She handed it down to me. It was very full and a few grains spilled onto my fingers. "I'll replace it tomorrow. Thank you," I said.

"Please don't bother," she replied.

I had to leave. The lawn seemed vast. I crossed towards the hard edge of the wall, behind which the world was slowly materializing again. I had an extraordinary sense as I walked, somewhat stiffly, with the sugar trickling onto my fingers, that no eyes were on me. No one was watching me. I wanted to look back, but I couldn't. I couldn't confirm such an obvious insult.

I was mad as hell. I was in my lounge, where everything was still the same. I was mad as could be. I smashed up a chair. Still the rage wouldn't leave me. I smashed up a table. Then I started to feel better, pacing around among the splinters with a bottle of Scotch in my hand. Who the hell did they think they were, treating me like a dog? Who the fuck were they anyway? Lunatics, blind people, fat slobs, smug shithouses.

I should have gone right into their house and smashed up a few things. That would have been perfect, with the news in the background. I would have shown them unrest and rioting and burning, in three dimensions. I would have given them wanton destruction of private property. I would have given them hell in the eye-level oven, and stonings with the bric-a-brac from the room divider. And then I would have left them uneasy calm after yesterday's violence.

But was it all worth it?

I sat down in the surviving chair and thought about it more carefully. They were such perverse people. What were they planning to do behind that ridiculous wall? *Volkspele? Nude braaivleises?* Secret nocturnal rituals accessible only to people in helicopters?

Fuck them. I had to tidy up.

17 August

The wall is almost finished.

I have not been thinking about it much. Of course, since the unfortunate incident with the sugar I've had to avoid them, to spare us all embarrassment. I have been going to work early and coming in late – and always careful to avert my gaze. Yet, out of the corner of my eye, as it were, I've watched the wall edge malevolently towards the end of the trench. There is not much space left for it to cross: scarcely a metre. That will be done next weekend and the betrayal will be complete.

I am no longer interested in them. They have blurred into the background out of which they came. But, for the sake of symmetry, I have decided to record the end of it all, the laying of the final brick. It seems necessary. Then I can be done with this journal.

24 August

He is almost finished. He is building the last panel from the garden side. I have watched him slowly obliterated by his wall. Now all I can see is a pair of hands reaching up.

I imagine that she is there with him, holding a bottle of champagne. No doubt I will see the cork flying up to the stars.

But is there cause for celebration? No. Is there reason for building when things are falling down? No. Is there reason for drinking beer when people are starving? Probably not. Do two people and a bottle of champagne make sense when citizens are pitched against soldiers, when stones are thrown at tanks? Does private joy make sense in the face of public suffering?

There he begins the last course of bricks. How bored I am with the tired repetition of gesture. How bored I am with the familiar shapes of words. How bored I am with this journal. It's just a wall. That must be clear by now. Even a child could see it. And the words that go into it like bricks are as bland and heavy and worn as the metaphor itself.

He lays the last brick. But I have the last word.

THE END

Later that same evening:

I am writing simply because I cannot sleep. And the reason I cannot sleep is that those bastards across the road are having a party. A wall-warming, I suppose. The music is too loud. And the buzzing of voices! They have strung coloured lights in the trees. Candles are burning in paper bags on top of the wall. I would phone the police, but I have already smashed the telephone.

I would gather to me, if I could, the homeless and the hungry, the persecuted, the pursued, the forgotten, those without friends and neighbours, to march around the wall. We would be blowing paper trumpets left over from office parties, and banging on cake tins, and raising up a noise to wake the dead and bring the wall tumbling down.

8 September

Today there was something new attached to the wall: a FOR SALE notice.

17 September

Today a SOLD notice.

2 November

Today they left.

I went across and stood on the pavement to watch their household effects being put into the truck. It is all as I expected: the knotty pine, the wicker, the velveteen, the china, the cotton print, the plastic, the glass, the stainless-steel, the beaten copper.

I stood right next to the truck with my hands on my hips. I dared them to meet my eye but they seemed not to notice me, or not to care. They put a few boxes on the back seat of the car and they followed the pantechnicon. I watched until they disappeared.

The wall looked ashamed of itself.

I went back home.

9 November

The new people have moved in. They are simply people carrying boxes and banging doors. Good.

Today the municipality pruned all the trees in our suburb. The sky has opened up. The wall turns its back on the street. It is a beautiful sunny day. I must get out.

And I must remember to take a stroll past the wall some time and see if I can spot my brick.

The Box

"There are forces in the outside world, and here within our borders," said the Prime Minister, fixing Quentin with an accusing stare, "who seek to overthrow my government by violent means. They wish to create the impression that we are weak, that we will capitulate. They even go so far as to suggest that the country is in a state of civil war. I say to these cowards – for that is what they are – that they will have to face up to reality. And the reality is that every act of cowardly violence will harden our resolve. The reality is that my government is committed to the maintenance of law and order."

Quentin put down the bottle of Southern Comfort and went to stand in front of the television set. "He's out of his mind," he said sadly. "That is the horrible truth. He's mad as a hatter."

The Prime Minister's face filled the screen. It looked as soft and pliable as a lump of clay.

"Do you mind not standing in front of the screen," Mary said. Quentin ignored her, and she moved to the other end of the sofa.

"Who seek to sow the seeds of discord and reap a harvest of bloody revolution," the Prime Minister said.

The camera began to zoom out and the Prime Minister grew smaller and smaller, until he was just six inches tall. He was seated behind a desk in an office filled with leather-bound books. He rose and came slowly round to the front of the desk.

"To those who approach us as equals in the community of nations, we extend the hand of friendship."

A chubby hand reached out to Quentin. He put out his own hand and it tingled as it approached the screen and then slipped through into warm custard. The screen went blank and Quentin groped, closed his fingers around the Prime Minister and jerked him out of the box.

In Quentin's fist the Prime Minister looked even tinier than he had on the screen. He flashed and flickered, filling the space around him with a dirty cloud of electrons. "Put me back! Put me back this instant!" he shouted, beating his tiny fists on Quentin's knuckles.

Quentin turned to Mary, who was getting shakily to her feet, and said, "Look what I just did."

"You can't do this!" the Prime Minister yelled. "By the powers vested in me I command you to put me back where you found me."

The voice was so full of authority and indignation that Quentin almost obeyed.

He took one step towards the television set. But then the Prime Minister sank his teeth into Quentin's forefinger, and Quentin gasped and dropped him. He careened off Quentin's knee, arms and legs flailing, and fell with a soft thud on a bean bag. He jumped to his feet immediately, looked challengingly around him and began to scramble down to the carpet.

"Get something to catch him in," Quentin said.

Mary ran to the kitchen. When she came back into the lounge with a salad bowl the Prime Minister was wobbling towards the television set. Quentin headed him off with a rolled-up newspaper and she dropped the bowl over him. There was a scratching sound against the inside of the bowl, and it inched forward. Then silence. Mary sat down on the arm of the sofa and looked at the message on the screen. We apologize for the short delay, it said, our technicians are working on the problem.

"I hope we didn't hurt him," Mary said.

"Of course not," Quentin replied, nudging the bowl with his toe, "the little bastard's as hard as nails."

Then he sat down heavily on the sofa and looked at his hand.

They sat in silence, Mary chewing her fingernails and Quentin drinking from the bottle, until the Prime Minister's office reappeared on the screen. A reporter was standing to attention in front of the desk. "Sorry about the break in transmission," he said. "We're sad to announce that the Prime Minister has suddenly taken ill and his address to the nation is therefore necessarily postponed. His doctor assures us that his condition is not serious. We will be issuing a full statement later this evening."

"Do you think he's all right?" Mary said. "He's very quiet in there." When Quentin didn't answer she went to the bowl, lifted it cautiously and peeped under it. "He's not moving," she said over her shoulder. Quentin studied the level of the liquor in the bottle.

Mary prodded the inert form with her finger. "Oh God," she said, "I think he's dead."

Quentin sighed and squatted down beside her. "Just answer me one simple question. Do we like him?"

"That doesn't matter," she replied. "He's human, isn't he?"

"Have we ever liked him?" he insisted.

"No," she was forced to admit.

"Then why the hell should we start liking him now?"

The Prime Minister groaned and sat up, rubbing his head.

"He's not even dead," Quentin said. He picked the Prime Minister up by the scruff of his neck and shook him. Then he held him up to his face and said, "Now what should we do with you?"

The Prime Minister began to struggle, kicking and punching at the air. Quentin smiled and rocked him back and forth.

"Please, Quentin," Mary said, tugging at his sleeve.

"All right then. What do you think we should do with him?"

"We could keep him…"

"*Keep* him!"

"My mother has a printer's tray full of little things that would be perfect for him: beermugs, teacups – "

"Who's going to feed him?" Quentin demanded.

"We could take turns."

"Out of the question. Here, hold him while I have a piss."

When he returned, Mary was sitting on the sofa with the Prime Minister cradled in her palm, his arms folded and his chin on his chest. Quentin sat down next to Mary and put his arm around her shoulders. He examined the bald patch on the back of the Prime Minister's head. Then he kissed Mary's ear and whispered, "You're right. It could be a lot of fun to keep him – for a while at least."

Mary crept down the passage, avoiding the floorboards she knew would creak, and peered into the kitchen. She could see the cage on the counter of the breakfast nook, bathed in cold moonlight from the window. She went closer slowly. The Prime Minister had his back to her. He was slumped – disconsolately, she thought – on a pile of sunflower seeds, with his head resting against the bars. He had taken off his jacket and folded it into a pillow, and that was under his neck; he had loosened his tie and slipped his braces off his shoulders. His feet were propped up on a corner of the water bowl. As she watched, one hand moved up to his face and a pinprick of coal glowed briefly.

There was a pause, and then a small cloud of baby-blue smoke drifted up. Mary pulled up a stool and rested her elbows on the counter so that her face was just inches from the bars.

The Prime Minister's eyes were closed. He could have been asleep, except that his hand rose and fell, and his face brightened and faded in the glow from his cigarette.

Mary tapped a fingernail on one of the bars. The Prime Minister's lip curled and then his eyes opened slowly and looked into hers.

"Hello," she said, smiling.

He stared at her.

She reached a finger in through the bars and scratched the side of his head. He jerked his head away, strode angrily to the other side of the cage and sat down with his back to her.

Mary turned the cage around so that she could see his face. "You're incredibly cute," she said.

The Prime Minister ground his cigarette out, lay down on his side and pulled the collar of his shirt up over his ears.

After a while Quentin called from the bedroom and Mary went back to bed.

The first meal Mary gave the Prime Minister consisted of a morsel of mashed potato, a sliver of steak, and a pea, all carefully laid out in the lid of a milk bottle. The Prime Minister took one look at it and threw it in a corner. The whole of the next day he refused to eat. On the following morning he ate some oats and a raisin, and banged his plate against the bars for more.

That night Mary got up for some water and heard a strange squeaking sound coming from the kitchen. Going quietly nearer she saw the Prime Minister, stripped to his underpants and with his tie knotted around his head, jogging on the treadmill.

And in this haphazard fashion things settled into a routine.

Mary fed the Prime Minister and saw to it that his cage was kept clean. She provided him with little things from toyshops, most of which he threw out of the cage when her back was turned. The one object he seemed pleased with was a recliner, complete with a miniature antimacassar and lace-edged scatter cushions. One morning Mary found the Prime Minister's clothes in a pile next to his breakfast dishes, so she washed them for him. She also gave him a bowl of water and retired discreetly to another room. Though she heard him singing as he splashed around in the bath, he still refused to speak to her.

Mary found the Prime Minister fascinating. She spent hours each day watching him as he paced around with his hands clasped behind his back, or sat day-dreaming in his chair, or did his exercises. In the evenings, after Quentin came in from work, Mary had to watch over the Prime Minister to protect him.

Quentin's hatred for the Prime Minister did not diminish with time. He seized every opportunity to torment him. He poured water over him, he threatened him with cigarette lighters, he banged things down on the counter next to the cage when he was napping. Every evening over supper, while the Prime Minister ate his miniature version of the meal with his back purposefully turned, Quentin would read out the latest official news.

"This morning the Prime Minister was discharged from hospital. His doctor is still refusing to comment on the precise nature of the illness that struck him down mysteriously last Saturday. However, he described his condition as satisfactory. After his discharge the Prime Minister retired to his country residence to recuperate."

The Prime Minister would carry on chewing as if he hadn't heard.

Only once did Mary feel the desire to hurt him, and this was in an attempt to provoke him out of his stubborn silence. She was washing the dishes one morning, chatting away to him about her childhood, her parents, her sister who had emigrated, and looked up to see that he wasn't listening at all. He was lying on his back examining the mechanism of the treadmill. She grabbed an old newspaper off the vegetable rack and was about to bang on the cage with it, but her eye caught the headline and instead she tore off the front page and stuffed it in through the bars. She smiled as the Prime Minister wrestled with it and then, when he had succeeded in spreading it out, paced out its meaning with his hands behind his back and a tear on his cheek.

The page showed a photograph of the Prime Minister's wife, smiling bravely into the camera, and below that a report to the effect that the Prime Minister was still not well enough to speak to reporters. There was also an editorial which speculated that the Prime Minister's political career was over, and listed the five people most likely to succeed him. When he wrung his hands over that, Mary started to laugh. The Prime Minister flew into a rage, overturning his chair and kicking sawdust through the bars.

After this incident Mary felt terrible. She apologized at length, assuring him that she wasn't really at all like Quentin, but the Prime Minister maintained a wounded silence.

One evening the three of them were watching television. At Mary's insistence the Prime Minister's cage had been placed on a kitchen stool quite close to the set. Although she had motivated the concession to Quentin on humanitarian grounds, her main concern was to keep a protective eye on the Prime Minister.

During the commercial break before the late news the Prime Minister heaved himself out of his chair and went to urinate in the cup Mary had provided for that purpose in a corner of his cage.

Quentin suddenly burst out: "That's it! I can't take it any more!" He grabbed the cage and stormed through to the kitchen.

"Please, Quentin," Mary pleaded, running after him.

Quentin put the plug in the sink and turned on the water. "I won't tolerate his presence in this house another minute!" he shouted. "What the hell are we going to do with him? We can't just keep him until he dies. He could live for another thirty years." He turned off the tap and reached into the cage. The Prime Minister clung tenaciously to the bars, but one firm tug was enough to pull him loose. Mary flung herself on Quentin but he shoved her away and plunged the Prime Minister under the water.

A stream of bubbles boiled to the surface.

"He's talking under water," Mary said in a small voice.

Quentin pulled the Prime Minister out of the water and threw him down on the counter. "This is fucking impossible!" he shouted, and went back to the lounge to watch the news.

Mary put her finger on the Prime Minister's damp belly and pressed. Water spilled from the slack lips, and then his chest shuddered and began to rise and fall. She lifted him gently, laid him out on a dishcloth and blew in his face. After a while he stirred and sat up, choking. He was trying to say something. Mary patted him on his back.

"He's crazy," the Prime Minister finally said in a gush of water.

"There there," Mary said, pushing him down onto his back, "you must rest. You've been through a horrible experience."

The Prime Minister lay quietly for several minutes while Mary stroked his forehead. Then he pushed himself tiredly into a sitting position. "In the circumstances," he said, choking back a sob, "I'm ready to talk."

It was a formal meeting, with Mary in the chair.

Quentin sat on a stool at one end of the breakfast nook counter, the Prime Minister sat in his recliner at the other. The cage had been put away where he couldn't see it. Once he was out of the cage the Prime Minister seemed to grow in stature. He sat with an air of dignified despair, appropriate to an honourable surrender, his fingers meshed together in his lap, his legs crossed, one shiny black shoe swinging.

"I declare this meeting open," Mary said.

The Prime Minister rose, looked around the room as if acknowledging a silent audience, then cleared his throat, and began: "Ladies and gentlemen. You see before you a man who was once the proud leader –"

"You're not half the man you used to be," Quentin put in.

The Prime Minister looked gravely at the toe of his shoe, then began again. "Ladies and gentlemen. My friend's manner may be insulting, but there is a measure of truth in his words. I stand before you alone, humiliated –"

"Belittled," Quentin said.

The Prime Minister stamped his foot. He addressed himself to the chair. "In the name of decency, will you stop this man from interrupting me."

"Please, Quentin," Mary said, "let him have his say."

"He's not in parliament now," Quentin said.

"My boy…," the Prime Minister said.

"Ha!" Quentin shouted, banging his fist on the counter so hard that the Prime Minister lost his footing and fell on his hands and knees. Quentin burst out laughing. The Prime Minister picked himself up, dusted the knees of his suit, and sat down in his recliner. He crossed his legs deliberately and said, "I demand an apology for this childish behaviour."

Mary looked at Quentin.

"You're not serious," he said.

He saw that she was.

There was a silence in which Quentin tapped his cigarette on the edge of the ashtray, and the Prime Minister rubbed his knees.

At last Quentin said, "I'm sorry."

"Apology accepted," the Prime Minister said.

"Let's begin again then," Mary said. "Quentin, please control your temper. Mr Prime Minister – proceed, and please make it brief."

"Ladies and gentlemen. Forgive me if I do not rise. Through no fault of my own, my knees hurt. Let me come straight to the point.

What we have here is a classic case of interdependence. I need you, for practical reasons: food, water, a roof over my head. Incidentally, the question of living-quarters is one I'd like to come back to later on. As I was saying, I need you. You also need me. The reasons you need me are rather different. I amuse you. I keep you company. Don't think I haven't noticed the dearth of human fellowship around here. But perhaps I could come back to that as well later on."

The meeting lasted four hours. Quentin smoked fifteen cigarettes. The Prime Minister, who was dying for a cigarette himself, bit his nails and jogged his foot. He wrung his hands. He limped around on the counter waving his fist and wagging his finger. Quentin spat at him and bombed him with peanuts. Eventually the Prime Minister, in a frenzy of frustration at his inability to overturn the ashtray, scooped up handfuls of ash and rubbed them into his face.

At last the meeting was over. The minutes, as Mary set them down, recorded that

(1) Quentin would attempt to secure the Prime Minister's wife without using unnecessary force or causing her unnecessary anguish.

(2) The Prime Minister's living-quarters would be improved.

(3) Quentin would refrain from taunting the Prime Minister without due cause.

(4) The Prime Minister in turn would do his best not to antagonize

Quentin by refraining from, among other things, urinating in his presence or trying to escape.

After the meeting Mary installed the Prime Minister in one corner of the spare room. The Prime Minister, in his new spirit of conciliation, offered to carry the recliner through himself, but eventually gave up halfway down the passage and allowed Mary to carry him and his furniture the rest of the way.

That night the Prime Minister couldn't sleep. He roamed the expanses of the wall-to-wall carpet and charted the limits of his new homeland.

For seven full evenings they sat in front of the television set, Quentin perched on a stool within easy reach of the screen, hands tingling, the Prime Minister in his recliner on top of another stool, holding thumbs conspicuously, Mary sitting quietly on the sofa behind them.

Getting the Prime Minister had been a simple enough task; getting his wife proved to be more difficult. It required calculations of scale and definition that hadn't occurred to Quentin before. In the weeks after her husband vanished she made frequent appearances on the box (or in the box, as Quentin put it). They saw her almost every night, looking bravely into the camera and describing a relapse or a recovery. But the camera was usually focused on her face, and the opportunity for snatching her was lost. On the one occasion when she was shown in full figure, she must have been all of twelve inches tall, and Quentin, on the point of making a grab for her, saw the look of horror on the Prime Minister's face and stopped himself.

On the eighth evening the Prime Minister's wife suddenly appeared in perfect proportion. In the middle of a car chase the screen went blank, a voice said, "We interrupt this transmission for a special news report" and there she was. She was floating in a cloud of peach chiffon and she was weeping. In the distance behind her a flag was flying at half-mast. There was one small problem: standing next to her, with one hand on her elbow and a grim expression on his face, was a man in a military uniform. He was wearing a peaked cap, and there was a bright row of medals on his tunic.

"Now!" cried the Prime Minister, jumping to his feet.

"Don't," said Mary.

The Prime Minister's wife dabbed at her eyes; the Minister of Defence opened his mouth to speak. And at that moment Quentin plunged his arm in up to the elbow and scooped.

A broken flagpole, trailing gravel and sparks, a whirl of peach chiffon and a blur of khaki exploded into the room.

The Prime Minister's wife landed on a fern in one corner of the room, and that broke her fall. The Minister of Defence struck

Quentin in the chest, rebounded and, borne down by the weight of his medals, dropped headfirst towards the floor. Quentin dived from the stool and caught him just before he hit the carpet.

The Prime Minister shouted "Gys!" in a voice so loud it could have belonged to a fully grown man.

The Minister of Defence scrambled out of Quentin's grasp and ran several paces, then threw himself on the carpet, rolled over, and rose up on one knee with a revolver in his hand. He pulled the trigger and Quentin felt a sharp sting on his cheek. Quentin swatted the Minister with the back of his hand and was surprised to see him fly across the room, smash into the wall and drop in a heap onto the carpet.

Mary turned the body over. The head was caved in like an eggshell and leaking. She began to drop large tears onto the corpse. The Prime Minister had meanwhile slid down the leg of the stool and retrieved his wife from the pot plant. The chiffon was a little bruised, but otherwise she seemed to be in good health. After a brief embrace they went over to the body; and now the Prime Minister's wife began to wail, and her wails rose up to meet Mary's large sobs.

Quentin stormed out in pursuit of a drink.

Mary recovered the body from the rubbish bin and did her best to straighten it out. She wiped the blood off its face and pulled up the knot of its tie. She put the cap on its head and rearranged the medals.

Then she fetched a spade from under the kitchen sink and buried it, with due ceremony, in the bottom of the garden.

The Prime Minister and his wife stood solemnly at the graveside. The Prime Minister made a short speech in which he praised the deceased's devotion to duty. The Prime Minister's wife sang a plaintive hymn, which almost started Mary crying again.

The following night, just before the epilogue, Quentin took the managing director of a supermarket chain. Mary gave him blankets and food and took him through to the spare room. She introduced him to the Prime Minister and his wife, and left them to make one another's acquaintance.

Quentin was lying in bed with his hands behind his head. Mary sat down on the edge of the bed next to him. "We need to talk about this thing," she said.

"I agree," Quentin said, sitting up. "It can't go on like this."

"I'm glad you also think so," she said.

"So far it's been far too random," he went on. "One here, one there. What we need's a strategy. Maybe a list." He scratched around on the bedside table for a pen and paper.

"That's not what I had in mind. I don't think you should be doing this."

"Why not?"

"Why?"

"I'm not sure yet," he said, "but I think it will become clearer as we go along. Right. Who's next?" He opened a notebook and poised a pen over the page.

"I don't want to play this game," Mary said.

"It's not a game. It's serious stuff."

"Let's forget it. I don't like you like this."

"Well, I've given you a chance," Quentin said. "If you don't want to take it, fine. Who's that woman with the face – you know, the TV personality, the one you said looked like a basset?"

The next evening Quentin took a continuity announcer whose vivacious insincerity particularly annoyed him. Mary carried the hysterical woman through to the bathroom to calm her down, and while she was in there Quentin took the captain of the Northern Transvaal squash team and a country and western duo. When Mary came out of the spare room, having handed the continuity announcer into the capable hands of the Prime Minister's wife, she heard a tiny rendition of "Oh, lonesome me" coming from the lounge, and she locked herself in the bedroom and cried herself to sleep. Quentin slept on the sofa.

In the week that followed, Quentin concentrated on priests, aiming for a representative selection of denominations. The week after that, he told Mary over supper, it would be professors.

"We can't have a stupid republic developing here," he said.

Mary gave all the new people blankets and put them in the spare room. In the mornings she put in a large bowl of ProNutro; in the evenings she dished up a third plate of food and put that in the room. Every two or three days she went in with a broom and swept out the rubbish and the bodies.

The professor week didn't work out too well. After an argument with a professor of divinity Quentin changed his mind, and started taking handfuls of spectators at sports events. "Ordinary people, that's what we need," he said to Mary, who was standing by with a picnic basket to ferry the new arrivals through.

Mary was awakened one night by a rumbling of voices. It was a small noise, far away and muted, and not altogether unpleasant. She lay listening to the sound as it rose and fell in the room next door.

"Are you awake?" Quentin said.

"Yes," she answered, turning on her side to face him.

"I've been meaning to talk to you," he said. "The spare room's starting to smell. Maybe it would be better if you cleaned it every day."

The evening after Mary left, Quentin misjudged his timing and took the torso of an opera singer. He watched the thing thumping its stumps on the carpet. Then he took a mouth out of a toothpaste ad and propped it up on a coffee table. It smiled at him. He smiled back. He speared the torso on the end of a fork and brushed it against the teeth. The lips slobbered open and the teeth began to gnash. For the hell of it he took the leg of a statue, half a building, and a cubic metre of Indian Ocean. Then he gathered it all up and went through to the spare room.

Movements

I

He slams the door hard on the sound of his name and it rumbles back down the passage at her. Now, at the bottom of the steps with the echo still lurching he wants to turn around but cannot, because she is still standing in the lounge with the image of his back and the slam of the door in her eyes and her hands.
The Italian neighbour under buttery verandah light raises his helmet-haired head from the dominoes, and watches.

He lights a cigarette at the gate, waiting for the anger to leave his stride. Converts this departure into a stroll to the shop, where he has to buy something to bring back as evidence. He buys a Coke, and feels uneasy: the man behind the counter begrudges small purchases and hates his clientele for refusing to make him rich.

She comes into the room, does not look at him lying on the bed with his face up to the ceiling, pretending to listen to the music while the

Coke goes flat on the table. His music, and it spreads itself out on the walls to colour them his colours.

I'm going out.

She finds her key, some money, a jersey. Goes out. And in the passage, with the door clamping shut behind her, she hears him scream and something smashes deliberately.

So she goes down the stairs.

The Italian neighbour packs up the dominoes and goes inside.

When he comes out of the gate he sees her sitting at the bus-shelter, he sees their loneliness made public. But turns purposefully right. Hears her call his name. Twice. Three times. Turns around on the third because she may not call again.

She sits on the bus-stop bench like a little girl, in the middle, with her feet dangling. She refuses to be angry.

Let's go home. Come home. The buses aren't running.

I don't want to. I don't feel like being in that house.

Please.

Silence, as she watches her foot swinging. Her silence folds its arms, dares him to be angry.

I'll go back. I'll pack my things. I don't have to stay.

Silence answers him so he turns and goes back slowly across the street, replaying the script in his head, convincing himself. Stops at the gate, suddenly afraid. That she will allow it to happen. Make him label things with yours and mine although the smell of her is in everything. That she will wait till he has shaken her out of things and folded them and packed them, before she comes to stop him.

He goes back to her more slowly, defeated. Stops close to her, wants to sit down, but her silence occupies everything. Reaches out to her profile softly with her name.
Don't make me.
You always win.
You make me say things.

She turns over the tape and her music laps at the corners. He lets her draw him onto the bed, take the shard from his fingers.
It's all right. It's all right.
But I didn't want to break it. I thought you'd come back if I broke it.
It's all right.
The walls are changing colour.
He lets her pull his head down to cry into her shirt, lets her cover him with her shadow.

II

He cries for the first time, in black and white.
This is during a confession, in a parked car. The radio provides a
soundtrack. The sky co-operates with rain. The windscreen mists
over. A streetlight tosses in some lighting. He puts the car into reverse
so that the gear-lever won't get in the way of the embrace.
She thinks his weeping is beautiful, sensitive, almost brave.
She says she has not been able to cry for years. "Once I held my hand
over the spout of a steaming kettle, to make myself cry, but it didn't
work."
He doesn't tell her how long it is since he was able to cry. He puts the
car in neutral, starts the engine, puts on the wipers, and drives home.

He cries as often as he can, not just during confessions.
Once he cries because he is happy.
He cries – clearly, articulately, he thinks – as metaphor for his sensi-
tivity, his courage. He cries because he is different from other men.

She cries for the first time after all these years.
A tear slow-motions down a hazy cheek.
She thanks him for making it possible, as if he is an onion.

They cry together.

She cries more often. He can't keep up.
She cries in technicolour, in broken English, as if it were real.
It strikes him one day that it is real. But he is always more convinced
by his own emotion than by hers.

He cries as counter-espionage. Behind her back, smearing his own
spit on his cheeks, trying a few sobs, waiting for her fingers to seek
out his eyes, the proof.

He starts to enjoy it when she cries.
In it he finds a reason to be gentle and sad.

He stops crying.
She doesn't notice.

He begins to predict her tears. A silence precedes them, like the pro-
phetic silence between tracks on a record, when the beginning of the
next song echoes out of memory.

One day she notices that he has stopped crying. "You don't cry any
more. Not even when you're unhappy."

For a while he manages to be her: incapable of crying. He even punches the walls once, trying for tears.

For a while she manages to be him: sensitive, beautiful, brave.

He has broken the ashtrays. Now he is regretting it, trying to pick up pellets of ash with his fingertips.

She puts on a tape and turns up the volume. Her colours, her dark blues. She goes away to fetch a dustpan. He hears her fill the kettle. He sits on the bed, rests his head against a greasy spot on the wall. His legs stick out at a broken angle. He has to keep his shoes off the duvet. He looks at the wall next to the window. The paint is flaking off in precise pieces, as if someone has been punching the walls, shadow-boxing. Isosceles triangles and parallelograms lie on the floor. The room is turning into an educational toy.

She comes in with the dustpan, begins sweeping up geometry and ash.

Freeze him, watching. He is composing a poem without capitals or punctuation.

Freeze her. (She also has a shadow, pasted on the wall, and a thought-bubble.) He will write a poem and leave it by the kettle, because he still needs me.

III

She hesitates with her fingers on the door-handle, wishing that she could go out surely, that she could achieve the finality of a door, shut. But she hesitates because she wants to be comforted. It intrigues her that she would let herself be comforted if he would let himself come to her. But the doorway of his bedroom holds him like a frame. That is the safe place, after all, behind him there is light and colour, a shelf of books, an unmade bed, and he guards it with his body. But the door where she is standing is a frontier: there is nothing beyond it but the night and the street.

Perhaps, she is thinking, with one hand on the door-handle and the other against the cold glass, he will see how small I am, imagining me in this black frame, against this empty night.

He sees that she wants him to come to her and it drives him back. He feels safer in the doorway of his room. She has occupied the hallway. It is hers, her hands are everywhere. Her hands move in gestures that he cannot understand, and so he allows them to assume the shape of hands that are reaching for door-handles and keys. He finds himself in the doorway of his bedroom, stepping in and out of it, trying to break its hold. Then her hand does settle on the door-handle, and the night begins to open in him.

He goes to her. Perhaps he goes too quickly. He is sure that she will be gone by the time he reaches the door. She will be gone leaving nothing but the scent of her fingers on the glass. He will be able to call after her, hopelessly. But she is still there, hesitating, and now he has to reach her and he doesn't know what to do with his hands. He puts one hand on her shoulder, softly, as if not to frighten her. That hand wants to comfort her, draw her back to him.

But the other hand argues: it presses on the small of her back, as if it wants to push her out into the night.

She listens to the hands, just the hands.

The one on her shoulder, curled like a crook, she hears, is pushing her out through the crack of the door. The one on her back, that flat palm, is pulling her in.

She turns herself in to him, his hands turn her in to him. She opens him like a door, it is easy, and she walks through. He sees her getting smaller and smaller down the passages to the small place where he is waiting, where he will be able to speak to her without fear.

I am coming, she says, and soon my voice will be small enough for you to hear it above the clamouring of your busy heart.

He looks at his grey hands.

He hears her car start in the street below.

He finds himself in the doorway of his room.

He sees that she has gone out, closing the door behind her. It is light behind the frosted panes, it is morning outside, where she is.

We Came to the Monument

I have a few things to tell you and a lot of time.

I stand with my back to the world, my hands in my pockets. To tell the truth I have no hands: these pockets are empty. I am only surface. There is no more to me than meets the eye.

Except that I have a heart and a brain. And I can invent a tongue. That is all I need to make a monument as quick and fickle as a kite.

We came to live in the Monument, more or less by chance. We were on our way to the city, but we came to the Monument and it seemed like a place to stay. That was months ago.

News came from the north that the city had been abandoned. After the long years of siege, the defenders gave up hope. They put aside their guns, they turned to dust, they took flight. The attackers, storming triumphantly through the deserted streets, were surprised to find nothing worth possessing. They smashed a few statues (according to the reports) and went away.

For a long time we had been dreaming about a return. So we left our place in the bush and came north. We were five families in all. Our leader's name was Steenkamp; I am his only daughter.

I lived in the city once. I lived there for a long time. I stood on my pedestal at a busy intersection, and I thought I was fortunate to find myself at the heart of it all, in a place so full of people and incident.

I watched carelessly over the people. Generally, they watched carelessly over me. Few of them knew what I stood for. Industry, some might have said, or Courage, or the People Themselves, their Past, or maybe their Future.

I remember a few of them. An old woman, for example (I watched her grow older). Her head became a broken bird's nest, her body a twisted branch. She used to scatter breadcrumbs from a plastic bag. She planted her feet like roots in the dry grass and the birds settled around her like scraps of blackened paper.

I also remember those who were cleaning up, because they were always there: trimming the edges of the lawn, cutting the trees into solid geometry, spearing pieces of paper on sharpened wire. I thought then: One day soon one of them will spear a pigeon, or the old woman's chattering brain, and roast it over a brazier in front of the iron gates.

But this is all beside the point.

I remember especially my love.

I lived in a city of rock. In the morning a tide of flesh and blood came in, it surged through the streets and crashed against the buildings, voices slid over one another like pebbles. In the evening the tide receded, leaving the streets full of sand.

I remained behind, a monumental silence, dry and hollow. I waited my turn to speak through my love's talkative hands, her fluent skin.

On the last day of our journey north we camped within sight of the Monument.

It stands on a hill overlooking the city. When I was a child the Monument was floodlit every night so that you could not forget about it. It was visible from every window, summoning us. We entered that cavernous space as if it were a cathedral. Signs told us to be silent. The walls inside were lined with marble friezes. My father would lead us around, stopping in front of each panel to read the inscription on a brass plaque and point out certain details. Clockwise, we would go, for it was a chronicle, telling the whole story of our people: a story of origins and pioneers, battles and massacres, and long journeys marked by heroism and suffering. The names of the places, the heroes, the battles won or lost were familiar to me. But the friezes filled me with a small, private horror. The people were frozen, half in and half out of the stone. It was not a passive element. It sucked them in, it cunningly enslaved them, while allowing them the illusion of liberty. The folds of a woman's dress flowed secretly into a rockface. A man's boots were rooted to the stony ground. The manes of the horses, at full gallop, hooves trampling the bodies of our fallen enemies, blew back in a stone wind.

On the last evening of our journey, there were no floodlights on the Monument, just the sordid backdrop of the sunset. Even when the sky faded to grey the black block on the broken hills persisted. As we ate, gathered around the fire, my eyes went again and again to the hills. I saw that some of the others also looked to the Monument, and then turned their eyes away and stared into the flames.

Just before bedtime my father called us all together. "I have been thinking," he said, "that the scouts should go first to the Monument tomorrow morning, to pay our respects. From there they can also observe the city and judge whether it is safe to return."

It was agreed.

But I knew then, in a way I have of knowing what is inevitable, that we would never go further than the Monument. We had come home.

I lived in the city, and I wept, when the weather permitted. Sometimes I could see the place reeling between monument and ruin, and I could not flee.

The wind was ravenous; it peeled a skin of dust from the hills, it carved numbers on the faces of the buildings, it chewed the trees down to the bone, it ambushed people, exploding under skirts and coats, it swallowed and spat out fragments of bone and cloth.

The wind blew all sorts of madness into people.

I was troubled by a recurring dream: One morning I see a crowd coming my way, laughing and singing, carrying ropes and crowbars and hammers. They have come to topple me, to drag my body down into the street. I am afraid that I will fall to pieces if I move. I do. I expect that they will leave me to rot, as a warning to all those whose hearts were hardened. But no, they scavenge me for souvenirs. My eye becomes a paperweight, my foot a doorstop. What bits of me will make bookends, flowerpots, stepping-stones, a wreck for the bottom of the fish-tank? Those who pull me down are surprised to see a sticky heart pacing out the confines of my broken ribcage.

The dream troubled me, but my love troubled me more.

Always heads turned to watch her as she passed. An old man on a bench, a student with a clipboard under his arm, the businessman, the bus-conductor, those who were cleaning up – they watched her as though she were public property, the way I am, or the fountains, or the bust of a dead statesman. Only I did not need to turn my head. I kept my eyes fixed on a space next to the bus-shelter, a space shaped just like her. And when she suddenly filled the space, I was pleased with the inevitability of my love for her.

At other times it drove me to distraction to be so implacably myself. My heart betrayed me. I felt my veins begin to tingle, my skin begin to itch. I told myself this desire to be a man was foolish. There are more than enough men in the world.

But I wanted to go with her. I began to prepare myself.

My hands had been frozen into two permanent gestures, one open, one shut. Always like that, in the mornings, in the evenings, one open, one shut. But then the local historians, who wanted to give our city a history with footnotes, began to say that sometimes the hand that was open in the morning was shut at night. They said I was some kind of miracle or, at least, that I contradicted myself.

The people paid no attention. There were no tour buses full of pilgrims. The people knew that a statue is only a statue.

The scouts came back from the Monument to say the place was in ruins. They said nothing about the city.

We held a meeting to discuss our course of action. Some said that the ruined Monument was a sign we should turn back. Others argued that it summoned us on to some task of reconstruction. My grandfather said it was our duty to go up to the Monument and do what we could to clean it up and make repairs. Finally it was agreed that any decision would have to wait until we had all seen the place for ourselves.

The road up the hill was cratered and overgrown, and the ascent, with all of us pushing and pulling the loaded handcarts, took many hours. It was mid-afternoon before we emerged at last from a grove of bluegums onto the slopes below the Monument. Where once there had been lawns as smooth as carpets, the grass now grew wild, spilling over the terraces and pathways. The trees, once sculpted into leafy cannons and bombshells, had exploded into disorder.

And the Monument itself. An acidic wind had scoured the sheen off it. Lightning had branded it and thunder had rubbed its hard edges to powder.

We circled the enclosing wall until we found an entrance and steps leading up to a sagging door. My father stopped in the doorway and the rest of us crowded around, peering into the gloom. He pointed, and I saw that a narrow beam of sunlight, marbled by dust motes, fell from a crack in the ceiling onto a dead, unintelligible face. My grandfather dropped to his knees and began to wail. Grandma tried to comfort him.

We lit torches and went in, hesitantly, my father in the lead. Dry leaves crunched underfoot. The place had a warm, furry stench. We followed my father, clockwise, stopping in front of each panel. The torchlight flickered on discoloured faces, slimed chins, cobwebbed mouths. At the first panel – the settlers erect a stone cross on a beach, curious natives look on, a stunned sea – my father held his torch to the plaque, but could not make out the words.

I covered my mouth with my shawl. The figures on the walls twitched and turned their eyes away from the light. We waded through the warm air, slow as the hands of a clock, in silence. At last we emerged into the glare.

"We'll camp out here," my father said, indicating the wild grass between the steps and the enclosure.

We spent the rest of the afternoon making camp.

When night was falling and the other women were preparing supper, I picked my way to the rear of the Monument, hoping for a view of the city. Instead, I discovered an unaccountable absence. Each of the four corners of the Monument had once been guarded by sentinels, great stone warriors with their backs fused to the walls and their hands clasped around the barrels of their rifles, whose stocks rested between their boots. But one of the sentinels, the one who had looked to the city, had abandoned his post. I climbed up onto the empty ledge and rested my back against the corner. I looked into the distance, to the factories he had watched over, a ragged skyline of chimneys, toothed roofs and pylons. When I was a child that sky would be red with the flames from the furnaces. Now a cold grey night poured in, filling in all the spaces between things, congealing on every surface, until my back grew numb.

I cracked myself loose and went back to the fire.

The wind blew a war into the city.

The city fathers put up lights everywhere to turn night into day. On a whim, they would switch them all off, and then the darkest of nights rang through the city like a cracked bell.

Some people left. I saw the convoys, the families carrying creaking suitcases, the lonely ones and twos.

Others stayed. They bought uniforms and held meetings at night. Then it was as if spaceships had landed in the stadiums. The lights were blue against the sky, the stars were washed out. I thought the people of the city were fortunate that they no longer needed the stars, neither for navigation, nor prophecy, nor hope.

I itched all over. Every night I schooled my heart to beat and moved my hands. I would fetch her from the space next to the bus-shelter, and together we would leave and find a place where the night was left in peace.

I waited too long. One morning, I knew that she was gone. The space had crept into me while I slept and now it ached like a tooth socket. I sought it again and again with my tongue, urging blood into my cold limbs. And when the blood had seeped to the tips of my fingers, to my toes, I knew that I could walk.

When I was younger I longed to be a man. I wanted to wear Christmas hats of crackling paper, I wanted to clean my nails, clear my throat, put on socks, wait at the robot looking impatiently from side to side. Now I wanted simply to leave. But something kept me rooted to the spot.

One day a man with a long feather-duster tickled my face until I almost split my sides. He connected a hose to a tap and washed me down as if I were some artefact, caked with dirt, unearthed from the tomb of a dead civilization. He sat under a tree, with his back against the trunk, and waited for me to dry. Then he came to look at me, squinting into the sun, as if he saw the outlines of a new man.

That night when the tide had gone out I climbed down from my pedestal, stretched, and walked away.

I walked through the gutted city. I walked past the survivors, asleep in the ruins, in their stainless-steel beds, in their striped pyjamas, above their patient shoes, next to their incorruptible clocks. I walked out of the city, along the route taken by the refugees. And so I came at length to the Monument and it seemed like a place to stay.

I took the place that had been kept for me among the sentinels. There, with my back pressed comfortably to the walls, I could watch the city from a distance. The busy lives and deaths of the people could take their course in the corner of my eye.

I never cried for my lost love; sometimes the rain wet my face. I never laughed for my found freedom; sometimes the wind pasted a leaf against my mouth.

I said: I am just a monument to a night I wept with my ear against your *breast, a morning I touched your sleeping eyes and your dreams brushed off on my fingers, a moment between darkness and light when, at last, the planets turned on the brittle stem of your wrist.*

But I didn't believe a word of it. After all, none of it happened. Still, a sense of loss was necessary.

And in this way many years went by.

The day after we made our camp in the shadow of the Monument, I rediscovered the museum. I remembered clearly where it had stood, dug into the rocky slope, but still it was hard to find. Rock falls had almost buried the building. When I eventually found the entrance it was blocked by rubble, but I managed to squeeze through.

The torch showed me a broken display-case, an upturned desk. A woman used to sit there, I remembered, selling tickets and souvenirs: scale models of the Monument, teaspoons with engravings of the Monument, Monument dishcloths and paperweights, Monument letterboxes. I righted the display-case: tarnished teaspoons.

I went down a passage and came to a room behind glass. The Living Room of a Typical Farmhouse. A man sat at a table with the family Bible open in front of him. Two well-behaved children sat on either side of him, their chins resting on their hands. A woman stood behind the man, one hand resting on his shoulder.

I smashed the glass and climbed through into the room. There was a film of dust on the table, rat-droppings in the teacups. I tried shifting the little boy, but he would not budge: closer inspection revealed that he was bolted to his chair, the chair was bolted to the floor.

I went through a low doorway into the kitchen. The light from my torch flickered on copper pots and pans, and on the painted coals that glowed in the oven. The pot on the coals was empty.

In room after room I examined the set faces of these statues, touched the rough fabric of their clothes, their cold hands. I turned the dusty pages of their hymnbooks and Bibles. I tested their clumsy implements, their hard chairs and lumpy mattresses.

I took back with me an embroidered bonnet to show the others.

That evening when we gathered around the fire there was an argument. My grandfather started it by asking me about the bonnet.

"I found it in the museum," I said. "There are all sorts of wonderful things down there, maps and – "

"You must put it back," he said flatly.

"Why should I do that?"

"If you had any respect for the dead," Grandfather said, "you would not have taken it in the first place. You should know better."

I told him there were all kinds of useful things in the museum, clothing, blankets, buckets – things we needed. It would be foolish to let them lie there. Grandfather accused me of treachery. Others joined the argument, most of them arguing that we needed to be practical. Grandfather persisted. "You don't need a fancy bonnet," he said.

And he was right, although I did not admit it. It amused me to start a fashion. By tomorrow, I thought, all the women will be wearing these ridiculous bonnets. By next Sunday, when we gather for prayers, half the men will be wearing top hats and coarse black suits, and clutching prayerbooks in a language we hardly understand.

Eventually my father joined the discussion. "Our situation is difficult," he said. "It is not unlike the one our forefathers found themselves in. We must take a lesson from them. They improvised, they endured, they made do. The rains will be here soon and the tents are inadequate. We must build better shelters for ourselves. Perhaps there are things in the museum that will make our task easier."

He did not mention the city.

"I have an idea," Grandfather said sarcastically. "Why don't we just move into the Monument?"

And that, of course, is exactly what we did.

My grandparents stayed on in their tent for a week after the rest of us moved. Then one night there was a storm. Grandma moved inside. Grandfather lasted another day on his own, speaking to no one, but when it rained again the following night, he too moved in with us.

All the best places along the walls had been taken; my grandparents had to make their home in the middle of the room. They put up a canvas lean-to next to the sarcophagus of the unknown pioneer.

I have made myself a bed on a marble bench in the corner. In the frieze just above me is a statue who intrigues me. He has turned his back on us.

This particular panel depicts the signing of a treaty. Two men are seated at a table. One of our early leaders sits on the left. Behind him stand our people, his people. Some of them hold rifles; all of them wear hats. Our leader looks at the man opposite him, but he appears not to see him. He looks through him to the distant mountains. Immediately behind our leader stands a woman. She too looks to the mountains. One of her hands rests on our leader's shoulder. To her left, a priest who holds a Bible. He looks at the man on the other side of the table with determined tenderness.

The enemy. He sits awkwardly on the edge of his chair. He looks like a man who has never sat in a chair before. He holds a quill in his left hand. He is about to make a cross on the document our leader pushes towards him. He does not look at the mountains. He looks at the end of the quill. Around him, his people kneel.

Behind these kneeling people, stands my friend. I cannot see his face, but I know that he is not unhappy with the stone world in which he belongs. He turns his back on us. He cannot hear us.

The life of a sentinel suited me. I watched the city crumble. I heard bombs and I saw fires. Sometimes bombs fell on the hillside or in the carpark. The Monument endured. The streams of refugees dried up. Fewer and fewer people were left in the city. But still the siege continued.

For a long time no one came to the Monument at all. I was happy with myself. The foolish desire to be a man left me.

Then one day, out of the corner of my eye, I saw three men appear from the trees. They studied the Monument with telescopes. Then they came on, and passed out of my vision, heading towards the steps. I heard them exclaiming and breaking through the undergrowth. After a while they left, going back the way they had come.

Later that day they returned, bringing with them many others, carrying bundles and drawing handcarts. I knew then that they would stay here. They were bringing their voices, their smells, their sour breath. They would make fires and sit around them talking, laughing, disagreeing. My feet began to itch. The blood was rising in me.

But there was something worse. She was with them. She was moving towards a space I carried in me and she would fit it perfectly.

I cried out: You may touch me, but not enter. Here in my untouchable heart nothing needs to move. But already my heart had awakened. It was beating softly, forcing blood into my dry veins.

I fled inside. I scrambled from frieze to frieze, trying to find a place to

hide, pushing aside the quiet women, trampling the toys of the children,
kicking over kettles, stumbling across battlefields strewn with thorns and
assegais and the bodies of the dead.

   I heard their feet on the steps.

   I found myself in a corner, among the vanquished.

   I heard the beating of her heart.

   I turned my back and sank into the stone.

   She has made her bed just below me. That was inevitable. I hear her
dimly, talking in her sleep. I feel her warm breath on the back of my neck.
She wills me to turn around.

We came to live in the Monument, more or less by chance.

   It seems to me sometimes as if the earth stopped dead on its axis
then, like a globe blocked by a child's hand, and slowly began to
revolve in the opposite direction. It gathers up the long thread of
history, so carelessly unwound into space. A wind is blowing in the
hourglass and it lofts the grains of sand into the night. When the
people are asleep the sand settles in the blood, the streets. I try to resist
by dreaming up storms and floods.

Sometimes I think I hear storms deep in the earth, and lightning striking
upwards to the surface, to break me from these walls. At last, a destiny

of stone. From my skull, cracked open like an egg, hopes and hungers as improbable as birds take flight against a steep grey sky and disappear.

Except for one, which digs its claws into the earth and howls her name. It turns on me its ancient face of joy and grief. It will not let me go.

A Science of Fragments

In memory of Lulu Davis

> Fragments neither close
> nor open meaning:
> they may mean anything except
> wholeness, except certainty.
>
> — Lionel Abrahams

An Unposted Letter

On the day of her death he sat down to write and took her death, or rather his grief, as theme. He found disturbing the haste with which he needed to convert grief into fiction. Yet he admitted that his grief, her death, became more believable with every word he set down. He read the words over as if he had chanced upon them in the flyleaf of a borrowed book. He was moved to tears by his own face, in a mirror.

On the day of her funeral he rewrote the piece three times and typed it up. It hardly filled a page. Rereading it, moved once again to tears, he found an error, and had to type it over. It had to be perfect.

He unpinned two paper figures, a dancer and a sleeper, from his notice-board and folded them in his page. Now that it was folded into quarters the page became a letter. He sealed it in an envelope and put it in his pocket.

It was late. He dressed hurriedly, and while he was dressing he realized that he intended to post his letter in her grave. It amazed him that this had been his intention all along.

The need to post the letter stayed with him, a voice speaking softly in his pocket, as he walked with the other mourners to the open grave.

In the end, he did not post the letter. A spadeful of sand came to seem the adequate gesture, a sheet of white paper an affront. But another consideration urged restraint: he had become too attached to his own words to part with them.

Fruit

She props herself in a fork of the apricot-tree and picks fruit. She is a lilac shadow in the quiet green heart of the tree. In her hands the apricots are succulent suns. She bites into them gleefully and spits out the pips.

He sits on the verandah in an armchair and watches her out of the corner of his eye.

She picks five apricots and drops them in the lap of her lilac dress. Then she discovers that she needs both hands for climbing. So she eats two of the apricots, stores three in her mouth, and climbs down. The hem of her dress snags on a branch and the cloth tears.

She goes to where he is sitting. Her cheeks bulge with fruit. He stifles laughter.

An indistinct fanfare from her full mouth, and then her lips open slowly and she pops the apricots out one by one. She does this with a flourish, like a magician, but he is reminded of a fish; a bird regurgitating from its crop; an insect laying eggs. He looks at the fruit, shiny with spit, in his hand.

It hurts her that he goes to wash the fruit under the garden tap, but she says nothing.

Versions of Himself

Once, at an exhibition, he bought a photograph she had taken: "The Waiting Room." A cardboard box full of chaos and decay. A looming matchbox. Two giant moths. Mulberry leaves as tall as trees, uprooted. Silkworm cocoons stuck to the grey walls. Silkworm droppings. Pink scented sweets. Bones. Electric flex. A crashed dove. A die toppling onto its lucky face. A dead pig. Five plastic people on a bench (from l. to r.):

The watcher
holds an object in his lap and looks into it, rather than at it: a book, a crystal ball, a mirror, a reliquary.

The lovers,
man and woman, their heads resting together, their hands meshed, inanimate. Her eyes are closed. Or perhaps they are simply lowered to look at his hand.

The listener
holds an object to his ear: a telephone, a shell, a bloody rag.

The other man,
the dark one, cut off by the edge of the photograph, in shadow, his head down, his hands hidden. Below the brim of his hat, a face without features.

Conversation

With the dawn a grey chill came into the room. He reached for the bottle and she suddenly burst out: "I used to like your hands but I've changed my mind. They're the hands of a clerk."

He replied, trying to be cruel, "You have the hands of a plumber."

Her head jerked, as if he had struck her, but she laughed. She clapped her workman's hands, full of scratches, the nails chipped and rimmed with black, and she snorted with delight.

Broken Mirror

In the Cavalier Bar at the Flashback Hotel he turned an empty glass in a pool of its sweat on the counter. On the back of a Laughing Cavalier serviette he wrote:

"You crossed the border. You came to rest in a homeland of deaf earth and dumb stone. Now and always, you are travelling on a foreign passport."

He asked the barman for the date and wrote it next to the laughing face. The ink ran. He put the serviette in his pocket.

Meanwhile, she floated in the immense calm beyond the waves. She opened the valve in one of her water-wings and it jetted stale air below the surface. She puttered in circles, on her back, looking up at the circling clouds.

Under one arm she carried a story, her own, missing a chapter or two, wrapped in bright yellow oilskin and tied up with string. The story refused to sink. She forced it under, boiling bubbles as if it were drowning, but it twisted out of her hands and bobbed stubbornly to the air.

She swam back to the shore, towing the bright package behind her.

In the margin of the sea, in large letters, he wrote:

"Forgive me my story, as I forgive you yours."

He sat down to watch the sea erase his message. But the tide was going out and

"Forgive me my story"

persisted. He had to cross it out himself with the palm of his hand.

No one saw him leave. While her eyes were closed he walked out in the sunshine at Jan Smuts airport, his head turned purposefully away, his collar up. He phoned the Flashback from a booth. Reception said the number rang and rang.

In the gardens then, in a childhood place, in the beautiful gardens of the Flashback Hotel, her veins slow with sleep, one leg drawn up, her bones heavy with words, her eyes wide open and dark, she curled at last into cactus-needle, leaf-vein, moss, lichen, loam.

Conversation

She said, "I have the mind of a forty-year-old divorcee in the body of a sixteen-year-old schoolgirl."

He replied, "Or vice versa."

She did not hear, or pretended not to. She looked at the grey morning behind the window-panes. The look on her face was so unexpected that he almost laughed: a jaded, adult expression, signifying worldliness, cynicism, regret.

Versions of Herself

Once, for his birthday, she gave him the fragments of an animated film she had made. A cardboard box spilled out the bits and pieces of a puzzled world: paper people, two inches tall, wax-crayon rainbows, trees, hungry eyes and mouths.

There were hundreds of versions of the heroine, herself, each differing slightly from the next.

For an evening he amused himself, hunting out the figures that could be placed one after the other to build the raising of a hand, a single step, a leap over an obstacle, a pirouette. Then he put the box in a drawer.

Years later he came across the box when he was tidying up. He kept two versions of the heroine and threw the rest away. He pinned the two survivors to the notice-board above his desk:

The dancer

wears a tattered lilac frock. She stands on one foot, her other leg drawn up almost to her chest, her arms stretched for balance. Her hair explodes over her shoulders. Startled eyes, two full stops, are the only features of her face.

The sleeper

wears the same frock, lies on her side, one knee drawn up and hugged. Her hair pours over a turned shoulder and obscures her face, which she presses into a pillow of earth. Just visible, one heavy-lidded eye, shaped like a comma, closed.

Crossing

They waded into the waves to cool their feet, and he scared himself with a joke about sharks. Then the word "shark" kept circling under the conversation. They walked on in silence towards the wreck.

The wreck, when they reached it, disappointed him. From miles away it had promised to be a monument, something magnificently wasted. From close it was merely metal, dead, rotting into rock. Even the gulls left it alone.

She was more than satisfied. She wanted to swim across to the wreck. She said it was an island worth exploring. He dissuaded her, mentioned sharks again, pointed out the cross-current, threatened to go home.

They climbed up to the dunes, where they had imagined shade. But as he lowered himself onto the sand, the dune shifted with his weight and slid into heat.

She settled down and slept. The sun put a gloss of sweat on her skin, a hot fluff on her shoulders. He came close and watched her sleeping face. This crossing held no dangers. This space could be bridged by a hand or a word. An image slid out of the blue: a finger stirring chips of shell to catch the light. He drew back, unaccountably afraid, spilling sand around him.

She dreamt (she said, when she awoke) that she braved the crossing. The sea was wild. She was washed, exhausted, swallowing salt-water, into the hold. A shaft of light showed her a ladder, but high and out of reach. She scrabbled against the sheer walls and tore her palms on rust. She went under once, twice. Then a wave lifted her gently, as if she was a child, and guided her hands to the rungs. She climbed up to the deck and was saved.

Debris

In the waiting room, in the shadows, the dark man speaks:

    if I should stay up all night with a lucky-packet watch on my wrist, in the dawn, in the corner of a room, in the mysterious symmetry of wall meeting wall, if I should lie on my back with the curtains open wide, in Braamfontein, the sky, from my dirty window, the Hillbrow Tower with a polka-dot bow-tie, a bruised sky full of blood, in salmon, puce, cerise, peach, apricot, plum, a thorn-tree, the musical fountains at Wemmer Pan, a papier mâché Dromedaris, a fibreglass Van Riebeeck, the gilt-edged dumps, the laundromat in Pretoria Street, dirty linen dancing in the suds, in the butchery at the Restless Supermarket, a butcher with three fingers and a bloody Band-aid, if I should smell salt, tea-rose, turpentine, if I should see, in the rearview mirror, rows of mealies arrive-depart-arrive, in a telephone booth, if I should open at random to a name, to a number, in the pages of a notebook bound in black, with a red spine, on the last page, or the first, in a margin, if I should hear in the ribcage of the hardest word its soft heart beat

Echo

On the anniversary of her death, his grief, he takes two versions of her, a dancer and a sleeper, from their shroud. He can no longer remember why he chose these two from among the hundreds. He pins them up, pushing the pins carefully into the familiar wounds.

Tsafendas's Diary

1 Granny is knitting me a thinking-cap, in pink and blue. It is shaped like a turnip, with a long, curling tail. I'll be able to pull it down over my ears, I'll be able to pull it down right over my face, and look out through the two eye-holes she has thoughtfully provided.

"You need to do some thinking," Granny says, "and it is always better to do your thinking incommunicado."

2 Granny in her wicker rocking-chair.

In the twilight Granny's moonface comes and goes, comes and goes, while her crochet-hook knots the giddy momentum of the planet into little coloured squares.

Granny is off her rocker.

3 Granny rocks and rocks. The wicker squeals. Her shadow comes and goes on the wall behind her.

"We must have Tsafendas's Diary," Granny says. "We are its rightful owners. It's a shame to keep it locked up somewhere, away from the world."

I agree.

"Do you know what it is, child?"

I do not answer.

Granny laughs and the shadow laughs with her. "I shouldn't have asked."

4 Granny gives me the thinking-cap. It fits me well. She seems pleased, plumping the cap up on my head and tugging the tail so that it hangs down at a jaunty angle.

"Now you are ready to do some thinking," she says. "The first thing you must think about is Tsafendas's Diary."

I pull the cap down over my face and look out through the eye-holes.

Granny smiles. "You must fetch it for us," she says. "Tsafendas's Diary is the key to all mysteries. The mysteries of meat and the imagination."

5 In the mean time, Granny keeps me busy feeding the hole in the backyard.

"Food for the earth," Granny says. "Excellent stuff. Full of goodness."

I carry the buckets of food out from the kitchen and empty them on the edge of the hole.

"Don't just stand there, you impossible child. Down to business. Feed it. It cannot help itself. You must be willing to get your hands dirty."

I climb into the hole. The bottom is marshy, it sucks at my feet. Granny rocks closer to the edge so that she can look down on me. Her eyes are as pale as the sky behind her. Her face comes and goes on the horizon. With the flat edge of my spade I scrape the piles of food along the rim into the hole. Potato peelings, bones, bread-crusts, meat. I dig it in. The mixture bubbles and steams.

6 Granny has the meat-hook. She tacks the meat together. She pulls the meat-blanket up to my ears and tucks it in. By morning it will be rotting.

7 In the coldest winter in living memory I wear my thinking-cap to bed. I notice a distinct improvement in the quality of my dreams.

I dream I am the curator at the Houses of Parliament.

I lead a party of tourists across a desert of pale-grey carpet to a square of stainless-steel pillars and chains, which marks the spot where Tsafendas slaughtered the Prime Minister. The tourists dam up around the chains. I step into the empty space. I stoop and lift a square of plastic, and there they are: the historic bloodstains.

8 Granny says Tsafendas's Diary is kept in the Police Museum in Pretoria. She won't tell me why. But she takes from her wooden basket a rambling, lopsided blanket. It is a breeding-colony of tassels, pom-poms, fringes and frills.

"What on earth is it?" I ask.

"It is a map of the Police Museum," Granny says. "When you set out to find Tsafendas's Diary you shall take it with you."

9 My dreams continue to improve.

Granny and I set out on the motorized rocking-chair. We are going to Pretoria to recover Tsafendas's Diary. Granny drives. I sit on her lap. On the Ben Schoeman highway, snug under the meat-blanket which Granny has thoughtfully provided, with my thinking-cap pulled right down to my chin, I am happy, I think. We narrowly avoid a collision with a Mercedes Benz. We arrive in Pretoria.

Granny pulls over in front of the prison.

"He's there," Granny says, pointing with her crochet-hook. "He's been there all these years. Sitting on his secrets, hatching them out, feeding them from his filthy mouth, caring for them until they are dark and ugly enough to be sent out into the world. He's there all right. I can smell him."

"Who?" I ask.

"You haven't learned a thing," she says, pinching me. "It goes in one ear and out the other."

10 Granny is knitting a long black ribbon. Its fanged head is buried in the fleshy folds of her hands. The throat curves to the floor, where the blade of the rocker pins it, lets it go, pins it, lets it go. The body is fat and bloated, heaped coil upon coil. The narrow tail flicks in a corner of the room.

"What is it?"

Her fingers twist, easing the ribbon from her skin.

"What do you think it is, child?"

11 I see the killer. He crosses the pale-grey carpet and comes to a door. I smell the fearful sweat on his palm as he reaches for the doorknob. He opens the door. He looks from side to side. He goes out into the street.

He goes out into the street!

I wake up choking. The thinking-cap has fallen down over my face, my mouth is full of warm fur, my nose is full of its stench. Meat stew.

I pull the cap off and throw it in a corner. Still I can smell it. I retrieve it and bury it at the bottom of the laundry basket.

In the morning, Granny: "Where's your thinking-cap?"

12 Granny is angry with me. It's back to the hole. I pile the scraps up on the rim. Granny sits on her rocker. I bring her the hose-pipe and she soaks the stew down.

"Dig it in. The earth is hungry."

I climb into the hole. I sink into the stew, up to my knees, it is hot down there, the steam rises, I think my feet are cooking.

13 Granny parks the rocking-chair in the street outside the Police Museum. She sets me down on the kerb, takes off my thinking-cap.

"The time for thinking is over," she says. "It's time to act. Go in and get it. Do not be afraid: no one will suspect a child. Remember, we are its rightful owners."

She hands me the map. I go up the stairs, between the tall, fluted columns, into a tiled lobby.

Behind me I hear the rocker squeaking. Granny is a pendulum. She keeps time.

A pom-pom marks the spot where Tsafendas's Diary should be. I make my way there (past Dangerous Weapons, Forgery, Terrorism and Ritual Murders). I find myself in an empty room.

14 "Have you got it, child?" Granny asks, looking at my empty hands.

I shake my head.

"It doesn't matter," she says. "Perhaps I already have it. Perhaps I've had it all along." She taps the lid of her wooden basket with fingernails like beaks.

15 In a dark corner of the Police Museum, behind musty black curtains, in a glass cabinet, lies a miniature landscape. In the west a hill, in the east a suburb, between the two an expanse of open veld. It is midnight, but lights still burn in a few of the houses.

A man stands on the hill. He points a rifle at the sky, his finger has just squeezed the trigger. In one of the houses, in a bed, a child has just stopped breathing, but her blood still runs, slowly, her hair and her fingernails are growing.

Between the barrel of the rifle and the roof of the house stretches a perfect fluorescent arc. It is violet, it hums in the stale air. It indicates the path the bullet took between the barrel of the rifle and the brain of the child.

In a separate glass cabinet is a piece of corrugated iron with a hole in it and a bullet dangling on a length of string.

16 Tsafendas's Diary comes to me in my sleep, word by word, drifting down from the dim ceiling of my head.

In the morning, before breakfast, a fried egg leaking like a sunrise on my white plate, I am composing Tsafendas's Diary, dredging it up from my dreams, bringing it back in a bottle. I line the words up one behind the other.

Tsafendas's Diary has a grey cover, like weathered wood, and more than enough pages on which to carve the relentless passing of the days and nights.

17 My thinking-cap outdoes itself.

I find myself in a forest of fluorescent arcs. They burn violet and green and electric blue in the pale air, and each one has a beginning and an end.

One arc has its roots in the sweaty palm of Tsafendas's right hand. It passes through seven doors of stainless-steel, it sings in the burnished sky over the capital, it comes home to the earth, it sinks through granite, loam and lead, it shafts the Prime Minister's brittle skull, and bursts into bloom.

Another arc begins in an empty socket of that same skull, loops through the tangled canopy overhead and skewers Granny to her rocking-chair.

I move among the stems.

Everything goes dark. I hear the rhythmic squeaking of Granny's chair. Then a blister bursts in the darkness and a needle of light, red as blood, springs from Granny's forefinger. It scribbles on the air, it hums like a mosquito around Granny's head, it ricochets off the walls – the room grows hot and bright – it knits and purls the air into a thick, bristling blanket, and then it comes for me. I am its end.

18 I give Granny Tsafendas's Diary, wrapped in brown paper and tied up with string.

"What is it, child?" she says, turning on me her pale eyes. Her fingernails peck at the wrapping.

I look down at my feet, and the tail of the thinking-cap hangs over my face.

Granny slits the package with her crochet-hook. She pulls out the Diary and rests it on her knees. Her hands circle over the copperplate script on the grey cover. Then the beaks rattle on the pages, the hands begin to fly, past calendars, a map of the world, a map of South Africa, lists of public holidays, members of parliament, embassies, the capitals of the world, the currencies, timetables for buses and trains, the hands come to 1 January and settle.

Granny reads in silence. The hands lie panting on the open page.

I am suddenly ashamed. I pull the thinking-cap down to my chin. I cannot look up, not even when the leaves begin to fall around me one by one, blown into drifts around my ankles by a furious wind from the rocker.

Granny plucks the thinking-cap from my head and stuffs it up her sleeve. She rummages in the wooden basket. "Here it is," she says. She draws out the long black ribbon. "I've had it all along. Why are your eyes so wide, you useless child. It cannot harm us any more."

Rocking, rocking.

Her hands peck at the threads. The ribbon unravels. A pile of crinkled wool grows next to the chair, larger and larger, looms over Granny, ingests her. From the writhing heap her voice, muffled, shrinking: "Here it is. Here it is. Here it is…"

19 I am lost without my thinking-cap. All day I carry my naked head from room to room, but cannot find a thought large enough to fill it.

When I get into bed I find my thinking-cap under my pillow. Granny has added a large D in silver sequins.

20 I dream I am Death in my thinking-cap with the spangled D, I dream I am Death, coming with my crochet-hook and my wooden basket, which is dusted with talcum powder, which smells of death, lined with brass, which tastes of death, I am coming with my fluorescent thread and my iron hook to knot the world into my blanket.

21 Granny, her body swathed in the meat-blanket, her feet sticking out like boiled hams, rocking, rocking, to the mouth of the grave. She comes and goes on the precipice. She rocks herself over the edge.

I hear her cooking, bubbling and squeaking, in the meaty broth at the centre of the earth.

22 I'm digging it in. I have to feed the insatiable earth. I put in bones, leaf-mulch from the gutters, vegetable peelings, blankets, papers. I soak it all down. The ink begins to run. I take up my spade and I dig it in.

When My Hands Burst into Flames

Wednesday afternoon, mid-winter, finds me at the counter in the United Building Society (Hillbrow), minding my own business, making a cash withdrawal, when my hands burst into flames.

I react predictably: fling myself on the floor, cry out, roll around, try to beat out one flaming hand with the other. I keep this up until a man grabs hold of me and pins my shoulders to the floor with his knees. Another person sits down on my stomach. This unexpected behaviour brings me to my senses.

The man pinning my shoulders is a security guard. He opened the door for me when I came in here and I saw my face in the plastic peak of his cap. The person sitting on my stomach is a cashier, the very same young woman who was attending to my financial needs a moment ago. As she counted out my money I noticed her fingernails, which are long, hooked, flame-red.

The cashier's pointed heels dig into my calves and make me squirm. She produces a spoon and performs aerobatics with it in the space above my head. She could be planning to feed me, except that the spoon is empty. The spoon zooms towards my face and I see my misshapen reflection. Her nails are like tongues of fire. Her skin smells of Lux. I am suddenly seized by the absurd fear that she is going to scoop my eyes out of their sockets.

I screw my eyes shut and thrash about. The security guard's knees tighten like a vice on my head. The soapy hands flap against my face.

This reminds me of my own hands, the cause of all this bother. I stop resisting and look around. I am surrounded by a circle of old faces. It is the end of the month and the place is full of pensioners. Their mouths open and close. I speak but I cannot hear my voice. The cashier is wearing too much eye-shadow: her lids look bruised. The security guard's cap has fallen over his eyes.

I spot one of my hands, the left I think. By chance this hand has come to rest on the cashier's thigh. It is burning brightly, like a heap of kindling. The cashier's stocking melts away under my hand. A circle of glowing fibres.

I taste metal. While I have been otherwise occupied the cashier has inserted the spoon into my mouth. A diagram from a first-aid manual pops into my head. I get it: they are seeing to it that I don't swallow my tongue. I nod my head appreciatively and the security guard's knees clamp again.

I can't hear a thing. The mouths of the old faces open and close. I think I can decipher expressions of concern and dismay, and this banishes less charitable thoughts from my mind. I have seen people behave in this way at the scene of an accident.

My other hand, presumably the right, comes into focus. It lies burning on an island of smouldering carpet. I raise it tentatively to get a better view of it. Two comforting thoughts strike me. I feel no pain (under normal circumstances my pain threshold is rather low). And my hand is encased in a perfect glove of fire, tailored snugly at the wrist and showing no sign of spreading. I move my fingers and watch the play of the flames. This keeps me occupied for some time.

The security guard shifts his weight off my shoulders. Although I am relieved, I do not move. I listen to the muttering of the old faces. Soon the cashier stands up and a man in a suit, a manager I would say, puts a supporting hand under her elbow and steers her away. The circle of faces closes again.

Another diagram comes into my head. I mesh my fingers together on my stomach so that the flames form a neat camp-fire. I stare into the flames, lost in thought, camped out under the stars. In the heart of the fire I see my hands clearly, composed, intact. No crumbling charcoal and ash, which is a relief.

The security guard rouses me from this reverie by hooking his hands under my arms and lifting me to my feet. The pensioners return to their queue between stainless-steel pillars and chains. An old woman dusts me off unnecessarily. Everyone is smiling kindly now and avoiding my eye.

I extend my right hand towards the security guard. Without blinking he takes my hand and shakes it. I watch his hand sink into my flames. I hold his hand a little too long and he snatches it back. Too late. It is burning nicely, quite a blaze. He puts it in the pocket of his trousers. Clever blighter. A stream of smoke pours from the pocket.

I head for the door, beating my hands against my thighs, but the cashier calls me back. She calls me by name. At first this strikes me as odd, but then I remember that she has my Help-U card. That is what she is waving like a flag. I go over to the counter. I take the card and the wad of ten-rand notes she pushes under the glass. The money bursts into flames at once.

Cupping this small fire in my palms, careful not to drop any cinders, I walk out into Kotze Street. I dump the charred papers in the gutter and trample on them. My flames are pale in the afternoon sun, but the heat is intense. Apparently my hands are an inexhaustible fuel.

Pedestrians passing by look at me curiously and I show them my hands and shrug my shoulders.

I cross the street. Some schoolboys block my entry into Fontana. I wander this way and that, waving my hands. One of the boys points me out to the group and they laugh. There is nothing I can do. I cannot put my hands in my pockets for fear that I will ignite my trousers.

There is a gift shop nearby, with a mirror in its window, and I go there, enduring stares and sniggers, to observe this spectacle for myself. To my consternation I see that the spoon is still sticking out of my mouth. I spit it out. Then I concentrate on the sight I have come to see: Man with burning hands. I look at myself from various angles, in profile, hands at sides, hands outstretched, hands covering face, and so on. For a moment I am filled with horror and fear. But this quickly passes.

With my hands hanging at my sides like two forgotten torches I go along the arcade towards Pretoria Street. There is a queue of people at the Computicket kiosk, but not one of them stares at me. I retrace my steps with my hands more prominently displayed. No reaction. It seems that without the spoon I am an ordinary man. I find this irritating.

I wander aimlessly for half an hour. I seek out the public toilet and try to douse my hands in a basin of water, but succeed only in producing a lot of steam. I think of taking some photographs in a coin-operated booth, but cannot figure out how to draw the curtain without starting a fire. Finally I enter a shoe-shop with the express intention of setting something alight.

A cowboy boot takes my fancy. But the damn thing won't burn.

A salesman collars me but I ignore his persistent chatter and concentrate on my task. This makes him suspicious. He is about to become abusive when the boot catches. I put it back on its pedestal and hurry around to the plate-glass window to watch it burn. The salesman glowers at me through the glass.

I go along the pavement to the curio-sellers and set fire to a dozen wicker baskets. They burn beautifully, all it takes is the touch of a finger. I watch a German tourist buy a conflagration and carry it away proudly. I follow her to the Chelsea Hotel, sniffing the smoke and watching the embers scatter.

I am starting to enjoy myself. I am highly inflammable. Better, I am incendiary.

I go into Exclusive Books and browse. When the place is going merrily I leave and watch from across the street. Customers come and go without a care in the world, strolling between the blazing shelves, turning the red pages, leafing through the ashes.

Suppressing a host of foolish pranks, I head for home. At the corner of Harrow and Abel I buy a newspaper and page frantically while I wait for the lights to change, gathering what news I can from the curling pages. By the time I reach the other side of the street the news is ashes. I fling it aside.

I sit on my balcony. There is nothing much to do. The coffee boils in the mug cupped in my palms. It is too hot to drink. Night falls.

I go inside. I hold my hands up to photographs in frames. I brand some letters on the ceiling. I switch on the TV and watch until the set collapses in a charred heap. I keep warm.

Later I think I will torch the park across the street. Meanwhile, I am content to play with fire.

The Terminal Bar

"Time, gentlemen!"

Another night in the Terminal Bar, in the Transit Lounge. Another kick-out time, another unhappy hour. It is always closing time here in the Terminal Bar, but no one leaves. I switch off the aquarium lights and switch on the fluorescent tubes. No one takes any notice.

I empty the ashtrays, collect the glasses, rinse them (the dregs go into a bucket for the New Year punch). I move so quietly among the drunken and disorderly that they hardly see me. I am the night watchman. I watch over broken veins, gaping pores, greasy lips, scars, age-spots, acne. My patrons. I try hard to feel sorry for them, let the sleepers sleep, leave those who are maudlin to weep, those who are nauseous to vomit. In the morning Josephine (who was abandoned here by the Weinbergs, they had to leave in a hurry, their plane was revving up at the end of the runway) Josephine can clean it up. I put up with the mess. There is a place for everyone – almost everyone – in the Terminal Bar, there is a home away from home.

"Time, gentlemen!"

Perhaps a few will roll out through the batwing doors into the

Transit Lounge, where their wives and children lie asleep. There is a place here for women and children too, a home of sorts.

I wipe the counter down for old times' sake, switch off the fluorescent tubes and, in the glow from the Castle Lager sign above the dartboard, make my way to my bunk in the storeroom. I check the refrigerator door: I was happier before Mrs Boshoff and Little Bossies were put in there, among the perishables. I lie down on my bunk.

Another night in the Terminal Bar, Wilson assumed responsibility for the refrigeration of the corpses because, he said, he was a friend of the family.

Another night Wilson said, "Take your average Kreepy Krauly."

And Boshoff said, "You should see what I did to a guy once with a Kreepy Krauly."

Another night a woman moved slowly around the room, looking at my patrons one by one. I followed her to the men's room. She listened at the window and I listened too. I could have thrown her out, I'm the proprietor, we have rules, but something held me back.

In the end, it is enough to know that the Terminal Bar is my place.

I did all the alterations myself, put in the wood-grain wallpaper, the antique mirror behind the counter, the stained-glass panels – plastic actually, you wouldn't think so – depicting naked peasant girls trampling out the vintage, the linoleum (because it's easy to clean) and the clock, embedded in the sawn-off end of a wine barrel. Plastic also. Too bad it doesn't work. Stuck on 11 o'clock. But that serves us well: it is always kick-out time in the Terminal Bar, even if no one leaves.

I'm a stickler for detail. You will see that the dishcloths are dollar bills, in cotton – a gift from an American who was passing through. Over the bar there's a springbok head and that thing next to it is a Kreepy Krauly. The coasters show scenic attractions from the four corners of the earth and portraits of famous sportsmen.

I wanted to keep a bit of the old place too. The wall behind the dartboard – that's the original colour. Pale green is a good colour for the Terminal Bar. The light in here is watery, aquarium light, very atmospheric, it leaks from cylindrical plastic shades, it drips on the walls. Aquarium light is good too, because drunk people are like fish.

That's a quote from Smith, the film director (he calls them motion pictures). Just let a voice be raised during a game of Killers and Smith comes blundering in here, throwing his fat stomach around, and Moloi after him, pointing the camera, sticking his nose in. "The fish are at it," Smith says, "let's catch them." Then Boshoff throws Smith and Moloi out because they're disturbing the clientele. The two of them aren't allowed in here any more.

Pale green is a good colour for the Terminal Bar if you ask me, but a lot of people disagree. It takes all kinds, they say, and it's hard to keep them happy. Boshoff, for example, likes pale green: it reminds him of an officers' mess somewhere and makes him feel at home. Then again Wilson, the Kreepy Krauly salesman, can't stand the colour. He said so plainly on the day he pitched up.

We don't have too many new arrivals. Wilson came out of nowhere. Josephine heard him knocking at the window in the men's room while she was cleaning the urinals and she called me. I took a good look at him first – you can't be too careful. Fat and freckled, grubby white suit, tie with the knot undone. Looked harmless enough. I gestured to him to go round to the front, to the entrance through the Transit Lounge.

He comes in carrying a five-litre bottle of pool chemical, a Cadac Mini-Braai and a canvas duffel bag. He's pouring sweat. I give him a drink and he collapses into a chair, swigs, stares at the pale-green wall. "This place looks like a swimming pool badly in need of a Kreepy Krauly," he says. Can you believe it?

Boshoff rises to the bait. "Listen, you."

"Wilson," the newcomer puts in, "salesman."

"You're not at home," Boshoff continues. "You don't have opinions."

But even while Boshoff is speaking Wilson heaves himself to his feet, opens the duffel bag and unpacks a Kreepy Krauly. A magnificent specimen, thirty foot long if it's an inch, with a livid head and a pale sucker trailing filaments of slime. The men gather round.

"Who the hell do you think you are barging in here and passing comments about the decor," Boshoff says.

Wilson plugs the tail-end of the Kreepy Krauly into the cash register and the long, ribbed body shudders. He calls for water, and Weinberg, who was still with us then, sends Josephine to fill a tub. Officially, Josephine is still in Weinberg's employ, so I don't mind.

"You're a big baby."

Josephine brings the tub. Wilson takes off his jacket, rolls up one shirtsleeve and tests the temperature of the water with his elbow. Apparently he's satisfied, because he submerges the Kreepy Krauly's head.

I can see trouble coming. Boshoff is getting angry. No one's listening to him, they're all crowded around the tub, where the Kreepy Krauly is gasping and gurgling as it comes back to life. I turn my back on them and polish some glasses: that way I can watch them in the mirror.

Here it comes. Boshoff pulls out his revolver and fires a shot into the ceiling. Fists fly, the tub overturns, Smith rushes in with Moloi hot on his heels. A woman's face appears at the batwing doors. The Kreepy Krauly, liberated unexpectedly from the tub, creeps away between the tables.

Jesus, these people.

Then Father O'Reilly takes me aside, points out Wilson's Cadac and suggests we have a braai. That should restore the peace and boost the morale. The idea doesn't grab me – stinking up the Bar with the smell of burning meat, splashing grease all over everything – but the situation's getting out of hand.

I switch on the fluorescent tubes – they generally have a sobering effect – and Father O'Reilly climbs up on a chair and calls for order. While he's explaining the plan, I take Josephine into the storeroom and instruct her to rustle up some meat. By the time I come back into the Bar the men are piling the tables and chairs – making space for dancing, they say – and setting up the Mini-Braai. The Kreepy Krauly has climbed the wall behind the dartboard, leaving a trail of slime and blistered paint, but I bite my tongue. The men are in a festive mood. They draw chairs into a circle around the gas bottle and start to discuss fire-building techniques. Wilson lights the gas but has to turn it off again: the meat hasn't arrived yet and resources are scarce.

Weinberg and I take a luggage trolley to the fridge to load up the cabbages. He won't do it on his own because of Mrs Boshoff and Little Bossies. Afterwards, from my post at the batwing doors, I watch him push the trolley over to the counter at Budget Rent-a-Car where the women are standing by to prepare the salads. There's a party atmosphere in the Transit Lounge too. The children are playing hide-and-seek among the shanties. The curtains, which we usually keep drawn across the tinted plate-glass windows, have been opened. Each window frames an identical segment of cold grey runway and empty veld. It is always winter, it is always twilight, beyond the glass. That's why we keep the curtains closed.

Josephine appears at last with a bundle of meat on her head and Wilson lights the gas again.

Boshoff has speared the first chop (horse-meat actually, but you wouldn't say so) on the end of a fork and is about to throw it into the fat when the peace is shattered by a burst of gunfire and a crash of breaking glass. We take cover behind the counter. Boshoff draws his revolver. Silence, broken only by the slurping of the Kreepy Krauly as it edges along the murky waterline where the pale-green wall meets the ceiling. Then a loudhailer: "You are surrounded! Give yourselves up!"

"Over my dead body," Boshoff mutters.

We lie still. More gunfire, more breaking glass, children crying.

"Someone should do a recce," Boshoff says.

Wilson volunteers. He crawls over to the batwing doors, peers under them, motions us to join him.

The Transit Lounge is full of soldiers in combat gear, their faces smeared with boot polish, their cuffs and collars stuffed with grass and twigs. They all carry rifles – "of foreign origin," according to

Boshoff – and one has a mine detector and is sweeping the floor around the delicious monsters. Another has a pistol and shouts a lot: obviously the leader.

"He's in charge all right," Boshoff says. "And only a captain. Just shows you. I could wipe him out with one shot."

"What about the women and children?" Wilson asks.

The women and children huddle together at the Information desk. A soldier guards them while the others search the tents and lean-tos. Two of our windows have been broken in the attack and these rectangles of hot, white runway and bleached sky stand out like overexposed frames in a strip of film.

Smith and Moloi appear from behind a pot plant and creep on their hands and knees towards the captain. Moloi has his camera pointed at the captain's boots.

Weinberg shivers. "Those jokers are going to get us into a lot of trouble."

"Damn right," Boshoff says. "Any second now the terrorists are going to start performing for the camera."

"Maybe someone should tell them the camera doesn't have film in it," Weinberg suggests. "They ran out six months ago."

"I'll do it," Father O'Reilly says. "They wouldn't harm a man of the cloth."

Father O'Reilly goes over to the captain and they speak briefly. The captain shoots Father O'Reilly in the foot. He gives orders. The soldiers start poking around in the salads with their bayonets and blowing up hand luggage.

I feel like crying. You grow to love a place, even a place like the Transit Lounge. Boshoff's a bok for mounting a counter-attack. He keeps waving the revolver and taking aim, but Wilson stops him with: "What about the women and children?"

After a while the captain comes towards the Bar and we hide behind the tables. As he pushes through the batwing doors the Kreepy Krauly reaches the corner of the room and lets out a contented sigh. The captain raises his pistol and fires.

The bullet hits the Kreepy Krauly in the head, spattering cogs and sprockets. A spasm runs through its body and bursts into the cash register, causing the drawer to spring open. The sucker cannot find purchase, the neck bends, the head slides slowly down to the floor and rolls over, gasping and rattling.

The captain, who's been watching the Kreepy Krauly's last moments curiously, bangs on the counter with his waterbottle. The men look at me. Forget it! Wilson sits up. "I'll handle this," he says, and goes over to the counter with the bottle of pool chemical. He spends a long time mixing something and decanting it into the waterbottle. I look out under the batwing doors. Father O'Reilly is hopping around on one foot, and Smith and Moloi are walking backwards and sideways, pointing the camera.

The soldiers withdraw, taking with them the cabbages and one of the women (fortunately no one's wife).

We leave Wilson weeping over the Kreepy Krauly and go into the Transit Lounge to assess the damage. Not too bad. Apart from the broken windows and a few craters everything is normal. Josephine starts tidying up and we get the women to tend to Father O'Reilly while we go back to the braai. But the flame has been burning all this time and the gas bottle is empty. Boshoff flies off the handle. He says Wilson was supposed to be looking after the fire, he'll break his fat neck.

An ugly scene was developing, but monkey nuts and drinks on the house restored order.

Another night in the Terminal Bar – no, later that same night – the discussion turned to civil defence. Boshoff recalled the speech he once made to a women's club on the proper procedure for dealing with terrorists, and the men asked him to repeat his presentation. "You never know when it might come in handy," someone said.

Boshoff needs props. First he calls for a stick of grissini. He knows there's a whole box of the stuff in the storeroom, a gift from an Italian who got out of here by hiding in some laundry. Then he needs a pair of pliers. I can't help him with that, but he settles for a nutcracker. Finally, he wants Wilson, he says he'll be perfect as the captured terrorist. To a T, is how he puts it.

All this time Wilson's been tinkering with the Kreepy Krauly, trying to coax it back to life, and he doesn't even look up when his name is called. Boshoff gets angry again. "Ek is Bossies!" he shouts and rips open his shirt. His name is tattooed across his chest in letters six inches high and coiled around with serpents, the "i" dotted by a hairy nipple.

Suddenly Wilson's happy to oblige. He lets himself be bound with his own tie to a chair standing in the space cleared earlier for dancing. Boshoff now calls this space the Interrogation Room, explaining that the similarity between the word "interrogation" and the word "terrorist" is no coincidence.

"This is how it works," Boshoff says. "I come into the room and put my pliers here where the prisoner can get a good look at them." He leaves the nutcracker on the floor and goes off to play Killers with Weinberg. Smith tells Moloi to get a close-up of the pliers and then a shot of Wilson's face.

Soon everyone gets restless.

"See how it works," Boshoff says, and pauses to throw his darts. "You're all dying to know what happens next and imagining terrible things. Now let's say that after an hour I come back and pick up my pliers. Are you ready to talk?"

Wilson is.

"Let's also say that you're a tough nut," Boshoff says, flexing the nutcracker and clamping a stick of grissini in its jaws.

It is quiet in the Terminal Bar. The silence is thicker than blood.

Then Father O'Reilly hobbles in and orders a Bloody Mary, and Boshoff goes back to the dartboard, while the men squabble over the rest of the grissini and try out the nutcracker. It's left to me to untie Wilson and give him one on the house. Smith and Moloi sit down at a table with Father O'Reilly for the exclusive interview. They're convinced that Father O'Reilly is the man of the moment because of his wound.

It was another night – possibly even the very next one – Boshoff took his wife (whom we knew as Mrs Boshoff) and his daughter (Little Bossies) into the duty-free shop and blew their brains out.

I saw it coming. I said to Father O'Reilly: "Talk to Boshoff. The man's unhappy here, he keeps ripping his shirt. That's twice in one week. He's used to the wide open spaces."

Another night then, Boshoff takes his wife and daughter into the duty-free, between the perfume and the chocolates, and blows their brains out. Then he turns the weapon on himself, but can't pull the trigger. "He discovered," says Father O'Reilly, "that he had too much to live for."

There's a crush at the shop as everyone presses in around the corpses. The air is thick with whisky fumes and aftershave, the floor is sticky with blood and soft centres. Here they come now, tramping the mess back to the Bar, with Wilson in front shouting out the order.

"Dirty pigs! You aren't coming in here with those shoes."

That stops them in their tracks. Some of them go off to sulk in the leatherette chairs or sit on their luggage like schoolchildren waiting for a bus. A few smart alecs leave their shoes outside the door and creep over to the counter in their stinking socks.

I dish out the gin and they pick over the corpses. Wilson wants to keep them in the refrigerator as facts, just in case there's ever a trial. He says he badly wants to be Boshoff's friend. Weinberg says we should send the bodies on as unaccompanied luggage.

It is still 11 o'clock when Boshoff comes out of the men's room, where he's been pleading with Father O'Reilly for absolution, and goes sheepishly to the dartboard, followed by Smith and Moloi. No one else looks at him: they all look at their reflections in the mirror. Boshoff throws a few darts, and Moloi follows the flight of each one wistfully with his camera.

Then Wilson goes over, puts an arm around Boshoff's shoulders and lets him sob a little on his lapel.

"I know how you feel," Wilson says. "It's like when you lose a sale."

Later that night, while the men were playing darts and Wilson was explaining how the bottom had fallen out of the Kreepy Krauly market, the women came for Boshoff.

It was very quiet in the Transit Lounge, too quiet, and that's why I was at the batwing doors and saw them mustering. I spotted the ringleader at once, with my experience of these things. So here they come with this woman in front, they're pushing in through the doors, without so much as a by-your-leave or may-I, they're marching between the tables, they're heading for the dartboard where a game of Killers is in progress.

"We want no trouble here," the woman says, although they're carrying sticks and stones and pieces of concrete from the bomb craters, "we just want Boshoff."

They were going to string him up, I suppose, or give him a talking-to.

In any event, Boshoff's middle name is trouble (he always says so). He steps forward. "Ek is Bossies," he says, and rips open the front of his shirt.

The women recoil in horror. Now the men surge forward, carrying Bossies like a banner, and drive the women out. Stones rain down on the counter and the mirror smashes. The men were unhappy about that afterwards, looking at their puzzled faces in the cracked glass.

Usually when Bossies ripped his shirt we'd rally round to find the buttons for him so that his wife could sew them back on again, but this night we left them where they fell.

There was a great deal of drinking that night in the Terminal Bar, and a great deal of weeping and vomiting. I think they all slept over, I don't think one of them made it back to the Transit Lounge. I didn't even try to kick them out: I couldn't bring myself to switch on the fluorescent tubes and watch over that unthinkable array of stains and blotches.

The next morning when I was scouring the floor for small change I found the buttons and stuck them there against the mirror as a memento.

Another night Wilson says, "Take your average Kreepy Krauly."

And Boshoff says, "You should see what I did to a guy once with a Kreepy Krauly."

And I say (don't ask me why, I usually keep my nose clean), "Talk is cheap but money buys the whisky."

Another night there's the sound of a plane revving up at the end of the runway, and Weinberg takes his wife and runs for it. Without even saying goodbye. "It isn't done," Father O'Reilly says.

Another night Wilson presents me with the head of the Kreepy Krauly mounted on kiaat; there's a small ceremony and it's hung behind the bar.

Another night Smith tries to get a close-up of Boshoff's tattoo, and Boshoff beats him to within an inch of his life. Wilson does likewise to Moloi, out of a sense of loyalty to his friend, he says. That's the last time Smith and Moloi set foot in the Bar. They have to live with the women and children in the Transit Lounge. I take them a couple of beers occasionally when the others have gone to sleep.

Another night, it was still kick-out time, although it was dawn. I'm there among the sleepers, among the dislocated dentures, the gummed-up eyes, the wet lips, I'm picking up small change on the murky bottom before Josephine starts to clean, and the woman comes in. She moves so quietly I don't hear her, but I feel the stale air shift. At first she doesn't see me on my hands and knees between the tables. She moves slowly around the room, looking at my patrons one by one. I think perhaps she's looking for Boshoff. She comes to him, balanced like a fallen statue between two bar-stools, his big shoes jutting like a pedestal. She goes on to Wilson in his crumpled suit, his lips pressed to the cold surface of the counter, and Weinberg – no, Weinberg is gone. She looks them all over. She comes to me and looks me over too, and what makes this difficult is that I look back. She goes into the men's room and stands with her face pressed to the small window, listening for something. I listen too. A jet engine, perhaps, or distant gunfire, or someone calling, or the grinding of the earth's axle. She goes out. I follow as far as the batwing doors.

Josephine brushes past me with her mop.

I switch on the aquarium lights. "Morning!" I move among the sleepers, nudging them with the tip of my shoe, and they stir in the silted air, bloated and pale, like drowned men.

Another night in the Terminal Bar, don't ask which, it is always night here, night has always fallen like a drunkard between the tables.

Let's say the woman will come tomorrow. I'll follow her to the men's room and we'll listen to whatever it is we're expecting to hear. Then she'll go out and I'll move among the sleepers, watching over them, nudging them with the tip of my shoe.

"Time, gentlemen!"

Propaganda by Monuments

For Chas Unwin

The Tuba

The darts started when Cliffie brought home a Saddam Hussein dartboard. Basil went out and bought them each a set of darts, plastic flights for Cliffie and feathers for himself. Every Saturday afternoon from then on someone or other would drop in for a game – Cliffie's friend Larry, or John de la Porte, or Beachball Buitendag, or Sergeant Dundas from across the road, or a little Irish chap with a bad skin who did not like them calling him Smurfie. An odd number of beer-drinkers, peanut-tossers and dart-pushers – you don't throw a dart, lady, you *push* it. And blou wildebeeste would not drag them away from the board. When the weather warmed up they moved from the kitchen to the front verandah. They hung Saddam Hussein on the door to Cliffie's room at the side of the house, and kept the braai fires burning, and played on in the summer evenings under a string of jaundiced moons.

My boy Richie would be roped in to keep score, to fetch and carry cold quarts from the fridge, to baste the chicken with a paintbrush. I told Basil and Cliffie: your pals better watch their language in front of Richie. He's only a child, and you know how he is, he picks things

up. But as soon as my back was turned Cliffie would give him beer –
mainly froth, but still – in a tumbler with a cancan dancer on it, a two-
faced tart flicking her petticoats quite coyly at the outside world, while
under the drinker's nose, on the froth-laced inner curve of the glass,
she revealed more naked flesh at every sip. Richie would perch on a
bar-stool with a kindergarten blackboard propped on his knees and
a cigarette of chalk between his fingers, his tumbler on the window-
sill beside him, like one of the boys. But he was not one of them. He
was not one of us. He was always drifting off, he didn't answer when
he was spoken to, he looked through us with his round eyes.

Then I would say: he's somewhere else.

Most of those Saturdays went the same way: the more they drank
the angrier they got with Saddam Hussein. A few months earlier
not one of them would have known him from Adam, but now they
couldn't stand the sight of him. When the face behind the wire began
to fade, just as it had faded from the newspapers and television screens,
they recognized in its pock-marked features other faces that enraged
them: politicians and priests; members of parliament and talk-show
hosts; managing directors and their wives; half-remembered head-
masters, playground bullies, army corporals; ex-wives, bad friends.
And in the small hours, invariably, their brothers, themselves.

On pay-days the boys were always a bit wild, but in the festive season they became ungovernable. They forgot about pushing the darts

and threw them like assegais. It's a wonder no one was hurt. They aimed for the eyes or the nose, but sometimes they didn't even hit the board. One night Smurfie launched a dart into the rafters and shattered a reindeer in the Christmas lights. Beachball Buitendag managed to throw a dart into the doorpost with such force they couldn't pull it out again; Basil unscrewed the flight the morning after and worked the barrel out with a pair of pliers. In the end there were so many holes in that door it took two coats of Wall and All to cover.

The Salvation Army band came round as usual in the week before Christmas. I heard them from the kitchen window, when I went in to fetch Cliffie's famous sosaties and Basil's chops; they were playing "While shepherds watched their flocks" in the next block.

I took the meat outside. Sergeant Dundas and Basil had started another game of 301, and the Sergeant was losing. "This kid of yours is blind," he said, ruffling Richie's hair, "or his arithmetic's up to *sherbet*." Sergeant Dundas's prickly italics were for my benefit, proof that he was watching his tongue. Richie double-checked the sum in the Sgt D column. Then he went back to colouring in the holes in the alphabet stencilled across the top of the blackboard, his marbled irises vivid and intent.

The Salvation Army trooped around the corner into Chromium Street. In front was a man carrying a music stand and a white baton.

He was wearing sunglasses with wraparound frames and reflective lenses, incongruous under the melodramatic peaked cap with its puffed up crown.

"And here comes Richie Richardson from the golf-course end," said Cliffie.

My Richie glanced up at the sound of his name and then returned to his drawing. But Sergeant Dundas came to the end of the verandah and glared at the conductor. His lips were pursed, his cheeks were swollen, his fingers were kneading the stodgy flesh of his paunch. Sergeant Dundas was a musician himself – he played the tuba in the Correctional Services orchestra – and when he started puffing away at an invisible instrument it was always an omen.

The band gathered on the pavement in front of Sergeant Dundas's house, and I hoped they would stay there. A dozen black men, in sober uniforms and pious boots, with saxophones and side-drums and trumpets and trombones all of stainless steel, as practical as a hospital kitchen. There was one woman too, carrying a Bible and a little white collection tin.

"Nineteen double twenty," said Basil behind us and threw it. Practice was making perfect.

Cliffie was supposed to play the winner, but the coals were ready and he didn't want to leave them. He opened the plastic pack with his teeth and put the sosaties on the grill. Basil and the Sergeant started another game.

"Just watch me whitewash you, china," said the Sergeant.

"You and whose army?" said Basil, and opened with his first dart.

The members of the band spoke among themselves and looked at us shyly. Then the conductor picked up his music stand and led them across the street towards our house. The itchy-ball tree in the corner of our yard overhung the pavement and I thought he might choose its shade, but he set up the stand in the sunshine at our front gate and opened a book of music on it. The band gathered round him in a semicircle, facing us. A trumpet cleared its throat discreetly. Then he flourished the baton and they began to play. O come, all ye faithful, joyful and triumphant. Richie ran to the fence to listen.

I turned down the volume on the portable TV set, which was standing on a kitchen chair at the top of the verandah steps where Cliffie could keep half an eye on it. Cricket from the Wanderers.

"Turn it up," said the Sergeant, wincing. "These jokers are giving me earache. Funny thing about *blacks,* you know, they can't hold a tune. Not one of ours, I mean. Their ears are different."

The same breeze that brought the devilled smoke from Cliffie's sosaties to our noses kept rifling through the pages of music, turning them in flurries and carrying off the melody. The conductor went on regardless, as if the music stand was just for show. The darts thudded into the board in trios. The Sergeant poured another cane – for the pain, he said. Then he put his hands over his ears and said, "Me me me." .

Chri-i-st the Lord...

The cricket commentary became audible again. A Mexican wave was going round in the stadium, tossing up a spume of paper plates, beer tins and cheers. Sergeant Dundas applauded ironically and took his turn at the board. He was still trying to open, but Basil had whittled his score down to double figures.

The conductor turned and gave the slightest of bows. Basil put his arm around me. He smelt of brandy and Sta-soft. Cliffie burnt his fingers flipping the sosaties over and cursed. Sergeant Dundas italicized the curse in the background as his dart bounced off the bullseye and fell to earth. Basil pinched my side and made me jump.

I felt that the conductor was looking at me through his ridiculous glasses, as if I was a character in a three-dimensional film. They were all looking at us. You would think we were the show and they the audience.

I called Richie to go and fetch my purse. The conductor turned away again and the band struck up "Good King Wenceslas."

"I hope you're not going to give them money," said the Sergeant.

"Why not?"

"Don't want to encourage them. Worst version of "Old King Cole" I ever heard."

When the snow lay round about, deep and crisp and even. The grass rank and juicy between Richie's toes, his dusty footprints on the red steps. I have never seen snow. A white Christmas is inconceivable.

The Sergeant was the musical expert, so I just said: "It's for a good cause."

"They'll spend it on booze." He scratched his pot-belly with the point of a dart.

"Double bull," said Basil, and threw it.

"Uncle Colin..." I was going to explain how Uncle Colin, who hit the bottle a bit, ended up in the Salvation Army home, but thought better of it.

"We weren't watching so it doesn't count."

"I saw it," said Cliffie. "Perfect cherry."

"How do you know they're really from the Salvation Army?" said the Sergeant. He always had something up his sleeve.

"The uniforms, for one thing."

"The uniforms! What does that prove? They look like bloody bus conductors. Haven't you heard about these chancers dressed up in orange overalls, pretending to be dustbin boys and coming round for Christmas boxes? These guys are probably also trying to make a fast buck. The prisons are full of con-artists, you know. There's big money to be made in charity."

Big money. It resounded in the back of my mind like a cymbal.

Richie came back with my purse.

"You should give them some of that big money of yours, Cliff," said the Sergeant. "That would be a hoot."

"The Big! Money!" Cliffie sang out from the braai, like a quiz-show host, and sprayed beer over the flames. "There's only one left."

"Come on, Cliff. It'll be worth it. You can take it back afterwards."

"Shanghai!" said Basil, starting and finishing another game. He was becoming superhuman.

Bring me flesh and bring me wine, bring me pine-logs hither.

Cliffie caught Richie by the arm and whispered something in his ear. The boy went into the house.

Cliffie worked in Lost Property at Jan Smuts. It was an endless source of gifts and novelties. But the best find of all, the one that had given him the most pleasure, had come from a friend in Customs, where it had been abandoned by an economic mission returning from a trade fair in Montevideo. It was a treasure chest, an old army-issue trommel covered with papier mâché barnacles and oversized padlocks, and filled to the brim with krugerrands. The coins were the size of dinner plates and made of wood, with a bust of Paul Kruger painted on one side and a leaping springbok on the other.

There were a hundred coins in the chest to start with and Cliffie spent them lavishly. He handed them out to beggars at robots, he tipped roadhouse waiters with them, he gave them to newspaper vendors. The memory of these transactions made him laugh until the tears ran down his cheeks. "You should have seen his face!" As the supply diminished he became thriftier, because a good laugh is hard to come by, but in the end the coffer was empty. Now it stood next to the stove full of dead men. The very last coin had been resting on the mantelpiece in the lounge for a month, waiting for some special occasion.

Richie came out of the house with the coin. Cliffie piled his sosa-ties on the edge of the grill, put down the tongs and bent to wipe his hands on the lawn. Richie actually held out the coin to him, but at the last moment he snatched it back. Cliffie thought he was playing some silly game and made a grab for it. The boy turned and ran up the driveway at the side of the house, and Cliffie chased after him.

They went round the house twice, but Cliffie could not catch up. After the third circuit Richie ran across the lawn with Cliffie at his heels. At the foot of the itchy-ball tree he had time to stuff the coin down the front of his shirt before he scampered up the trunk and disappeared in the greenery.

"I can't even see him," said Basil. And then in a different voice, loosening his belt: "Richard, if I have to fetch you from up there you'll be sorry."

"Forget it," I said. "In your condition you'll break your neck. And I won't let you lay a hand on that child."

"Just throw down the money," said Cliffie.

"If he was my son I'd turn the hose on him," Sergeant Dundas said to me. "Let him get away with little things like this, he'll end up burning down the house."

"Stay away from the phone wires, boy!"

We barged around under the tree, staring up into the foliage, shouldering one another aside.

Richie was always otherwise. He would be staring down at us absently, through eyes too full of colour, as if the irises had been stirred into the whites. The doctor said his eyesight was perfect though, better than average. What does he think of us, I thought, baying like hounds, baring our teeth. What does he see down our pink throats?

"It's the same all over," Sergeant Dundas shouted as "Away in a Manger" swelled up on the other side of the fence and surged over us. "The kids telling the grown-ups what to do. I see it every day. The prisons are bursting at the seams. Me me me me me me me."

Basil tried to hoist himself up into the tree but the branch broke off in his hands and he fell on his backside. A raspberry from the trombone.

"Bugger this for a joke," Sergeant Dundas burst out. "He's making us look like fools. They're laughing at us. Just look at them, in their fancy dress, with their pips on their shoulders. This one with the sax is a bloody brigadier."

They did seem to be enjoying themselves. One of the trumpeters was actually smiling as he blew. I hadn't thought it was possible.

"It's the same wherever you go, some *black* face laughing at you. They'll be toyi-toying in your front garden just now." The Sergeant went over to the fence and shouted at them. "Enough of your stupid music you *clowns*. Go away!" And then, abandoning the italics, cursed them to high heaven.

The round mouths of the instruments looked mildly shocked. The little Lord Jesus lay down his sweet head. A string of saliva drooled from the end of the trombone to the dust.

The idea that the Salvation Army had come especially to ridicule us seemed suddenly feasible. Why did they carry on playing like this? Did they deem it their duty to provide a soundtrack for our squabbles? Why wouldn't they shut up? Why didn't they go away?

"It's not us they're laughing at," said Cliffie, as if I had spoken aloud. "It's you Sarge."

"Is that so?"

Cliffie was always a troublemaker. We all looked at Sergeant Dundas, at his lumpy knees, at his fat stomach, at his red-veined cheeks puffed up with air. The sun glanced off the iridescent frames of the conductor's glasses. Sergeant Dundas flushed.

"They'll laugh on the other sides of their faces!" And he marched across the street to his house.

"Now throw down the money, Rich," Cliffie called into the greenery.

The last of the big money had changed hands once before. A man had come knocking at the door on a Saturday morning, asking to weed the flowerbeds and mow the lawn. He wanted twenty rand for the morning's work, but Cliffie offered him a bonus if he would wash the car. When he was finished we were summoned as an audience, and Cliffie handed him the wooden coin.

After their initial surprise, the victims of Cliffie's pranks usually became angry and started to argue with him. Some of them begged for the real money that was owed them. A few joined in with the laughter – and they were nearly all white, Cliffie said, which just went to show that your blacks didn't have a sense of humour, it was the funny thing about them. But this one saw the joke immediately and began to weep, resolutely, in a language we did not understand.

He walked to the end of the verandah and back, while I stared at the sponge in the bottom of the bucket. Then he laid the coin on the top step and walked out of the yard. His reflection slid over the polished surfaces of the car in the driveway. Cliffie called after him, but he did not even look back.

I thought Richie would cry too, but his eyes were hard and dry. It made my lids itch just to look at them.

The tuba started up in Sergeant Dundas's house. I heard it before anyone else, my ears were always good. But I think the conductor heard it too, because he waved his arms, scooping the music up in his hands and splashing it over them, and they played louder and began to shuffle from foot to foot. Ding dong! merrily on high.

The tuba grumbled and spluttered as it warmed up. It was not a melody, just a noise, like the beery passing of wind in the belly of an oompah band, and soon it settled into a two-stroke rhythm: oom-pah oom-pah oom-pah. Then Sergeant Dundas appeared in the doorway of his house. He stooped as he crossed the threshold, so that the brass bell of the tuba could scrape under the lintel, and chugged down the garden path.

A few members of the band turned their heads to look over their shoulders but the conductor jerked them back as if they were attached to strings.

"Give them hell Sarge!" Cliffie shouted.

The Sergeant crossed the street, picking up his feet and plumping them down to the rhythm of his own music. His cheeks blew out like bellows. He was jammed into the instrument, with his fat breasts propped on the tube above and his belly bulging out below. He bore down on the band and shouldered his way into the semicircle. He puttered up and down in the space between the conductor and the musicians, huffing and puffing louder and louder, trying to drown them out or break their rhythm.

The music faltered for a moment, the sounds dislocated one from the other, seemed about to fly apart into chaos. Sergeant Dundas swelled up inside the tuba, his flesh peeled over the valves, the big mouth boomed. But the conductor, with his head thrown back, gazing up into the sun, gathered the drifting parts and pulled them together again. A new melody assembled itself from the disjointed components of the old one and to our great surprise, and his own, Sergeant Dundas was at the heart of it. He stopped short and the band rolled on without him. It was a tune I had never heard before, a flow of sound with the careless power of a river.

In this extremity Sergeant Dundas found a new rhythm, a difficult one he had never conceived of until now, three rising notes full of hurt and resentment dredged up from the depths of his being, which he began to blast out, as if he was hurling stones from the throat of the tuba. This time the faltering was barely perceptible. The music closed over the Sergeant like brown water.

Harrumphing, bleating, wheezing, waving his head from side to side, he churned up and down, butting at the players with the bell of the tuba. They whirled aside and shuffled along beside him, as if they were all being dragged hither and thither by the same currents. Suddenly they were swirling on the pavement, in a gathering cloud of dust, and with each pass there seemed to be more of them, and the music grew louder and more forceful. In the midst of the mêlée Sergeant Dundas thrashed, pawing at the tuba as if it were no longer a weapon but a serpent in whose coils he was entangled, trying to throw it off, trying to escape. But they would not let him.

Then the woman was on one side of the Sergeant and the conductor on the other. All smiles. The woman shook the tin in his ear and the conductor tapped on his shoulder with the baton. Sergeant Dundas's legs jerked, his arms twitched, he began to dance, nodding his head and stamping his feet, swimming in slow motion. They all moved off along Chromium Street and as the din faded I heard the television commentators chattering on about the wicket, and the pages on the music stand fluttering, and the wooden coin clattering down through the branches.

I would choose to be with Richie, in the tree, nested in leaf-green shade, with rough bark scratching pleasantly against my spine, with the tang of the itchy-balls stirring a monumental sneeze in my nostrils. I would be the one to let fall this useless currency. But I am unable.

What does he see from up there?

Basil, crossing the lawn, carrying the puzzle uncomfortably in his body like a full bladder, saying: "Now I've seen everything."

Cliffie, with tears of laughter hardly dry on his cheeks, tipping the charred meat into the ashes, saying: "I went all the way to Greenside for these, and they cost a bomb – but it was worth every cent."

Me, rooted to the spot, earthbound, saying: "It's all right boy, you can come down now."

And I imagine he sees a multitude, something more than a mass, growing larger and clearer as it recedes, and Sergeant Dundas borne along in it, his spot marked by the big mouth of the tuba, growing smaller and fainter, passing out of our neighbourhood, our lives, and our times.

Propaganda by Monuments

I
Grekov

Pavel Grekov paused for a moment in the overheated lobby of the apartment block to turn up his coat collar and smooth down his hair. He glanced sceptically at his watch – five to two – and then at the pinched face of the city behind the glass. He would have to hurry, which he was not in the habit of doing, but at least a brisk walk would get the circulation going. He pulled on his gloves, jammed his fists into his pockets and shouldered through the door.

He walked with his head pulled down into his collar and his eyes fixed on the toes of his boots. He saw from above the tentative splay-footed gait foisted on him by an icy pavement, and was not amused by it. The streets were almost deserted. Did it get this cold in the Transvaal? he wondered. Did it snow? Probably not, it was too close to the Tropic of Capricorn. Then he pulled his right hand out of his pocket and pressed three fingers to his chest, where a letter from those unimaginable latitudes was stored in an inside pocket. He might have been taking the letter's temperature through the thick cloth, or trying to feel the patter of its heart above the pounding of his own. Get more exercise, Grekov! he lectured himself. Out from behind that desk!

Grekov was a junior translator in the Administration for Everyday Services, an English specialist. Slowly but surely over the years he had established an interdepartmental reputation for his command of a fractious and somewhat eccentric English vocabulary. In recent months he had discovered his forte: rendering broken English in indestructible Russian. In the departmental estimation this was a highly desirable skill, and there were rumours, none of which had made an impression on Grekov himself, that he would soon be transferred to Foreign Affairs. He would have leapt at the opportunity.

The fact is that Grekov was bored. In the course of nearly five years in the same position no more than a handful of interesting documents had crossed his desk, precious messages in bottles carried to him on a tide of mundane communiqués and news clippings. It goes without saying that these rarities never originated in Everyday Services, but rather in the Ministry of Culture, or Foreign Affairs, or even Sport and Recreation, and they were so scarce that he was able to remember them all without effort.

He remembered them now, in chronological order, as he hurried through the snow-struck city. His career had started auspiciously with an exchange of telegrams about an inheritance and an itinerary issued by a travel agent in Kingston, which he could have sworn was in code – although this notion may have been put into his head by the security restriction stamped on the docket. In any event, this scoop had been followed by a dry spell of several years, until at last he was called upon by Culture to translate a menu for an official function. How many people could there be in Moscow who knew what a madumbi casserole was? Then another drought. More recently the tempo had started picking up: he'd done several love-letters full of double entendres and a set of instructions for assembling a Japanese exercise bicycle. There had also been poems by a Malawian dissident and the lyrics of a song by a band called The Dead Kennedys. But nothing had gripped his imagination like the letter he now carried over his heart.

It had washed up in his in-tray a week ago, and its contents struck him as so unlikely that at first he thought someone higher up was pulling his leg – probably that Kulyabin character in Housing. Just the day before, Kulyabin had made faces at him in the men's room and told him to keep his pecker up.

But the letter proved to be genuine. The Chief confirmed it: the translation had been requisitioned by Foreign Economic Relations. Still Grekov wasn't convinced. He phoned the Ministry himself, on the pretext of finding out how urgently the translation was required, and got hold of a certain Christov, the aide whose signature was on a covering note pinned to the envelope. Christov was adamant: the letter had come all the way from the Republic of South Africa, signed, sealed, and delivered. He hadn't actually opened it with his own two hands, but he had seen it done with his own two eyes. Grekov knew where South Africa was, of course? Of course.

As he neared the river Grekov became anxious that he had somehow lost the letter, or left it at home, and he had to lean against the parapet and fumble it out of his pocket. The envelope was green and edged around with blue and orange chevrons, and it was grubby, as if it had been dropped on a dusty floor. In the top left-hand corner was a pale blue rectangle containing the phrases PER LUGPOS, BY AIRMAIL, and PAR AVION in a tidy stack, and beside it, in a smaller orange window, some sort of winged mythological creature, a crude representation of Pegasus, perhaps, or a griffin with a human face. In the right-hand corner were three stamps, crookedly affixed: the largest, apparently the most valuable, depicted a pastoral scene, with herds of fatted sheep and cattle grazing on fertile steppes; the smallest symbolized energy and industrial progress in a collage of cooling towers, dynamos and pylons; the other was a portrait of a man – a politician, he assumed, or a king. All three were shackled together by a postmark that read PRETORIA – 6.01.92.

The address was in blue ballpoint pen, in a hand that had something childishly precise about it. The letters were all flat-footed, as if the writer had ruled lines in pencil to guide him and rubbed them out afterwards. The wording itself suggested a touching faith in the reliability of the postal service. It read:

The Ministir of Foreign Affairs
PO Kremlin
Moscow
Russia ("USSR")

If he hadn't been wearing gloves Grekov would probably have taken out the letter and read it for the hundredth time. Instead he held the envelope up to the light to see the rectangular silhouette of folded paper inside. He turned the envelope over. On the back, in pencil, he had jotted down Christov's telephone number. He had also taken down some directions given to him by an acquaintance in Roads and Pavements. He studied them now, plotting his course to the monument, and suddenly regretted that he had spoilt the envelope by scribbling on it. He put the letter away with a sigh and went along the embankment towards Borovitskaya Square.

The people he passed were like himself, bundled up in their own thoughts, and he saw nothing out of the ordinary until he reached the end of Prospekt Marksa, where a dozen middle-aged men – tourists, to judge by the primary colours of their anoraks – were standing together in a frozen clump gazing at the outside of the Lenin Library. He was struck firstly by the fact that they were all men, and then by the more remarkable fact that every last one of them wore spectacles.

He went up Prospekt Kalinina, looking out for the park that was his landmark, and when he found it turned left into a side-street. He became aware of a high-pitched buzzing in the distance, like a dentist's drill, and felt reassured that he was going in the right direction. In the middle of the next block he came to an even narrower street, a cul-de-sac called Bulkin, and at the end of that was the nameless square that was his destination.

The square at the dead end of Bulkin Street was surrounded by apartment blocks. In the middle of the cobbled space, on an imposing pedestal, was a large stone head. Not just any old head – a head of Lenin. And not just any old head of Lenin either. According to Roads and Pavements it was the largest head of Lenin in the city of Moscow. If Roads and Pavements were correct on that score, Grekov speculated, why should this not be the largest head of Lenin in Russia, or the broken-down Union, or even the whole out-of-order world?

The eyes in the head of Lenin looked straight at Grekov.

On this particular afternoon, as expected, two workers in overalls were standing on Lenin's bald pate, one wielding a noisy pneumatic drill and the other a gigantic iron clamp. A ladder rested against the cliff of a cheek, and at its foot a third worker was lounging against the pedestal. A lorry surmounted by a crane, and braced at each corner by a huge hydraulic leg with an orthopaedic boot on the end of it, stood to one side. Grekov judged that he was in good time, and so he crossed to the opposite pavement, which had been shovelled more recently, slowed his steps and strolled on at a leisurely pace, his usual one, enjoying the progressive revelation of detail.

Naturally, the stone head loomed larger the closer he got. The features, at first indistinct, now clarified themselves. The eyes were still looking straight at him, even though he had changed pavements. On a smaller scale this phenomenon might have qualified as a miracle; on this scale it was undoubtedly a question of perspective. They were kindly eyes, if not quite grandfatherly, then more than avuncular; but as the mouth came into focus, beneath the sculpted wings of the moustache, the whole face changed, it became severe and irritable, it took on the cross expression of a bachelor uncle who didn't like children. And then, quite unaccountably, as he came closer still, the face foreshortened into friendliness again.

The workers clambering about up there made the monument seem even more colossal than it was, and Grekov couldn't help but admire their gleeful daring and lack of decorum. The one with the drill was skating around on the great man's icy dome like a seasoned performer; and even as Grekov watched, the skater's companion, the one with the clamp, slid audaciously down the curvature of the skull, unloosing a shower of scurfy snow from the fringe of hair, and found a foothold on one of the ears.

Along one side of the square stood a row of empty benches, five in all, and Grekov made his way there. With a characteristic sense of symmetry he chose the one in the middle, wiped the slush off it with his cuff and sat down, tucking his coat-tails underneath him. He gazed about the square. Two little boys had climbed up on the lorry and were using the crane as a jungle gym, dodging the snowballs thrown by their earthbound companions. The yells of the children clanked like chains against the frozen facades overlooking the square. There were a few smudged faces at peep-holes in the misty windows, but apart from the workers, who presumably had no option, Grekov was the only grown-up who had ventured out to watch this monumental lump of history toppled from its pedestal. The workers themselves, in their oversized mufflers and mittens and boots, looked to him like children dressed up in their parents' cast-offs.

How soon people become bored with the making and unmaking of history, Grekov thought, remembering the hundreds of thousands who had taken to the streets to watch the first monuments fall. Looking about at the empty square, becoming conscious of his singularity, he felt an uncomfortable sense of complicity with the overalled figures and their vandalizing equipment.

The driller finished his trepanation and called for an eye. This turned out to be a huge metal loop with a threaded shaft. It was toted up the ladder by the lounger from below, and the same man brought down the drill. The man balancing on the ear secured the eye with the clamp and screwed it into place. Three similar eyes already protruded from the skull, and the fourth completed the all-seeing square. The man with the clamp now climbed down, leaving the driller alone on the summit with his hands on his hips and his nose in the air, like a hunter dwarfed by his trophy.

The clamp, lobbed carelessly onto the back of the lorry, woke up the crane operator, who had been dozing unseen in his cubicle. Under the clamper's directions the operator began to move the boom of the crane so that its dangling chains and hooks could be secured to the eyes.

The lounger, still carrying the drill, shooed the children away to the other side of the square and then came and sat on the bench next to Grekov, who at once tried to strike up a conversation.

"Another one bites the dust," he said cheerfully.

"Seven this month," came the gruff reply.

"You don't say! Where do you put them all?"

"Scrap heap … of history."

"No, seriously," Grekov insisted, and demonstrated his good faith by taking off one glove and offering a cigarette, which was gladly accepted. "What happens to them? I'm a student, you see. I'm making a study of monuments."

"A man after my own heart," said the worker, adopting a tone that was ingratiatingly earnest. "Let's see now. First, the bronze ones. The bronze ones are melted down and reshaped into useful objects like door-knockers and railings. Then the ones of stone: those are crushed into gravel and scattered on the paths in our public parks so that the citizens don't come a cropper. Now for the marble ones – not too many of those – and the ones of display-quality granite: the beautiful ones are sliced up for tombstones and carved into monuments of the new heroes – only smaller, of course, to accommodate the new noses and ears. But the ugly ones, like this one, have to be kept, or rather *preserved*, because they were made by famous artists long ago, whose names escape me for the moment, and they have to be cleaned up and put in museums. There's a heap of them at Vnukovo, behind the bus terminus."

"At Vnukovo, you say."

At that moment the crane's engines began to roar and drowned out the conversation.

The head wouldn't budge. The chains sang like rubber bands and the lorry rocked on its hydraulic legs, but the bone and sinew of that stubborn neck held fast. The pedestal shivered. Then there was a crack like a whiplash, a ruff of white dust burst from under the jawbone and the head tore loose and bobbed wildly at the end of the chains. It was so startling to see this gigantic object bouncing playfully on the air, like a child's ball, while the lorry swayed perilously on its legs, that Grekov recoiled in fright.

The head was lowered onto the lorry and secured with a multitude of cables. It was made to look backwards, but whether by accident or design Grekov could not tell. A fifth worker, who had been sleeping in the cab, now came to life and drove the lorry away down Bulkin Street. His comrades posed on the rigging around the head like revellers on a Mardi Gras float. One of them had his foot propped in a dilated nostril, another scratched his back on the tip of a moustache. But despite all these little distractions, these buzzing flies, the eyes gazed back unflinchingly, and there was such a forbidding set to the bottom lip that Grekov took his hands out of his pockets and stood up. The lorry turned right at the end of the street and at last the stony gaze was broken.

The children had gone indoors, the watchers had withdrawn from the windows and the peep-holes had misted over again. Grekov was alone. He went to the pedestal and walked around it in both directions. There was no inscription. A single thread of iron, a severed spine twisting from the concrete, marked the spot where the head had stood. The head of Lenin. It was hard to imagine something else in its place. But that's the one certainty we have, he thought. There will be something in its place.

He sat down with his back against the pedestal and took the letter out of his pocket. He examined the winged beast again, and failed to identify it. Then he took off his gloves, opened the envelope and spread flat the sheet of white paper it contained. Although Grekov had almost forgotten the fact, this was not the original letter, but a version of it twice removed. He had dared to keep the envelope, but keeping the letter itself had been impossible. Instead he had made a copy of the letter in his own hand, and this was a carbon copy of that. The original English was there, word for word, but there were also notes of his own, in parentheses and footnotes – guesses at meanings, useful turns of phrase culled from memory and the dictionary, corrections of spelling mistakes. This was a translation method he had devised himself, in the absence of tape recorders and word processors, and although it was primitive he was proud of it.

There were also speculations – contained in a series of marginal notes and questions – that exceeded the bounds of his responsibilities as a translator and partly explained why the seat of his pants was stuck to the plinth of an empty pedestal in a public square on a Sunday afternoon: Who is this man Khumalo? Is he serious? What does he really want? Will he get it? Who will help him? Me (of all people)?

Grekov read the letter through again, although he practically knew it by heart. In a dimple in the middle of the sheet his eye came to a tight spring of black hair. It was in fact a hair from Boniface Khumalo's head, which Grekov's brisk walk had dislodged from a corner of the envelope and shaken into the folded sheet. But Grekov, understandably, failed to recognize it. He blew it into space in a cloud of steam.

II
Khumalo to the Ministir
(with selected notes by P. Grekov)

"Boniface Tavern"
PO Box 7350
Atteridgeville 0008
Tvl [Transvaal – peruse map]
5th Jan[uary] 1992

TO WHO[M] IT MAY CONCERN

Re: SURPLUS STATUES [in the matter of/concerning]

I am greeting you in the name of struggling masses of South Africa,
comrades, freedom fighters, former journeymen to Moscow – you
may know some … [Never met a military trainee, but believe they
existed.] Also in the name of boergious countrymen known up and
down [business "contacts"? class alliances?] here at home. I myself
am very much struggle [struggling – infamous Apartheid].

My particular personality is illustrious. I am doing many things
well: initially gardening assistance, packer O.K. Bazaars [so-called
"baas"], garage attendance, petroljoggie [prob. brand-name cf.

Texaco], currently taverner and taxi-owner, 1 X Toyota Hi-Ace 2.2 GLX (1989) [Japanese motor vehicle] so far – "See me now, see me no more." But especially now I am going on as Proprietor (Limited) Boniface Tavern, address above-mentioned, soon revamped as V.I. Lenin Bar & Grill. This is my very serious plan. You must believe it!

Hence it is I am taking up space to search out whether spare statues of V.I. Lenin are made available to donate me or if necessary I would be obliged to purchase on the most favourable terms (lay-by). [In a nut-case: His overweening desire is to buy a statue of Lenin. One can't help but bravo.] Please state prefference [one f], down payment, interest rates, postage, etc. etc.

Apartheid is crumpling as you know. Recently you visited a New South Africa to espy trade opportunities. [Trade Missionary to S.A. – check w. Grigoriev.] Here is one! I mean business! Fantastical benefits may amount to all of us. V.I. Lenin Bar & Grill is opening (1st May for publicity stunts) with unheard parties and festivities, free booze, braaid sheep [barbecued mutton], cows [beef], chipniks [prostitutes], members of the medias (TV 2 and 3, Mnet [!]), Lucky Dube [sweepstake?], Small Business Development Corporation (SDBC) [Grig?], wide-scale representatives from organizations (SACP, ANC, PAC, ACA, FAWU, MAWU, BAWU, etc. etc.). [Check] It will be a big splash [make a splash – attract much attention] for tourism and international relations.

As far as I'm concerned nothing can prevent my request to pass. I have pedestals galore and many other statues to compliment my favourite V.I. Lenin. Also recognition to be attached viz. [videlicet: namely] "This Beautiful Monument was donated to Working People of Atteridgeville by Kind Masses of Russia, unveiled 1st May 1992 (Is there time?) by Jay Naidoo (for example)."

After three weeks and no reply has forthcome I'll write again, not meaning to plead to you.

Amandla! [*interj.* Power! Usually A. ngawetu]

Yours faithfully,

Boniface Khumalo
Proprietor (Ltd)

PS If you are not the right person please forward this letter to the same. Thank you.
PSS Toyota 10-seater is blood-red. MVM325T. Thanks.

III
Lunacharski and Lenin
(an offcut)

and in 1918 *Proletkult* declared that the proletar-
iat should assimilate existing bourgeois culture
and "recast the material in the crucible of its own
class-consciousness".[6] Lunacharski himself argued
against gimmicky experimentation: "The independence of proletarian art does not consist in artificial
originality but presupposes an acquaintance with
all the fruits of the preceding culture."[7] We may
assume that as Commissar of Enlightenment – he
had become head of the People's Commissariat for
Education and the Arts (NARKOMPROS) in 1917
– Lunacharski knew only too well that experimental work would be incomprehensible to the illiterate
masses. In the coming years Lunacharski and Lenin
would clash over the position of *Proletkult,* with
Lenin trying to subordinate it to NARKOMPROS
and the Party, and Lunacharski arguing for a measure of independence.

These differences notwithstanding, Lunacharski

looked back on the immediate post-revolutionary years with some nostalgia. In 1933, the year of his death, he recalled Lenin's scheme for "Propaganda by Monuments" and sought to revive it. His reminiscences tell us something about the complex relationship between the two men and the vexed question of the role of art in the revolution.

Lenin's taste in art was conventional; he was fiercely opposed to the avant-garde, especially to futurism. Lunacharski recalled an episode during the 1905 revolution when Lenin passed the night in the house of Comrade D.I. Leshenko. Here he came across a set of Hermann Knackfuss's books on great artists and spent the night paging through one volume after the other. The next morning he told Lunacharski how sorry he was that he had never had time to occupy himself with art. "What an attractive field the history of art is. How much work there for a communist."[8]

How did "Propaganda by Monuments" come about? According to Lunacharski, the idea was sparked off by the frescos in Campanella's *La Città del Sole (The City of the Sun)*. In the Utopian state depicted in this work, frescos were used to educate the young. Lenin, mindful of the straitened circumstances in which many of the artists of Moscow and Petrograd found themselves (the latter would be renamed Leningrad only in 1924), but mindful too that frescos would hardly suit the Russian climate, proposed that artists be commissioned to sculpt "concise, trenchant inscriptions showing the more lasting, fundamental principles and slogans of Marxism"[9] on the city walls and on specially erected pediments, in place of advertisements and posters.

"Please don't think I have my heart set on marble, granite and gold lettering," Lenin went on (in Lunacharski's reconstruction of their dialogue). "We must be modest for the present. Let it be concrete with clear, legible inscriptions. I am not at the moment thinking of anything permanent or even long-lasting. Let it even be of a temporary nature."

"It's a wonderful idea," Lunacharski said, "but surely what you propose is work for a monumental mason. Our artists will become bored if they have to spend their days carving inscriptions. You know how they lust after novelty."

"Well, it happens that I consider monuments even more important than inscriptions: I mean busts, full-length figures, perhaps – what do you call them? – bas-reliefs, groups. And let's not forget heads."

Lenin proposed that a list of the forerunners of Socialism, revolutionists and other heroes of culture be drawn up, from which suitable works in plaster and concrete could be commissioned.

It is important that these works should be intelligible to the masses, that they should catch the eye. It is also important that they should be designed to withstand our climate, at least to some extent, that they should not be easily marred by wind, rain and frost. Of course, inscriptions on the pedestals of monuments could be made – if such trifles are beneath your artists, perhaps the stonemasons will oblige us – explaining who the man was and so forth.

Particular attention should be paid to the ceremonies of unveiling such monuments. In this we ourselves and other Party members could help, perhaps also prominent specialists could be invited to speak on such occasions. Every such unveiling ceremony should be a little holiday and an occasion for propaganda. On anniversary dates mention of the given great man could be repeated, always, of course, showing his connection with our revolution and its problems.[10]

Lunacharski was consumed with the idea and immediately set about putting it into practice. Some inscriptions were set up on buildings, and quite a few monuments by sculptors in Moscow and Petrograd were erected. Not all the monuments were successful. Some of them broke. Perhaps the artists had misjudged the climate after all. A full figure of Marx by Matveyev cracked in half and was replaced by a less impressive bronze head. Other monuments were simply too ugly, and here the artists were definitely at fault. Moscow's statue of Marx and Lenin in "some sort of basin"[11] was the most notorious failure. The citizens dubbed it "the whiskered bathers" or "Cyril and Methodius," because it made Marx and Lenin look like a pair of brotherly saints emerging from a bath-tub.

The modernists and futurists ran amok. Korolev's statue of Bakunin was so hideous that horses shied when they passed it, even though it was hidden behind boards. It proved to be "of a temporary nature." No sooner had the statue been unveiled than the anarchists, incensed by its depiction of their hero, smashed it to pieces.

But although the manufacture of monuments left much to be desired, "the unveiling of monuments went on much better."[12] Taking to heart Lenin's suggestion that "we ourselves could help," Lunacharski himself unveiled a string of monuments.

A contest was organized to choose a design for a statue of Marx, and both Lunacharski and Lenin participated enthusiastically in the judging. A well-known sculptor proposed a statue of Marx standing somewhat acrobatically on four elephants, but it was rejected – after personal adjudication by Lenin – as inappropriate. In the end a rather splendid design by a collective, working under the guidance of Aleshin, was chosen. It showed Marx with his feet firmly on the ground and his hands behind his back. The group built a small model of the statue in Sverdlov Square in time for that year's May Day celebrations, and Lenin approved of it although he did not think it a good likeness. The hair in particular was not very well done, and Lunacharski was asked to tell the artist to "make the hair more nearly right."[13] The torso was also too stout: Marx seemed about to burst the buttons of his coat, and some subtle tailoring was called for. Later Lenin officiated at a ceremony in the Square to "place the podium"[14] and made a remarkable speech on Marx and his "flaming spirit"[15] – but the statue was never erected.

Lenin was disappointed by the quality of the monuments erected in Moscow, and not reassured to hear from Lunacharski that those in Petrograd were better. "Anatoli Vassilievich," he said sadly, shaking his head, "have the gifted ones all gathered in Petrograd and the hacks remained here with us?"

And so "Propaganda by Monuments" petered out.

A decade later, when Lunacharski tried to revive the scheme, he used Lenin's own words (although he closed his ears to the echo):

> For the time being, I do not expect marble and granite, gold lettering and bronze – so appropriate to socialist style and culture. It is too early as yet for this – but, it seems to me, a second wave of propaganda by monuments, more lasting and more mature, also more effective for being enriched by the vital human element of sculpture, could be instituted by

IV
Christov to Khumalo
(translated and annotated by P. Grekov)

Ministry of Foreign
Economic Relations
32/34 Smolenskaya Sennaya
MOSCOW 121200
28 January 1992

My dear Mr B. Khumalo,

It is with rather a great deal of pleasure that I pen this missive, reactionary to yours of the 5th inst.

Some weeks may have passed, indeed, as your request flew from subtropical Pretoria, administrative capital of the Repudlic of South Africa, to our correspondent temperate urbanity, and henceforward overland to various ministries and departments, videlicet Foreign Affairs – to whom it had been addressed on the bottom line, so to speak – Trade, Tourism, Defence, and Foreign Economic Relations, where it still resides and from whence this missive now therefore emanates. I am a member of the same Ministry, sad to say in a somewhat subsidiary position (Protocol Department), but nevertheless by good fortune required to acknowledge the landing of your letter of the 5th inst. [I, contrarily, am a respected colleague of Everyday Services Department, City of Moscow, which we write "Mockba."– Tr.]

I am instructed to inform you that your letter is receiving considerate attention at many and various levels, local and national/ international. Soon we will pen additional missives to impart the final decision-making process and details.

[Feeling overwhelmingly cocksure that your request re: SURPLUS STATUE will meet with a big okey-dokey fairly forthwith, I make bold to expand the range and scope of the instructions by informing, firstly, that the surplus statue videlicet "Head of V.I. Lenin" which is in mind for dispatch to you is somewhat a national treasure. Materially it is stone. Proportionally it is large, without laying it on thick one says "colossal," being by estimation 7 (seven) metres high, chin to crown, and 17 (seventeen) metres in circumference, at hat-brim level (but has no hat). Imperial equivalences for convenience: 23 feet by 56 feet approx. Will this serve? It will necessitate Herculean efforts in the transportation, but well worth it.

On a new thread. What is doing in the Transvaal? Do the cows and sheep graze on the veldt nearby free from harm? Much has been said and supposed vis-à-vis socio-political machinations of reformism in your motherland of which I am always an amateur or eager beaver as they say. But the horse's mouth is what you are. Your tidings have captivated me boots and all. Please correspond. – Tr.]

We look forward to hearing from you in the near future. [And who knows how long ago hence we may eat beefsteaks and drink vodkas – our patriotic highball – in V.I. Lenin Bar & Grill of Atteridgeville! – Tr. Tr. is for "Translator," being me, Pavel Grekov, same as below.]

Yours faithfully,

A. Christov
Tr: P. Grekov

Postscript: Please correspond to me personally at 63-20 Tischenko Str., Apt #93, MOSCOW 109172. No doubt it will suffice. Conclusively, do you question why the monuments, large and small, have no hats? The head of Lenin in history was fond of hats, precisely caps.

V
Khumalo

Boniface Khumalo put the letter in the cubby-hole along with the tub of Wet Ones. On second thoughts he took it out again and slipped it under the rubber mat on the passenger side. Then he caught his own furtive eye in the rearview mirror, and asked himself why he was playing postman's knock. There was nothing compromising about the letter. The Total Onslaught was over, even if a stale scent of danger still wafted from the exotic landscapes of postage stamps and the unexpected angles of mirror-script print. He retrieved the envelope again and put it in the pocket of his jacket, which hung from a hook on the door-pillar behind his seat.

That everyday action dispelled the threat and left nothing in the air but the caramel tang of new imitation leather and the cloying lavender of the Wet Ones with which he had just wiped his hands. He checked that his fly was buttoned. He checked that his door was locked. Then he looked out of the window at the drab veld of the valley dipping away from the road, straddled by electricity pylons with their stubby arms akimbo, and dotted with huge, floppy-leaved aloes like extravagant bows of green ribbon. On the far slope of the valley was a sub-economic housing complex, a Monopoly-board arrangement of small, plastered houses with corrugated-iron roofs, all of them built to exactly the same design. The planners of Van Riebeecksvlei had sought to introduce some variety into the suburb by rotating the plan of each successive house through ninety degrees, with the result that there were now four basic elevations which repeated themselves in an unvarying sequence down the long, straight streets.

Khumalo had driven past Van Riebeecksvlei on his way to Pretoria a thousand times. But he was struck now, for the first time, by the fact that he could tell at a glance it was a white suburb, even though there wasn't a white face in sight. Was it because the walls of the houses were pastel plaster rather than raw face-brick? Or precisely because there was no one to be seen? Even at this distance it looked like a ghost town. Where was everybody? He thought of the stream of people that flowed up 5th Street from the taxi rank and cast his regulars up on his doorstep.

Khumalo buckled his safety-belt. He tweaked the ignition key and the engine sprang to life. He goaded all six cylinders with petrol, and then let them idle. The advertising was getting to him: he could almost hear the engine panting.

He gentled the car over the ruts at the edge of the tar and accelerated, watching the rev-counter. It was a Sunday afternoon and there was not much traffic. He flew past a bakkie laden with crates of vegetables and a mini-bus called "Many Rivers to Cross," one of Mazibuko's. The car practically drove itself, as he liked to tell his envious friends, just the way the tavern ran itself and the taxi paid for itself. One of these days I'll retire, he said, because there won't be anything left for me to do. Made redundant by progress.

The Boniface Tavern was Khumalo's pride and joy. He had started the shebeen ten years earlier in his garage, adding on a room here and a room there until it was larger than the house itself. The "Tavern" of the title had been prompted by the medieval ring of his own first name – his late mother had named him for St. Boniface, English missionary among the Germans, martyred in 755 at the ripe old age of eighty.

The Boniface Tavern had certainly been unusual in its day, but lately all licensed shebeens were being called taverns. "I was ten years ahead of my time," he would boast to his patrons, "I was a taverner long before the Taverners' Association came along." Secretly, the change made him unhappy. Now that every Tom, Dick and Harry had a tavern, the Boniface Tavern lost its special flavour. He began casting around for an alternative.

A new decade dawned. On the day Nelson Mandela walked from the shadows into the glare of daily news, Khumalo decided that his establishment needed more than a change of name to face the future in; it needed a change of clothes. It happened that the taxi he'd acquired a few months before was proving to be lucrative, and he was confident that he would soon be in a position to finance the new wardrobe.

The style he settled on had a touch of the "taverna" about it: he wanted red plush, wrought iron, vine leaves, lashings of white plaster and crowds of venerable statuary. He saw the very thing in Nero's Palace, a coffee shop in the Union Hotel, and that became the model. He made a few enquiries about Nero's decor, and one Saturday afternoon went out to Hyperplant in Benoni, a nursery that specialized in garden statues. It was expensive – a common or garden gnome would set you back R44 – but he came away with two disarmed goddesses, several cement amphorae with cherubim and seraphim in relief upon them, sufficient numbers of caryatids and atlantes to prop up a canvas awning over the courtyard, and a bench with mermaid armrests. He stockpiled his purchases in the backyard, where the elements could age them while his funds recuperated.

So far so good, except that the new name continued to elude him. He thought of exploiting the obvious political angle by honouring a popular leader. But in this capricious epoch how could you tell who would be popular in the new year? In any case, the old guard was getting on. The way of all flesh was fleeting, whereas decor had to last. He looked further afield: The Richelieu? Never mind The

Napoleon! He was still undecided when a new possibility bobbed up unexpectedly in the pages of the *Pretoria News*.

One evening he read on page two that the Moscow City Council, in concrete expression of their commitment to the reforms sweeping through the Soviet Union, had decided to take down 62 of the 68 statues and other memorial structures in the capital devoted to V. I. Lenin. "All Lenin memorials in schools and other institutions for children also will be removed," the report concluded. What other institutions for children are there? he wondered. Orphanages? Hospitals? Reformatories? And then he thought further: What will become of all those statues? I could make good use of a couple myself, to string some coloured lights from.

That's probably as far as the fancy would have gone, had there not been a comment on the statues in the editorial column of that same newspaper. Although the tone was mocking – the simple act of giving "Vladimir Illyich" in full was a sure sign of satirical intent – the idea struck a chord with Khumalo.

SURPLUS STATUES

Calling all enterprising businessmen! The import opportunity of a lifetime presents itself. The Moscow City Council has decided to dismantle the hundreds of monuments to Vladimir Illyich Lenin which grace its crowded public buildings and empty market-places. Cities throughout the crumbling Soviet Union will follow suit. We ask you: Where else in the world is there a ready market for statues of Lenin but in South Africa? Jump right in before the local comrades snap them up for nothing.

Khumalo parked his car next to a building site in Prinsloo Street. An entire city block was being demolished, and all that remained of the high-rise buildings that had occupied the spot was one ruined single-storey facade with an incongruously shiny plate-glass window in it. It had once been Salon Chantelle, according to the sign. The departed proprietor had written a farewell message to her clients on the glass in shoe-white: We apologize to all our ladies for the inconvenience caused by demolition. Please phone 646-4224 for our new location. Thank you for your continued support. XXXXX. C.

Khumalo got out of the car. The building site looked as if it had been bombed, and the impression of a city under siege was borne out by the empty streets. He suddenly felt concerned for the welfare of his car. It only had twelve thousand k's on the clock. Then he heard a metallic clang, and traced it to an old man with a wheelbarrow scrounging among the collapsed walls. Perfect. He could keep an eye on the car. Khumalo called out to him, in several languages, but was ignored. In the end he had to go closer himself, through the gaping doorway of Salon Chantelle, stepping carefully over the broken masonry in his brown loafers.

The old man was salvaging unbroken bricks and tiles from the rubble.

"Greetings, Father," Khumalo said.

The man glared at him suspiciously.

"What are you collecting there?"

It was obvious. The old man spat with surprising vehemence and accuracy in the dust at Khumalo's feet, picked up a brick with three round holes through it, knocked a scab of cement off it against the side of the barrow and dropped it on the pile.

"Are you building your own place?"

Another brick fell.

"Do you sell these things? I may have need of some building materials myself one of these days. Are you a builder?"

"This rubbish belongs to no one," the old man finally said in a broken voice. "It is just lying here. You can see it yourself."

Khumalo gave him a one-rand coin and asked him to watch the car. He pocketed the money noncommittally, spat again with conviction, and went back to work. Feeling as if he had been dismissed, Khumalo walked up Prinsloo Street towards the State Theatre.

At the Church Street intersection he waited for the robot to change even though there was no traffic. He looked right, and left, and right again towards Strijdom Square, and caught a glimpse of the dome like a swollen canvas sail over the head of J.G. Strijdom.

When the Strijdom monument was first unveiled a story had gone around that its unconventional dome defied the laws of architecture, and therefore of nature. A group of city architects – the rivals whose tender had been rejected? – were so intrigued by it that they built a scale model in perfect detail out of chicken-wire and plaster of Paris. The model fell over. No matter how much they tinkered with it, it fell over.

The lights changed, and Khumalo crossed the street with the same jaunty stride as the little green man.

J.G. Strijdom had been leader of the National Party in the 1950s and Prime Minister of the Union from 1954 to 1958. He was one of the great builders of apartheid. The details were on the pedestal. But though he had passed the monument often, Khumalo had never bothered to read what was written there. All he knew about Strijdom he had gleaned from the words of a popular political song. "Sutha sutha wena Strijdom!" the song said. "Give way, Strijdom! If you don't, this car, this car which has no wheels, will ride over you!" In Khumalo's mind Strijdom's face had never borne the serene, far-sighted expression he saw on it now, as the bronze head came into view over islands of greenery. Rather, it had a look of stupefied terror.

It was the face of a slow-footed pedestrian, a moment away from impact and extinction, gaping at the juggernaut of history bearing down on him. *This* Strijdom is *that* Strijdom, Khumalo thought with a smile. As secure on his pedestal as a head on its shoulders.

In front of the monument, where one corner of the billowing dome was tacked to the ground, was a fountain: a thick white column rose from the middle of a pond and on top of it were four galloping horses, their hooves striking sparks from the air, their manes and tails flying. Usually jets of water spurted up from the pond and played against the column, but today they were still. Some crooked scaffolding leaned against the yellowed stone, and the stench of stagnant water rose from the slimy moat at the column's base. Khumalo sat on the dry lip of the fountain and looked at the limp agapanthuses and the grey river-stones embedded in cement on the bottom of the pond.

Then he looked at the head. His heart sank. According to his calculations, the head of V.I. Lenin promised to him in the letter from Grekov was at least three times larger than the head of J.G. Strijdom! The pedestal would hardly fit in his yard. Perhaps if he knocked down the outside toilet and the Zozo ... but surely it would cost a fortune just to build a pedestal that size. And who would pay for the installation? What if he approached the SACP, or the Civic, or a consortium of local businessmen? Atteridgeville needs a tourist attraction, after all, something with historical value. I'll donate it to the community, he thought, they can put it up on that empty plot by the police station. My name can go on the plaque, I'll unveil the bloody thing myself!

Still, it would be a pity to give it away, when *I've* gone to the effort to get hold of it. Has he promised it to me? I think he has ... But who is this Grekov anyway? Can he be trusted? On whose behalf is he speaking? He doesn't sound like a very important person. Although he seems to know more than Christov, at any rate.

Khumalo shrugged off his jacket and took out Grekov's letter. He didn't think of it as Christov's letter, it had been so ruthlessly invaded and occupied by the translator. The fingerprint in ink from the typewriter ribbon, which was clearly visible in the top left-hand corner of the page, may have settled the question of authorship once and for all, had Khumalo been able to check it against flesh and blood.

He read the letter again. It had been typed on an old typewriter and all the loops of the letters were closed, like winking eyes. There were things he didn't understand. Colossal? Please correspond? He put the letter back in the envelope. The Cyrillic postmark read: Mockba.

For a reason he couldn't put his finger on, Khumalo felt better. He jumped up and paced out the dimensions of the pedestal. He multiplied them by three in his head, and had to chuckle: the pedestal alone would be the size of a double garage! He studied the poetic verse inscribed on the salt-and-pepper stone but could not make head or tail of it. His Afrikaans had always been weak. He walked around the pedestal and at the back discovered two more inscriptions, twins, one in English and one in Afrikaans. He read the English version out loud in a cracked impersonation of the old scavenger.

The monument had been unveiled by Mrs Susan Strijdom on Republic Day, 31 May 1972. The Honourable B.J. Vorster, then Prime Minister, had made a speech at the unveiling ceremony. The sculptor of the Head of Strijdom was Coert Steynberg. The sculptor of the Freedom Symbol (the bolted horses) was Danie de Jager. With an admirable concern for fair play, the inscription went on to record the names of the architects of the unnatural dome (Hans Botha and Roelf Botha), the quantity surveyors (Grothaus and Du Plessis), the engineers (W.J.S. van Heerden and Partners, viz. Bruinette, Kruger, Stoffberg and Hugo), the electrical engineers (A. du Toit and Partners) and, with disappointing anonymity, the building contractors (Nasionale Groepsbou Korp.).

The sun was shining through the finely veined bronze ears of Johannes Gerhardus Strijdom.

Khumalo went and stood at a distance, upwind of the stinking Freedom Symbol, with his eyes half-closed, squinting. And after a while he began to see how, but not necessarily why, the impossible came to pass.

Autopsy

Um.

Basically, I was seated at the Potato Kitchen in Hillbrow partaking (excuse me) of a potato. Nothing very exciting had happened to me as yet: I was therefore dissatisfied and alert. Then the King Himself came out of Estoril Books, shrugged His scapular girdle, and turned left. It was the King, no doubt about it, I would know His sinuous gait anywhere. Even in a mob.

It was suppertime, Friday, 15 May 1992. Scored upon my memory like a groove in wax. I lift the stylus, meaning to plunge it precisely into the vein, but the mechanism does not have nerves of steel: the device hums and haws before it begins to speak. (The speakers, the vocal cords, the voice box, the woofers, the tweeters, the *loud* speakers.) So much for memory, swaddled in the velvety folds of the brain and secured in the cabinet of the skull.

My potato was large and carved into quarters, like a colony or a thief. It had been microwaved and bathed in letcho with sausage and bacon. Also embrocated with garlic butter (R0.88 extra) and poulticed with grated cheddar as yellow as straw (R1.80 extra). Moreover, encapsulated in white polystyrene.

I was holding a white plastic fork in my left hand. I was stirring, with the white plastic teaspoon in my right hand, the black coffee in a white polystyrene cup.

The slip from the cash register lay on the table folded into a fan. It documented this moment in time, choice of menu item and price including VAT (15.05.92/letch R9.57/chee R1.80/coff R1.90/garl butt R0.88).

Although it was chilly, I had chosen a table on the pavement so that I could be part of the vibrant street life of Johannesburg's most cosmopolitan suburb. A cold front deep-frozen in the south Atlantic was at that very moment crossing the mudbanks of the Vaal. The street-children squatting at the kerb looked preternaturally cold and hungry with their gluey noses and methylated lips.

One of the little beggars was an Indian. Apartheid is dead.

I found myself in the new improved South Africa, seated upon an orange plastic chair, stackable, but not stacked at this juncture. It was one of four chairs – two orange, two umber – drawn up to a round white plastic table with a hole through its middle, specially engineered to admit the shaft of the beach umbrella, which shaft was also white, while the umbrella itself was composed of alternating segments of that colour and Coca-Cola red. My legs were crossed, right over left. The toe of my right shoe was tapping out against a leg of the table the homesickening heartbeat of "O Mein Papa" throbbing from the gills of a passing Ford Laser.

The King chose that very moment to exit Estoril Books with a rolled magazine under His arm. He paused before the buffet of cut-price paperbacks on two trestle-tables. He examined cracked spines and dog-ears. He scanned the promotional literature.

A saddening scenario presented itself: every book will change your life.

Bundling Himself up in His diet, He turned left, took eight sinuous steps, choreographing heel, toe, knee and hip by turns, all His own work, and turned left again into the polyunsaturated interior of Tropical Fast Foods. He was a natural. He passed under the neon sign: a green coconut palm inclined against an orange sunset while the sun sank like an embolus into a sea of lymph. Las Vegas Motel – Color TV – 5 mi. from Damascus – Next exit.

Adventure beckoned.

I had consumed no more than 25 per cent of my meal – let's say R3.00's worth – and hadn't so much as sipped the coffee, but I rose as one man, dragged on my trench coat and hurried inside to pay the bill.

My white plastic knife remained jutting from the steaming potato like a disposable Excalibur.

"*Danke schön*," I said, in order to ingratiate myself with the Potato Woman of Düsseldorf.

"*Fünfzig, fünfzehn*," she replied, dishing change into my palm, and banged the drawer of the cash register with her chest.

Los!

On my way into the night I skirted five children squabbling over my leftovers: three-quarters of a potato (75 per cent), divisible by five only with basic arithmetic.

I sauntered across Pretoria Street, dodged a midnight-blue BMW with one headlight, cursed silently. In the few short minutes that had passed since the sighting, a grain of doubt had jammed in the treads of my logic, and now I paused on the threshold of Tropical Fast Foods, in the shadow of the electric tree, suddenly off balance. Where am I? Or rather: Where was I? Hollywood Boulevard? Dar es Salaam? Dakar? The Botanical Gardens in Durban?

Oh.

The man I had taken for the King was leaning against the counter with His back to me, gulping the fat air down. Blue denim jacket with tattered cuffs; digital watch, water-resistant to 100 metres (333 feet); tracksuit pants, black with a white stripe; blue tackies (sneakers), scuffed; white socks stuck with blackjacks.

The Griller assembled a yiro (R9.50). He pinched shavings of mutton from an aluminium scoop with a pair of tongs and heaped them on a halo of unleavened pita-bread. He piled sliced onions and sprinkled the unique combination of tropical seasonings. I turned aside to the poker machine and dropped a rand in the slot.

The machine dealt me a losing hand.

Meanwhile, the spitted mutton turned at 2 r.p.m., like a stack of rare seven-singles in a jukebox. A skewered onion wept on top of the pile. Where the Griller's blade had pared, the meat's pink juices ran, spat against the cauterizing elements, which glowed like red neon, and congealed upon the turntable.

I drew the Jack of Diamonds *and* the King of Hearts.

The man I had taken for the King turned to the Manager and spoke inaudibly from the right side of His mouth. There was no mistaking the aerodynamic profile, the airbrushed quiff as sleek as a fender, black with a blue highlight, the wraparound shades like a chrome-plated bumper, the Velcro sideburns, the tender lips.

The Manager amplified the whispered request for more salt.

The Griller obliged.

I kept the Jack *and* the King, against my better judgement.

The Manager cupped a paper bag under a stainless-steel funnel and tipped a basketful of chips (fries) down it. He dashed salt and pepper, shook the bag, and handed it to the King. The King throttled the bag and squirted tomato sauce (ketchup) down its throat like advertising.

The Griller finished assembling a yiro (r9.50). He rolled it expertly in greaseproof paper and serviette (napkin), slipped it into a packet and handed it to the Manager, who passed it to the King. The King took the yiro in His left hand. With His right hand He produced a large green note (bill), which the Manager held up to the light before clamping it in the register.

A flash of snow-white under the frayed cuff when the King reached for His change. Not a card up His sleeve but a clue: sunburst catsuit, doubling as thermal underwear.

The King dropped the coins into a money belt concealed under His belly. He took up the (fries). He swivelled sinuously and tenderly. Anatomical detail: sinews and tendons rotated the ball of the femur in the lubricious socket of the hip. (Nope.) Of the pelvic girdle? (Yep.) He slid onto an orange plastic stool. His buttocks, sheathed in white silk within and black polyester without, chubbed over the edge.

He pushed the shades up onto His forehead. He took out a pair of reading-glasses with teardrop rims of silver wire, breathed on the lenses (uhuh), buffed them on His thigh and put them on.

Now I might have hurried over, saying: "Excuse me. I couldn't help noticing."

Instead, I looked away.

In the screen of the poker machine His reflection unrolled not one magazine but four: the February issue of *Musclemag International (The*

Body-Building Bible), the April issue of *Stern*, the Special Collector's issue of *Der Kartoffelbauer* (March) and the November 1991 issue of *Guns & Ammo*. He spread them on the counter, chose the *Stern*, rolled the other three into a baton and stuffed them into a pocket.

He opened the magazine to the feature on Steffi Graf and flattened it with His left forearm. With His right hand He peeled back the greaseproof paper and with His left He raised the yiro. His Kingly lips mumbled the meat as if it were a microphone.

The menu said it was lamb, but it was mutton.

A full-page photograph showed Steffi Graf serving an ace. It captured her racket smashing the page number (22) off the top left-hand corner of the page and the sole of her tennis shoe squashing the date (April) into the clay. It captured the hem of her skirt floating around her hips like a hula hoop. The King gazed at her thighs, especially the deep-etched edge of the biceps femoris, but also at her wrists, with their eight euphonious bones – scaphoid, semilunar, cuneiform, pisiform, trapezium, trapezoid, unciform, os magnum – enclasped by fragrant sweatbands, and her moisturized elbows scented with wintergreen.

Er.

Then He gazed at the talkative walls. The muscle in His mandible throbbed, the tip of His tongue simonized the curve of His lips with mutton fat. He spoke with a full mouth, He pronounced the lost opportunities under His breath: Hamburger r4.95 – Debrecziner r6.50 – Frankfurter & Chips r6.95 –

He chewed. He swallowed.

Eating made Him sweat. He was fat, He needed to lose some weight. He'd lost (six and a half pounds) in the fifteen years since His last public appearance, but still He was fat. An eight o'clock shadow fell over His jaw, He needed to shave. He needed to floss, there was a caraway seed lodged against the gum between canine and incisor, maxilla, right, there was mutton between molars. He needed to shampoo, His hair bore the tooth-marks of the comb like the grooves of a 78.

He ate, it made Him sweat. A bead of sweat fell like a silver sequin from the end of His nose and vanished into a wet polka dot on His double-jointed knee. He swabbed His brow with the (napkin). He licked His fingers and wiped them on His pants. He got up and walked out.

Wearing His shades on His forehead and His reading-glasses on His nose, He glided over the greasy (sidewalk).

I hurried after Him, pausing momentarily to pluck: the *Stern*, which He had left open on the counter, the corners of the pages impregnated with His seasoned saliva; the (napkin) bearing the impress of His brow; and the sequin. (I have these relics still.)

He took eight sinuous steps and turned left into the Plus Pharmacy

Centre and Medicine Depot. He padded down the aisle, between the Supradyn-N and the Lucozade (on the one hand) and the Joymag Acusoles: Every Step in Comfort (on the other), to the counter marked Prescriptions/Voorskrifte.

The Pharmacist was a bottle-blonde. She was neither curvaceous nor bubbly, wore a white coat, bore less than a passing resemblance to Jayne Mansfield. The King spoke to her out of the left side of His mouth. He proffered an American Express traveller's cheque and a passport.

Two other customers were browsing: a man in a blue gown, a woman in a tuxedo. She shooed them out and closed the door in my face. There was a poster sellotaped to the glass: Find out about drug abuse inside. Under cover of studying the small print I was able to gaze into the interior.

The King pulled a royal-blue pillowslip embroidered with golden musical notation and silver lightning bolts out of the front of His pants. He swept from the laden shelves into His bag nineteen bottles of Borstol linctus, sixteen bottles of Milk of Magnesia, twenty-two plastic tubs brimming with multi-vitamin capsules (100s), fifty-seven tubes of grape-flavoured Lip-Ice, three bottles of Oil of Olay, four aerosol cans of hair lacquer, twelve Slimslabs, three boxes of Doctor McKenzie's Veinoids, five bottles of Eno, twenty-five tubes of Deep Heat, a king-size bottle of Bioplus, five hot-water bottles with teddy bear covers, an alarm clock, six tubs of Radium leather and suede dye with handy applicators, a jar of beestings and a box of Grandpa Headache Powders.

The Pharmacist tagged along, jabbing a calculator.

He signed the cheque.

I rootled in a bombproof (trash can).

He took eleven sinuous steps.

The Pharmacist held the door open for Him, and shut it behind Him when He had passed, breathing in His garlicky slipstream.

He found Himself once more upon the (sidewalk) among the hurly-burly of ordinary folk.

I might have made an approach with right hand extended: "Long time no see."

Instead, I hid my face.

He breathed. He took off the reading-glasses, He pulled down the shades. He settled His bag of tricks on His left shoulder. He turned right.

The King moved on foot through the Grey Area.

Now He took five hundred and seventy-one sinuous steps and turned right again. Attaboy.

Window-shopping:

He passed Checkers. He passed the hawkers of Hubbard squashes. He passed Fontana: Hot roast chickens. He passed the Hare Krishnas dishing out vegetable curry to the non-racial poor on paper plates. He passed the International Poker Club: Members Only, and the Ambassador Liquor Store: Free Ice. He passed the Lichee Inn: Chinese Take-aways. He gave a poor girl a dime. He passed the hawkers of deodorant and sticking-plaster. He passed the Hillcity Pharmacy, Wimpy: The Home of the Hamburger, and Summit Fruiters. He shifted the bag of tricks to His right shoulder. He passed Hillbrow Pharmacy Extension (a.k.a. Farmácia/Pharmacie). He passed the hawkers of wooden springboks and soapstone elephants. He dropped His Diner's Club card in a hobo's hat. He passed the Cafe Three Sisters, Norma Jean, Look and Listen, Terry's Deli, The Golden Egg, Le Poulet Chicken Grill, Gringo's Fast Food, Bella Napoli and Continental Confectioners: Baking by Marco. He passed the hawkers of block-mounted reproductions of James Dean with his eyes smouldering and Marilyn Monroe with her skirt flying. Late, both of them. He passed the Shoe Hospital: Save Our Soles. He passed the hawkers of block-mounted reproductions of Himself with the white fringes of His red cowboy shirt swishing, and the black fringes of His blue hairstyle dangling, and the grey shadows of the fringes of His black eyelashes fluttering. Himself as a Young Man. His name was printed on His shirt, over the alveoli of His left lung.

He felt sad to be a reproductive system.

Sniffing, He turned right into the Wurstbude.

"*Guten Abend*," He said. "*Wie geht's?*"

"*So lala*," said the Sausage Man of Stuttgart.

The King extracted a pickled cucumber as fat and green as His opposable thumb from the jar on the counter. "*Ich möchte eine Currywurst*," He said, sucking on the cuke, "*mit Senf, bitte.*"

(R4.70.)

He held His breath as the wurst went down the stainless-steel chute. One flick of the lever and the blades fell: the wurst spilled out in cross-sections two-fifths of an inch thick.

"*Fünfundzwanzig … dreissig, sieben, zehn*," the Sausage Man said.

"*Ich bin ein Johannesburger*," the King replied. "*Auf Wiedersehen.*"

At the barrel-table outside He ate the lopped sausage expertly with a brace of toothpicks, in the time-honoured manner. He broke the bread and mopped the sauce. He dusted away the crumbs.

Momentarily satiated, shaded, the King moved once more through the Grey Area; once more He moved sinuously; once more He appreciated the cosmopolitan atmosphere. (We both did.)

Now He took two hundred and seventy-five steps (Squash and Fitness Health World, Tommy's 24-Hour Superette, Bunny Chow, Bengal Tiger Coffee Bar and Restaurant, hawkers of baobab-sap and the mortal remains of baboons, Econ-o-Wash, Magnum Supermarket, Jungle Inn Restaurant, Quality Butchery: Hindquarters packed and labelled) and turned right.

He stopped. He parked the bag of tricks. He hitched down the tracksuit pants with His left hand and unzipped the catsuit with His right. He reached into the vent and abstracted a dick.

I was too far away, propped against a fireplug like a gumshoe, to determine whether this organ had charisma. But I was close enough to hear a musical fountain of urine against a prefabricated bollard and to see afterwards on the flagstones a puddle shaped like a blackbird.

He moved. He took one hundred and one steps (Faces Health and Beauty: Body Massage, American Kitchen-City, Hair Extensions International) and turned left into the dim interior of Willy's Bar.

The fascia of Willy's Bar was patched with the gobbledegook of the previous tenant's plastic signage: Julius Caesar's Restaurant and Cocktail Bar, upside down and backwards.

Willy's Bar was licensed to sell wine, malt and spirits, right of admission reserved.

The King and I felt like blacks, because of the way He walked. Everyone else felt like whites. Nevertheless, apartheid was dead.

I ordered a Black Label and went to the john.

The King sat at the counter. He put on His spectacles and fossicked about in the bag of tricks. He swallowed a handful of pills. He swallowed a Bioplus on the rocks and chased it with a Jim Beam.

He had a fuzzy moustache of curry-powder on His upper lip.

It affected me. I hid my face behind the *Star* (City Late) so that I wouldn't feel spare.

We watched the Weather Report together. The cold front was on our doorstep, they said. The King was dissatisfied. I thought He might draw a handgun, but He did not. He just took a powder and pulled a mouth.

I read the Smalls.

Spare is another word for lonesome.

We watched Agenda: The ANC's economic policy.

Ah.

While a party spokesman was explaining the difference between property and theft, the strains of "Abide with Me" drifted in through the batwing doors.

A faraway look stole over the King's features. He gulped His drink, slapped a greenback on the counter and went out.

I followed after, lugging the depleted bag of tricks and the change (R3.50).

O Thou who changest not, abide with me, the Golden City Gospel Singers beseeched Him. In a moment He had insinuated Himself into their circle, between the blonde with the tambourine and the brunette with the pamphlets.

A chilly wind blew over the ridge from the Civic Theater. It picked up a tang of Dettol from the City Shelter and Purity from the

Florence Nightingale Nursing Home. It swept sour curls of sweat and burnt porridge out of the Fort and wrapped them in dry leaves from the gutters. Tissue-paper and handbills tumbled over the flagstones. The wind coughed into the microphone.

Ills have no weight, and tears no bitterness.

The King opened His mouth. Then He gaped, as if He'd forgotten the words, and shut it again. He would not reveal Himself.

I wept. I wept in His stead. For what right had I to weep on my own behalf? To weep for the insufferable bitterness of being dead for ever and the ineffable sweetness of being born again?

The hymn came to a sticky end. A siren bawled on Hospital Hill. The brunette pressed a pamphlet into my hand: Boozers are Loozers.

I seized His arm and felt a surprisingly firm brachioradialis through the cloth. He shrugged me off – a sequin shot from His cuff and ricocheted into the darkness – but the damage had been done: no sooner had I touched Him, than He began to vanish.

I was moved to call out, "The King! The King!" The brunette embraced me and cried, "Amen!" Two hours later I still had the imprint of her hairclip on my temple.

While I was being mobbed, someone walked off with the bag of tricks.

Laughter: involuntary contractions of the facial muscles, saline secretions of the lachrymal ducts, contortions of the labia.

Vanishing-point: a crooked smile, a folderol of philtrum, nothing.

I hunted high and low for the King, in karaoke bars, escort agencies, drugstores, ice-cream parlors and soda fountains, but found no trace of Him.

I have a feeling in my bones – patellae, to be precise – that He is still out there.

Appendix

The very next morning I saw Steve Biko coming out of the Juicy Lucy at the Norwood Hypermarket. I followed him to the hardware department, where he gave me the slip.

The WHITES ONLY Bench

Yesterday our visitors' book, which Portia has covered in zebra-skin wrapping-paper and shiny plastic, recorded the name of another important person: Coretta King. When Mrs King had finished her tour, with Strickland herself playing the guide, she was treated to tea and cakes in the cafeteria. The photographers, who had been trailing around after her trying to sniff out interesting angles and ironic juxtapositions against the exhibits, tucked in as well, I'm told, and made pigs of themselves.

After the snacks Mrs King popped into the gift shop for a few mementoes, and bought generously – soapstone hippopotami with sly expressions, coffee-table catalogues, little wire bicycles and riot-control vehicles, garish place-mats and beaded fly-whisks, among other things. Her aide had to chip in to make up the cost of a set of mugs in the popular "Leaders Past and Present" range.

The honoured guests were heading back to the bus when Mrs King spotted the bench in the courtyard and suggested that she pose there for a few shots. I happened to be watching from the workshop window, and I had a feeling the photographs would be exceptional. A spring shower had just fallen, out of the blue, and the courtyard was a well of clear light. Tendrils of fragrant steam coiled up from a windfall of blossoms on the flagstones. The scene had been set by chance. Perhaps the photographers had something to prove, too, having failed to notice a photo opportunity so steeped in ironic significance.

The *Star* carried one of the pictures on its front page this morning. Charmaine picked up a copy on her way to work and she couldn't wait to show it to me.

The interest of the composition derives – if I may make the obvious analysis – from a lively dispute of horizontals and verticals. The bench is a syllogism of horizontal lines, flatly contradicted by the vertical bars of the legs at either end (these legs are shaped like h's, actually, but from the front they look like l's). Three other verticals assert their position: on the left – our left, that is – the concrete stalk of the Black Sash drinking-fountain; in the middle, thrusting up behind the bench, the trunk of the controversial kaffirboom; and on the right, perched on the very end of her seat, our subject: Mrs King.

Mrs King has her left thigh crossed over her right, her left foot crooked around her right ankle, her left arm coiled to clutch one of our glossy brochures to her breast. The wooden slats are slickly varnished with sunlight, and she sits upon them gingerly, as if the last coat's not quite dry. Yet her right arm reposes along the backrest with the careless grace of a stem. There's an odd ambiguity in her body, and it's reflected in her face too, in an expression which superimposes the past upon the present: she looks both timorous and audacious. The WHITES ONLY sign under her dangling thumb in the very middle of the picture might be taken up the wrong way as an irreverent reference to her eyes, which she opens wide in an expression of mock alarm – or is it outrage? The rest of her features are more prudently composed, the lips quilted with bitterness, but tucked in mockingly at one corner.

The photographer was wise to choose black and white. These stark contrasts, coupled with Mrs King's old-fashioned suit and hairdo, confound the period entirely. The photograph might have been taken thirty years ago, or yesterday.

Charmaine was tickled pink. She says her bench is finally avenged for being upstaged by that impostor from the Municipal Bus Drivers' Association. I doubt that Strickland has even noticed.

There seems to be a tacit agreement around here that *Mrs* King is an acceptable form, although it won't do for anyone else. When I pointed this out, Charmaine said it's a special case because Mr King, rest his soul, is no more. I fail to see what difference that makes, and I said so. Then Reddy, whose ears were flapping, said that "Mrs King" is tolerated precisely because it preserves the memory of the absent Mr King, like it or not. He said it's like a dead metaphor.

I can't make up my mind. Aren't we reading too much into it?

Charmaine has sliced the photograph out of the unread newspaper with a Stanley knife and pinned the cutting up on the notice-board in Reception. She says her bench has been immortalized. "Immortality" is easy to bandy about, but for a while it was touch and go whether Charmaine's bench would make it to the end of the week.

We were working late one evening, as usual, when the little drama began. The Museum was due to open in six weeks' time but the whole place was still upside down. It wasn't clear yet who was in charge, if anyone, and we were all in a state.

Charmaine was putting the finishing touches to her bench, I was knocking together a couple of rostra for the Congress of the People, when Strickland came in. She had been with us for less than a week and it was the first time she had set foot in the workshop. We weren't sure at all then what to make of our new Director, and so we both greeted her politely and went on with our work.

She waved a right hand as limp as a kid glove to show that we shouldn't mind her, and then clasped it behind her back. She began to wander around on tiptoe, even though I was hammering in nails, swivelling her head from side to side, peering into boxes, scanning the photographs and diagrams pinned to chipboard display stands, taking stock of the contents of tables and desks. She never touched a thing, but there was something grossly intrusive about the inspection. Strickland wears large, rimless spectacles, double glazed and tinted pink, and they sometimes make her look like a pair of television monitors.

After a soundless, interrogative circuit of the room she stopped behind Charmaine and looked over her shoulder. Charmaine had just finished the "I," and now she laid her brush across the top of the paint tin, peeled off the stencil and flourished it in the air to dry the excess paint.

I put down my hammer – the racket had become unbearable – and took up some sandpaper instead. The people here will tell you that I don't miss a thing.

Strickland looked at the half-formed word. Then she unclasped her hands and slid them smoothly into the pockets of her linen suit. The cloth was fresh cream with a dab of butter in it, richly textured, the pockets cool as arum lilies.

"What are you doing?" Strickland asked, in a tone that bristled like a new broom.

Charmaine stood back with the stencil in her hand and Strickland had to step hastily aside to preserve a decent distance between her suit and the grubby overall. Unnoticed by anyone but myself, a drop of white paint fell from the end of the brush resting across the tin onto the shapely beige toe of Strickland's shoe.

The answer to Strickland's question was so plain to see that it hardly needed voicing, but she blinked her enlarged eyes expectantly, and so Charmaine said, "It's the WHITES ONLY bench." When Strickland showed no sign of recognition, Charmaine added, "You remember the benches. For whites only?"

Silence. What on earth did she want? My sandpaper was doing nothing to smooth the ragged edges of our nerves, and so I put it down. We all looked at the bench.

It was a beautiful bench – as a useful object, I mean, rather than a symbol of injustice. The wooden slats were tomato-sauce red. The arms and legs were made of iron, but cleverly moulded to resemble branches, and painted brown to enhance a rustic illusion. The bench looked well used, which is often a sign that a thing has been loved. But when you looked closer, as Strickland was doing now, you saw that all these signs of wear and tear were no more than skin-deep. Charmaine had applied all of them in the workshop. The bruised hollows on the seat, where the surface had been abraded by decades of white thighs and buttocks, were really patches of brown and purple paint. The flashes of raw metal on the armrests, where the paint had been worn away by countless white palms and elbows, turned out to be mere discs of silver paint themselves. Charmaine had even smeared the city's grimy shadows into the grain.

Strickland pored over these special effects with an expression of amazed distaste, and then stared for a minute on end at the letters

WHI on the uppermost slat of the backrest. The silence congealed around us, slowing us down, making us slur our movements, until the absence of sound was as tangible as a crinkly skin on the surface of the air. "Forgive me," she said at last, with an awakening toss of her head. "You're manufacturing a WHITES ONLY bench?"

"Ja. For Room 27."

Strickland went to the floor plan taped to one of the walls and looked for Room 27: Petty Apartheid. Then she gazed at the calendar next to the plan, but whether she was mulling over the dates, or studying the photograph – children with stones in their hands, riot policemen with rifles, between the lines a misplaced reporter with a camera – or simply lost in thought, I couldn't tell. Did she realize that the calendar was ten years old?

Charmaine and I exchanged glances behind her back.

"Surely we should have the real thing," Strickland said, turning.

"Of course – if only we could find it."

"You can't find a genuine WHITES ONLY bench?"

"No."

"That's very hard to believe."

"We've looked everywhere. It's not as easy as you'd think. This kind of thing was frowned upon, you know, in the end. Discrimination I mean. The municipalities were given instructions to paint them over.

There wasn't much point in hunting for something that doesn't exist, so we decided at our last meeting – this was before your time, I'm afraid – that it would be better if I recreated one."

"Recreated one," Strickland echoed.

"Faithfully. I researched it and everything. I've got the sources here somewhere." Charmaine scratched together some photocopies splattered with paint and dusted with fingerprints and tread-marks from her running-shoes. "The bench itself is a genuine 1960s one, I'm glad to say, from the darkest decade of repression. Donated by Reddy's father-in-law, who stole it from a bus-stop for use in the garden. It was a long time ago, mind you, the family is very respectable. From a black bus-stop – for Indians. Interestingly, the Indian benches didn't have INDIANS ONLY on them – not in Natal anyway, according to Mr Mookadam. Or even ASIATIC. Not that it matters."

"It matters to me," Strickland said curtly – Charmaine does go on sometimes – and pushed her glasses up on her nose so that her eyes were doubly magnified. "This is a museum, not some high-school operetta. It is our historical duty to be authentic."

I must say that made me feel bad, when I thought about all the effort Charmaine and I had put into everything from the Sharpeville Massacre to the Soweto Uprising, trying to get the details right, every abandoned shoe, every spent cartridge, every bloodied stitch of clothing, only to have this jenny-come-lately (as Charmaine puts it) give us a lecture about authenticity. What about our professional duty? (Charmaine again.)

"Have we advertised?" Strickland asked, and I could tell by her voice that she meant to argue the issue out. But at that moment she glanced down and saw the blob of paint on the toe of her shoe.

I had the fantastic notion to venture an excuse on Charmaine's behalf: to tell Strickland that she had dripped ice cream on her shoe. Vanilla ice cream! I actually saw her hand grasping the cone, her sharp tongue curling around the white cupola, the droplet plummeting. Fortunately I came to my senses before I opened my big mouth.

It was the first proper meeting of the Steering Committee with the new Director. We hadn't had a meeting for a month. When Charlie Sibeko left in a huff after the fiasco with the wooden AK47s, we all heaved a sigh of relief. We were sick to death of meetings: the man's appetite for circular discussion was insatiable.

Strickland sat down at the head of the table, and having captured that coveted chair laid claim to another by declaring the meeting open. She seemed to assume that this was her prerogative as Director, and no one had the nerve to challenge her.

The report-backs were straightforward: we were all behind schedule and over budget. I might add that we were almost past caring. It seemed impossible that we'd be finished in time for the official opening. The builders were still knocking down walls left, right and centre, and establishing piles of rubble in every room. Pincus joked that the only exhibit sure to be ready on time was the row of concrete bunks – they were part of the original compound in which the Museum is housed and we had decided to leave them exactly as we found them. He suggested that we think seriously about delaying the opening, which was Portia's cue to produce the invitations, just back from the printers. Everyone groaned (excluding Strickland and me) and breathed in the chastening scent of fresh ink.

"As far as we're concerned, this date is written in stone," Strickland said, snapping one of the copperplate cards shut. "We will be ready on time. People will have to learn to take their deadlines seriously." At that point Charmaine began to doodle on her agenda – a hand with a stiff index finger, emerging from a lacy cuff, pointing at Item 4: Bench.

Item 2: Posters, which followed the reports, was an interesting one. Pincus had had a letter from a man in Bethlehem, a former town clerk and electoral officer, who had collected copies of every election poster displayed in the town since it was founded. He was prepared to entrust the collection to us if it was kept intact. Barbara said she could probably use a couple in the Birth of Apartheid exhibit. We agreed that Pincus would write to the donor, care of the Bethlehem

Old-Age Home, offering to house the entire collection and display selected items on a rotating basis.

Item 3: Poetry, was Portia's. Ernest Dladla, she informed us, had declined our invitation to read a poem at the opening ceremony, on the perfectly reasonable grounds that he was not a poet. "I have poetic impulses," he said in his charming note, "but I do not act upon them." Should she go ahead, Portia wanted to know, and approach Alfred Qabula instead, as Ernie suggested?

Then Strickland asked in an acerbic tone whether an issue this trivial needed to be tabled at an important meeting. But Portia responded magnificently, pointing out that she knew nothing about poetry, not having had the benefit of a decent education, had embarrassed herself once in the performance of her duties and did not wish to do so again. All she wanted was an answer to a simple question: Is Alfred Qabula a poet? Yes or no?

No sooner was that settled, than Strickland announced Item 4: Bench, and stood up. Perhaps this was a technique she had read about in the business pages somewhere, calculated to intimidate the opposition. "It has come to my attention," she said, "that our workshop personnel are busily recreating beautiful replicas of apartheid memorabilia, when the ugly originals could be ours for the asking. I do not know what Mr Sibeko's policy on this question was, although the saga of the wooden AK47s is full of suggestion, but as far as I'm concerned it's an appalling waste of time and money. It's also dishonest. This is a museum, not an amusement arcade.

"My immediate concern is the WHITES ONLY bench, which is taking up so much of Charmaine's time and talent. I find it hard to believe that there is not a genuine example of a bench of this nature somewhere in the country."

"Petty apartheid went out ages ago," said Charmaine, "even in the Free State."

"The first Indian townships in the Orange Free State were established way back in October 1986," said Reddy, who had been unusually quiet so far, "in Harrismith, Virginia and Odendaalsrus. Not many people know that. I remember hearing the glad tidings from my father-in-law, Mr Mookadam, who confessed that ever since he was a boy it had been a dream of his to visit that forbidden province."

"I'll wager that there are at least a dozen real WHITES ONLY benches in this city alone, in private collections," Strickland insisted, erasing Reddy's tangent with the back of her hand. "People are fascinated by the bizarre."

"We asked everyone we know," said Charmaine. "And we asked them to ask everyone they know, and so on. Like a chain-letter

– except that we didn't say they would have a terrible accident if they broke the chain. And we couldn't find a single bench. Not one."

"Have we advertised?"

"No commercials," said Reddy, and there was a murmur of assenting voices.

"Why ever not?"

"It just causes more headache."

"Oh nonsense!"

Reddy held up his right hand, with the palm out, and batted the air with it, as if he was bouncing a ball off Strickland's forehead. This gesture had a peculiarly mollifying effect on her, and she put her hand over her eyes and sat down. Reddy stood up in his ponderous way and padded out of the room.

Pincus, who has a very low tolerance for silence, said, "Wouldn't it be funny if Charmaine's bench turned out to be the whites' only bench?"

No one laughed, so he said "whites' only" again, and drew the apostrophe in the air with his forefinger.

Reddy came back, carrying a photograph, a Tupperware lunchbox and a paperknife. He put the photograph in the middle of the table, facing Strickland. She had to lean forward in her chair to see what it was. I wondered whether she fully appreciated the havoc her outsize spectacles wreaked on her face, how they disjointed her features. She looked like a composite portrait in a magazine competition, in which some cartoon character's eyes had been mismatched with the jaw of a real-life heroine.

Everyone at the table, with the exception of our Director, had seen this routine before. Some of us had sat through it half a dozen times, with a range of donors, do-gooders, interest groups. For some reason, it never failed to involve me. I also leaned forward to view the eight-by-ten. No one else moved.

I looked first at the pinprick stigmata in the four corners.

Then I looked, as I always did, at the girl's outflung hand. Her hand is a jagged speech-bubble filled with disbelief. It casts a shadow shaped like a howling mouth on her body, and that mouth takes up the cry of outrage. The palm Reddy had waved in Strickland's face was a much more distant echo.

I looked next at the right hand of the boy who is carrying Hector Peterson. His fingers press into the flesh of a thigh that is still warm, willing it to live, prompting the muscle, animating it. Hector Peterson's right hand, by contrast, lolling numbly on his belly, knows that it is dead, and it expresses that certainty in dark tones of shadow and blood.

These hands are still moving, they still speak to me.

Reddy jabbed the photograph with the point of his paperknife.

"This is a photograph of Hector Peterson, in the hour of his death," he said. Strickland nodded her head impatiently. "The day was 16 June 1976." She nodded again, urging him to skip the common knowledge and come to the point. "A Wednesday. As it happened, it was fine and mild. The sun rose that morning at 6.53 and set that evening at 5.25. The shot was taken at 10.15 on the dot. It was the third in a series of six. Hector Peterson was the first fatality of what we would come to call the Soweto Riots – the first in a series of seven hundred odd. The photographer was Sam Nzima, then in the employ of the *World*. The subject, according to the tombstone that now marks his grave, was Zolile Hector Pietersen, P-I-E-T-E-R-S-E-N, but the newspapers called him Hector Peterson and it stuck. We struck out the "I," we put it to rout in the alphabet of the oppressor. We bore the hero's body from the uneven field of battle and anointed it with English. According to the tombstone he was thirteen years old, but as you can see he looked no more than half that age … Or is it just the angle? If only we had some other pictures of the subject to compare this one with, we might feel able to speak with more authority."

This welter of detail, and the offhand tone of the delivery, produced in Strickland the usual baffled silence.

"Not many people know these things." Reddy slid the point of the knife onto the girl. "This is Hector's sister Margot, a.k.a. Tiny, now living in Soweto." The knife slid again. "And this is Mbuyisa

Makhubu, whereabouts your guess is as good as mine. Not many people know them either. We have come to the conclusion, here at the Museum, that the living are seldom as famous as the dead."

The knife moved again. It creased Mbuyisa Makhubu's lips, which are bent into a bow of pain, like the grimace of a tragic mask, it rasped the brick wall of the matchbox house which we see over his shoulder, skipped along the top of a wire gate, and came to rest on the small figure of a woman in the background. "And who on earth do you suppose this is?"

Strickland gazed at the little figure as if it was someone famous she should be able to recognize in an instant, some household name. In fact, the features of this woman – she is wearing a skirt and doek – are no more than a grey smudge, continuous with the shadowed wall behind her.

I looked at Hector Peterson's left arm, floating on air, and the shadow of his hand on Mbuyisa Makhubu's knee, a shadow so hard-edged and muscular it could trip the bearer up.

The child is dead. With his rumpled sock around his ankle, his grazed knee, his jersey stuck with dry grass, you would think he had taken a tumble in the playground, if it were not for the gout of blood from his mouth. The jersey is a bit too big for him: it was meant to last another year at least. Or is it just that he was small for his age? Or is it the angle? In his hair is a stalk of grass shaped like a praying mantis.

"Nobody knows."

Strickland sat back with a sigh, but Reddy went on relentlessly.

"Nevertheless, theories were advanced: some people said that this woman, this apparent bystander, was holding Hector Peterson in her arms when he died. She was a mother herself. She cradled him in her lap – you can see the bloodstains here – and when Makhubu took the body from her and carried it away, she found a bullet caught in the folds of her skirt. She is holding that fatal bullet in her right hand, here.

"Other people said that it didn't happen like that at all. Lies and fantasies. When Nzima took this photograph, Hector Peterson was still alive! What you see here, according to one reliable caption, is a critically wounded youth. The police open fire, Hector falls at Mbuyisa's feet. The boy picks him up and runs towards the nearest car, which happens to belong to Sam Nzima and Sophie Tema, a journalist on the *World,* Nzima's partner that day. Sam takes his photographs. Then Mbuyisa and Tiny pile into the back of the Volkswagen – did I mention that it was a Volkswagen? – they pile into the back with Hector; Sam and Sophie pile into the front with their driver, Thomas Khoza. They rush to the Orlando Clinic, but Hector Peterson is certified dead on arrival. And that's the real story. You can look it up for yourself.

"But the theories persisted. So we thought we would try to lay the ghost – we have a duty after all to tell the truth. This is a museum, not a paperback novel. We advertised. We called on this woman to come forward and tell her story. We said it would be nice – although it wasn't essential – if she brought the bullet with her."

"Anyone respond?"

"I'll say."

Reddy opened his lunchbox and pushed it over to Strickland with the edge of his palm, like a croupier. She looked at the contents: there were .38 Magnum slugs, 9 mm and AK cartridges, shiny .22 bullets, a .357 hollow-point that had blossomed on impact into a perfect corolla. There were even a couple of doppies and a misshapen ball from an old voorlaaier. Strickland zoomed in for a close-up. She still didn't get it.

"If you'll allow me a poetic licence," Reddy said, as if poetic licence was a certificate you could stick on a page in your Book of Life, "this is the bullet that killed Hector Peterson."

So we didn't advertise. But Strickland stuck to her guns about the WHITES ONLY bench: we would have the real thing or nothing at all. She made a few enquiries of her own, and wouldn't you know it, before the week was out she turned up the genuine article.

The chosen bench belonged to the Municipal Bus Drivers' Association, and in exchange for a small contribution to their coffers – the replacement costs plus 10 per cent – they were happy to part with it. The honour of fetching the trophy from their clubhouse in Marshall Street fell to Pincus. Unbeknown to us, the Treasurer of the MBDA had decided that there was a bit of publicity to be gained from his Association's public-spirited gesture, and when our representative arrived he found a photographer ready to record the event for posterity. Pincus was never the most politic member of our Committee. With his enthusiastic co-operation the photographer was able to produce an entire essay, which subsequently appeared, without a by-line, in the *Saturday Star*. It showed the bench in its original quarters (weighed down by a squad of bus drivers of all races, pin-up girls – whites only – looking over the drivers' shoulders, all of them, whether flesh and blood or paper, saying cheese); the bench on its way out of the door (Pincus steering, the Treasurer pushing); being loaded onto the back of our bakkie (Pincus and the Treasurer shaking hands and stretching the cheque between them like a Christmas cracker); and finally driven away (Pincus hanging out of the window to give us a thumbs-up, the Treasurer waving goodbye, the Treasurer waving back at himself from the rearview mirror). These pictures caused exactly the kind of headache Reddy had tried so hard to avoid. Offers of benches poured in from far and wide. Pincus was made to write the polite letters of thanks but no thanks. For our purposes, one bench is quite enough, thank you.

You can see the WHITES ONLY bench now, if you like, in Room 27. Just follow the arrows. I may as well warn you that it says EUROPE-ANS ONLY, to be precise. There's a second prohibition too, an entirely non-racial one, strung on a chain between the armrests: PLEASE DO NOT SIT ON THIS BENCH. That little sign is Charmaine's work, and making her paint it was Strickland's way of rubbing turpentine in her wounds.

When the genuine bench came to light, Charmaine received instructions to get rid of "the fake." But she refused to part with it. I was persuaded to help her carry it into the storeroom, where it remained for a month or so. As the deadline for the opening neared, Charmaine would take refuge in there from time to time, whenever things got too much for her, and put the finishing touches to her creation. At first, she was furious about all the publicity given to the impostor. But once the offers began to roll in, and it became apparent that WHITES ONLY benches were not nearly as scarce as we'd thought, she saw an opportunity to bring her own bench out of the closet. The night before the grand opening, in the early hours, when the sky was already going grey behind the mine-dump on the far side of the parking-lot, we carried her bench outside and put it in the arbour under the controversial kaffirboom.

"When Strickland asks about it," said Charmaine, "you can tell her it was a foundling, left on our doorstep, and we just had to take it in." Funny thing is, Strickland never made a peep.

I can see Charmaine's WHITES ONLY bench now, from my window. The kaffirboom, relocated here fully grown from a Nelspruit nursery, has acclimatized wonderfully well. "*Erythrina caffra*, a sensible choice," said Reddy, "deciduous, patulous, and umbrageous." And he was quite right, it casts a welcome shade. Charmaine's faithful copy reclines in the dapple below, and its ability to attract and repel our visitors never ceases to impress me.

Take Mrs King. And talking about Mrs King, *Mr* King is a total misnomer, of course. I must point it out to Reddy. The Revd King, yes, and Dr King, yes, and possibly even the Revd Dr King. But Mr King? No ways.

It seems unfair, but Charmaine's bench has the edge on that old museum piece in Room 27. Occasionally I look up from my workbench, and see a white man sitting there, a history teacher say. While the schoolchildren he has brought here on an outing hunt in the grass for lucky beans, he sits down on our bench to rest his back. And after a while he pulls up his long socks, crosses one pink leg over the other, laces his fingers behind his head and closes his eyes.

Then again, I'll look up to see a black woman shuffling resolutely past, casting a resentful eye on the bench and muttering a protest under her breath, while the flame-red blossoms of the kaffirboom detonate beneath her aching feet.

The Omniscope (Pat. Pending)

I am the one who invented the Omniscope – and I don't mind telling you that it came to me in a dream. The secret of my success as an inventor, modest as it is: turn no dream visitor away from your door empty-handed. Feed him, invite him to freshen up, send him out into the waking world in a suit from the Little Eden Charity Kiosk (or a frock as the case may be).

Hauptfleisch – that's me – reveals all.

This dream was no action-packed adventure; this dream was an invitation to attend.

I espied a person at a wooden bureau, below a lattice window, in a room enamelled with light. No monk in a cell limning parchment, no burgomaster's daughter making lace while the sun shines, but a man in an orange overall, patched at the elbows and torn at the knees, and on his bowed head a helmet with a miner's lamp, unlit, and on his feet rubber sandals made from tyres, and on his back the legend: BEARING WORLD (PTY) LTD.

On the slanted top of the bureau lay a wooden casket, nothing fancy, tomato-box pine inlaid with bottle-tops and drawing-pins, about the size of a telephone directory, and emerging from it, at an angle of 60°, a narrow brass-plated tube like a sea dog's telescope. (In the interests of depth, which is also distance, let me point out that "telescope" comes from the modern Latin *telescopium*, from the Greek *tele*, far off, and *skopeo*, look at, naturalized as *-scope*, an instrument looked at or through, a viewer, hence mutoscope, microscope, bioscope. The settler draws closer, acquires the accent, becomes a citizen. Acknowledgements to follow.)

As I looked on, which is what I do in dreams, the miner-monk bent his head to the eyepiece and looked into the casket, then fell into a reverie, beholding in slack-lipped wonder whatever it was he beheld at the end of the tube. From time to time he roused himself, took up the casket by two crooked handles twisted from coat-hanger wire, shook it gently, set it down, and looked into it again.

After endless minutes, during which I longed to go closer but could not – frustrating for a man of action, a man good with his hands – he sprang to his feet, knocking his chair over backwards, slapped his thigh, and cried out in a joyful voice: Swords! He took a striped carpenter's pencil with a chiselled black lead from behind his ear and wrote in a spiral-bound notebook which I saw for the first time as the pencil-point bore down upon the paper.

I was now able to look over his shoulder and on the blue-lined page, in cuneiform print, saw this list:

(1) ....   (6) behemoth
(2) fires   (7) mountain
(3) swords   (8)
(4) ....   (9)
(5) library

I looked down the tube.

Had the onlooker vanished? Had I been the onlooker all along? Am I a miner-monk?

The eyepiece was sweaty and smelt of Old Spice aftershave. At the end of the tube I saw a meaningless fragment of whorled silver. I took up the casket and shook it gently, as I had seen it done, set it down and looked in again.

Now it was revealed to me,

fluted silver, grey dove, corded light of the river in flood, water in flight, pewter purl and marbled midnight of the sky above, fluency of blue, buoyancy of floe, flesh and blood, fowl, fish,

I could have gone on in this fashion indefinitely, but I roused myself and slapped my thigh, as I had seen it done, and wrote on the list:

(8) river

Eight down, one to go.

If I am not the miner-monk, why do I understand the rules of the game so well?

I gave the casket a vigorous shaking and mumbled an incantatory phrase or two for luck. I looked in: mountain … already on the list. I shook again and looked: a corner of the library. Again: another corner. Again: mountain. What's this? A razor-blade. A razor-blade! Again! Again! Again!

In this way I rattled myself awake.

It was a Saturday morning. I was able to lie in bed for some time, with the pillow over my face as is my habit, breathing in the musty siftings of sleep lodged in the pores of the pillowslip, while the dream grew accustomed to the half-light. Then, yawning and stretching and tossing off the blankets, I rose and led the dream, pale and shivering with fright, to the window, drew the curtains and, by the gentlest of pressures between the shoulder-blades, with a great show of warmth and hospitality, pushed it out into broad daylight. Dreams are more easily domesticated than people think.

I nicked the sardonic corner of my lip, of all things, while I was shaving, bled a lot, annoying. The safety razor was invented in

Paris in 1762 by a cutler named Jean Jacques Perret (coincidentally the same year in which Jean Jacques Rousseau published his *Social Contract*). Perret's invention was based on the cutthroat razor and cost an arm and a leg. The conventional T-shaped safety razor, as we know it today, was invented by William S. Henson of London in 1847, let's give him his due. But the blade of Bill Henson's razor had to be sharpened by a qualified expert, which was costly and inconvenient. It was only in 1901 that King Gillette, a Boston commoner, began to mass-produce disposable wafer blades, which permanently transformed the act of shaving (the pogonotomy, if you like) and helped to drive the beard from the face of the earth. It was a blade of this sort I had seen in the casket in my dream. I wouldn't swear to it, but to judge by the characteristic hourglass shape of the central aperture, it may actually have been a sensational Blue Super-Blade, introduced to the public in 1932 when the $2 Kroman De Luxe was withdrawn from production. *Emphatically, and without reservation, these are the sharpest, smoothest-shaving blades ever produced.*

I would find it interesting to trace the whole question of facial hair back to antiquity, exploring developments in pogonology (to be technical again), quoting from the ancients, but you can have too much of a good thing. Let me just say then that even with a so-called safety razor it is possible to cut yourself, and I was only able to staunch the flow by applying a swab of tissue-paper liberally moistened with saliva to the cut. With this unsightly wad stuck to my lip I descended for breakfast.

The sunlight, seeping through the blinds and pooling on the chequered vinyl Marley tiles of the kitchen floor, reminded me of Vermeer, and then, by association of warm scented light, light that smelt of starched linen and churned cream, linseed oil and the nape of the dairymaid's neck, I was reminded of my dream, and of the casket with its perfumed eyepiece.

Why was the thing so fascinating to the onlooker? Let's say to me.

I puzzled over this as I prepared my cereal and set my coffee to perk. Here is my explanation, and a rather feeble one it is, in the way of the waking world. Firstly, the tube – the scope? – was of such a narrow gauge that I could gain only partial glimpses of the objects contained within the casket. (Set aside, for the moment, the seemingly impossible magnitude of the dream-made contents, the fact that I had glimpsed a *mountain* in a space that could not even accommodate a molehill. The effect – which was to entice, to offer and withhold – would have been identical had I glimpsed the mysteriously magnified curve of a thimble.) Secondly, the casket contained a finite number of objects: the allure was to identify them all. I felt sure that once all the objects had been identified, the device would lose its power: the onlooker would cast the casket aside and hold fast to the list, which he had made himself. (If only I hadn't woken up!) In both cases I, the poor onlooker, had been seized by an unwholesome urge to make a whole greater than the part that was given.

Hopelessly inadequate, I know. Already I was speaking of the casket as if the dreams had been drained out of it, and groping for an analogy that was bound to disappoint. It was a bit like a jigsaw puzzle, I said, and a bit like a kaleidoscope. Ah, but it was also a bit unlike a kaleidoscope! Brewster, my champion!

Breakfast was a disaster with all this thinking going on. The milk was sour and I had to mix up some powdered, which I detest. Then my bloodstained swab fell off in the Post Toasties, which spoilt my appetite completely. I took my coffee (black) onto the stoep. The day lay before me like an empty page, feint ruled, prepunched, marginated.

And it was then, as an act of resistance you could almost say, that I decided to build the first Omniscope – although I wasn't calling it that yet. I am the one who invented it, born Hauptfleisch and still going by that name.

People *will* ask me: How did you do it? Did you sketch it in advance? In pencil or pen? Felt-tip or fountain? In two elevations or three? What was the scale? Large or small? Did you cost it out on the back of a cigarette box? Filter or plain? What did it come to? Did you have a marketing strategy?

I tell them that I made it up as I went along.

Did you have a plan? Did you gather the objects together first? (You mean the offerings? I ask.) Or did you build the box (Casket, I correct them) first and choose the objects (Offerings!) afterwards. Did you use a hammer?

This is becoming complicated, but terminology is all-important, sad to say.

Once and for all, this is what I did, in chronological order, as far as I remember:

I looked around for a casket, or at least for a waking equivalent. There was a tomato-box in the pantry, but juice-stained, pustulated with spilt seeds from split fruit, splintery, spatulate (I could go on like this, as you know) and in any event, I did not feel like complicated joinery. There must be a shoebox somewhere? I found one in the bottom of my wardrobe. Grasshoppers.

Then I sat down in the kitchen with a fresh cup of coffee and a sharpened pencil to remember, if I could, the objects on the dream-list.

I called back five of the miner-monk's identifications – fires, swords, library, behemoth, mountain – and one of my own – river. Two others – the first and fourth on the list – were on the tip of my pencil, but remained unwritten. And of course I had never identified Number 9. But hadn't I? What about the razor-blade? No, that couldn't possibly belong in the casket, it was too ordinary. Razor-blades and swords?

And so I fumbled for the key that opened the Omniscope: substitution. A razor-blade would go into my shoebox instead of swords. I went up to the bathroom, removed from my so-called safety razor the very same blade with which I had nicked my smile, descended once again to the kitchen and placed the bloody item in the box. It was a Wilkinson Sword Contact II. *The first triple-coated twin-blade with reinforced edges to resist blade edge breakdown and stay comfortable. So comfortable it's like a new blade every day.*

I looked at the list. Fire. Fire was easy: I found a box of Lion matches in the kitchen dresser, in the drawer with the clothes-pegs and the disposable chopsticks. Library: easy. Behemoth: tricky. I didn't have a behemoth, of course, although I had a small dog. But even a small dog will not fit in a shoebox comfortably, so I went a step further and chose one of the beast's biscuits instead, a bone-shaped one the colour of mincemeat.

I don't want to bore you with the details. In the end (which was reached some ten minutes later) I placed in the box instead of fires, a matchbox; instead of swords, a razor-blade; instead of a library, a postage stamp; instead of a behemoth, a dog-biscuit; instead of a mountain, a thimble; instead of a river, a rubber washer; instead of the unwritten enigmas, a teaspoon and a nutmeg seed. And finally, for good measure, a pot-scourer and a magnet disguised as a water-melon slice.

Why ten items instead of nine? Blame the waking world.

Why such a preponderance of kitchenware? Ditto.

I put the lid on the box and sealed it with masking tape. Then I punched a hole in one corner with the kitchen scissors and pushed through it a cardboard tube from a roll of aluminium foil. One glance told me that I had erred: I could see too much. The tube was 35 mm in diameter and no sooner had I pressed my eye to one end of it than I observed the postage stamp at the other, in its entirety, and identified it instantaneously.

I patched the hole and replaced the cardboard tube with a drink-ing-straw. Better, except that it was so dark inside the box I couldn't see a thing. (It was a laborious process, as you can see, the whole thing did not come to me in a flash.) I put a bicycle torch inside the box and resealed the lid. And finally, there it was: the first Omniscope, rough and ready, but fully functional.

It took me twenty-eight minutes to identify all ten of the objects positively. In my opinion that was too fast, and therefore too easy, even allowing for the fact that a stranger unfamiliar with the contents might take, say, three times as long. What are eighty-four minutes on the great heap of time? Accordingly, my primitive prototype was the simplest Omniscope ever built. When I went into full-scale production, which was later that day as a matter of fact, I enlarged the casket (as I preferred to call the "box") and included no fewer than *twenty-five* offerings (as I called the "objects").

Omniscope I ... "Omniscope" is good enough; "I" is flat, to say the least, but I had to come up with something on the spur of the moment when I was filling out the form for the patent. "Hauptfleischoscope" crossed my mind, but even I could see that it would not do. I toyed briefly with "Pandorascope," which had the advantage of being entirely Greek in origin, but it was too clever by half. And then I hit on that bastard "Omniscope."

Omniscope I was made of pine, the three dimensions of the casket were 300 mm × 400 mm × 150 mm, the scope was 175 mm long and 15 mm in diameter with an optically correct lens at each end (depth again), and the whole device retailed at r19.95.

I built a round dozen of this model over a period of two years and sold them all at flea markets. Most of them were bought as toys for children, which is not surprising when you consider that they were painted all over with luminous stars, moons and balloons, like lucky-packet kaleidoscopes, and contained the following assortment of generous offerings:

the Aberdeen Angus,
the butter-ball,
the candy-cane,
the Dr Doolittle,
the eighty-eight,
the forty-four,
the Gitche Gumee,
the hobby-horse,
the invisible ink,
the Jet Jungle,
the kamikaze,
the loop-da-loop,
the Mickey Mouse,
the never-never,
the one and only,
the pudding and pie,
the quack-quack,
the Roy of the Rovers,
the sticks and stones,
the tip-truck,
the unicorn,
the Vauxhall Viva,
the water-wings,
the yo-yo,
the zigzag.

Golly.

The kaleidoscope was invented by Sir David Brewster in 1817, and patented too. The device enjoyed a popularity never seen before, and not seen again until our own crazed century. *Every person who could buy or make one had a kaleidoscope. Men, women and children, rich and poor, in houses, or walking in the streets, in carriages or coaches, were to be seen looking into the wonder-working tube, admiring the beautiful patterns it produced, and the magical changes which the least movement of the instrument occasioned.* (Acknowledgements to follow.)

Buy or *make*! It was so easy to dismantle a kaleidoscope, and so easy to understand the principles on which it was based, that the patent was not worth the paper it was printed on. Poor old Brewster never made a bean.

Brewster discovered these principles while doing experiments on the polarization of light. *Brewster's Law states that light reflected from a solid surface is plane polarized, with maximum polarization occurring when the tangent of the angle of incidence is equal to the refractive index.* Deep. But his purpose in building the device, he claimed, was to *exhibit and create beautiful forms and patterns, of great use in all the ornamental arts.* Kaleidoscope, for your information, from the Greek *kalos*, beautiful, *eidos*, form, and *skopeo*, look at, naturalized as *-scope*, an instrument looked at or through, a viewer, hence a device for looking at beautiful forms. To look at the beautiful forms! To lay bare the infinite possibilities generated by the narrowest principles; endless variety and inevitable repetition; the symmetries of chaos. A noble enough purpose. But the invention was taken up by children and adults alike as no more than an amusing toy. Damn the day a sticky little hand first closed around a homemade Brewsterscope!

Ditto for the Omniscope.

Omniscope II arose from my conviction that seriousness of purpose is best served by duplicity. You won't be interested in the technical innovations (stabilizers, black beadings, adjustable scopes with multiple lenses, false bottoms, deadlocks) but you will want to know that each of the new models contained potato peelings; flowers of speech; physical explanations of miracles; bare facts, walls; cartload of bricks; memorials of remote ages; mantelpiece crowded with ornaments; gifts from Providence; a quantity of baskets; an inexhaustible supply of fish; the floating population; examples of unconscious humour; a table spread with every luxury; cakes and buns; biscuits of several sorts; types so various as to defy classification; a half-cooked potato; asparagus served with butter; the six pips of the time-signal; three clear days; 20 measures of wheat; fresh herrings, butter, meat, fruit; a peacock proper; paperbacks with lurid covers; impressions from the outside; Milton's prose works; quotations from the Fathers; rampant theorists, violence; academic, experimental, material; nominal and essential distinctions; villainous weather; instruments of torture; river alive with boats; some soda-water; two litres or thereabouts; potatoes of our own growing; a name brand; fish, flesh and fowl; a literal flood of pamphlets; the prose of existence; vowel and consonant sounds; a simple form of pump; the bottom of a well; the problem of ventilation; kettle steaming on the hob; hole to permit escape of steam; calamities in rapid sequence; landscape framed in an archway; the rare atmosphere of the mountain tops; hills folded in mist; the tip of the iceberg; the icy summits of the Alps; expert evidence, expert witness; a long roll of heroes; sons of toil, freedom, darkness; a very human person; the waste periods of history; diplomats seeking a formula; calculus of probabilities, variations; bunches of flowers, grapes, keys; articles of clothing; clothing, fencing, sacking, scaffolding; writing over the signature "Disgusted"; broken heads; two-handed and single-handed swords; mechanism for revolving the turntable; dated fashions; the peasant look in knitwear; coat with the woolly side in; the great attraction; a face lined with pain; a blue tie with pink spots; a regulation sword, cap; an old book, suit, teapot; the one with a broken handle; white robe splashed with red; a small quantity of blood; sketch in the manner of Rembrandt; a picture by the same hand; a signed masterpiece of Turner's; several transcripts from the same original; the big book and the little one; an odd volume of "Punch"; novel by Scott, play by Shaw; a book, an essay, on grammar; pages 7 to 26 inclusive; a wealth of illustration, wit, fruit; facts locked up in hieroglyphics; a critical edition of Ibsen; a string of beads, onions, symbols; unread books gathering dust; a very representative selection, collection; all the refinements of reasoning, torture; a once-famous doctrine; an old party with spectacles; the science of optics, ethics, philology; harmonic series; 99 as against 102 yesterday; few words, only a few words.

Only three copies of this model were ever built, and I happen to know the unhappy fate of each one of them. The first, which I sold to a Mrs Bernstein, at that time a Public Relations Officer, was afterwards carried abroad in a container ship and sold to a collector of modern art. The second was bought by a Soweto businessman and given in turn as a birthday present to one of his many aunts, a soothsayer, who uses it to predict the outcome of sports events. I could wish my wonderful Omniscope smashed to kindling. The third, the most painful to talk about, a member of my own family donated to the Medical Museum of the University of the Witwatersrand.

But enough of this. Mere background. I am the one who invented the Omniscope, I am the very same Hauptfleisch. Omniscope. It fits after a fashion, like a second-hand suit or a bargain-basement ball-gown. You understand the derivation, I'm sure – *omni* is everywhere, and I hardly need to go over *-scope* again.

I embarked upon the construction of *the* Omniscope (Pat. pending) on the 4th of March last year. I was going to call it Mark III, but the grandeur of the conception shamed me into silence. I planned to put in 1 000 offerings – yes, 1 000! – to start with. Or 999. Or 1 001. But why stop at 999 or 1 000 or 1 001? Piffling, when you think about it, a lightweight trinket. I could already see it laughed out of town or commandeered by one of the crackpot systems of belief with which the waking world is riddled. Idolaters! An ever-present danger, even now. It was just as well to remove my name from the thing. Let me be almost an anonym, gone and just about forgotten, like Brewster, my champion, my charger!

I can't say precisely what now.

But I can say that I've built the casket, canister, caddy, caster, snuff-box, matchbox, mud box, metal box, black box, pepper box, pillbox, pick-a-box, pyx, reliquary, nest of boxes, and so far I've put in some *matter*, some brute matter, some stuff, a patch of plenum, a bit of hyle, a lump of prime matter, mass, material, a body, a frame, a *structure*, a spot of substance, a cup of corpus, oodles of organic matter, flesh, flesh and blood, the real world, Nature, an object, a tangible object, a bird in the hand, enough, two birds in the bush, cont. *Roget's Thesaurus* (Penguin, Harmondsworth, 1979 (first pub. 1852, revised by Hauptfleisch 1993)), pp. 127 ff.

The Book Lover

I first came across Helena at the Black Sash Fête. Of all the second-hand book sales in Johannesburg, this one has the finest catchment area – good, educated, moneyed, liberal homes. Thanks to the brain drain and death itself there is always a large and varied selection. The venue is a suburban garden and, weather permitting, the books are displayed outdoors, gift-wrapped in leafy shade. They have already been sorted into labelled cardboard boxes – Biography, Fiction, Classics, Industrial Psychology, Judaica, to name a few – and the boxes are on trestle-tables with generous spaces in between. These arrangements are a godsend: one does not have to endure the crush of human bodies one associates with jumble sales or, worse, the intimidating configurations of book-lined walls in the second-hand dealers.

I came away from the fête last year with a satisfying haul. Perhaps my favourite among the half-dozen was a battered little *Quattro Novelle* by Pirandello, in Harrap's Bilingual Series, published in 1943, with a dun cardboard cover and grey paper that more than warranted the declaration on the copyright page: Book Production War Economy Standard. This ugly child was crying out for love in

Italian. There were English-speakers too: *The Culture of the Abdomen* by F.A. Hornibrook, with a personal recommendation from Arnold Bennett, who claimed it had relieved him of his dyspepsia and thirty pounds avoirdupois. And *Non-Sporting Dogs: Their Points and Management* by Frank Townend Barton M.R.C.V.S., with a dedication to the author's mother.

A couple of South African works I had been hunting, Huddleston's *Naught for your Comfort* and Millin's *The Burning Man*, also gave themselves up. I hesitate to call these publications Africana – they are still too plentiful and too reasonably priced – but I was pleased to have them.

I should mention in passing that I also netted a jar of pickled onions entitled STRONG on a gummed label of the kind made for school exercise books; and a peace-in-the-home in a terracotta pot from the plant stall. Beat them both down to give-away prices.

I hurried home to breakfast and the pleasure of going through my finds more thoroughly. The Pirandello parallel text is endearing. Recto: "And Teresina slipped away into the dining-room, a rustle of silk." Verso: "*E Teresina scappò via in sala, tutta frusciante.*" I can't speak a word of Italian, but that did not stop me from declaiming a paragraph or two in rich tones, through a mouthful of Fruitful Bran. (The manufacturers, the Kellogg Company of New Era, Springs, call it "fruitful," but I'm sure they mean "fruity.")

Naught for your Comfort was worth buying for the dust-jacket alone. Father Huddleston reaches out from the front cover with both hands. He is making a telling criticism of apartheid, no doubt, but the gesture puts me in mind of a fisherman showing the size of the one that got away. Perhaps it's the background the portrait is floating on – wavy lines of clerical purple, a cartoon Galilee.

There was a signature on the flyleaf of Millin's book: Helena Shein, Johannesburg, 1956. I'd seen that light and airy hand somewhere before, with its buoyant loops and windswept ascenders. I turned to my other acquisitions. To my surprise I discovered that *The Burning Man, Naught for your Comfort,* the *Quattro Novelle* and *The Pocket Book of Poems and Songs for the Open Air*, fully two-thirds of my haul, pulled from their scattered pools on the Black Sash trestles, had all once belonged to Helena Shein. The coincidence banged a window open in my mind and the present billowed out like a lace curtain in a sudden breeze. Through a gap edged with geranium leaves I glimpsed a vanished world: a cool room with a high pressed-steel ceiling and a picture rail, a pile of books on the arm of a chair, their ghostly echo in the varnished wood, gleaming copper fire-irons, a springbok-skin pouffe, a ripple of piano music on the sepia air.

What held these books together, I wondered, apart from paste and thread and the name written with a fountain-pen in ink now faded to sky-blue?

The blurb of *Naught for your Comfort* said that Trevor Huddleston first became interested in missionary work during "Oxford vacations, spent with the hop-pickers in Kent." After his ordination he became curate at St. Mark's, Swindon. "I met, and immensely liked, the railwaymen of England," Father Huddleston said. In 1939 he joined the Community of the Resurrection and took the three vows of poverty, chastity and obedience. Later he came to be Priest-in-Charge of the Anglican Mission in Sophiatown, where he became a legend, "a legend that will endure long after his departure and perhaps intensify." Black people christened him "Makhalipile," the Dauntless One. "Those who have seen Fr Huddleston in action say he owes his success among the Africans to his great sense of humour and to his joyous nature, which are such strong characteristics of the African."

The book had been bought at Vanguard Booksellers (Pty) Ltd, of 23 Joubert Street, Johannesburg. Harry Bloom's *Episode*, due for publication in April 1956, was advertised on the inside flap of the dustjacket. There was a quote from Alan Paton, who must have read the book in manuscript. "It is the location itself (that part of every South African town set aside for the African people) which is the real character of the novel," Paton said, "and Mr Bloom portrays it with a fidelity and a skill that command my admiration. His story never happened, yet every word of it is true."

The Burning Man, the second book on the pile, had also been purchased at Vanguard Booksellers. There was an inscription in the front cover: To my dear Helena, With love, From Julius P. Lofsky. It was dated September 1952. According to the blurb, this novel told the story of Johannes van der Kemp, "a soldier, a scholar, a philosopher, a mystic, a rake, a gentleman in sackcloth." Van der Kemp, it said, had come to South Africa to preach the Word of God to the heathen, but had failed miserably: "… he was one of the first causes of South Africa's difficulties today, in that he was the leader of those missionaries whom the Boers, when they trekked northwards from the Cape, accused of bringing the hatred and odium of the natives upon their heads. Nevertheless, like Spinoza, he was 'God-intoxicated,' and also intoxicated with sex. Thus his tempestuous life makes an admirable subject for Mrs Millin's art; once again she shows herself a mistress of her scene and subject."

Next was *The Pocket Book of Poems and Songs for the Open Air*, which came to me at third hand. It had belonged first to N. Morris, who had acquired it new in 1933. Twenty-three years later it had fallen into Helena's possession, and she had added her name below Morris's. (I have since added my own bookplate and the year 1990 below these.) I brushed the husk of a fishmoth as delicately veined and pretty as a pressed flower from page 286 with the nail of my little finger, and read the second verse of "As I Walked Forth," which was marred only slightly by a faded bloodstain. (I wonder whether one ought to refer to the vital fluid of an insect as "blood?" I suspect that it is not "blood" so much as "haemolymph.")

Poems and Songs for the Open Air was part of Jonathan Cape's Travellers' Library; it was number 97 in that series, according to the numerical index published with the text. It was a self-proclaimed Pocket Book. But it was clear at a glance that it would not fit my pockets. I tried it in my shirt pocket anyway, but it was much too big. I tried it in the rear pocket of my trousers, but it would not fit there either. Among my jackets I found an old-fashioned blazer with an inner pocket that was large enough. It must be true that pockets have been getting smaller over the years. Disappearing altogether in some cases.

At the bottom of the pile was the Pirandello parallel text. I paged for the passage about Teresina, but before I arrived there the breeze dropped and the curtain settled. I found myself in my own breakfast nook again, hot and bothered, with the pungent scent of crushed geraniums on my hands.

As a rule I avoid bookshops. Books en masse repel me. I dislike crowds of people too, even relatively small gatherings of strangers in which everyone speaks at once. I find intolerable the babble that assaults my ears as I enter a bookshop. Especially the less discriminating sort of second-hand dealer, the so-called "book exchange," full of shabbily dressed, ill-proportioned, abused bundles of pages with their shameless hearts burbling away on their sleeves.

I only have to approach such a place to feel enfeebled and upset. There is a buzz in the air, a shrill of pages rubbing against one another. Hemmed in by those abrasive strata I cannot hear myself think. Dullness envelopes me like a dust-cloud. I have to focus: I must find a crooked seam and mine it to an uncertain conclusion, up and down, up and down, prying out the occasional nugget. It is undoubtedly true, as Augustine Birrell says, that the best books are necessarily second-hand – but what trials one has to endure to acquire them!

So it was nearly two full months after the Black Sash Fête before I ventured again into a purchasing situation, and then only because it was necessary to obtain some reading matter for the Christmas holidays. The shop I chose was Yeoville Books of 28 Rockey Street, because the South African literature shelves are close to the door. A sensible arrangement, I think, which allows a decent amount of air to waft in from outside. Sometimes I am able to satisfy my needs there: but if I am compelled to go on, I treat this part of the shop as a decompression chamber in which I accustom myself to the arid, book-moted air that awaits me in the interior. If my will or my lungs fail me, I can quickly retire to the street, where there is a large supply of air, tainted by exhaust fumes but nonetheless quite breathable.

Prepared though I was, my Christmas shopping expedition nearly ended in disaster. I had hardly set foot in the shop when I was overcome by the contentious racket of the book mob. My sense of self – I believe it was that – rushed to the backs of my hands and pulsed like a rash of quotations. The layers of books on all sides drew themselves up into verso and recto of a colossal tome, and tilted to swat me like an insect. I reeled about in the doorway with my eyes screwed shut, until I bumped up against the laminated gondola of new acquisitions and clasped it. As I crouched there, trying to remember what had brought me to this pass, I heard a small voice muttering my name. Opening my eyes, I found them focused on a book in the South African fiction section: Harry Bloom's *Episode*. It was calling me. The spine showed a black man, a riotous person of some kind, brandishing a blazing torch, and, in its flames, the title and the name of the author spelt out in white bones. I stumbled to the shelf and seized the book in my left hand. It was surprisingly cool to the touch and I pressed it gratefully to my burning forehead. The noise in the shop faded away momentarily, and in the hush I became aware that a woman in a pink tracksuit, the sort of garment that has no pockets whatsoever, was looking at me compassionately. I turned my attention to the books again, fumbled at the shelf to comfort the aching gap where Bloom's *Episode* had stood a moment ago, and found that a copy of *Cold Stone Jug* had somehow appeared in my right hand. I remembered that I was looking for that too. I pressed the two books together in a crude sort of cross, as if the stone in the title of the one could somehow extinguish the fire on the spine of the other, reeled to the till, threw some money down on the counter and fled.

I paused on a bench in Yeoville Park to regain my composure. And there I discovered that my new purchases had also come from Helena Shein's library.

But somehow the coincidence was less interesting to me now that it had become more pronounced. When I got home, I put the books aside and reached for *The Cricket on the Hearth* instead. I always read one of the Christmas Books over the festive season. I must make it clear, I suppose, that my own library does not have the same disconcerting effect on me as the bookshops. On the contrary, I feel at home among these familiar few. "The man who has a library of his own collection," says Augustine Birrell, "is able to contemplate himself objectively, and is justified in believing in his own existence." I agree with this statement, and I have no doubt that it applies with equal force to women. (Birrell and I differ, however, on the question of numbers. He hesitates to call a collection of two thousand books a "library," whereas I suspect that two *hundred* books might more than deserve the title.)

In my own modest library there is silence. The books speak only when they're spoken to. In their silent company, I believe that I exist.

Harry Bloom's *Episode* had been bought at the Methodist Book Depot, corner Pritchard and Kruis Streets, Johannesburg, and inscribed in May 1956. You'll recall that on *Naught for your Comfort* the projected publication date for *Episode* was April 1956. So the book appeared on schedule, and Helena acquired it immediately.

Between pages 234 and 235 I found a fragile notice from the Automobile Association to a Miss H. Shein of PO Box 4134, Johannesburg, reminding her that her annual subscription to the value of £1 11s 6d was due on 1 July 1956. It was signed by J.H.C. Porter, Area Secretary. I myself have never been a member of the Automobile Association.

On page 235 was a reference to Father Huddleston, Nelson Mandela and Mulvi Cachalia, which I couldn't help but notice.

Bosman's *Cold Stone Jug* had been purchased at the Pickwick Bookshop, 45 Kerk Street. Quite against the odds, or so I thought at the time, there was a card tucked into this book too, which showed that it had been a gift. On one side of the card was a guarantee: "Mr Pickwick cordially invites you to call in and exchange this gift, in its present clean and new condition, if for any reason you are not satisfied with it." Alongside the guarantee was a drawing of Mr Pickwick. On the other side of the card was the following message: With my very best Wishes for a Happy New Year, from Muriel.

I turned the card over on the flyleaf and studied Mr Pickwick.

Then my eye was drawn to the logo of the distributor – the Central News Agency – on the flap of the dust-jacket: two naked black men playing bows. Mr Pickwick, with his hat concealed behind his coat-tails in his left hand and his chin propped in his right, gazed at these men through his little round spectacles across a field of yellowed paper. They looked in the other direction.

Incidentally, my bookplate is based on a woodcut by Dürer: St Jerome in his cell.

Although Helena Shein's books were doing their utmost to attract my attention, I might still have turned a deaf ear to the call. But a fortnight later, as I paused on the threshold of The Booknook, 42 Bedford Road, and raised my knuckles to the glass door, meaning to summon the female proprietor out onto the pavement for an emergency consultation about my New Year reading, a voice hailed me from inside. It was a clear, hollowed-out voice, like the tone struck from an empty goblet, but it had an oversweet edge to it like sugar crystals on the rim. It was quite detestable: my immediate impulse was to fly. But at that moment the door swung open all by itself and a shaft of light that seemed to be refracted through the top of my head slid from the doorway to a far shelf and rested on a tatty hardback. My name rang out again (I don't think it's necessary to go into detail here, except to say that my Christian name was used in a way I found overly familiar). Screwing up my courage I tumbled headlong down the shaft and plucked the book from the shelf. It turned out to be Barbara Cartland's *A Ghost in Monte Carlo*. I bought it, a little shame-facedly; indeed, I threw in a copy of *Cry, the Beloved Country* which happened to come to hand, simply to raise the tone of the purchase, and scurried home.

An examination of *A Ghost in Monte Carlo* left me with two questions. The first was a question of quality: What was Cartland, a writer of romances, doing in Helena Shein's library, rubbing shoulders with the likes of Huddleston, an archbishop and patron of the Anti-Apartheid Movement, and Bloom, a lawyer and serious novelist? I am not a snob, you see, but I am a stickler for standards. At that point I was reminded of Birrell's comment that it is better to collect a library than to inherit one – "Each volume then, however lightly a stranger's eye may roam from shelf to shelf, has its own individuality, a history of its own" – and felt rebuked. How could I know what had moved Helena to keep the book (I say "keep," rather than "buy," for reasons that will soon become clear).

The second was a question of morality. This copy of *A Ghost in Monte Carlo* was the property of the Johannesburg Public Library. The slip pasted to the flyleaf, with its teetering stacks of rubber-stamped dates, said so clearly. Ever since the book had been published in 1951, until it had last been date-stamped on 5 March 1956, scarcely a week had passed during which someone had not taken it out. But despite this popularity, despite the letters JPL stamped all over the title-page, despite the attached printed notice that the book had to be returned to the library within 14 days and that there was a fine of sixpence for every week it was overdue, Helena Shein had kept it. She had written her name on it. She had even dated it March 1956, a little superfluously under the circumstances. I had been forming an impression of Helena Shein, and she did not strike me as the kind of person who would steal from a public library. Yet I held the evidence in my hands. I think it was precisely this uncomfortable sense of ambiguity that caused me to become enamoured of Helena Shein and her books.

I did a quick calculation. The book was 1 815 weeks overdue. Allowing for inflation and an unfavourable exchange rate, Helena owed the JPL twenty-seven thousand rand.

JPL? It rang a bell somewhere ... and at last I caught the echo: Julius P. Lofsky.

"All Monte Carlo was talking! The winter of 1874 was the gayest, most profitable and most brilliant season since the opening of the Casino. Yet among the Royalty, aristocrats and millionaires from every country, two women caused a sensation.

One was elderly, her handsome face malignant and secretive; the other was exquisitely lovely with huge dark eyes in strange contrast to the shining gold of her hair.

Registered at the hotel as Mademoiselle Fantôme, everything she wore was grey, including a fabulous necklace of grey pearls. But only one person learned that 'the Ghost,' as she was called, had come straight to Monte Carlo from a convent.

In that glittering, sparkling throng three men played desperate and decisive roles in her life – the sinister Rajah of Jehangar, the debonair Prince Nikolai of Russia and Sir Robert Stanford from England.

It is a story of good and evil. How Mademoiselle Fantôme walks to the very brink of the abyss of evil, how she is saved and finds happiness through her own intrinsic purity is told in this thrilling, exciting, unusual forty-second novel from the pen of Barbara Cartland."

My fall was all the more precipitate for having been resisted so long. I went to sleep that night with *A Ghost in Monte Carlo* under my pillow and Helena Shein on the tip of my tongue. When I awoke the next morning they were both still there. I rose in a daze, dressed in serviceable flannels, walking shoes and the blazer with the large inner pocket, and went out to look for Helena Shein's books. I began to collect them for no other reason than that they had once belonged to her.

In the beginning, they were few and far between. It took me two weeks to find the first dozen. But the more I found, the more I wanted. Conversely, the more I wanted, the more I found. In the end, they were everywhere. Sometimes the chorus of demanding voices as I strode through the doorway of a second-hand dealer was almost harder to bear than the unintelligible muttering of days gone by. It seemed as if every second book called out to me, as if every penny dreadful wanted to make my acquaintance. (For "penny" read "twelve rand ninety-five.")

I was obliged to overcome my aversion to crowds. I had to harden my heart by plunging it repeatedly in the raucous air. I learned to circulate among the shelves, brushing a spine here and there with my fingertips, like a personality at a cocktail party. How are you? So glad you could make it. There's someone I want you to meet ... now where's she hiding? *There* you are!

My question still resounded: What holds this library together?

As Helena's books piled up, patterns that promised to reveal everything kept emerging and then fading away before my eyes. Take Ilya Ehrenburg's *The Fall of Paris* and Alexei Tolstoy's *Road to Calvary*, for example, found at flea markets on opposite ends of the city. Note how the titles echo one another. Note how both carry the War Economy Standard certification, inscribed on the same open book and guarded by the same little lion. Both books were published by Hutchinson & Co. Both had won the Stalin Prize. Both were purchased at the People's Book Shop, Africa House, 45, Kerk Street, Johannesburg. Have you noticed that people don't use that comma any more? I mean the comma after the number. Have you noticed that the People's Book Shop and Pickwick Bookshop have the same address?

The Fall of Paris was translated from the Russian by Gerard Shelley. But *Road to Calvary* was translated from the Russian by Edith Bone.

Mistral, who was the only English girl in the convent, arrives at the home of her Aunt Emilie in Paris. Emilie announces that they will be going to Monte Carlo. She summons Madame Guibout, the couturière, to measure Mistral for "travelling gowns, morning costumes, Ball dresses, robes de style, manteaux, dolmans, paletots and casaques." Madame Guibout's assistants come bearing "satins, velvets, cashmeres, failles, muslins, foulards, alpacas, poplins, rolls and patterns in every texture and colour."

Some people lounge about in the book they're reading as if it were a bed in a cheap hotel, dropping cigarette ash and biscuit crumbs between the sheets. Someone has slept here before, you think, tucking in the crumpled flap of a dust-jacket and brushing away a strand of

blonde hair. There are initials carved in the margins, NBs and aster-
isks, obscene propositions, faint praise and futile rejoinders.

Helena was a light traveller, the kind for whom a single photograph lodged in a crack of the dressing-table mirror must stand
for home. She had passed through with a quick eye and clean
hands. There were no annotations, no underlinings. But there
were signs of her everywhere, mementoes pressed flat between
the leaves: letters, cuttings, invoices, receipts, playing-cards, ticket
stubs, banknotes. She had scattered so many papers behind her
that I began to feel she was leading me on.

And I followed her: to the tearoom at Anstey's for tea and scones,
and then to Sportswear on the first floor, where she purchased a
swimsuit, a Mary Nash original, in seagoing cotton, shell pattern,
with shirred front panel, "Butterfly" bra and tuck-away straps, for
only 69/6. To the Colosseum to see James Stewart and Doris Day in
The Man Who Knew Too Much. (She was alone: Julius P. Lofsky was
out of town.) To the Belfast for a poplin blouse marked down to 19/6.
I even crept up to the window of her room, with the eight of hearts
in my left hand, and watched as a pale woman dressed in flickering
shadows sat down in a chair turned away from me, took up a book
from the armrest and tried to find her place.

All these scattered signs were added proof that her books had been read. The pages fell open smoothly, the spines didn't creak, there were no uncut sections. On the contrary, the rough edges of pages 129 to 160 of *The Lying Days* suggested that they had been slit open with the sharp edge of a ruler. It was among these pages that I found the following letter, typewritten in red ink on paper the colour of nicotine.

Sunday, 15th

My dearest Helena,

I was extremely sorry to hear about your mishap yesterday over the 'phone. I do hope you will soon recover from the shock you must have sustained and that it will have no ill effects. I had not written you previously as I had thought you might have been away somewhere over the holiday season. I thought yesterday I would take a chance with a 'phone call to see if you were at home, but I was very sorry to have your news.

You will be interested to hear that Mrs Porter is returning to her house in August (it has been let for twelve months) with a husband, a local optician. It has been in the offing for quite a while.

Did I tell you that Mrs Tishman passed on during June? She had a long spell of suffering. Mr Tishman is not too good at the moment with bronchial trouble, and we have had one or two very cold days lately.

I did not have any luck on the July. There were so many "certainties" before the race that one got a little confused as to what to back. Last Ray saved me a little, as I had backed it for a place when it was in the 20's, so I made a fiver there.

Well, my dear, I hope you are going to get back to complete normal soon. As I mentioned yesterday, I leave here by car next Sunday or Monday, and I shall 'phone you from Bernie's as soon as I arrive. I had hoped to see you at once, not thinking of anything that had been likely to upset you.

I believe Muriel's mother has returned to Port Elizabeth. I could not see her visit lasting.

> With a warm affection for you.
> J.P.L.

I would have relished something more personal, but one was able to read between the lines too.

Sir Robert Stanford meets Mistral in the public gardens at Monte Carlo, at dawn. "She was wearing a grey cloak of some soft material which fell from her shoulders to the ground, the hood shadowed her hair, and in the pale light he could just see the outline of her face – delicate features, wide eyes dark lashed, and beautifully moulded lips which were parted excitedly as she looked out to sea."

The signs say: take nothing but counsel, leave nothing but book-marks. This particular bookmark, which I discovered in *Persuasion*, said: Don't let UNWANTED HAIR cast a shadow over your life! Have it REMOVED BY ELECTROLYSIS – the only medically approved, perma-nent way. Lisbeth Lewis, 302 Safric House, Eloff & Plein Streets, Johannesburg. On the left of the business card was a line-drawing of a woman's face, and below it the caption: Be FREE of unwanted hair by the KREE method.

Naturally I wondered what the Kree method was. Are the Krees not a tribe of Algonquian-speaking Indians? But what held my atten-tion was the drawing: in a few deft lines the artist had captured a heart-shaped face and a soft blonde permanent wave, pencilled eye-brows as neat as brackets, an impudent scoop of nose, lips glossed with sweet nothings. The face was bisected vertically by a dotted line, and the left-hand side, that side blighted by unwanted hair, was veiled by a half-tone screen.

As I examined the drawing my fingers began to tingle: I felt Helena's gaze skimming over the lettering, gliding from the cool and supple limbs of one typeface to the warm hollows of another. I tucked the card back into the book and turned the page. But the tingling continued. I smelt the incense of the ink fuming from the print, mingling with the scent of orange blossom from her blue-veined wrists. I saw her right hand on the page, taking flesh around my own, then her downy arm, and then her freckled shoulder spilled over by yellow hair, one thing leading to another like the rhymes of a love-song. She raised her right hand to her mouth, licked the tip of her forefinger deliberately, lowered the hand again. The paper sucked the spit from her finger with a thirsty gulp.

I wanted to know everything about Helena Shein, but I refused to set about it properly. I went back to the beginning and asked myself sensible questions. I gave myself sensible answers too. Why had her library been dispersed? She had left the country. Or, more likely, she was dead. And even if she were still alive, and living in Johannesburg, she would surely be old enough to be my mother. I myself am a youngish man with a normal sense of regard for the aged. I could have cleared up the mysteries easily enough, I suppose, by consulting the relevant authorities. Certainty was possible. But I declined it. I wanted to know *this* woman, the one who had inscribed her name in these books. Did I mention that her g's were like party balloons with dangling strings, that her i's had soap bubbles revolving over them instead of dots? I wanted to touch the hand that had smoothed open these pages when they were new. I wanted to turn it over and read its palm.

A book lay open before me, verso and recto curving voluptuously away from the spine. I put my nose into the fold and breathed. The pages smelt of caramelized sugar. I opened my left eye. Slightly blurred, gigantically magnified, I read the following words: "All in grey she seemed to move like a ghost across the room; and as she drew level with Sir Robert's table, he could see that, wreathing her hair, where other women would have worn flowers, were the softest grey velvet leaves almost like shadows among the dancing gold." I had opened *A Ghost in Monte Carlo* in the middle of the scene in which Mistral makes her first entrance into the dining-room at the Hôtel de Paris. Aunt Emilie and Mistral, or rather Madame Secret and Mademoiselle Fantôme, are the talk of Monte Carlo.

There seemed to be no end to Helena's books. As far afield as Boksburg and Benoni, insistent voices called my name when I stepped into the swop shops and charity kiosks. My powers amazed me. In the tawdriest of a string of Bookworm Book Exchanges, a dismal place in Primrose wedged between a pet shop and a hairdressing salon, I found a copy of Firbank's *The Artificial Princess* that I *knew* she had read, even though her name was not in it. There was an unmistakable trace of her on the pages, like a whiff of hair lacquer on a second-floor landing.

In time the dealers, who had never valued my custom much, began to despise me. I suppose I did make a nuisance of myself staggering around in the aisles, groping at the books, even those dumb ones that turned their backs on me, and mumbling through them. On more than one occasion I had to snatch one of Helena's books from the clutches of a browser. "Browser" is not a term I would apply to anyone lightly, and least of all myself, but it suited this one to a T, with his rude hands (as Birrell would put it) and champing jaws. The book was *The Way of All Flesh*. God knows what would have become of it.

It pained me to think that with every passing day Helena's precious books were being swallowed up by the libraries of perfect strangers. I redoubled my efforts.

Occasionally I gave myself a day off, and spent it visiting the sites of the vanished bookshops. First stop on my itinerary was always Vanguard Books, Helena's favourite, long since obliterated by an insurance company's high-rise. They were all gone – Pickwick's and Vanity Fair and Random Books and L. Rubin, Booksellers and Stationers. City Book Shop had become Bob's Shoe Centre. Resnik's was now the Reef Meat Supply.

I breathed freely in these spaces emptied of books. Marrowbones and cleavers and the tinkling bell of the cash register made music for my ears. But in the lobby of Africa House a foul smell rose up from the floor, as if a long-forgotten bestseller was rotting under the marble flags.

Aunt Emilie takes the life of Henry Dulton to prevent him from revealing that she is really Madame Bleuet, proprietor of a house of ill fame in the Rue de Roi. Mistral, confined to her room while the body is disposed of, remembers how lonely she was at the convent, and how Father Vincent saved her by giving her the freedom of his library. "She read a strange and varied assortment of books. There were books on religion, travel, philosophy, and books which, while being romances, were also some of the greatest achievements in French literature … There were dozens of others which at first she liked because they were English, but which later became, as books should, real friends and often closer than the real people in her life."

The relics yielded by Helena's books I filed away neatly in a Black Magic chocolate box that had once belonged to my mother, but the books themselves mounted up in odd corners of my house. I began to worry that this disorder would prevent the essential unities of the library from manifesting themselves, so one evening I carried all the books to my study and sat down to make a list.

To my way of thinking, alphabetical is still the order of choice. I created the categories A–I, J–R and S–Z and began to sort the books into them by author, constructing three ziggurats on the end of my desk as I went along. This arrangement, though architecturally sound for the first tower, proved to be impracticable for the others when a statistical imbalance was revealed. The first tower (A–I) contained just a dozen books, but the second and third (J–R and S–Z) had 111 and 77 respectively. So I razed the first tower, spread the books out in an alphabetical fan, slipped a sheet of Ariston bond into my Olivetti typewriter, and began.

BIBLIOGRAPHY

Austen, Jane, Persuasion (J.M. Dent, London, 1950)

Birrell, Augustine, Obiter Dicta (The Reprint Society, London, 1956)

Bloom, Harry, Episode (Collins, London, 1956)

Bosman, Herman Charles, Cold Stone Jug (A.P.B. Bookstore, Johannesburg, 1949)

Butler, Samuel, The Way of All Flesh (Collins, London, 1953)

Cartland, Barbara, A Ghost in Monte Carlo (Rich and Cowan, London, 1951)

Dickens, Charles, <u>Pickwick Papers</u> (McDonald, London, 1956)
Ehrenburg, Ilya, <u>The Fall of Paris</u> (Hutchinson, London, 1943)
Firbank, Ronald, <u>The Artificial Princess</u> (Duckworth, London, 1934)
Fowler, Gene, <u>Schnozzola: The Story of Jimmy Durante</u> (Hammond, Hammond & Co., London, 1956)
Gordimer, Nadine, <u>The Lying Days</u> (Victor Gollancz, London, 1953)
Huddleston, Trevor,<u> Naught for your Comfort</u> (Collins, London, 1956)

This latter was among the first volumes belonging to Helena I ever found. You will recall that I was particularly taken with the dust-jacket. I flipped to the copyright page to check the date. Then I ran my eye down the inside flap: This is the testament ... burning questions of the day ... burns like a beacon ... challenge which no person of conscience can ignore ... Jacket design by Kenneth Farnhill ... Price in Union of S. Africa 15/- net. I groomed a dog-ear with my fingernails. And it was then that I noticed a small white triangle protruding from between the black-edged board and the dust-jacket. I tugged it, and three photographs tumbled out.

I arranged these photographs under my reading-lamp. They were black and white snapshots, about six centimetres by eight, with wavy edges. Two of them were snaps of the sort people feel obliged to keep even though they're practically worthless. One showed a babe in arms with its face obscured by the fringe of a shawl. The other showed three men in swimming-trunks forming a pyramid, two standing side by side and the third straddling their shoulders. The pyramid was on the point of collapse, all three men were moving, all their faces were blurred. Even so, I could tell at a glance that none of them was Julius P. Lofsky.

Have you noticed that snapshots have been getting larger over the years? Very few of them will fit in a wallet these days – not that I'm the sort of person who would carry a snapshot around in a wallet.

The third photograph showed Helena and her parents. There was no caption on the reverse side, just the number 9056/3 written in pencil and the word EPSON, the trade name of the photographic paper, repeated in red ink seven times (and an eighth EP with the SON cut off), but there was no doubt in my mind that it was Helena. She looked nothing like my imaginings, and yet I felt an acute pang of recognition; in fact, the argument between these two contradictory certainties was what persuaded me that it must be her.

I gave the photo a sniffing, but all I turned up was the faintest hint of glue. It may be true, as I've been told, that the human nose is an organ in decline, habituated to stenches and increasingly incapable of drawing finer distinctions.

Helena and her parents are posed on a speckled tile path that runs at a diagonal across a patch of lawn. On either side of the path are beds of impatiens kept in check by toothy brick borders. The garden wall, angling away to left and right like the arrowhead to the pathway's shaft, is made of pale brick, solid for a dozen courses, then surmounted at intervals by square posts half a dozen courses high, with the spaces in between filled by panels of twirly wrought-iron. The gate at the end of the path, visible as broken corkscrews and drill-bits in the spaces between the three figures, has a matching design. From the disposition of the houses in the background, and two streetlights shaped like morning glories on delicate stems, I can tell that Helena's house is on a corner stand. Those houses are made of the same brick as her garden wall and have corrugated-iron roofs. Their windows are set into frames of chunky white concrete and dimmed by cataracts of venetian blinds. One of the houses has a porthole in the wall next to the front door. Another has a hedge as smooth as a concrete quay, and a ragamuffin palm-tree.

I know these bricks, these houses. Although the photograph is black and white, I can see the marmalade colour of them, the glazed rind of brick and the plaster thick and white as pith. This is a Highlands North house, a Cyrildene house, an Orange Grove house. The streetlights nod against a wan blue sky, crossed in one corner by telephone lines.

Helena is a head taller than her parents, who stand on either side of her. Mr and Mrs Shein are middle-aged and look like immigrants.

Mr Shein wears flannels, a loud tie, a bristly pullover. The cuffs of his shirt are pulled up with sleevebands, and this has the effect of enlarging his hands, which dangle in hollow fists at his sides as if they are dreaming of pushing a barrow. His pants are too short: you can see his socks, and shoes as round and shiny as aubergines. Mrs Shein wears a dark skirt, and a cardigan with raglan sleeves over a white blouse buttoned to the neck. She has strappy wedge-heeled shoes and a boy's haircut. Her left hand seems to be holding in her stomach. Her right hand rests on Helena's hip, disembodied, severed from the encircling arm.

It is hard to believe that two such dumpy, badly dressed Europeans could produce this statuesque beauty of a daughter, looming over them despite her flat black pumps. She is wearing a sleeveless halter-neck top in a dark colour, brightened by a chain and locket. Her skirt, which is soft and full, falls to mid-calf. The skirt is a moon colour with circular motifs – flowers or cogs – scattered over it. I imagine that they are earth colours.

What I have failed to imagine is her black hair, her dark eyes, her olive skin. She is no wispy blonde. With a name like Helena Shein, I might have known.

I saw her cross a tiled lobby. At the foot of the stairs she stepped out of her shoes and then quietly ascended. I followed, scooping up the shoes as I passed, watching her brown feet and the heart-shaped prints they left on the polished treads. On the second-floor landing it dawned on me that the photograph had been lying undetected for all these months. How many times had I held the book in my hands and failed to feel the warmth beneath its skin? The books had blunted my curiosity by surrendering their treasures too easily.

I'm ashamed to say that I fell upon the other books in a frenzy, ripping off their jackets, fondling their boards and flaps, turning them upside down and shaking them, thrusting my fingers into their spines, squinting into their pockets. I became so engrossed in the search that I forgot my Bibliography entirely. The search failed to turn up anything new.

The Rajah of Jehangar abducts Mistral with the intention of turning her into his concubine, but she escapes.

The next day I was reminded of the Bibliography and sat down to it again. But I think I was never meant to complete the task, for as soon as I ran my eye over the twelve entries on my list I was struck by a peculiarity so obvious that for the life of me I cannot explain how it had escaped my notice before (it surely cannot have escaped yours): the predominance of the year 1956.

I looked through the rest of the books. Scores of them had been published or purchased in that year too. Why had Helena read so much in 1956? Historically speaking, it was not the most memorable of years. The Soviet invasion of Hungary came to mind, and the Olympics in Melbourne. Of course, I was born in 1956…

Then it hit me like a ton of books: we were brothers and sisters, the books and I, Helena's offspring. Helena's abandoned children! Cast out into the streets, thrown upon the mercy of strangers. A sense of kinship with the books overwhelmed me as I gathered my long-lost family into my arms. "They are mine, and I am theirs," I said with Birrell.

When I had regained my composure, this new understanding of my relationship to the library made me a little uncomfortable about my feelings towards Helena and the rather overwrought way I had been burying my nose in my siblings. I resolved to adopt a more proper attitude towards them all.

Aunt Emilie reveals to the Grand Duke that his son, Prince Nikolai, is in love with Mistral – who is the Duke's lost daughter! "There was so much bitterness and spite in Emilie's passionate declamation that instinctively Mistral turned towards the Prince as if for protection and found him beside her. He took her hand in his and held it tightly. She clung to him, thankful for his strength. She knew that he was as astonished as she was at what was occurring. Yet neither of them could say anything. They could only cling together, two children lost in a wood of terror and bewilderment."

Naturally I now began to take a special interest in the books published in 1956, my peers. But close as I felt to them, there was one with which I acknowledged an even deeper rapport, and that was *A Ghost in Monte Carlo*.

I examined the triangle formed by *A Ghost in Monte Carlo*, Helena and myself with profound disquiet. I had seen the Cartland clan huddled together in the shops, under signs that said exchange only, chattering away. It amazed me to think that a book of their persuasion might be the one that held the key to our impossible love story – especially when there was so much other good literature to choose from.

A Ghost in Monte Carlo was Barbara Cartland's 42nd *Novel*. She had also published one *Political Novel*, called *Sleeping Swords*, under the pen-name Barbara McCorquodale; a work of *Philosophy*, called *Touch the Stars*; and a work of *Sociology*, called *You in the Home*. This precocious fecundity notwithstanding, who could have foreseen then that another four hundred and seventy-five books would issue from her imagination?

I neglected to mention, I think, that the photograph of Helena and her parents contained a priceless piece of information: leaning into the picture from the right, on a striped black and white pole, was a white sign with the words BUS HALTE painted on it in black, and below them the stencilled number 15. I hardly need to stress how important such a route number might prove to be in locating the house in which Helena grew up. But perhaps I could add a tangential comment: I believe that this bus-stop was for the exclusive use of whites. The sign for a black bus-stop would have included the words SECOND CLASS. The sign is beautifully painted. The question of whether the pole is white with black stripes or vice versa I leave to those with an interest in natural phenomena like the quagga.

Mistral, awakening from a six-day swoon occasioned by her aunt's death, finds that the Grand Duke has claimed her as his daughter and that her wardrobe has therefore been filled with clothes. "Never had she seen such an array of lovely clothes. There were gowns of every colour and description, and their hues rivalled the very colours of the flowers in the garden. There were dresses of blue, pink, green, rose and yellow. Mistral stared at them with wide eyes…The one thing she had noticed immediately was that there was nothing grey amongst them. There was not even a pair of shoes of that colour."

I came round, at last, to certainties. I took sensible steps. Enquiries at the Information Office on Van der Bijl Square revealed that bus route 15 went through Orange Grove. I was not surprised. Whether the route had remained unchanged since 1956 no one could say, but I was optimistic.

One morning in May, at 9.45, I boarded a number 15 doubledecker outside the magistrates' courts in Main Street. I sat at the top, in front, and had the entire upper deck to myself. As luck would have it we went up Rissik Street, and so I obtained unusual new perspectives on no fewer than three vanished bookshops. When the bus turned into 10th Street, Orange Grove, I alighted and began to walk. My plan was to follow the bus route through the suburb, paying special attention to corner houses in the vicinity of stops. If I did not locate the Sheins' house in this way, I would start a more wide-ranging search in the neighbouring streets and, if necessary, the adjacent suburbs.

I felt confident: considering my aptitude for finding books, turning up something as large as a house seemed relatively simple. Even so, it was laughably easy. I had not gone more than four or five blocks when I spotted one of the houses in the background of the photograph. The palm-tree louring over house and garden gave it away at once. I was almost disappointed.

Helena's house was exactly where it was supposed to be, although it had vanished behind an eight-foot wall. Where the twirly gate had been there was now a wooden door with a yellow and white striped awning and an intercom. There was a sign that said the property was protected by 24-hour armed response. Another sign gave the address of Mr Paving.

I sat down on the bus-stop bench facing the door and opened *A Ghost in Monte Carlo*. I had been saving the final pages for this moment.

Madame Boulanger tells Mistral that Sir Robert still loves her: he has called her name in a delirium. Mistral seeks him out at the Hotel Hermitage. "He held her closer to him, his lips against her hair. He knew then that this was what he had searched for all his life, that his search was at an end, his goal in sight. With a sense of urgency at the passing of time he sought her lips. 'I love you,' he whispered against her mouth and knew there was no need for words as she surrendered herself to the passion behind his kiss."

As I raised the book to my lips the door opened and Helena appeared. I gazed at her over the top of the book, while she doublelocked the door behind her and secured an enormous bunch of keys in a shiny blue handbag.

She didn't look a day older. She was wearing the skirt she wore in the photograph, but I was delighted to discover that it was a sunny yellow, and splashed with whorls of bright blue and green. A white poplin blouse set off her brown skin to perfection. There was a chill in the autumn air, but she didn't feel it. She swung her bag over her shoulder and walked in the direction of Louis Botha Avenue.

I stowed my book in the pocket of my blazer and followed, like a blind man, the tapping of her heels along the pavement. I floated in her fragrant wake, light-headed with the scent of orange blossom and patent leather. At every step the book in my pocket thumped like a heart against my chest. On the cool fabric of her blouse, between her sculpted shoulder-blades, I saw in English Times the legend: THE END – and I walked towards it.

Alphabets for Surplus People

I
A Day in the Life of
the Parper of the People

The woman who designed Parper's official residence came to breakfast.

"I still think it needs a louvre here," she said. "I can't see my aperitif." The last crowd lived in utter darkness.

"You're the Architect," said Parper.

This was a little joke: Parper is universally regarded as the Architect of our Freedom.

"Last time I was called to the bar," said Parper, "I had to use the tradesmen's entrance. Same again?"

Parper and the Architect were sipping Bloody Marmers (named for Parper's ex). Secret ingredients: bile, Tabasco. The Architect drew a line on her glass with a pointy fingertip to show the Barman when.

"I'm not a drinking man," said Parper, the autocrat of the breakfast nook. "Affairs of state demand a sober mind and judgement. I'm certainly unused to liquor on an empty stomach. By Jove, this is the stiffest porridge I've ever eaten. Compliments to the Chef."

Baroque laughter.

"Now if you'll excuse me…"

The Architect disappeared by perspectival increments.

"Duty calls," Parper sighed, and buzzed for his Driver.

Who arrived, flourishing a dipstick like an épée, to report that the official limousine was broken. There were spare limousines for just such an emergency, but Marmer's friends had borrowed them and forgotten to bring them back.

Thank heavens for the moped collection. The collection had been founded by one of Parper's predecessors after the Great War. Several of the specimens belonged in museums, it was said. The Equerry, whose task it was to service the mopeds – in the absence of horse-flesh – recommended that Parper take the antique Vespa.

"Never ridden a scooter," said Parper, "but I'll soon get the hang of it."

The Fashion Co-ordinator fastened bicycle clips to Parper's shins, which made his trousers look uncannily like jodhpurs. She attached rose-tinted goggles (a gift from the people of Denmark) to Parper's head. The Equerry patted the Vespa's velvety rump.

A pair of springbok horns had been grafted onto the handlebars. The Fashion Co-ordinator draped a scarf over them, and shuddered.

"It's ethnic, my sweet," said the Gamekeeper, who had performed the transplant.

In fact, the horns were a gift from a small-town butcher in appreciation of Parper's support for game conservation.

The Helicopter Pilot, happening to glance down from the heliport on the roof of the east wing, saw Parper mounting the scooter, and came abseiling down to offer his services.

"Goodness, I'd forgotten all about you," said Parper. And was whirled away to the seat of power, which is made of stinkwood.

Parper settled down with tea and thirteen newspapers. But he was interrupted by the arrival of the Interpreter from the Spanish, the newest addition to the staff. A sporty young woman. Parper had her installed in a corner.

"I'm not sure your services will be required, but one can't be too careful."

The hour between tea and lunch was for ministerial consultations. It being the first Tuesday of the month, Parper received various Jims, Johns and Jacks: a Jim Crow, a Johnny-Come-Lately, the Convener of the Jack-of-All-Trades Committee.

They had all been poets before becoming ministers, and enlivened proceedings with quotations from their works.

The luncheon menu was transparent, multicultural, democratic: polony sliced so thin you could see through it, reconstructed soya-mince in Parper's favourite poppadoms, representative crosssections of Black Forest gâteau.

An aide-de-camp was observed stuffing petits fours up his pull-over. Parper, surmising that the fellow was a Kleptomaniac, tactfully turned a blind eye, saying:

"Anyone have a telling tale?"

The Swedish ambassador tried the one about the Irishman, the Texan and Van der Merwe. She never reached the punchline. First the Attorney-General fell asleep over his sorghum beer. Then a

Lumberjack, late for his morning appointment, burst in with a basketful of sawdust he wanted blessed.

And then Parper's Minister without Substance came bowing and scraping with a lunchpail of breyani, all his own work, he said. He had even grown the ginger in his window-box in an effort to revive the spice trade.

"Too little too late," Parper said, and sent him packing. (Curries give Parper wind.)

Noddy hour. There were so many Noddymen today that the security guards herded them into the courtyard, where Parper might address them from the balcony, and rain down upon them blessings and the leftovers of the Black Forest gâteau.

Today's inspirational message: "Be the best Noddyman you can be. Multiply yourself inoffensively."

A party of tourists making their way to the rose-garden were outraged to see one man administering electrical shocks to another in the vaults beneath the official residence. But the tourguide set their minds at ease: it was the Organ-grinder and his monkey rehearsing for the gala performance at the Venezuelan Embassy.

Parper's Pogonologist, no mere barber and not to be confused with the Little Barber of the Piece, restored the grey symmetry to Parper's beard by a painstaking frosting of individual hairs. Then he stropped his cutthroat twenty-six times and discreetly severed the pricetag from Parper's skullcap. Parper looked more distinguished than ever.

"Who is known as the Parper of Venezuela?"
    "Bolívar."
    "What is the unit of currency in Venezuela?"
    "Bolívar."
    "What is the capital of Venezuela?"
    "Bolívar."
Parper tipped his Quizmaster six cents, the exact equivalent of one bolívar, wordlessly demonstrating that he knew more about Venezuela than that charlatan with all his encyclopaedias.

Twelve limousines, three buses, one armoured car. Parper declined the helicopter, because he wanted to see what was happening on the ground, and took the armoured car.
    Parper (as they trundled over the rockery): "I forgot to put out the cat!"
    Driver: "Not to worry. A Rotary Ann will see to it."

The road to the Venezuelan Embassy lay past the new public toilet on Freedom Square, and Parper decided to make a whirlwind tour. A Speech-writer riding in the seventh limousine (with the Quizmaster) rustled up a speech. Parper jogged on the spot for a minute to make water for baptizing the urinal.

When the moccasins were buffed, an oil-stain came to light on one of Parper's turn-ups. A Tailor travelling in the bus with the choirboys undertook the invisible mending in transit. Parper gratefully tried on a pair of the fellow's revolutionary "Long Jims," which are made of grass, and pronounced them "surprisingly comfortable."

The Venezuelan Embassy was also the work of Parper's Architect. Style: post-hacienda.

The Interpreter from the Spanish obliged at the buffet, but Parper preferred sign language to express his admiration for the sultry, cigar-coloured Under-Secretary. Whereupon the Ambassador donated her to Parper, to hold in trust for the people of the republic.

"You are most generous, comrade amigo," said Parper. "I have always wanted a Venezuelan."

(A white lie. Parper afterwards passed the unhappy woman on to Barber. She was supposed to improve his Spanish, but instead she taught him tennis – he fantasized that she was Gabriela Sabatini – and the love-songs of the Orinoco.)

When it was time for the speeches, Parper was nowhere to be found. But there was a happy ending: he was in the kitchen talking to the staff.

"I too have been a Waiter," he declared. "I started below the salt and worked my way up to the head of the table."

The Gringos' rumba rendition of the national anthem, with solo for Organ-grinder and Monkey, brought the house down. The Xylophonist played his instrument behind his head, with the help of two assistants. Parper sportingly joined in on maracas. Then Parper's Foreign Minister had to spoil everything by cha-cha-ing sideways into a fish-pond.

The Parpermobile, newly repaired, gleamed in the porte-cochère. Parper patted the Driver's back. Then they rolled through quiet streets. Behind glass, darkly, Parper sipped a Virgin Marmer.

People of God!

No job no money no house

Six hungry childrens
Please give work money food
read the cardboard sign of a stop-street Yahoo.

Parper read two newspapers and brushed his teeth. He looked in at the nursery.

Barber was in Spiderman pyjamas, watching CNN.

"How's Parper's Little Zuluboy?" Parper said, chucking him under the chin. Goatee stubble ... Parper disapproved.

"Everyone's got them," said Barber tearfully.

"Oh all right then," said Parper, pulling a human face.

II
The Comings and Goings around
the Marmer of the Nation

Marmer's Acrobats go before her turning cartwheels,
belabouring the ground with loofahs to drive out dust devils,
drawing dotted lines with the sweat of their brows.

Marmer's Bodyguards karate the grand piano into
occasional pieces, opuscules, skeleton keys, matchsticks, and
build in the trampoline pit a lyrical fire to braai a goat.

Marmer's Counsellors wield a lemon slice, a sundae spoon,
a jar of honey, and a stainless-steel funnel to ensure that
their sweet, refreshing counsel never splashes.

Marmer's Dilators apply rods and cones of every description,
animal, vegetable and mineral, to open therapeutically,
like a flinging ajar of doors, her duly congested passages.

Marmer's Electricians favour environmentally friendly
technologies for generating power: talk hot air, think bright
sparks, beat children with sugar cane on the soles of their feet.

Marmer's Footballers wear Israeli bomber jackets from military surplus stores, and woolly caps and mittens in patriotic colours knitted by concerned senior citizens for Operation Hunger.

Marmer's Glaziers install double glazing, because things look better through a vacuum; get for thanks tumblers of shatter-proof crystal, because things look better through a heeltap.

Marmer's Hootchi-kootchi-men gleam in the sun, peel kidskin from fingers like plantains, slick back their dubbined hairdos, pluck calculators from their waistbands, tot up the expenses.

Marmer's Illuminists install in her bedroom lampshades like big boiled sweets (humbugs, lollipops) and sconces for kraal-scented tapers: thatch, cow-pat, burnt pap to take her back.

Marmer's Jugheads return from their fact-finding missions brimming with duty-free rosy, reeking of Havana fumes, and answering only to "Toby" (for a happy hour or two).

Marmer's Kitchenboys admit to tenderizing a trigger-finger or two with the mallet, in the course of duty, but prefer dicing, chopping, grating, slicing, mincing and grinding.

Marmer's Lawyers put on dog Latin to intimidate the plaintiff,
object, bandy about malfeasance and misdemeanour, ipsissima
verba, adjourn, stand the defendant to a liquid lunch.

Marmer's Market Gardeners mobilize for her convenience living
catalogues of their wares: berries in barrels, root vegetables
in tubs, watermelons in trailers filled with potting soil.

Marmer's Nutritionists calculate the recommended daily
allowances of minerals and vitamins, add them, multiply by the
first number that comes into their heads, submit the invoice.

Marmer's Organ-donors lay at her feet, among other things,
dogsbody viscera, taste-bud ikebana, pot-belly tripe, white
meat, puppy-fat, cauliflower ears, the green apples of their eyes.

Marmer's Partypoopers turn up the lights, turn down
the volume, invalidate the wishbones, unpimento the olives,
spit in the dip, spike the punch, open the presents.

Marmer's Quartermasters accept payment in kind: bags of nails,
self-basting fowls, sheepskin seat covers, lashings of cream, tubs
of whitewash, guns, answering machines, medallions of lamb.

Marmer's Restaurateurs support revolutionary causes, including lamb on the spit, wheels of cheddar, whisking two egg-whites, rolling in breadcrumbs, cycling in the park in chef's hats.

Marmer's Silversmiths fashion serviette rings, little handles for corn on the cob, sosatie skewers, trowels for brie, spoons for scooping the flesh of granadillas, toothpicks, tips.

Marmer's Tasters are televised taking their lives in their hands, warming it in their palms, swirling, sniffing, tossing it back like destiny, pronouncing it unbearably sweet.

Marmer's Undertakers permit no eating or drinking in the presence of the dead, in deference to their insatiable hunger for movement, their unslakeable thirst for breath.

Marmer's Ventriloquists throw their voices downstairs: then utensils applaud her, the kettle sings her praises, the coal-scuttle declares itself willing and able to burst into love.

Marmer's Waterbabies understand the well-rounded language of Jacuzzi bubbles, know how to seed clouds and breathe through reeds, use cocktail umbrellas to dowse for bathtub gin.

Marmer's Xerographers reproduce her dinner menu in strict
proportion: fifty-two thousand for subscribers, twenty-six for
the press, and thirteen for handing out free at soup kitchens.

Marmer's Yebomen practise endlessly the doffing of caps in
unison and the bending of knees in counterpoint, never say no,
always say roger, okey-dokey, affirmative, absolutely.

Marmer's Zuluboy comes for the weekend under the
joint custody agreement, tags along behind on her coat-tails,
ensconced on a little beaded pouffe, chewing a candy-cane.

III
The Signature Tunes of
the Barber of the Piece

(Examples only.)

Arranger: Down the Orinoco, on a breeze as sweet as cocoa,
  Barber go.

Babysitter: Tooler too tooler Barber tooler twarner, tooler too
  tooler Barber tooler twarner.

Cheerleader: Parper's Little Man shouldn't blow his own horn,
  but: Parp! Parp! Parp!

All together now:

Courage

"My Mother's Love" ground to a halt at the picnic-spot just before the bridge over the Inyongo and set down a white man with a walking stick and a silver suitcase. It was the first time a suitcase as shiny as the foil from a cigarette box had been seen in our part of the world. Banoo the bus driver alighted as well. Able-bodied passengers were usually expected to bring their own sacks and boxes down from the roof-rack of the bus while Banoo revved the engine, but on this occasion he scaled the ladder himself and fetched a leather bag from under the tarpaulin. Years later, when I went to school in Piet Retief, I saw that the postmen carried their letters in bags like that.

These were the first days of our freedom and it was not really necessary to be nice to the whites any more. But Banoo brought the bag down carefully and placed it in the white man's arms. Then he hopped up on the whitewashed parapet before the bridge and pointed down into the valley. He gave directions, his hands bowing and scraping so earnestly in the air we could almost hear them. The white man smiled and nodded, and beat a tattoo on the toecaps of his boots with the end of his stick.

Banoo's bus was as blue as a swimming pool, and "My Mother's Love" was painted on both sides and the back in snowcapped letters, but inside it was like an oven. Soon there were impatient mutterings from the passengers. Banoo ignored them. Only when an arm crooked out of a window and a fist banged the "v" in Love did he hasten back to the wheel, scattering handfuls of directions as he went, and drive away.

From our hiding-place behind the concrete picnic table, Fish and I watched the white man. There was no need to hide from him, of course, except the thrill of spying itself. As luck would have it we were dressed for the occasion: we had clumps of grass stuck in our collars like freedom fighters, because we were preparing to sneak up on the girls washing clothes down at the river, but this new arrival was a worthier quarry. He was a youngish man with copper-coloured hair and a pink skin, running to fat and trying to conceal it under baggy floral shorts that hung down to his knees and a shirt dotted with assegais and shields in the colours of the new ruling party. He had shiny yellow boots and thick red socks. As soon as the bus was out of sight he hitched up one leg of his shorts and urinated against the parapet.

"Do you see?" Fish whispered. "His cock is made of rubber."

"He shouldn't piss there," I said.

"It has a valve like a bicycle tube." Fish had been to Fort Alexander to visit his sister and so he was an expert on whites.

The white man slung his bag over his shoulder, took the silver suitcase in one hand and the stick in the other, and started down the track. This had been the main road once, before Fish and I were born. It curved down to a drift over the Inyongo and then climbed all the way back up again to Lufafa, our village. Since the bridge had been built over the gorge the track was seldom used and the bush had almost reclaimed it. The descent offered memorable views of the sea and the spray against the rocks at the mouth of the river, but the white man did not have eyes for any of it. He was too busy trying to keep his balance. He kept losing his footing, despite the ferocious treads of his boots, and sliding down in clatters of shale. He made such a racket that stalking him was no challenge.

About halfway down he tripped over a root and skinned his knees. I wanted to go and help him then, I've always been a softie, but Fish wouldn't hear of it. There must be no collaboration with the enemy. "What does he want down by the river? Perhaps he intends to attack the women?"

But there was no need to worry. The girls saw the suitcase coming and fled to the other side of the river. The white man flung himself down among the clothes spread on the rocks to dry and thrust his head under the soapy water. He looked like a pile of dirty laundry, lying there in a heap. After a while he picked himself up and scooped water in his hands to clean his knees. Then he made a study of the stepping-stones across the drift, plotting his course with the end of his stick. The girls gathered on the opposite bank, pointing and waving. Although we were too far away to hear what they were saying, we could tell he was negotiating his passage with them.

Teetering from stone to stone, flailing with suitcase and stick, rocking perilously after every step, the white man crossed the Inyongo. He made such heavy going of it I began to hold thumbs for him. But the anticipation of dry land made him bold. He tried to take three stones on the trot, overbalanced on the last and plunged one of his wonderful boots right up to the strap in the muddy bank. He gave the girls the end of his stick and they pulled him out.

He took off the muddied boot and washed it in a pool. He rinsed the sock and wrung it out. Then he put the sock and the boot on again.

His behaviour thus far had been merely silly, but now it became annoying: he took a packet from his leather bag and dished out sweets all round. He checked the clasps on his suitcase and gave it to my cousin Pinky. He buckled the leather bag and gave it to Thabiso. While he was doing this the girls were rushing to bundle laundry and fill buckets. Surrounded by his bearers, and swinging the walking stick which he had decided to carry himself, the white man took the track up to Lufafa.

There was not much point in keeping our distance any more and so we hurried to catch up. As everyone knows, it is always easier going up than down, especially when the path is broad and clear. The white man was striding along quite cheerfully now, in a cloud of sweet-scented giggling from the mouths of the girls and sour anti-perspirant from his own armpits, swinging his stick and humming a tune. From close up he looked fatter and pinker. His knees were like bruised peaches. His boots creaked, especially the dry one. He reminded me of a picture-book pony.

Halfway up he ordered a halt, poked the end of his stick into the ground, unfolded a leather seat from the other end and perched on it. It was the first time a shooting-stick had been seen in our village too and it caused such a hullabaloo of laughing and jostling that one of the girls choked on her sweet. The white man took it all in good spirits, joining in the laughter and wobbling from buttock to buttock. When someone pointed out the damp spot around his boot he obliged us by stamping it so that water bubbled out of the stitching, and laughed louder than ever.

These were the first days of our freedom, as I've said, and there was no need to be especially mean to the whites. But there was a mean streak in Banoo, and I became aware of it as we reached the end of the track and emerged once more onto the main road. The white man's long march had brought him to the far side of the bridge over the Inyongo, a stroll away from where the bus had dropped him off. Banoo had sent him to the river and back, just to see how far it was. But he did not see the joke. Neither did anyone else and I decided to keep it to myself. He looked so pinkly pleased with himself for having found his way through foreign territory.

Thrillingly, he pointed to my mother's shop with his stick and we all went that way. The silver suitcase, which Pinky was balancing on her head, flashed in the sun, calling me to service. I wrestled it away from her. Fish tried to take the leather bag from Thabiso, but the white man wouldn't let him, and he slunk off cursing. So it was that I was marching at the head of the expedition, carrying the suitcase in my hand like a gentleman, when Peter Meyerhold Becker, artist, appeared among us.

Although I had carried the suitcase on the triumphal leg of its journey, the white man, whose name and vocation were still a mystery to me, rewarded Pinky with a Coca-Cola.

My mother shooed the other children out of the shop and had a difficult conversation with him over the counter. He took a letter from his bag and spread it out, and she pored over it, looking for all the world as if she could read, exercising the whole repertoire of critical grunts and approving murmurs she had developed to appraise my accounts of the day's takings. Then she gave him the chair from behind the counter, plucked some stalks of grass from my collar, and sent me to rouse Chief Phosa from his afternoon nap: "Tell him the government of the people has sent us a white man."

The chief was grumpy to be woken, but he cheered up when he heard my message. He put on his straw hat and his sandals, tucked his shirt into his pants and followed me to the shop. When he laid eyes on what the government had sent, however, his face fell back into wrinkles. He expected a suit and tie, I think. All three of them went into the little office at the back of the shop, leaving me to guard the till. The white man took his baggage with him.

I had to rehearse the story of our visitor several times in the hour that followed. The suitcase, polished more expertly with each retelling, grew so shiny you could see the future in it. There was quite a crowd waiting when the white man finally emerged, and they were as disappointed in the baggage as Chief Phosa had been in its owner.

"This one is my son," my mother said.

"We've met." The white man stuck out his hand and I was bold enough to shake it. It cleaved to my fingers like dough. He fumbled for my thumb afterwards and laughed when our hands grappled clumsily between us. He had lost some of his pinkness in the cool interior, but his ears and nose were brighter than ever.

"This white's name is My Old Becker," my mother said, and fished a key on a curtain-ring from her bosom. His name, bobbing on the surface of our mother tongue, made him smile. "Take him to the room. And show him where the toilet is."

I took the suitcase and led My Old Becker, as we called him, across the field to the clinic.

Like the track down to the river, the clinic was a vestige of the old days. It was a yellow-brick building with a corrugated-iron roof, three interlinked rooms and a stoep at the front with built-in benches, where the patients could wait in comfort. The university students who had built the clinic during their vacations as a contribution to the development of our rural district put in light sockets and three-pin plugs and taps, but the government of the day never got round to supplying the electricity and the water that would have filled these fixtures with purpose. They never got round to doctors and nurses either. For a while medical students came twice a year from the university in Fort Alexander, until the fighting kept them away.

Our house was next door to the clinic and so my mother was appointed caretaker. In return, she was allowed to grow vegetables on the plot at the back, which the builders had thoughtfully cleared of scrub. Once it became apparent that the students were not coming back, at least for the time being, my mother received Chief Phosa's blessing to use the building too. The metal tables and cupboards were stacked in the end room; once a year thereafter, in the name of care-taking, they were carried out to be washed. The middle room became a storeroom for the shop. The front room, into which boxes and bags sometimes spilled, was used for guests.

I ushered My Old Becker into his quarters.

The place was stifling. The air smelt thickly of carrot-tops, onions, green mealies, curry-powder, detergent, rat droppings, mouldering cardboard. My Old Becker sniffed and sweated, but kept on smiling. A sponge-rubber mattress as grey and crumbly as a stale crust leaned against the wall. I laid it out for him and put his baggage in the corner behind the door. He seemed to have forgotten about me. He patted the fat rump of a mealie-meal bag as if it were a cow and wiped his whitened palm on his shorts. He read the label on a box of tinned peas. When I left him he was turning one of our squashes over in his hands as if he had never seen anything like it. If he needs the toilet, I thought, he can follow his nose.

Cupped in the warm palm of a dune, with the sun setting over my shoulder, I watched My Old Becker on the rocks. He took off his boots, stuffed his red socks into them, placed them side by side on a ledge. His feet were so soft he could hardly walk on the barnacles, but he winced his way out towards the sea and clambered onto an outcrop. Beyond him the rock shelved away and then plunged sheer into the water. The tide was coming in. The waves doused him in explosive spray and seethed around him. High and dry, the boots admonished him for his recklessness, as the waves beat closer. But he stayed there, very still, gazing straight ahead, as if he was hoping to be swept away.

My Old Becker survived to have supper with us that evening, and we had tripe and tinned peas even though it was a Tuesday. He had an appetite and a peculiar way with the fork, folding long strips of the tripe into concertinas on the tines. He had blistered his feet so badly that he could not put on his boots and was wearing rubber sandals instead with soles as thick as sandwiches. His feet put me off my food. They were pale and fleshy like vegetables, with blue veins in the ankles and sprinkles of red hairs on the toes, and the heels were extravagantly patched with sticking-plasters. There were plasters on his knees too.

That afternoon on the track I had seen myself reflected in the lid of the suitcase and heard it rattle as if it were full of pills, and I had concluded that My Old Becker was a doctor. The plasters confirmed it. But when he had mashed the last of the peas into the gravy and cleaned his plate, he began to talk about the purpose of his visit, and I learned that he was an artist. My mother, who had understood less of the discussion with Chief Phosa than she cared to admit, encouraged him with questions. I interpreted, glossing over what I didn't grasp, inventing a little.

It seemed that he had been commissioned to make a statue for the government of the people. A statue of a man, life-size, made of metal, he said, like a hoe. We had seen statues of the saints at St. Joseph's Mission – made of plaster, it's true, but we understood the principle. He had to warn us, then, that it was more complicated than that: although this statue would have the shape of a man, it had to show not the man himself but an idea – the idea of courage. The government wished to honour the people for the courage they had shown in the struggle for our freedom. The statue would be put up in Fort Alexander, outside the house of the government, to remember those who had died for our freedom and those who had suffered and survived. Because, he said, some of the brave were dead and some were still living.

We were not stupid people, my mother and I, not incapable of what you might call abstract thought. My mother ran a successful business and I kept the books. We thought, with some justification, that we were two of the brainiest people in Lufafa. But we had never met an artist before.

"Ask him why he has come to make his statue here in our village," my mother said.

"He says," I said, "that he is not going to make it here. He is doing research. He is looking for a man to use as a model."

"Is he going to take one of our men away with him?"

The worried look on her face made him laugh. "He finds your concern amusing," I said. "He says your men are safe. He is just going to take photographs and make measurements, which he will take back to the city."

"I find him amusing too," said my mother, "he looks like a pig, but never mind. What makes him think he will find a brave man in our village? Doesn't he know that most of the fighting was up north? He would do better looking for his model there."

"He says the courage of the individual doesn't matter. He wants somebody who looks like courage."

"There are people like that everywhere. Why has the government sent him here?"

"He says Comrade Mhlandhla told him about you."

Mhlandhla was the Minister of Finance. My Old Becker kept a straight face, which I translated, and when my mother got the joke we all laughed together.

We offered him a candle, but he had a torch with a beam as strong as the headlight of a car. I watched it bowling across the field, flashing now at the ground before him, now at the clinic ahead. In the middle of the field he suddenly stopped and stood on one leg to examine the sole of his sandal in the light of the torch. He took off the sandal to look at it more closely, propping his bare foot on his knee. Then he saw me in the lighted doorway, shouted something I couldn't understand, lost his balance, and hopped around on one leg, laughing, while the beam of the torch tumbled against the sky. His laughter, brash as the light in the darkness, embarrassed me, and I went in.

"I'll never understand these whites," my mother said. "If it doesn't matter who this statue is, then it doesn't matter. To come all this way for something that doesn't matter. . . It makes you worry about the government. I think this My Old Becker, who is actually quite a young man as you can see, is taking a free holiday. But once he's here, I say there is only one man in this district who looks like courage, and that is Chief Phosa. You can tell him I said so."

Fish said: "I know about artists. I remember one from Fort Alexander. My sister used to work for him. This one of ours is a sculptor, of course, but hers was a painter. He painted pictures of flowers and trees, and once a fire in the bush. But mostly he loved to paint fruit and vegetables. Every Sunday he would go to the greengrocer for onions, peppers, mealies, sweet potatoes, garlic. Sometimes it was bananas, oranges, granadillas, whatever was in season. He put the food in a bowl on a table and it had to stay there for a week. Mercy was not allowed to dust it. Then this so-called artist put on an apron, like the ones our mothers wear, but very dirty, all covered in paint. He had paints in tubes like toothpaste, and he squeezed them onto a plate, and he put this paint on the picture with a knife and fork. When you saw him doing it, Mercy said, it looked like he was eating something. On Friday, when the vegetables were not so fresh any more, he gave them to her to cook for her supper. He himself was very thin, because he never had enough to eat. But he was always drinking. Artists are like that."

During the following days My Old Becker limped all over Lufafa, with his rubber sandals snapping at his heels, gazing into the face of every man he met as if he expected to recognize an old friend. He startled us by sticking his head in at the classroom window and staring at Mr Namabula. He had bought himself a straw hat like Chief Phosa's at our shop, but the damage had already been done: the back of his neck, which a deep crease divided into two fleshy humps, was like a segment of lobster shell slicked with some buttery ointment, and there were puffy blisters on the tops of his ears, from which, said Fish, a host of hairy red spiders would soon hatch.

The word got around that the strange white man was an artist, an official artist, with instructions from the government to immortalize one of us. The prospect didn't appeal to everyone. Some of the men said they didn't want to be a statue, of courage or anything else, and that they would refuse to do it, even if they were chosen. When these men saw the artist coming towards them, sweating in his wind-breaker like a loaf of bread in a plastic bag, they turned away their faces; the extremists among them even ran off into the fields. But most of the men were taken with the idea. They went out of their way to bump into him, and when they did they pursed their lips and narrowed their eyes, and caused the muscles in their jaws to pulsate. Every evening, as we sat eating, a string of hopefuls came to our door, on the flimsiest pretexts, and dangled their faces in the light.

Although My Old Becker had said clearly that he was looking for a man, some of the women thought they had an equal chance. "Women fought for our freedom too," I overheard one of them saying. "Women are also courageous." When my mother tried to explain the finer points of My Old Becker's project, she was unmoved. "If it comes down to appearances, women are just as courageous-looking as men. More so."

We children had no illusions about our suitability as models. If Fish and I took to following My Old Becker around, sometimes with and sometimes without his knowledge, it was simply that we wanted to be the first to know when he made his decision. And, for my part, I wanted to learn about the ways of the artist.

One afternoon we followed him down to the beach and spied on him from the dunes while he bathed. I had thought of him as a pink man, as if "white" was just a way of speaking – but the parts of him usually concealed by clothing were as white as paper. I pointed out to Fish that his cock did not seem to be made of rubber, but of the same pale flesh as the rest of him, although it jutted comically from a nest of hair like a rusty pot-scourer. He had shocking quantities of hair on the white bulb of his belly and in the small of his back, and even on his plump shoulders, like tufts of wiry coir peeling from an old armchair.

He chose the worst place to swim, in a little bay where the currents hoarded seaweed. I might have shown him a better spot, but for Fish's judgemental presence. My Old Becker didn't seem to mind the mess at all. He flung himself down in the shallow water and bobbed there with the wrack in the cross-currents. He let the sea spill him out on the sand and drag him this way and that in the backwash, spinning him around, running him aground and refloating him again and again, scraping and scouring him on all sides. He let himself be bumped against rocks and rolled over in the jagged shells and slimy kelp on the waterline, until a wave finally beached him. He lay there for a moment, with his limbs at crooked angles, like driftwood, then roused himself with a fearful glance at the sky, and quickly dressed.

"This white is mad," said Fish.

Later, when he tired of digging things up at the water's edge and gazing into pools, he went and sat on his usual ledge, with a pad on his knees, and began to draw the sea. At last: the artist at work. We scampered out to watch.

It was an education. He was drawing with wax crayons, like those we used in the classroom. I had pictured an elegant pen, like Mr Namabula's, or long, slim pencils striped like drinking-straws. Instead, these stubby, childish things. He held them back to front what's more, with the point cupped in his palm like a cigarette coal on a windy day, and drew with the blunt end. The paper had the texture of a crêpe bandage, and he was covering it with little marks, jabbing at it irritably, as if the wind was strewing sea sand on his picture and he had to keep brushing it away with his knuckles, dropping one crayon and taking up another every minute. His whole body rolled over the drawing, buffeted by memories of waves, and his pale feet flip-flopped on the rocks.

Fish and I came closer and closer, drawn by the tidal swirl of colour, until we were each gazing over one of his shoulders. At close quarters his flesh was overpowering. His temple was stuck with sea salt and grains of sand. His cheek was like a well-seasoned steak. The blisters on his ears had burst and the skin was peeling off in curls like pencil shavings. I held my breath. The thought of breathing in the slough of My Old Becker turned my stomach. He seemed totally unaware of our presence. Soon I too forgot everything but the hand on the page and the sea spilling out of it.

At last he stopped. He tore the page from the pad and held it out for us to inspect. I had never seen anything like it. When you looked at it properly it was nothing like the sea, just a solid mass of wriggles and curls, something the sea might have spat out. But under the impulse of mysterious laws, which the eye could not fathom but had to obey, the mass would liquefy. Running water.

"What do you think, boys?"

I searched for words to contain what floated on the page. But before I could speak Fish said, "It's rubbish. I can draw better than that. It looks like spinach." And spat.

"Don't be unpolite, Fish," I said in English, so that My Old Becker would appreciate my support.

But My Old Becker had the audacity to rebuke me. "Let him have his say. He doesn't have to like it if he doesn't want to."

He was trying to teach me a lesson, and it was one worth learning. Why should I stand up for him, after all? He was big and fat enough to stand up for himself. All the same, his words stung.

"What do you think?" he asked, with one of his fixed smiles.

My answer took both of us by surprise. "It's like shit from a cow. The colour."

He turned his smile on the drawing. It's a thing of no worth, I thought, perhaps he'll give it to me, so I can draw on the other side. But instead he said, "You're right, it is a piece of shit," crumpled it up and threw it into the water.

That night Chief Phosa came to supper at My Old Becker's invitation. It was unorthodox, but what could we do. We had meat for the third time that week.

"The men are making my job very difficult," My Old Becker complained.

"How can that be?" You could tell from his tone that Chief Phosa did not think of My Old Becker as a man with a job.

"Many of them are avoiding me. When they see me coming they run off into places where I can't follow. They are hindering my research. I want you to call a meeting of the whole village so that I can see everyone."

"Have you taken a look at Namabula?" Chief Phosa asked. "He is a fine-looking man, and educated too."

"The teacher? Yes, he has a beautifully shaped head, and lovely thoughts inside it, I'm sure. But his eyes are too close together. Makes him look shifty."

My mother understood perfectly the gesture My Old Becker made with two fingers. "That's just what I always thought!" she said, and tinkled like a cash register. Mother had taken a shine to the white man, which made my disillusionment with him complete.

"Shabangu then? A brave fighter with a stick."

"Shabangu! What about his ears?" my mother said, and pulled out her own for My Old Becker's entertainment. She was enjoying herself. My Old Becker confirmed all her prejudices.

They proceeded to work their way through the presentable men of Lufafa. My Old Becker recalled most of them, and he had something good and something bad to say about each one. It seemed that our village demonstrated just how unequally physical resources were distributed in a population. Those whose bodies were well shaped invariably had something wrong with their heads, and vice versa. Those whose bodies and heads passed muster were always let down by their faces. And the faces themselves were a mixed blessing. They had too much chin or too little, the eyes wouldn't stay put, the noses rebelled.

"Why don't you take all the best parts and stick them together," Chief Phosa was inspired to say. "You could come up with a perfect man."

"A monster!" My Old Becker cried with a knowing snort. "Try the worst bits rather, you might have more luck."

Chief Phosa dangled his face resolutely and waited for my mother to nominate him, and I waited too, but she disappointed us.

Chief Phosa departed with My Old Becker's letter of appointment on the letterhead of the new government, and so on Saturday morning the entire village gathered on the field in front of the clinic. The Chief and my mother sat on the benches in the shade, with My Old Becker between them, while everyone else sweltered. The children were playing on the edges of the crowd, but I was seated next to my mother, a small, asymmetrical appendix to these historic proceedings. Like most villages we had our share of the old and the misshapen, but we had strong, healthy men and women too, fishermen and farmers, people who worked hard, people we admired. Today I looked on them all with new eyes. They seemed like a sorry lot, full of unexpected weaknesses and little flaws that disqualified their claims on posterity.

Chief Phosa made a long speech about My Old Becker and his quest, although there could not have been a soul in the district who did not already know. The fact that attendance at the meeting was compulsory had deepened the rift between those who did not want to be a statue and those who did. The former slouched around in their work clothes and huddled under cowardly sunshades. The latter were baking courageously in their Sunday best. There was a smattering of camouflage gear, designed to make the wearer stand out in the crowd. The bravest ones strutted up and down with their chests stuck out or adopted statuesque poses. Some people from other villages had turned up uninvited, and not everyone thought they should be allowed to stay.

At last Chief Phosa sat down and My Old Becker stepped forward. He was wearing, for the occasion, a purple beret with a toggle like a teat sticking out of it. He had put on his boots and slung a camera around his neck. His nose was painted white. He paused on the end of the stoep and with agitated circles of his arms stirred everyone to their feet. Then, fixing a look of troubled concentration upon his face, he limped out among them.

An excited, embarrassed silence fell. It was the sort of fidgety silence we knew in the classroom, when Mr Namabula patrolled the rows to see who had done their homework and who not. Like a privileged monitor, I saw all the people of Lufafa as Mr Namabula might have seen our class, cupped in the palm of my hand. My Old Becker went up and down, gazing at bodies and faces, adjusting a pose with a flick of the wrist, circling and squinting, patting here and there, as if he was at a livestock auction.

The attention of the crowd rolled in on My Old Becker like a tide. Waves of glances beat forward and spattered us where we sat on the stoep. Then the waves began to clash and churn, for those in the front were turning to watch My Old Becker as he passed. There was a moment of disturbing calm, when he reached the middle of the mass and the attention swirled around him, like ripples round a fisherman's float. Then he bobbed on and the tide of attention turned and beat out to the backwaters of the crowd, and beyond, to the green slopes and the distant blue of the ocean.

In the stagnant reaches at the back of the crowd My Old Becker stopped. There was a man there sitting flat on the ground. My Old Becker's fingers fluttered around his bowed head, as if he was chasing flies. Then he stooped and raised up the chosen one. The people fell back in alarm.

In the clearing we saw Kumbuza.

My Old Becker walked towards us. The people parted. Someone handed Kumbuza his crutch and he skipped along in the artist's wake.

When Kumbuza was a young man he had gone to Johannesburg to work on the mines. He was one of my mother's suitors, and she remembered well how he looked in those days – the shape of his hands, the details of his smile, the green of the shirt he wore on the day he left, just like a particular leaf in the kitchen linoleum. And she remembered that while the other men clustered around the recruiting agent, falling over their own feet, Kumbuza lagged behind, walking backwards down the river track – the agent had left his truck on the other side of the drift – and ticking off on his long fingers the goods he would bring with him when he returned. As it happened he came back with nothing but a tin chest full of pots and pans and bottles of brandy. He left behind in Johannesburg the three longest fingers of his beautiful right hand. In later years, when the war of freedom lapped at the edges of the district, his absent trigger-finger became a joke in our village.

Kumbuza acquired a wife who was less choosy than my mother and became a farmer. He got drunk as often as he could. In his second season he slipped under the plough and mangled his left foot. Unfortunately our medical students were not in residence at the time. The foot was poulticed and bound, but it did not heal. The young doctors duly appeared and sent Kumbuza back to Fort Alexander with their driver. When he returned three months later his foot was missing and so was his wife.

In time people came to feel unsafe in his company, and so they left him to pursue his reckless course on the outskirts of their lives. He became a fisherman. He kept lobster traps for liquor money and he fished for his own dinner from the shore. The thumb and little finger of his right hand had evolved into a marvellously dextrous tool. He could open a bottle or bait a hook as deftly as any man. His crutch was as good as a leg, we said, although it sometimes failed him, as a leg will. Once he slipped and fell on the rocks, not far from where My Old Becker made his drawing, and lacerated his left leg from ankle to thigh. He fell off a stile and knocked out his front teeth. On another occasion he tore off the lobe of his right ear with a carelessly cast fish-hook. Then he went rushing up and down on the stoep of the clinic, cursing the absent doctors and pouring more blood than I had thought was contained in the human body.

This was the man My Old Becker had chosen for his statue of courage.

The choice aroused unexpectedly strong feelings among the men and women of Lufafa. They were outraged. They were filled with shame. In the few days that remained of My Old Becker's sojourn among us Chief Phosa refused to speak another word to him. The people, especially those who felt that they themselves deserved the honour, did the same. My mother was incensed. That night we sat down to samp with a relish so hot it brought the sweat out on My Old Becker's brow, and before the bowls were empty she demanded an explanation.

Was it not the case, she said, that My Old Becker had rejected the best-looking men we had to offer, because of the tiniest imperfections, only to settle on this wreck of a human being.

"It is not the business of the artist," he said pompously, flourishing his red face, "to give a man what he has never had. But when a man has lost a part of himself, it might well be the business of the artist to return it to him."

To pick up the pieces, to make broken things whole, to restore the lost unity. It was a laughable claim and I could easily take issue with it now. But then I was delighted. It was obvious to me, as perhaps it would have been to other children of Lufafa, that the right choice had been made. Kumbuza's missing bits and pieces might have filled our parents with horror, might have given them aches and pains in the corresponding digits and limbs, but to us they were marvels. I still remember running my finger over the scars on his leg as if they made a map of the future. I remember the drunken smell of his laughter and how deliciously he tickled with the pincer of his right hand. I remember, in my bones, stirring a loose milk-tooth with the tip of my tongue while Kumbuza reeled through the door of the shop with a bloody rag pressed to his mouth.

"I'll be glad to see the back of him," my mother said. "He's eating us out of house and home."

Had My Old Becker's choice of model not already redeemed him in my eyes, my mother's growing hostility would have done the trick. When he invited me to assist with the photographing and measuring, I forgave him everything.

The photographing of Kumbuza took place in our backyard on Sunday morning at the crack of dawn. It had something to do with the light. My Old Becker demanded total privacy, but there was really no need. Kumbuza behaved admirably. He let himself be photographed standing up, sitting down, crouching, kneeling, rising, falling, lying. He wielded the crutch and then the shooting-stick like a rifle, a flag, a hoe. He twisted his face into a wide range of expressions. My Old Becker wallowed around him with the camera, smiling and sweating and getting thorns in his bare feet.

By mid-morning My Old Becker was exhausted. He sent Kumbuza away to rest and retired to the room. While he slept the silver suitcase at last revealed some of its secrets to me.

Kumbuza was supposed to come back at four o'clock to be measured, but it was dark before he staggered through the kitchen door. His account of the morning's session had been worth more than a drink or two, and he was so drunk he could hardly stand. My Old Becker and I arranged him in a chair.

We had already rehearsed my part in the operation. I sat at the table with a notebook containing lists of body parts and diagrams of heads and bodies in several elevations. There were curly brackets and arrows sticking out of these bodies, and dotted lines where I had to fill in the figures.

My Old Becker sharpened my pencil with a scalpel. Then he produced from the silver suitcase a leather folder, which I had peeped into that afternoon but did not have the nerve to unpack. Inside was an array of silver objects. They looked to me like surgical instruments, although they also reminded me of Mr Namabula's maths set.

There were rulers and clamps, a little hammer, a spatula and a small pair of calipers with a brass screw. There was a second pair of calipers too, but much larger and made of wood. My Old Becker took up the silver calipers and screwed open their jaws.

Kumbuza appeared to have nodded off. But when My Old Becker approached his face with the calipers raised he opened his eyes with a cry of horror. Showing remarkable agility for a man in his condition he scooted under the table, butted a chair out of the way with his head, and hopped up on the other side. He seized his crutch from a corner and shook it at us over the table, cursing and raving. My mother appeared in the doorway to the lounge but My Old Becker calmly shut the door in her face.

It took half an hour to get Kumbuza back in the chair. It was only after My Old Becker had demonstrated the calipers on my own nose and ears that he consented to be measured.

My Old Becker homed in again and gripped Kumbuza's broken nose gently in the calipers, twiddled the screw, held the calipers against his ruler and called out a figure. Kumbuza squinted down his nose as if he was surprised it was still there. I found the appropriate space on my diagram and wrote the figure down in my best hand.

For as long as My Old Becker worked on his face, Kumbuza sat in terrified immobility, except for his eyes, which squinted and rolled, and the thumb and little finger of his right hand, which echoed every movement of the silver jaws. But when the wooden calipers were applied to his limbs, he proved ticklish and began to squirm and shriek with laughter. I had been on the verge of laughing all evening and now it burst out. My Old Becker began to laugh too. All three of us laughed and measured and laughed again until the room was swimming.

It was this tumult, pouring from our house in precise measures, which lent credence to Fish's story that he had looked through our window and seen My Old Becker torturing Kumbuza, tearing strips of flesh from his body with a pair of pliers, while I sat by laughing.

The next morning "My Mother's Love" carried My Old Becker out of our lives. He left me his wax crayons and some plastic lens caps. He left Kumbuza the shooting-stick, which I would have preferred. He promised to send us photographs of the statue, he promised to invite us to the unveiling. But we never heard from him again.

Our new-found freedom broke its promises too. It did not bring us the things we expected, like water, electricity, prosperity and peace. It brought new battles and new factions to fight them. Within a few years the war returned and this time we were not spared.

My mother sent me to live with her sister in Piet Retief to complete my schooling. I went on the back of an army truck: the burnt-out wreck of "My Mother's Love" lay on its side in a gully on the road to St. Joseph's. The following year I left for England.

I came back to Fort Alexander a month ago, when the cease-fire was signed, as an Education Officer of the British Council. On my first Sunday back home, in a park near my hotel, I found My Old Becker's statue.

As a statue of courage it is not a great success. There is nothing abstract about it. It is not an idea. It is a soldier. He wears boots and he carries an AK47. He turns Kumbuza's face towards the enemy, but the expression on it is not courageous. I would call it bemused, almost as if he is trying not to laugh. He has reason to feel pleased with himself, this freedom fighter, for he has all his working parts in their proper places, including his trigger-finger.

I watched the statue from a distance.

"Mister." A youngster with a large and flashy camera around his neck tugged my sleeve. "You want a picture with the General. Five rands."

I thought he was referring to the statue, but he went on: "That man there is the General himself. He can be in front of his statue with you, two by two."

The General was lounging on a bench in the shade, but when we looked his way he lurched out into the sunlight. The combat uniform, with its empty trouser-leg pinned back, threw me for a moment, but the face was unmistakable.

I reached for my wallet.

"Five rands is nothing," the boy assured me. "He is a true hero of the people."

Isle of Capri
Tempo di Tango

> But this is neither here nor there – why do I
> mention it? – Ask my pen, – it governs me, – I
> govern not it.
>
> – Sterne, The Life and Opinions of
Tristram Shandy, Gentleman

Somewhere far away,
Over Naples Bay,
I thought I heard the Sirens singing as I set foot on the beautiful Isle
of Capri and found that I had nothing but antic dinars, doubloons
and zlotys in the capacious pockets of my pea-jacket.

There was no one to meet me: it was dinner-time.

I hauled the jolly boat *West Wind* up among the fishermen's dories
and row-boats for hire. Then I sat down on the stone groyne at the

end of the beach to empty the brine out of my gumboots and put on my velskoene. The left boot offered up a Mastercard in a rheumy marinade and I remembered with relief that I had stowed it there at the start of my journey, proof against pirates. The right boot coughed up a pickled krugerrand. Useful too.

I dried the card under my arm and looked at the lights in the windows of the houses, and then at their slick reflections on a sea the colour of Tassenberg vin ordinaire. The sighing of the waves as they leaned their glossy heads against the pebbles and the fishy smell of the seaward breeze reminded me that I was sleepy and hungry.

That's where my thoughts keep on turning:
sleep and food, as I follow my nose along the cobbled way that slants steeply up from the harbour, lined with double and treble storey houses, white plaster shaled away to ruddy brick, doorways arching Moorish eyebrows over little balconies with wrought-iron balusters shaped like spare parts for lyres. I sniff out the fifth house on the left. Scents of fish, lemon and dill-tips stream from the letter-slot in the door, where a bicycle with balloon tyres and a wicker delivery basket over the front wheel leans against the wall. I knock twice, and then thumb the bicycle bell for good measure. The wicker is sequinned with fish-scales and beribboned with verdigris kelp.

Picture me: Sun-burnt, wind-whipped, salt-encrusted. Over my left shoulder, trussed by my left arm, my duffel bag, which recently did duty as ballast, containing my clothes, a mix-and-match assortment of panama, dinner-jacket (maroon), shirts (open-neck and starched), bow-tie, cummerbund, flannels (white), Bermudas (Paisley), pumps, plimsolls. In my right hand my guidebook, which features concise information on the principal attractions, scenic and historical, and useful phrases in a handy appendix. **Dove siamo?** ~ Where are we? **Come si chiama?** ~ What is your name? **Questo ventolino è delizioso.** ~ This breeze is delicious.

A crack opens and oozes a man.

"**Buona sera.** ~ Good evening," I say, tilting my book to the light. Then I have to drop the duffel bag to turn over a new leaf. "**Si può avere alloggio per la notte?** ~ Can one get lodging for the night? **Sarà possibile avere da mangiare?** ~ Will it be possible to get something to eat?" And by way of conversation: "**Come sono graziose quelle vele.** ~ How pretty those sails look. **Suppongo che siano paranze da pesca.** ~ Fishing-boats I suppose."

"What has washed up on our doorstep?" the man says in unguent English. "Let's take a look-see." He shoves the door wide, and in the light from the passage I feel my face develop features for him like a Polaroid snapshot. While he studies me, inviting me to gaze back with becoming frankness, my eyes are drawn to the doorway at the end of the passage, in the shadow of the stairs, where another man is silhouetted. That man raises his right hand in a clipped gesture of greeting.

"How long will you be staying?"

"A few days. **Vorrei vedere le cose notevoli, di maggiore interesse.** ~ I want to see noteworthy things, of major interest. Just the Villa Jovis and the Blue Grotto, and then I'll be on my way."

"Have you done Naples yet? Oh you must. It isn't necessary to die afterwards, you know."

I chuckle in my Italian accent. "Later perhaps. **Cosa è piatto del giorno?** ~ What is the dish of the day?"

"There's no board here, I'm afraid. We're nothing but servants in these quarters. But you're welcome to lodging, for a small fee. My name is Vincenzo."

"All the better, Vincenzo – **grazie infinite** ~ very many thanks – I like to see how the locals live," and I give him my name in return. We negotiate a price: the conversion tables in my book come in useful. Then he turns away and calls out in an oily voice. The man at the end of the passage, freed at last from the thrall of the threshold, walks towards me, his outline softening with every step.

He hefts my bag and I follow him into the house and up the stair-case. Fish smells circle in the still air of the stairwell and rub their fatty gills against the banisters. When my porter turns the light on in my room, I see that he is as black as ebony, a perfect curio, with his heavy-lidded eyes and petulant lips.

I introduce myself. He doffs his name: Pietro.

This Pietro pockets the cowries and annas and pieces of eight that I trawl from my pocket without a glance or a word and leaves, shutting the door behind him.

Down by the sea,
Where romance came to me,
like a rosebud carved out of a marbled radish floating in a finger-bowl of lemony water, I dined in style, alone, it being out of season, in my velvet dinner-jacket, in the cavernous depths of the Ristorante la Grotta Azzurra, on a *frittura di pesce*, consisting mainly of shrimps and fillets of a fish called by the locals *red roman*, all soused in olive oil from the mainland groves and tasting of the deep. The fry was served on a bed of rice spilled from a cornucopia of red cabbage leaves and nuggeted with knobs of butter, garnished with sprigs of parsley and curly kale. First square meal in weeks and it hit the spot.

Discussed the decor with the waiter, one Gianni, according to the plastic sea shell pinned to the breast of his toga. (The soothing effect of the robe was spoilt, I thought, by a bloody conic section of fez with a tassel like a burst aorta.) Reassured to hear from him that the nets billowing from the ceiling had been used in former times to haul the so-called red romans and other delicacies from the Bay of Naples, and that every last Chianti bottle that hung gasping there had been drained at these very tables. **La lista di vini, per favore.** ~ The wine list, please. I myself chose a Lacrima Christi grown on the slopes of Vesuvius to kindle a fire in my belly, and a cassata to douse.

Halfway through dessert sirens howled, the ship's lanterns which served as lights blinked off, and neon rods tumesced in the gloom above the nets. Gianni appeared in a swirl of toga, flourishing the bill like a search warrant. In the sudden glare I saw that he was in fact a mulatto.

"What's the hurry?" I asked. "Where's the fire? **Cosa pensi, Gianni?** ~ What do you think, Jack?"

"*Zitto!*" He waved the haemorrhaging fez. "Goddam yankee! Your time is finish."

I dropped my Mastercard in his fez and he swept out. I was still rummaging in the guidebook for pointed questions to winkle out the meaning of this unseemly haste, when he returned with the slip, which I had to sign, and in another glaring moment was gone.

For a while I gazed into the open mouths of the bottles overhead and waited for the return of Gianni, but as time went by that seemed increasingly unlikely. The useful phrase I had fuddled from the stream of consciousness – **Cosa significa ciò?** ~ What is the meaning of this? – gaped and drifted back into the shallows.

I tried to find my way to the reception desk, but could not. I was eager to see again the men's room, with its cut-glass atomizers of eau-de-Cologne and porcelain jars of green hair-oil, to read again the graffito on the door of the third cubicle from the left: THE PENIS MIGHTIER THAN THE SWORD, to view the tropical fish in their football jerseys, to rifle the treasure chest full of after-dinner mints, and to milk the espresso machine of firelit copper. Nothing doing. Place was empty. Let myself out through a side door, conveniently marked USCITA, into an alley paved with grimy flagstones. Rubbish bins like broken Corinthian columns ankle-deep in their own solemn rubble lurked in the corners. Had to walk off my dinner on the waterfront, where there were boys sniftering fragrant cigarette smoke in their palms, young men reeking of bravado as acetous as aftershave, and old men with mothballs in the secret pockets of their overcoats to mint the funk of mortality. Pissed into the Bay of Naples from the foot of the dog-leg pier of Marina Grande, and watched the lights dance in the foam.

Tossed and turned, hauled out of sleep by lust like an angle through the flesh of the mind's eye, cast ashore on the low-maintenance linoleum of the landing, spilled into the toilet, unbattened the hatch, upped periscope, clung to the jaundiced enamel for a bout of volcanic spewing, until my bilge was emptied out, flat as the silver bladder from a Cellarcask claret. Becalmed suddenly, with my sea legs folded under me, focused on the manufacturer's name traced in letters as delicate as veins in the throat of the bowl: SHANKS. Has my skinny digestive tract grown so unused to landlubberly food?

Picturing the scene,
And what might have been,
I lay in bed with my heavy head primed and lolling in the catapult of my hands, until the manservant Pietro knocked and entered with bucket and spade. His sour face told me that my eruption of the night before had already been remarked and, indeed, he sniffed around in the four corners of the bedroom and looked relieved that they had escaped my attentions.

I tried to discuss my itinerary with him – shopping for souvenirs (better to get that over and done with), lunch and writing postcards at a cafe in the Piazza Umberto (ditto for postcards), the Blue Grotto in the afternoon. Would there be time for the other grottoes too, I wanted to know. "The lovers of marine grottoes will do well not to confine their visits to the Blue Grotto," according to my guide-book. "There are others, just as beautiful and not so sought after, that the island boatmen know about and enjoy showing to those who are capable of appreciating them... He who has not 'dreamed in the grotto where the mermaid bathes,' as Gérard de Nerval said – whether it be the Red Grotto, with its porphyry reflections, the Green Grotto, resembling an enormous liquid emerald, the Yellow Grotto, all of gold and topaz, the Pink Grotto, the colour of coral and flowers, the White Grotto, even more secret and mysterious – does not know the major spells of Capri." I strung together a couple of very inventive improvisations from the list of useful phrases to convey the gist of this to Pietro, addressing him amiably as **Facchino Mio** ~ Porter Mine, but he refused to be drawn. Instead he took some coins from the bedside table and performed an elaborate mime with them, which I misinterpreted at first as a request for a tip, but finally understood as a warning against pickpockets.

I found it hard to focus on his performance, being constantly distracted by the pads of gnarled leather which he wore strapped to his knees, the likes of which I had come across only once before in my travels – on the gold-fields of the Witwatersrand – and which gave his robust figure an air of intolerable servility.

I rummaged in my list and found: "**È un piccolo albergo eccellente, tranquillo e pulito.** ~ It is an excellent little hotel, clean and quiet. **Vorrei delle cartoline illustrate.** ~ I want some picture postcards." But he had already sneaked away.

I had to find my own way then to the Via delle Botteghe. My

guidebook renders this as The Shops Street. No ring to that at all. I would have said: The Street of Shops, by analogy with La Rue des Boutiques and Strasse der Kaufladen, also given, which show some respect for the Italian. The Street of Shops seems to be the centre of attraction here. The most common item of merchandise is the straw basket shaped like a toadstool hung in clusters from the fascias, closely followed by the T-shirt with a motto safety-pinned to wooden trellis-work. I picked up a basket and a couple of T-shirts that say "My master went to the Beautiful Isle of Capri and all I got was this lousy T-shirt." Also a wineskin with the Castello di Barbarossa painted on it. The shopkeeper wouldn't take my dinars, but he fawned over the krugerrand which I fished from my shoe. Then the little money-grubber gummed it in his cheek and stuck it on his forehead, right between the eyes. My change, which I bore away in the basket, included dollars, pounds and other sensible currencies, but also a mass of coins and banknotes I did not recognize at all. Some of the coppers were square, and others were round but had holes through them.

To the Piazza Umberto for lunch, a pizza I imagined, a Napolitano of course (cheese, tomatoes, olives, anchovies). But the smell of fish in the air turned my stomach, so I ordered espresso instead and sat back to observe. The coffee hadn't even come yet when some fracas brewed up over a backgammon board at a table in the corner. Couldn't tell what it was all about, language too strong for the guidebook no doubt, just a flurry of men flinging up their palms and striking their thighs with the hairy backs of their hands. A man I took to be the manager of the cafe went over, but instead of restoring order, as I anticipated, produced a pistol as slick as liquorice and shot one of the players dead. Three thuds, like a monk beating a carpet, tango time. More gesticulating. Then two men picked up the leaking corpse and carried it inside. The manager, if that's what he was, chewed the silencer off the end of the barrel, pocketed the pistol, strolled away across the square, took a flight of stairs one at a time and disappeared down an alley.

I was alarmed. No one else blinked. They just kept their bruised Neapolitan eyelids drooped over the windows of their souls like weather-beaten awnings.

When the waiter arrived I fired off a salvo of useful phrases, like persistent echoes – "**Si porti soccorso, subito!** ~ Bring help, immediately! **Chiami un medico!** ~ Call a doctor! **Ho male al petto.** ~ I have a pain in my chest. **Non mi piace vivere pericolosamente.** ~ I don't like to live dangerously. **Prepotenti!** ~ Tyrants! **Birboni!** ~ Rascals! **Non voglio vedere più, sono stanco** ~ I don't want to see any more, I'm tired. **Ha un dizionario italiano-inglese?** ~ Have you an English-Italian dictionary? **Cameriere, il conto!** ~ Waiter, the bill!"

But he just grinned and said, "*Cinema! Cinema!*" He kept boggling his eyes and revolving his fist next to his head, which I took to mean that he thought I was mad. Then I realized he was representing a camera. Can't say I noticed any cameras rolling during the murder. When in Rome is all very well, but I wish I could speak the language.

But it's in vain that I'm yearning,
especially now that I've muddled my brain with a bottle of plonk de blanc on the terrace at the Ristorante la Grotta Azzurra, where I repaired to settle my empty stomach after the killing in the piazza. Gianni – I think it is he – brings me a ballast of olives and grissini. I feel safe there in the fog. But I can't find my way home. All the streets look the same. All the houses look the same. They all have the same little outdoor pizza-ovens and braai-spots, the same myopic judases in the front doors, the same flagged porches and loggias overhung by the same personalized bougainvilleas. I had hoped that each little dwelling would have a character all its own, but you can't have everything, I suppose. In the end I have to bray like a donkey to attract attention – and it works. Pietro comes out in his birthday suit to find me, and takes me under the elbow familiarly, as if I am his venerable grandfather. This suffices as far as the foot of the stairs, where less respectful measures become imperative and he up-ends me in a fireman's lift. As we mount the stairs I try to get to the bottom of this inexplicable sameness of things, but he says nothing. I have a feeling though that he understands English, and simply pretends not

to, in order to avoid complications. I notice, from my upside-down position, that he is wearing the knee-pads. I wish I could confront him about it. He deposits me on my bed and withdraws quietly.

Somewhat sobered, I turn to the salutary history of the Grotta Oscura recorded in my guidebook and it sends me to sleep with a tear on my cheek: this grotto, more beautiful by far than the blue one, was engulfed quite suddenly one day in 1808 by a rockslide, which also carried away two donkeys grazing overhead and a stout Martello tower. "Fate changed it all," the guidebook says, "with a capricious roll of her hips." Then my mind reels again, and the words avalanche down the page and seal off the magnificent past, rendering it permanently closed on account of the weather.

Fate changed it all,
And I'm left to recall
the taciturnity of servants and the prolixity of guidebooks as I eat my breakfast. Today the Grotta Azzurra would seem like second best, so I bend my steps towards the Parco Augusto instead. Flanked by two marble lions I look down on the Faraglione Rocks. These lions are plump fellows, with manes as smooth and fat as plaited mozzarella, crouching like bulldogs on a leash. Nothing like lions at all, really. The beast on a box of Lion matches bears more resemblance to the real thing. A passing stranger pats one of the pets on the rump and

says, "Good boy," in perfect English. I try to strike up a conversation, but he just points to his ear and hurries off.

I find a bench under a walnut tree and do a bit of reading on the area. I must start planning ahead. Tiberius's Villa Jovis is a must, the guidebook says. "You will climb, if you are stout-hearted enough, the old stone steps to the Villa of Jupiter, where Tiberius frolicked with his little fish – or so they say." Then there's a statue of the poet Tasso in the piazza at Sorrento it might be interesting to view. He had a house on this coast too, I'm told, but it fell into the sea. Things keep collapsing around here. The whole region must be geologically unstable. The house of Tasso's sister Cornelia is still standing, but I can't see what good that would be.

Then voices greased by the sea's long windpipe probe beneath my skin, insinuate themselves and screw up the tourniquet between hand and eye.

I look high and low, but of course I cannot find the source.

'Twas on the Isle of Capri that I found her,
Beneath the shade of an old walnut tree,
Oh! I can still see the flowers blooming round her,
Where we met on the Isle of Capri,
I sang as I tramped home all alone in the dusk, in the dark.

Soft Italian eyes,
Dark as midnight skies,
the tourguide-cum-boatman had, and a wispy black moustache that he tried to starch with saltwater drawn up in his hand, just to pass the time of day, as we queued at the entrance to the Blue Grotto. **"Desiderei una guida che parla inglese.** ~ I should like a guide who speaks English." *"Che? Che?"* A score of boats captained by a spectrum of quadroons and octoroons bobbed in the calm under the cliffs. The boats bearing parties rafted along in twos or threes, grapnelled together by loud talk and barbed laughter, whereas the singletons like me sat in the bows in attitudes of stiff repose, signalling their ease with solitude by the smoke from their pipes, dangling their hands in the water, humming an air, while the oarsmen plied the furry tongues of the waves with their salt-bleached spatulas.

"**Desidero un rimedio contra il mal d'aria.** ~ I want a remedy against seasickness."

There was something palpably ridiculous about queuing in rowboats and it curdled my stomach. The awestruck expressions on the faces of the initiates as they issued from the arch in the cliff-face back into the light of day I found cumulatively pathetic and by the time I reached the front of the queue and was propelled into the grotto – *Olà!* – I had resolved not to look. There was a principle involved, a principle of resistance. I kept my eyes screwed shut, although I tilted my head from side to side and oohed and aahed as the guide droned on behind me through his moustache, *magnifico* this and *bellissimo* that, and dabbled me in circles.

In the end his babbling exasperated me so, that in a moment of spite, without even opening my eyes, I took my guidebook with its list of useful phrases from my pocket and committed it to the dark water. I imagine that it sank like a stone.

When my pilot thrust me back into the outside world the regulation five minutes later I had fixed upon my face a look so utterly dull, like the death-mask of a man who died of boredom, say, that the sightseers peering avidly over the bows of the waiting craft fell back in fright into bilge-water.

So I have done the Grotta Azzurra, though I honestly cannot say I have seen it; whereas I have seen the Grotta Oscura, though no human has drawn breath in it for nearly two hundred years.

By the time we bumped against the landing-stage at Blue Grotto Tours I had developed a healthy antipathy for my mustachioed friend. Tipped him a brass farthing and a plugged nickel, damned him, left.

Strolling back to my lodgings in Marina Grande, lost in thought, I became aware that a car was idling along beside me. It was the first motor vehicle I had seen since my arrival. Shadowy figures sat motionless behind the smoked glass windows, men I would say, from the hunch of shoulder and neck. I stopped. The driver's window slid smoothly down and a monkey-suited arm tossed out a ball of paper. While I stooped to retrieve it from the gutter, the car drew slowly away and turned down a side-street.

I sat down on a bench and spread the crumpled sheet flat on my knee. I had high hopes of finding some intriguing message in Italian, and was already regretting the impulse that had cost me my guide-book – but the note was in English.

Reconstructing the episode afterwards, it struck me forcibly that the car was a Ford *Capri*. Can't help thinking that it means something.

Sleeping or waking they haunt me,
the shadowy men, eyeless behind their dark glasses. I dream that they kill me. I dream that they are the men who do all of the killing, everywhere. They killed the backgammon player in the Piazza Umberto. They slew the stone lions in the Parco Augusto with the jawbone of a quagga. They pushed Tasso's house into the sea because they thought he was asleep inside it, dreaming.

Their magic thrill
Holds a spell on me still
as I return to the piazza to seek out my waiter, the cameraman. I find him easily enough, and he remembers me too. In the burnished skin

of his face the eye seen in profile is as dark and luscious as a Sorrento sloe. He informs me with a syrupy wink that his name is Tiberio. Not Tiberius, please.

Should I give him my name? It seems the obvious riposte, yet I decide against it, and silently hand him the assassins' note, now neatly folded into a cocked hat. Instead of opening the note as I anticipate he extracts a pen from the ring-binding of the menu and prints his name on the paper lining: Tiberio, and then a three-digit telephone number.

This is tiresome.

Then Tiberio presents me with a wine bottle wrapped up in linen. The usual Lacrima Christi. The swaddling-clothes smell of dishwater. Something prods me through the grey folds. I accept it: his ballpoint pen. He winks again, waves the napkin with a magician's flourish and sits down at the chair opposite to uncork the wine. He clamps the bottle between his knees and drives the corkscrew into it.

I peep at the pen under the edge of the tablecloth: it is an ordinary BIC, a hexagonal yellow plastic tube with a coppery cone sticking out of one end and a red plastic plug in the other. I glance at Tiberio's handwriting to confirm that the ink is red. It is. In the middle of the shaft, midway between warhead and tampion, is a little hole, a fistula that a pinhead could seal, of indeterminate purpose.

Tiberio has broken the cork in half. He speaks to me in sign language: makes a hoop of the index finger and thumb of his left hand and thrusts the middle finger of his right hand into it. He means to push the broken cork into the bottle. I hand him the pen, it does the trick.

The wine has bits of cork floating in it, but I grit my teeth and decide not to let it bother me.

Tiberio hands me the pen again. What is the significance of these multiple exchanges, I ask myself, as he balances the tray on the peduncle of his left hand, loads it swiftly with glasses holding melting ice-cubes, mangled paper umbrellas and the dregs of bloody sunsets, and exits towards the kitchen. First he gives me the pen, then he reclaims it, then he gives it back again. Does he mean me to have it? Whose pen is it anyway? Is it really his to dispose of or does it belong to the establishment?

I consider these questions at length while I quaff the corky wine. Does it taste of ink or is it my imagination?

When I want to pay the bill a yen spills from my hands, and in retrieving it I make a discovery that drives the pen from my thoughts altogether. The old cobblestones of the piazza are not stones at all, but solid concrete embossed with a labyrinthine design to make it resemble individual cobbles. By hand signals I am able to convey my astonishment to Tiberio. In reply he takes me by the arm and leads me to a corner of the square, tactfully skirting the ketchupy bloodstains from the shooting, shifts aside a wrought-iron table and shows me a metal plaque embedded there: BOSS-CRETE, PO BOX 9372, Alberton 1450. Is this a clue? Another five-letter island beginning with a "C"?

I find my room – which I must remember to describe in more detail – ransacked when I get back, and me in no condition to cope with another mystery. Feathers all over the place, you'd think someone had been plucking chickens. By chance a chicken is roasting in Vincenzo's oven downstairs, and the aroma of crisp skin basted in lemon juice with garlic and a hint of oregano floats up to make my mouth water.

In the privacy of my hunger I examine the pen closely. It is sticky and smells tipsy. A BIC, as I've said, an Orange Fine Point. The trade name is printed on it. In front of the name, in a frame shaped like a TV set, the letters S, A, B and S are arranged like points of the compass around a lozenge. I recognize the symbol from my travels: the stamp of approval of the South African Bureau of Standards.

After the name, another symbol: a person armed with a pen. I recognize him too. Although he has no primary sexual characteristics, I feel sure this little person is a man, a dragoman, a logoman, with his pen slung over his shoulder like a bazooka. A foot soldier bearing a gigantic pen, tattooed on the plastic skin of an even mightier pen, which I in turn hold in my hand. I extract the plastic plug from the end of the pen with my teeth: it looks like a bullet, but it tastes of ink. I suck the air out of its hollow point so that it sticks to the tip of my tongue.

Can I speak with the bullet stuck to my tongue? Yes I can. I go onto the landing and call down into the stairwell for Pietro to rise and restore order. I miss my guidebook more than ever. The bullet dances on the tip of my tongue and rattles against my teeth.

BIC. A coded message no doubt. What on earth could it mean?

In the middle of the night I awake with an acronym speeding to the surface of my mind like a cork popped on the seabed. BIC: Beautiful Isle of Capri.

Now all the pieces should fall into place; but they lightly resist the demands of gravity.

Tho' I know for me
This love may not be
are strange terms in which to couch a death-threat, I thought, studying the note yet again as I caught my breath in the shade of a blue-gum tree on the haul up to the Villa Jovis. Then I folded the note precisely to frame the bloody echo of an infamous name. The red letters and double-jointed digits of Tiberio's name and number had been smudged by my sweaty palms. I put the note away, and guzzled the mentholated air.

From the picturesque ruins of the villa I made an unpleasant discovery: I am not on an island at all, but in a walled city. The ocean rubs its belly against our northern shore, where the Marina Grande sprawls, suckling a litter of yachts, dories and rubber dinghies, among them the redoubtable *West Wind*. In every other direction the city is encompassed by high walls, and beyond them are rolling hills covered with seas of sugar cane as far as the eye can see. It is easy to imagine how a misunderstanding might have arisen, when swells roll through the cane and spend themselves against our walls. These walls are crenellated, as thick as a donkey, topped with broken glass embedded in cement, superseded in places by specially manufactured and easy to install strips of metal spikes, supplanted in turn by staves of electrified wire upon which a musical death might be arranged.

To the east and west our walls seem to run right into the sea, jaywalking across streets and beaches and plunging directly into the water.

You would think, to look at it, that this is not the Isle of Capri at all, but a time-share resort in some subtropical holiday destination; or a maximum-security retirement village in a province ravaged by civil war. Somehow such possibilities have eluded me until now. This failing has implications for these eyewitness accounts of mine, these reports from abroad.

Why does a sweet voice still taunt me
as I wend my way home, bearing on my shoulders a head stuffed
with second thoughts.

On a path near the Street of Shops I am accosted by bandits armed
with cowhide shields, wooden spears and canvas bags emblazoned
with the names of banks and building societies. They threaten to cut
my heart out chop-chop unless I surrender to them everything of
value, which I do. It comes down to the BIC pen and the ransom note
with Tiberio's name and number on it, which items I was keeping for
sentimental reasons; some chicken feathers; a coaster from the cafe
in the Piazza Umberto; the last of the zlotys; and a Mastercard slip
from the Ristorante, which I'd kept for tax purposes. The bandits
hold open the hungry mouths of the bags and swallow everything.

They're disappointed with their haul. They insist on taking all my
clothes, and we almost come to blows over the velskoene. In the end
they let me keep my shoes. In this lucky way I also get to keep my
Mastercard, which is sitting snugly against the instep of my left foot.

She was as sweet as a rose at the dawning,
But somehow Fate hadn't meant her for me,
And though I sail'd with the tide in the morning,
Still my heart's on the Isle of Capri,

I sang as I tramped home all alone and footsore, covering my naked-
ness with a loincloth of eucalyptus leaves, in the dusk, in the dawn.

Pietro was outraged. He summoned Vincenzo, whom I hadn't
seen since the night of my arrival, ages ago, so that he could give me
a dressing down in my own language. They say it's all my own fault,
I should have been more careful.

Summertime was nearly over,
Blue Italian sky above
the Campanile, from which it had become so fashionable to fling
oneself in recent years that a permanent guard had to be mounted at
the little door, the diners and coffee-drinkers at the cafe having not
unnaturally wearied of the spectacle and complained to the management. I couldn't sit still. I was absolutely broiling in my dinner-jacket,
feeling like a fish out of water and attracting too much attention.
The eyes of the onlookers told me that they thought I was a madman
dressed up for my own funeral, overdressed in fact, probably just
casing the Campanile to plan my plummet. Tiberio was nowhere to
be seen; his locum was a blond Adonis called Barend, but before he'd
brought the stiff whisky I'd ordered, I made tracks.

In a street west of the piazza, which I would have sworn I had
traversed without hindrance a few days before, I came to the wall
I'd spotted from the Villa Jovis, and decided to follow it down to the

sea. A no-man's-land two metres wide had been carved out of the town beside the wall, and it was in this space that I walked, stepping over bricks and potholes, crunching through drifts of broken glass, marvelling at the innards of buildings laid bare in cross-section, the heartwood of dissected arbours and split loggias. I came to a quadrangle surrounded by cloisters, cleaved open to the outside world as grimly as a carcass, and a little further crossed a road onto a pebbled beach. The wall extended out into the water, with such a gentle declivity that it finally slid beneath the surface a hundred metres or more from land. There at the vanishing-point some people were gathered with the sea swirling around their ankles.

At the water's edge a wooden ladder rested against the wall and I used it to mount to the top. A wavy line of beige sand stretched away into the distance, the border between a sea of greenery and an ocean of aquamarine. Beneath the roar of the surf the drowned guidebook burbled away about the intense and multiform harmonies of sea and sky, a ruined civilization, a world outside time.

A butcher's dozen of men wearing I♥CAPRI T-shirts and clutching beaded spears twelve inches long were lined up on the wall with their backs to the water. I had seen the T-shirts and the spears on sale in the Street of Shops, prices slashed, everything must go, and I concluded that these men were tourists, and very probably Zulus. A second row of men, a reciprocal team of locals, Italians to a man, conceivably soccer players, faced the Zulus at arm's length, which was the greatest distance the wall allowed. The Zulus kept glancing over their shoulders into the deep water at their backs, and I looked too and saw my old friend from Blue Grotto Tours bobbing there in his row-boat.

As I drew closer the Zulus began to sing. I recognized the song at once: "Arrivederci Roma." One of my favourites. Their voices were magnificent, a regal drapery of sound, like bolts of maroon velvet and purple satin tumbled down from under thatched eaves and spilling out swaths over ochre walls. But their phrasing was disgraceful. They couldn't get their tongues around the r's at all.

Allibadezi Loma, they carolled, *Goebaai, Goebaai, Goebaai.*

This made the Italians irritable. They threw up their hands and eyebrows and slapped their foreheads. The Zulus sang on heartily. When they got to

I'm sorry I must leave you

the Italians reached out as one man and pushed them into the sea.

Apparently none of the Zulus could swim. My friend from Blue Grotto Tours rowed closer and beat the drowning men with his paddle, battering their hands to pulp against the gunwales, shoving them under like dirty laundry, bundles of overalls and limp gloves, while the men on the wall called out encouragement and advice.

The sea boiled up into a red froth of shibboleths.

I said, "Lady I'm a rover,
Can you spare a sweet word of love?"
an old geezer was singing on the Terrazza della Funicolare, and
going through the languid motions of a tango. Someone should tell
him it takes two.

I myself was reduced to beggary. Say, mister, can you please spare
me a dollar? Coins, buttons, bottle-tops, washers, medals, pebbles,
curtain-rings and peppermints rattled into the panama.

When I had built up a little stake, Pietro was kind enough to ferry
my souvenirs and provisions down to the Marina in the basket of his
bicycle – I think they're all pleased to be seeing the back of me, actually. I toted my duffel bag myself. Time to cruise pleasurably away,
to greener waters.

Men without substance, you may have your Island and do there what
you please. I personally shall carry your memory in my heart and in
a charming little folder of picture postcards called Ricordo di Capri
(32 Vedute) with the Blue Grotto on its cover, which Vincenzo has
given me as a going-away present, accompanied by a stern injunction
to keep in touch.

I sail for the mainland tomorrow. Across the bay I expect to find
not Bloubergstrand or Umgababa, but Sorrento. I have faith. I hope
to visit the statue of Tasso, to pay my respects. Also the spot where his

house used to stand. I imagine some scar on the landscape might still be visible, perhaps some rubble in a gully will yield up a memento, if only a pebble shaped like an eye to store in the cheek, to ward off thirst.

Then, all going well, it's onwards, onwards to the Galli rocks, if some well-disposed local will give me directions, where I hope the Sirens will sing for me an inconsequential love-song, worth more than a thousand learned disquisitions on the subject, as I turn the *West Wind*'s head to open water:

She whisper'd softly, "It's best not to linger,"
And then as I kissed her hand I could see,
She wore a plain golden ring on her finger,
'Twas goodbye to the Isle of Capri.

"Kidnapped"

This notice was in the *Star* today, in the People in Crisis column, between the Johannesburg Parent and Child Counselling Centre (484-1734) and Lifeline (728-1347). It's easy to imagine how it landed up there: counselling services are listed in the entertainment section, on the same page as the theatre and titbits from the world of books.

KIDNAPPED SHORT STORY COMPETITION —
To celebrate the centenary of the death of Robert Louis Stevenson, one of Scotland's best-loved storytellers, the David Thomas Charitable Trust is offering £1 000 in prize money in a unique short story competition. To enter you must write a story with the title "Kidnapped," which is, of course, the title of the novel Stevenson published in 1886. Write to Competition Department (Kidnapped), DT Charitable Trust, c/o Writers News Limited, PO Box 4, Nairn IV12 4HU, Scotland for competition rules and entry forms.

I'm opposed to literary competitions on principle, especially when they require one to play the bespoke author and make the goods to measure. But it's almost a shame to scruple when I have a soft spot for old RLS and a special affinity for his work, if I say so myself.

I dreamt last night that Louis and I were camped out in the Magaliesberg ("Louis" is familiar, but then we were comrades in my dream, as close as shipmates). After a day's march over the veld I was nodding off with a mug of chocolate in my hand, while he was reading by firelight, Hazlitt's "On Going a Journey."

"This is so good," he remarked suddenly, as if to himself, "that a tax should be levied on everyone who hasn't read it."

The observation made him smile, and he wrote it down in his notebook. Then he put the notebook and Hazlitt away in a pocket of his velvet jacket, which he folded into a pillow, crept into his sleeping-sack and lay down curled to the fire. In a minute he was asleep.

He will say too, I speculated, when he comes to write about the subject, that a walking tour, to be properly enjoyed, must be gone upon alone. We'd argued about it earlier, as we clambered out of Kiepersol Kloof, and every point I made on the side of companionship seemed only to support his claims for the joys of silence and surrender to the world around.

The face sticking out of the sheepskin was pale as paper, its gaunt angles hardly softened by sleep. Wrapping myself in my plaid, I stepped away from the fire and looked down into the valley, where I could see lights in the windows of the self-catering chalets at the Utopia Holiday Resort. And with that I felt myself dispersed like a wisp of smoke, like a figment of his imagination.

Strangely enough, the dream left me feeling tenderly protective of RLS and his legacy. I decided to write off for an entry form. Surely it can't harm.

The possibilities are endless. I could write something about Stevenson writing *Kidnapped*. Or I could dramatize an incident from his youth which casts an interesting light on the book; a glance at the biographies suggests that his visit to Earraid in 1870, when his father was building the Dhu Heartach lighthouse, is the obvious choice. He wrote about it himself in "Memoirs of an Islet," which would make my task easier. But perhaps I should leave the author in peace and concentrate on the work. Say: someone is reading *Kidnapped*. A political prisoner? A prison warder? An assassin in a dentist's waiting room? Or: a country boy takes the book out of the travelling library and sees himself reflected there. Where should I set my story, or rather my tale? In the Highlands or on the Highveld? When? If I want Stevenson himself to show his face, and not just in dreams, the period defines itself neatly. But if the book is my protagonist, I have more than a century to play with.

On the other hand, I could write a story called "Kidnapped" that has nothing whatsoever to do with Stevenson or his book. Or with kidnapping, for the matter of that.

In any case, there's no point in starting until I've seen the rules, which might set limits to my creative licence. I should use this time to reread the book. I remember that David Balfour was carried off on the *Covenant* and afterwards shipwrecked – but all that fuss about Jacobites and the Campbells … I suppose the DT Charitable Trust plumped for *Kidnapped* because Stevenson himself thought it his best book, but I would have preferred *Treasure Island* or *Dr Jekyll and Mr Hyde*. I wonder who they are exactly, these charitable trustees? It doesn't bode well that they have an entire department devoted to competitions.

Idea: Louis and Fanny Stevenson are living in a boarding-house in Bournemouth. It is February 1885. Until recently Louis has been working on an adventure story called "The Great North Road," but now he has given it up. The following month, when he and Fanny move to Skerryvore, their new home in the town, he will begin to write *Kidnapped*. A little romance might cling like ivy to the Stevensons' new house, which has fruit trees in the garden and a model of the Skerryvore lighthouse at the door; but the boarding-house is emblematically dingy. Louis is all but bedridden. When he looks back on this time he remembers living "like a weevil in a biscuit." The Great North Road! He says in "A Gossip on Romance" that the very words sound in his ear like poetry. Why does he cast the story aside then? The household bills need paying, we are told. But there must be more to it than that. How can he be sure that *Kidnapped* will fill the coffers? What does the sea story satisfy that the landfast adventure cannot?

My story is set in the interval between "The Great North Road" and *Kidnapped*. The scene shifts between Dorset and the Highlands, between the author and his hero, as half-formed fragments of the new book, which has been brewing in his mind for ten years or more, come to him in fevered dreams. Stevenson is not quite himself, and neither yet is David Balfour. Scotland I think I can manage, with the help of Fodor and back numbers of *The Scots Magazine*. As for Bournemouth, it will be merely rumoured, a smudge behind grimy panes.

I have begun to read *Kidnapped*. To tell the truth, it was the Introduction to the book that gave me the idea for the Bournemouth story. I am keeping a list of aromatic phrases, not just the obvious "muckle" and "mair" and "wouldnae," but things like "rowans in the kirkyard" and "prodigious wild and dreadful prospects" and "bogs and hags and peaty pools," which one can toss into the brew like fistfuls of peppercorns.

And another list of syntactical principles. Why should "said I" have been put to rout by "I said" in English prose? What could such a reversal represent if not egotism?

"And here I must explain," Stevenson writes at the beginning of Chapter XII, "and the reader would do well to look at a map."

I took his advice, and mair's the peety.

At first it was pleasant enough, identifying Little Minch and the Isle of Tiree and the Sound of Mull. I put my finger on the spot where the *Covenant* lay becalmed on the morning after the battle of the roundhouse, in which David and Alan Breck bested their attackers. Then my eye began to wander. I called in at the Isles of Muck and Eigg and Rhum and Canna, and then beat hastily back to the mainland. I still hadn't got my bearings. I headed inland and meandered down the Tweed. There was quite a romance to the place-names. My hero – I mean Proto-Balfour, the boy Stevenson sends out from his sickbed in Bournemouth – could pass this way on his travels. My eye picked out a route for him: Dundee, Blairgowrie, the Forest of Atholl. It was easy going.

But then a peculiar sensation came over me; for a terrifying moment I recalled the apoplexy that carried RLS off in the end. I was choking. There was something too rich in the nomenclature, something that made it stick in the craw like drammach (shall we say): Pitlochry, Strath Spey, Cromarty, Dornoch, Lairg, Tongue, John o' Groats. As for the topography, it was improbably intricate, like crumbling parchment. Who could memorize the shape of such a country?

The place rose up before me, behind a mist of words, the familiar mixed in with the strange, brae and burn, crag and moor, meadow and brake, heathery hill and mossy dale, ragged grey heath and new-mown field as tidy as tartan. Every scrap of it trodden upon and named, and a net of footpaths and lanes and high roads and low roads flung over for good measure. What lives were lived on the face of this earth, and who could begin to comprehend their outlines?

It came in on me that it would be effrontery to write a story about the other side of the world, the other side of time ... it was presumptuous enough to write about the other side of the street. To write anything at all, to make anything up, to set anything down was to act in bad faith. The world was too immense and complicated. A short story! Hoot-toot.

And then Stevenson bobbed up in his velvet jacket and silk tie, with Hazlitt bulging in his breast pocket, and he remonstrated with me, just as he once remonstrated – rather more respectfully, let it be said – with no less a personage than Mr Henry James, for these primitive anxieties about art and reality; and naturally his darts wounded me more deeply, seeing that a century had passed since they were first flung and I ought to have known better, and especially seeing that I am only an aspirant author, with no body of work to shield me, whereas Mr James was padded thickly all over with famous books. I stood in the surf and felt foolish and old-fashioned. Art and reality, said Stevenson, bobbing, are not in competition, you simpleton. Art stands in the same sort of relation to reality as a geometry theorem. And then he cast off the good ship *Romance* and sailed boldly away, tacking expertly to windward and sounding as he went.

Resolving to make the best of my unhappy situation, I prepared to explore the island. And found myself still bent over my atlas, gazing at Loch Ness. I saw a *National Geographic* documentary on the Monster once. And here we have the bonny, bonny banks of Loch Lomond … Lockerbie, upon which an aeroplane fell … Motherwell, whose soccer team was always mentioned on CNN…

When he was writing *Kidnapped,* Stevenson recalled, the characters grew to be so real that they stepped off the page, turned their backs on him and walked away. From then on they made up the story and he just wrote it down, like a stenographer. How I wish that this might happen to me one day.

My nasty experience with the map of Scotland bothered me for weeks. Stevenson wrote that he found it hard to believe there were people who did not care for maps. Well, I found it hard to believe that I was one of those people! On the contrary, I had always thought of myself as a map lover. Then why had looking in the atlas paralysed my creative faculties? Many another author, and RLS pre-eminently, reported that maps inspired them to write. In the end, I reasoned it out for myself as follows.

The whole story of *Treasure Island* grew out of a map of the place, which Stevenson and his stepson invented to amuse themselves. As he gazed at the map, the characters began to appear there, peeping out at him (stepping off the page again!). But this was to be expected, because he had invented the island himself. He made it small enough to be traversed in a day and left it uninhabited (Ben Gunn was marooned there for just three years). It was a country of the imagination.

Kidnapped was written with the aid of maps too, but now the romance was spun out of real places. Propped up in bed at Skerryvore, with the maps scattered around him like another land of counterpane, Stevenson set about planning David Balfour's travels, recalling places he had known as a boy and finding adventures to justify them. This was a country of the memory.

But I proposed neither to invent a place nor to remember one. Perversely, I wished to remember a place I had never been and invent a place that already existed. What path could be more full of pitfalls? The prospect was sure to make one feel ill, especially when confronted with evidence of an irrecoverable, unimaginable world.

To test my theory I opened the atlas again (at Hungary as it happened) and felt dizzy immediately. Bingo.

As an antidote I looked for Nairn, which I had annexed by means of a letter in my own hand, but couldn't find it. I had to look in the Index. It's not where I thought it would be, a penny stonecast from Edinburgh, but up in the sticks, or their heathery equivalent. No wonder the entry form is taking forever to reach me.

It occurs to me that a story set closer to home might be just the ticket (it would certainly obviate the need for maps). These DT chaps in Nairn have cast their net in foreign waters; they must expect to land some strange fish. Then again, kidnapping in all its facets is such a big thing down our way, I'm sure to be at an advantage: we've got dirty tricks, hijacking of vehicles, stealing of children, muti murders, witchhunts, shanghaiing of illegal aliens, to mention just a few. I almost feel spoilt for choice. The political angle might be worth pursuing, something which stresses those elements of *Kidnapped* that chime with our recent history – notably an oppressed, dispossessed population and an exiled leadership.

Idea: A Jim Comes to Jo'burg story, being a South African version of *Kidnapped*, in which each element is an echo of the original. Mid-1980s. Jim, newly orphaned – his father has died unexpectedly of natural causes somewhere in the Midlands – arrives in Egoli to find his Uncle Ebenezer. But Uncle Ebbie is hiding a guilty secret and wants to be rid of the boy. One afternoon he takes him down to the White Horse shebeen, where they meet a taxi-driver called Hosea (the Captain Hoseason of my story). Ebbie strikes a deal with Hosea to pack Jim off to a relative in Lebowa who could do with another pair of hands in the fields. Jim is lured aboard Hosea's taxi, a Toyota Hi-Lux called *Promises, Promises* (too much?) and spirited out of the city on the N1. It's the Easter weekend and the great north road is clogged with pilgrims. In a traffic jam outside Pretoria they are involved in a minor collision with a bakkie. Before they get under way again one of the bakkie's passengers insinuates himself into the taxi. This is Jabulani, the Alan Breck of the story, not a Jacobite but an ANC activist. Jabu is organizing the passage of recruits across the border. He demands that Hosea set him down in a remote corner of the province; Hosea, who has taken the newcomer's dandyish appearance as a sign of wealth – it is in fact a shrewd disguise – in turn demands an exorbitant fare, and they argue. The conflict comes to a head in Naboomspruit, where they stop for petrol. Jim overhears

Hosea and his conspirators among the other passengers making plans to rob Jabu, and alerts him to the danger. They barricade themselves in the restroom and beat off several attacks. A truce is sealed and Hosea accedes to Jabu's demands. Jabu and Jim become firm friends. The older man is grateful to the youngster for his brave stand; he also sees him as a potential recruit. Hosea has never been in this part of the country before and they lose their way. Then, on a rocky back-road the vehicle overturns. Jim is thrown clear of the wreck. And so on.

It is thought clever, Stevenson says sarcastically, to write a novel with no story at all, or at least with a very dull one. This new idea of mine avoids that problem: the master himself has thrown me a storyline. Is there sufficient romance in it though? The plot is a thicket of circumstance, which is to the good, and I suppose I might persuade the occasional reader to identify with the hero. But a few essential ingredients are lacking: where is the clean, open-air adventure, for instance? I could probably build it in later, when Jim and Jabulani are on the run – "the flight in the veld," I'll call it. But is there *romance* to be found where the troops of the counter-insurgency unit pursue their quarry through the wastes of a rural slum? Can a Toyota Hi-Lux demand adventure in the same way as a sailing-ship? Will a Shell Ultracity refreshment plaza do for a roadside inn or a Caltex restroom for a fo'c's'le? I suspect not.

I should look to the past, as Stevenson did.

Idea: My story is set in the mining-camp of Johannesburg, mere months after the discovery of gold. My hero is a young man newly arrived from Scotland (there is just one woman in the whole of *Kidnapped,* and "Kidnapped" must conform). In his pocket he is carrying a precious possession: a first edition of *Kidnapped* (published in July 1886). I haven't quite got the storyline yet – but surely there is scope for romance here. I could fit in an ostler or two, a band of footpads, a stretch of moonlit road and a hurricane-lamp, buried treasure. Possibly even a potato-bogle.

The temporal symmetry appeals too: Stevenson set his *Kidnapped* a century or so before his time, and I shall do the same with mine.

The entry form arrived in this afternoon's post and knocked all my plans agley. I knew I should have waited.

To start with, the envelope contained several annoying enclosures from the chaps in Nairn: advertisements for the International Writers Club and the Writers Book Society – the absence of apostrophes was an added irritation – and enrolment forms from the Home Study Division. They also want me to subscribe to something called *Writers News,* which they say is full of useful tips and inspiring success stories. I'll be damned. The whole competition is an exercise in promoting their products. No doubt, if you don't subscribe to the rag your competition entry will go straight into their waste-paper basket. I shan't give them the pleasure, I thought, and threw their junk mail into my own.

Retrieved it a bit later, and had a closer look at the rules. It seems I might have been overhasty in my judgement. Rule 2 says there will be two classes of entry – those who subscribe to *Writers News* and those who don't – with £500 for the winner in each class. So far so good.

But what about Rule 5: "Entries must be accompanied by the entry fee of £2.50 minimum; £3.50 is the preferred fee while £5 would be welcomed to assist with the work of the DT Charitable Trust." On this scale, I should think £10 would be the mark of a truly generous nature.

And Rule 6, which states that the entries must be between 1 600 and 1 800 words long. Now that's a problem. I'm in an expansive mood. None of the ideas I've come up with so far could be crammed into five pages. I know what it's about too: they're trying to make things easy for the judges.

Then there's Rule 7, read together with Rule 10: entries must be postmarked by 20 January 1995 and the winners will be announced at a ceremony in London in March 1995. Thinking of dates reminded me that RLS died on 3 December 1894 (which means that the centenary of his death falls on Saturday next). Now I had to ask myself how a competition supposedly celebrating the centenary could ignore this date. It scarcely gave me confidence in the chaps in Nairn. If it had been left to me to make the arrangements I would have seen to it that the prize-giving ceremony was actually held on 3 December 1994. That way it might have been quite moving and meaningful. What luck that it fell on a Saturday too, the day most suited to such an occasion.

If I did win, by any chance, I wonder if they'd fly me to London for the ceremony? I'll bet the winners have more economically viable addresses. But I shouldn't even bother myself about it, because, on balance, I think I should forget the whole thing.

Last night (Saturday the 3rd) I organized my own little memorial dinner, the sort of thing I might have writ large for the prizegiving. There was negus with rum and lime-juice to give the flavour of an island night. The main course took its cue from *Travels with a Donkey*. I thought of chocolate and Bologna sausage, which is what Louis ate for dinner in the birch wood near Fouzilhic, and black bread, which was Modestine's share – but I settled instead for a leg of mutton and a tomato salad. I made a mayonnaise – that is what Louis was doing when he was struck down. It sounds macabre, but it went off bitter-sweetly. At exactly ten past eight a solemn toast was drunk in burgundy (given longer notice I might have rustled up some kava) and passages from the works were read. By good fortune, something very like a tropical storm blew up, complete with tantrums of lightning and squalls, and so the proceedings were concluded with the two prayers in time of rain.

What with burgundy, negus and brandy abominable to man, I had a restless night, and it tossed up an idea for a story that I've a good mind to write. It's fairly autobiographical, but no one need know.

Idea: The narrator is an aspirant author. For several months he has been trying, without success, to write a story for the Kidnapped Short Story Competition. In the course of researching his story he has grown to feel very close to RLS, to the point of beginning to affect his mannerisms; he has even grown a Stevensonian moustache. The story is set on the evening of the centenary of Stevenson's death, which the narrator is celebrating in a private ceremony. He is dressed up as the author, in grubby white flannels and a linen shirt; he half imagines, in his cups, that he *is* the author. An idea for a story finally comes to him: Bournemouth, 1886. The evening after Louis finishes the first draft of *Kidnapped*. Fanny has spent the day reading the book and dislikes it so much that Louis throws it into the fire. He vows never to think about it again – and indeed he never does. A story that erases *Kidnapped* from Stevenson's canon would be perfect for the Kidnapped Short Story Competition… The idea tickles our narrator (three sheets in the wind by now and easily amused) and he decides to put it down on paper. He fetches a notebook and writes "Kidnapped" at the top of the first page. No sooner is that done than his excitement dissipates. He stares for a time at the blank page. Then he uncorks a bottle of burgundy, to get the creative juices flowing again, fills a glass, raises it – and is felled by a stroke.

Spent most of December fleshing out this idea. My intention was to have the first draft down by the end of the year, but what with the disruptions of the holidays I only made a start on New Year's Day. To my distress I discovered that my plan for the story was 5 000 words long. I could have gone at it with the blue blade, I suppose, but it seemed a pity to give the idea less space than its due, so I decided to keep it in reserve and work on something else.

I took up my plan for a story set in early Johannesburg again. I'd established an appealing interplay there between past and present, memory and experience, Europe and Africa, fiction and fact, and so on, full of potential. But it seemed more like a novella, the sort of work in which the characters might rise up breathing from the page, or chatter away to one another in perfectly natural English, and after giving it more thought I decided to lay that idea down as well in a dark place and produce a stopgap story for the competition. Funnily enough, the idea I came up with on the spur of the moment seems just right. I can feel it in my bones. What I might call its elegant simplicity will appeal to the judges.

Idea: Kidnapped comes to a rather abrupt end. How many readers must have been left wondering what became of David Balfour in after years. Why not carry his adventures further? The story will take the form of an additional chapter at the end of the book and be called "Kidnapped: Chapter XXXI." It will be exactly 1 800 words long. I haven't decided what happens yet, but there will be nothing to suggest that the chapter wasn't penned by RLS himself. It will be the *Kidnapped* style to a T. (I must dig up my list of phrases and principles, and look again at *St. Ives*, which Quiller-Couch finished after Stevenson's death, to see how it's done.)

My one concern is the timing. The deadline's hardly a fortnight away.

I've been studying the rules again. Rule 10 says that the best entries will be published in *Writing Magazine* (another venture by the same chaps). It also says that each of the winners and each of the six runners-up in each class will receive six commemorative Robert Louis Stevenson £1 notes.

Rule 11 is more provocative: "*Each entrant* will receive a Scottish Robert Louis Stevenson commemorative £1 note. This will be sent in the final week of January 1995" (my emphasis).

What exactly is a Robert Louis Stevenson £1 note? It's explained on the back of the form. Scottish banks are allowed to issue notes of their own design, and the Royal Bank of Scotland has commissioned one with Stevenson on it for the centenary. The form shows a portrait of RLS in blue, in a little oval cameo frame, but printed all over with useful information. This must be the very image that appears on the money.

I wouldn't mind laying my hands on one of those notes, for a keepsake.

I've been struggling to get "Kidnapped: Chapter XXXI" going. I've always been a slow worker, but then I feel that writing a good story is like making a mayonnaise: you have to add the crucial ingredients slowly, drop by drop, being careful not to curdle the whole mixture. Frankly, it's become clear to me that I'm not going to finish by Friday. The prize money doesn't bother me – although I like to think I had as much chance of winning as the next chap – but losing the commemorative note is a blow … I've got just the frame for that note, made of bamboo and raffia. Some friend brought it back from a holiday in the South Seas. I can see old Tusitala gazing out of it from my study wall, as if he were leaning on the verandah of the house at Vailima.

All I have to do is enter. I could count off a thousand words of one of my plans and post them that, and they'd be obliged to send me my quid. I could post them some bits and pieces from the newspaper.

It would hardly be fraudulent either – I'd have to pay £2.50 for the exchange. But somehow it doesn't seem right.

When Louis was a lad of five he and his cousin Robert invented countries for themselves. Bob's was called Nosingtonia; Louis's was Encyclopaedia. He tells us, in "Memoirs of Himself," that they were constantly drawing maps of these lands.

At the same time Louis's Uncle David first quickened his interest in writing by organizing a literary competition for the Stevenson cousins. To enter you had to write a "History of Moses," and the prize was £1.

Phoned the embassy and spoke to what seemed like a very nice Mr Campbell. I thought I'd establish how easy it would be to get hold of one of those Robert Louis Stevenson pounds through the usual foreign exchange channels. Mr Campbell said it shouldn't be too difficult at all. In fact, he kindly offered to secure one for me personally on his next home leave. That would put the middlemen of Nairn up the burn without a paddle.

It turned out that Mr Campbell is a great lover of Stevenson himself. He was fascinated to hear all about the competition and the rules. I even tried out a few of my phrases on him. That set him going too

– of course, it came quite naturally to him, being a Hielandman – and we had a braw old time muckling and mairing one another.

"Afore ye gang awa," I said at one point – we'd been talking whisky and this was a joke – "might ye be so guid as to hearken to my tale?"

"Good heaven, man," said he, "would I turn my back on you in your chief need?"

"Say nae mair," said I, and began to explain my scheme for writing another chapter of *Kidnapped*.

At that he burst out laughing: "It's already been done, laddie, by the author himsel'. And no just a wee bit chapter, but an unco thick book."

Catriona! The sequel to *Kidnapped*! Being memoirs of the further adventures of David Balfour at home and abroad. It came back to me like a thunderclap and took the wind right out of my sails. The fact is that *Catriona* is the one novel by Stevenson I haven't read. There was no point in lying about it.

"Ochone! Never read *Catriona*? A lover of Robert Louis Stevenson, such as yoursel'? Who would have owned it?"

I noticed he said "Lewis" this time instead of "Louie," which is what I'd been saying, but let it pass.

"Fall to then, and be brisk," said he, "or ye'll bauchle it at the first off-go."

"Ag, it's too late," said I.

"It pains me to say it," said he, "but ye're a man of small contrivance."

I would cast all my plans for stories into the fire, if I had a fireplace; building a fire in the garden for that express purpose would be going too far, I suppose. When Fanny criticized the first draft of *Jekyll and Hyde*, Louis threw it into the fire and started over. If he could dispense with thirty thousand words so blithely, I could surely part with five or six. But I hate to think what that manuscript would have fetched today if she had kept it.

At the last, when the vein of stories in his mind burst, Stevenson demanded: "What's that?" As if a stranger had entered. There was no answer. He turned to Fanny and asked, more urgently: "Do I look strange?" And then he fell into a coma, and died.

Give them their due, the chaps in Nairn let me know that the Kidnapped Short Story Competition was officially over. Did I want to subscribe to *Writing Magazine*? If I did, I would be able to read the winning entries. They said the response to the competition had been overwhelming. Stories poured in from lovers of Stevenson's work everywhere. They said it was less a competition than an outpouring of love for one of Scotland's, nay, for one of the world's best-loved storytellers.

There was a list of all the winners, those who had won £506 and those who had won £6 in £1 notes. I saw that a chap from Braamfontein had made it to the finals. I said all along this competition was made for a South African. But I wonder if the blackguard appreciates those commemorative notes?

Well, I subscribed. It can't harm, I thought, I might even pick up some tips. Also, I wanted to read the winning entries. And when I was finished I was sorry I'd bothered. Not a real story among them. Is it any wonder that writers today are no longer loved, that even the best of them are merely admired? They've lost the knack. They are fine fellows, it's true, but they cannot write like Stevenson. You'll get no yarns out of them, just a handful of junk; no living flesh, just skin and bone. Faith, they're not even anatomists – they're resurrection men.

The Firedogs

The registered item waiting for me at the post office was not the cheque from the Receiver I had been expecting but a large parcel wrapped in brown paper. It wouldn't fit through the gap under the glass, and so the clerk opened a hatch between the windows and passed it to me through there. It was heavy, and plastered with rows of postage stamps like clips from a French film. There was a return address, an apartment in the Rue du Sabot, but no name.

At home I went straight to the dresser to fetch the kitchen scissors. There my eye was caught by the headline on the *Sunday Times*, under the cat's milk dish: MEMBERS OF TRUTH COMMISSION ANNOUNCED. I'd read the report the day before and one of the nominees had stayed in my mind – a priest whose hands had been blown off by a parcel bomb. Now I was reminded of him again, and a half-forgotten fear suddenly seized me … the fear of bombs. There should be a word for it.

Once, walking down President Street, it occurred to me that the rubbish bin at the foot of the steps to the City Hall contained a bomb. I resisted the urge to run away, crossed the street calmly, only to find an even more suspicious bin in my path, attached to a signpost at a bus-stop. I turned left into Rissik and saw another bin up ahead, and another beyond that, all ticking with explosive potential. Then I began to run, but inconspicuously, like any businessman hurrying to an appointment, holding my briefcase in my right hand because the explosion would come from that side.

Lydia, my girlfriend at the time, my live-in lover as they're called, had been sympathetic about the bins, but when my anxiety extended to letters and parcels she drew the line: What possible reason could anyone have for blowing you up? You've never been involved in anything in your life.

You never know, I would argue, with bombs floating around in the postal system. They make mistakes. I was the kind of person things happened to – she said so herself – as opposed to the kind who made things happen. I am still that kind of person, nearly ten years later. Nowadays some petty thief in the sorting office would probably blow himself up first, but one couldn't be too careful.

I approached my surprise package from Paris, scissors cocked. How did a parcel bomb work anyway? Would the detonator be rigged to the string? Unlikely. What scared me most was being blinded. Losing a hand would be terrible of course, but with a prosthesis one might regain some sort of grip on the world. Your vision was another matter. I closed my eyes and snipped the string. Gingerly, turning the vital organs away from the force of the blast – not too far, one didn't want to expose that other soft target, the spinal cord – I tore off a thick layer of paper and opened the cardboard box underneath. An object lay mangered in white polystyrene, and I lifted it out and set it upright on the table.

It was a devil, made of cast iron, nine or ten inches tall from fork-tip to cloot. He was a gloomy looking Father of Lies, a trouper in a provincial melodrama, with a dusting of polystyrene straw on his shoulders and two blunt-ended, calfish little horns on his head. He was wielding an enormous toasting-fork in one hand, rather like the one I kept for flipping chops over on the braai. His devil suit – or was it meant to be mortified flesh – fitted him poorly: it was crumpled around the ankles and sagging in the seat of the pants, where the tail curved from an elasticized vent. A length of rope was looped around the wrist of his free hand, and at the other end was a dog, a fluffy, button-nosed hound of hell with its tongue lolling.

I recognized the hand of the sculptor at once. It was perfectly predictable that Lydia would end up leading the artistic life in Paris. And that I would end up sitting here. She had probably left her name off the parcel deliberately, just to upset me. It must have cost her a fortune to mail. I plunged my hand into the polystyrene, searching for a card or a letter, and found instead the devil's identical twin.

Then the penny dropped: they were firedogs. I could see them standing in the flames, shouldering their burden without complaint, like middle-aged brothers in a queue at the post office, and keeping their charred, long-suffering faces straight, while the archangels floated above on the warm air. As for the mongrels, these firedogs had dogs of their own! How literal could you get. And being destined for my hearth, the point was to show how literal *I* was, as if the idea had been mine rather than hers.

She was having a little joke at my expense. But then it was a private joke, just between the two of us, and it was almost touching that she felt the need, after all this time.

The fireplace was one of the reasons Lydia and I took the house. I had seen more beautiful fireplaces in other Johannesburg lounges, ornate constructs of black iron inlaid with Italian tiles in blues or greens as vivid as powder paints, but there was something comfortably homely about this one. The mantelpiece was plain and solid oak. The hearth was deep, wide and thickly crusted with soot, and framed by an arch of red brick, rising on each side from a platform of red tile. It had been built for use and it worked superbly. That first winter we made a fire almost every night.

But there was something missing, as if the fireplace was incomplete. From long nights at the fireside, gazing into the domestic drama of flames, I came to the conclusion that those tiled platforms at each end of the arch needed to be occupied. They were like empty rostra on a stage – the arch hinted at a proscenium – distracting the eye from the real action by their conspicuous emptiness. A kettle or a flat-iron might do the trick; they were nothing more than hobs, I supposed. To test the proposition I put my brandy snifter there to warm one night, but the glass got greasy and black from the smoke. Electricity seems to have estranged us from fire once and for all. No, it needed something sculptural. We were an arty family after all, on Lydia's side.

I suggested figures, the keepers of the fire, stokers or smiths, one on either side like household gods.

You're so literal, Lydia said. She said that kind of thing affectionately then, as if there was something endearing in a literal cast of mind. According to her, it wasn't the platforms that needed to be filled, but the curve of the arch that should be echoed, an arc of action to link the one side with the other, some "conceptual leap" over the flames, so to speak. She would think of something.

I thought I saw what she was getting at. I said I would defer to her artistic judgement.

In the meantime, and to show that my imaginative effort had not gone unnoticed, she set upon the platforms two sullen stone heads which she had picked up in some craft shop, puny Easter Islanders to stand in for the keepers of the fire, and not exactly Promethean either. The heads did their job well enough until the night of the housewarming, which it took us a year to get round to, when one of the friends, the poetic Justin as it happened, tossing the dregs of his wine into the coals in an attempt at a Russian gesture, splashed the one on the left. Whereupon it "burst asunder," as he himself put it when he had recovered his composure, like a graven image struck by a bolt from above. Someone might have been hurt, but it was worth the risk to see their faces. It's remarkable how sensitive artistic people are about their physical safety (to be honest, I nearly jumped out of my skin myself). The repentant Russian was all for moving the surviving head with the tongs, to prevent another accident, but I told him to leave it where it bloody was. Lydia said afterwards I'd made a scene, they were just a couple of curios anyway, but I could see him dropping the thing and burning a hole in the kelim.

In the early evening Annie called to say she was working late, she would be home after supper. I decided to surprise her with a welcoming fire. I wanted to initiate Beelzebub and his brother, of course, but the weather was perfect – the first chilly night of the winter. I had logs left over from last winter's municipal pruning and half a bag of anthracite in the garage. I went out to fill the scuttle.

All summer the grate had been piled with pine-cones, put there by Annie in the spring as a scented promise of the next season's fires. I emptied out the cones and cleaned away cobwebs and leaves that had drifted down the chimney. I like to start with a clean slate; I can't understand how people can leave their hearths full of cinders and ash. Lydia used to say all that cleaning was wasted effort, like housework in general and other tidy habits of mind, which were suited to clerks and quantity surveyors and so on but irksome for everyone else. But God forbid one should call her Bohemian.

While I was about it I took a feather-duster to the archangels and rid the wings of cobwebs and the glorioles of dust. For the first time in years I had been reminded that they were not part of the furniture. Lydia fashioned these things, I thought, flicking at well-rounded rumps (a bit like her own) and thick-skinned feet. I wanted her to take them with her when she moved out, but she was adamant that they belonged where they were. Even if she could find a fire-place somewhere else with an arch like this one, of just this curve, which was highly unlikely, it wouldn't be right to resettle the angels when she had made them for here. I believe she said they were "site-specific." Exactly the sort of claptrap that made her impossible to live with.

I stood the devils on the hearth. You could see the family resemblance now with the angels above. They were created to the same scale, for one thing. But they were uglier, coarser, cheaper; poor relations, you could say. I speared a firelighter on each tine and rested a few logs between the two forks. The logs were a stroke of good fortune, much more aesthetically pleasing than splintery pine from the corner cafe. A couple of cones as a finishing touch, a sprinkling of anthracite, and the inferno was ready to blaze, just as soon as my supper came out of the microwave.

Although I had said I would defer to Lydia's judgement in the matter of the "piece for hearth," as it came to be known, I couldn't stop my literal mind from making a few conceptual leaps of its own. I dreamed up some wonderful schemes, all full of moving parts, by which I mean that they were kinetic.

My favourite was probably the cannon. On one of the empty platforms at the side of my hearth would be an old-fashioned cannon, of the sort you might see at the circus, and on the other a target – perhaps a man in an armchair, reading a book of poems. Cannon and target would be linked by an arc of thin wire, following the graceful curve of the brickwork. But the idea was this: when the fire got hot enough it would ignite some charge in the cannon, propelling a cannonball along the wire track and onto the little man, who would fly into a dozen pieces.

When I imagined this I always pictured the fireside dozers – invariably Lydia's friends, the movers and shakers – jolting in their chairs and spilling their sherry.

Then there was the tightrope walker. He would be standing on one of the platforms, and a high wire – which was actually a tube – would stretch to the other. This time the mechanism was hydraulic: the warmth of the fire would heat the liquid in the tube and bear the tightrope walker slowly aloft. It might take an hour for him to reach the apex, but then gravity would carry him headlong down the other side, and he would strike his skull against a gong. Consternation among the nodders!

There were others, variations on a theme, conversation pieces to kill conversation, all equally impractical: the runaway train, the test-your-strength machine, William Tell's cousin Gottlieb.

Lydia was dismissive. "Typical man. Engines and toys, and all so violent – and phallic."

That was another thing about Lydia: no sense of humour.

It needs something sculptural, she said seriously (as if I didn't know), I've had a few ideas.

She wouldn't let me see the "piece for hearth" until it was finished. Then a fellow sculptor – that sculptor fellow Barry, I called him – helped her to cart it over from the studio on the back of his bakkie and install it. There was an unveiling with a bath towel.

It was an arc of fairies.

Not fairies, she said crossly. Angels.

Angels were all the rage at the time, thanks to some film, I believe.

You could get them on wrapping-paper and bathroom decorations and so on. The Christmas before, one of the painters had given Lydia a coffee-table book on the subject.

Lydia's angels rose in a solid curving column, as if they had been sucked out of the ether by the breath of God (Justin said). A squirming mass of angel-flesh, I said. They were clinging to one another like soccer players after one of them has scored a goal. At either end of the arc was a puff of cumulus which doubled as a plinth and was secured to the tiles. Two very muscular angels supported the entire structure, like the anchormen in an acrobatic team, standing ankle-deep in the clouds. Most of the others were grappling one another, but here and there an individual, held in place by his fellows, had both hands free for clasping in prayer or playing the harp. Lydia insisted that they were dulcimers, although there was no sign of a hammer anywhere.

The friends were very complimentary. They said the angels seemed to be dancing over the flames, treading air, warming their soles. Frank, who was specializing in the history of art, said that the over-scaled feet were a marvellously parodic reference to the township style.

Lydia said the major references were Italian.

Michelangelo, I said, naturally.

Raphael, actually.

Très quattrocento, Karen said.

Personally, I thought they were too well-fed to be angelic, like art-school types got up as saints. But then Lydia always said I didn't understand how things worked – anything important, that is, the soft, human things, as opposed to the hard facts and figures.

In the end the archangels (my joke) did much to deepen my appreciation of the arts. I spent hours at a stretch, with my feet on the fender, gazing at their robust limbs and cheery faces, until they were as familiar to me as people I knew. There was the Archangel Barry, for instance, strumming something jazzy on the harp, and the Archangel Justin with his hand up the vestments of his celestial neighbour.

It was to be expected, I suppose, after the commercial success of the heavenly host, that devils would come back into fashion too.

I took my dinner to the lounge and put a match to the pyre. I half-expected some practical joke of the kind I might have dreamed up myself: the devils would drop their forks, or the puppy-dogs from hell would lift a leg and douse the fire. Once a squealing of sap in the wood seemed to issue from a dog's mouth, but the illusion quickly passed. They just stood there, with the fire blazing all around them.

When the logs were whole, and the flames were leaping up into the flue, my devils were majestic. Holding the conflagration up above their heads, they lost the taint of pantomime and looked almost biblical. But as the logs caved in on them, and I had to shovel on more anthracite, the devils' gloom returned. When you took a good look at them, they were seedy, unshaven, unfit, like dried-out old soaks, with hollow cheeks and maudlin eyes, thickening middles and stubby horns butting the air, ash mounting around their ankles. It really made you wish that they'd do something, flick their tails, or curse, or spit. Their acquiescence in these domestic duties was shameful.

Don't you want to do something with your life? Lydia used to ask, just to annoy me. Don't you have a sense of adventure?

I decided to renounce them, to deny their origins; it was too complicated to start explaining about Lydia now. I would tell Annie I had picked them up in a second-hand shop.

Better get rid of the evidence. I tore off the lid of the box and threw it on the fire. Then I tossed in a handful of the polystyrene but it let off such a noxious reek I went to dispose of the rest in the outside bin. When I up-ended the box a postcard drifted out. Cézanne's *Still Life with Apples and Oranges*, according to the useful caption. And on the back that familiar, creatively illegible scribble.

Dear Duncan,

What's it like living in Gauteng? Paris is wonderful. I really feel at home here, if you know what I mean. There's so much happening

– movies, exhibitions, music – you don't really know where to start. Yesterday I was at the D'Orsay (to look at their Rodins) but I saw this too, which you might like. You would definitely like the museum – it used to be a railway station. Excuse my scrawl, I'm writing this on the train. I still think Jo'burg would be better if it had a metro. And I don't want to hear about the unstable dolomite or whatever. Anyway, these are for those cold Highveld nights (I'll leave you to figure out what they are). I hope they remind you of the old days.

Always,
Lydia

Busy, busy, busy. So busy she hadn't even bothered to check whether I was still at the same address. I tore the cardboard box into small pieces and fed it to the fire.

Mercifully, the explosive mechanism of Lydia's departure has vanished almost entirely from my memory. But I remember as if it were yesterday the melodramatics with Justin which primed it. It was at this very fireside. Lydia had invited Justin and Barry and Karen and so on to a poetry evening. Justin read some of his poems, odious things about silky – or was it milky? – thighs and tonguetips in navels, all made for Lydia's exquisite ears.

I don't know anything about poetry, but I engaged him on the veracity of some anatomical detail. He was quite put out.

Lydia was embarrassed. It's a poem Duncan, she said to me, not a medical journal. You have to use your imagination.

So then I said that poetry was a dead art. Who bought the stuff anyway? You're history, I said (meaning poets in general).

What would you know about books? Justin said.

Very little, I said. But who cares? The book has been superseded by the computer.

That always gets to them.

Your problem – the friends had never diagnosed me before, although Lydia had set a fine example – your problem is you don't understand the difference between an object and a device. I could tell Justin was very angry because he began to speak with a peculiar Slavic intonation. He seized a book from the mantelpiece – it was some Folio Society thing in a slip case, which suited his argument rather well – and waved it at me. This is an object, an artefact, not a bunch of dots and dashes on a screen. There's a difference between turning a page and pressing a button you know. There was a lot more about the differences between paper and silicon, appreciation and consumption, sensuousness and sensory abasement, but I soon lost track. Then he looped back to his own poems and enduring values.

Enough is enough. The folder containing Justin's poems was lying on the coffee-table next to my chair and a devilish impulse made me pick it up and throw it into the fire.

How I wish I could let that stand, that I'd actually done it. But I did not. Whether it was a failure of the imagination or a victory for common decency I cannot say. Lydia always said I had no imagination; but then didn't she also say I was a decent sort? Wasn't that one of the things she saw in me? Wasn't that what she said she saw in me when they asked? Anyway, I hesitated and was lost. Justin snatched the folder out of my hand and threw it into the flames himself. I should think it was the most Russian thing he'd done since blowing up the curio; he was quite overcome by himself. Barry or someone tried to rescue the pages with the tongs, while Lydia clapped her hands.

It only occurred to me later that the little poseur probably had carbon copies at home. Or in his head (he set so much store by recitation).

Later on, when everyone had gone home, Lydia and I sat by the fire, not talking, just feeling silly, the way people do when they've behaved like characters in books. The object Justin had waved at me was on the couch, and she tipped it from its case and leafed through it, running her fingers over the paper as if to demonstrate a point about literature which I did not grasp, and then fell asleep with it open on her chest. I should have checked to see what it was. She took the better books with her when she moved out, and left me the "manuals."

Annie came in at ten and woke me up by putting her cold knuckles against my neck. The fire was dead, the surprise spoilt. She said it was cosy anyway, she'd get it going again in a minute. I went to the kitchen to put on the kettle and heard her exclaiming over the firedogs.

I bought them at that place in Queen Street, I lied. They go with the angels.

They're cute.

I heard her scrabbling in the scuttle. Did you finish the firelighters? Use a cone.

I can't get it to catch. Won't you bring some paper with you when you come.

The newspaper rack was empty. I took the *Times* from under the cat food.

The devils looked even more pathetic now, knee-deep in ashes. The toy poms had vanished entirely under the debris.

I took the poker from her and raked over the coals, crumpled the front page into a ball and tossed it on top. As the paper blackened and curled, the corners of my mind darkened too. The Truth Commission. The very idea filled me with dread. Not because I personally had anything to hide, but because the exercise was bound to be so repetitive. They would be digging over our sorry history, dragging things to the surface, corpses, crimes, injustices, everything that had been buried and could stay that way as far as I was concerned. Why was everyone so obsessed with the past? Why did time pass in the first place if not to conceal from us our own unpleasantness? Now the scar tissue would be torn off in the name of healing and the guilty secrets excised and hauled out into the light. We would have to go over it again, the killing, the stealing, the lying, the whole list of broken commandments.

You know, Duncs, they remind me of you.

What's that?

The firedogs. They remind me of you.

At least Annie has a sense of humour.

I'm being serious. She leaned closer to the hearth as the paper flared. How odd, they actually look like you. Is that why you bought them?

Who was I to argue?

Acknowledgements

Some of these stories first appeared in *English Academy Review, New Contrast, Sesame, Staffrider, Stet, TriQuarterly, World Literature Today* and in the anthology *Obsession*, edited by Sarah LeFanu and Stephen Hayward (Serpent's Tail, 1995).

Part III of "Propaganda by Monuments" draws on A. Lunacharski, "Lenin and Art," in *International Literature*, No. 5, 1935. "Isle of Capri" words and music by Jimmy Kennedy/Wilhelm Grosz © 1934, KPM EMI administered by Gallo Music Publishers (SAMRO), all rights reserved – used with permission. The description of marine grottoes is from *Italy*, edited by Doré Ogrizek (McGraw-Hill, 1950). "The Book Lover" quotes from Barbara Cartland's *A Ghost in Monte Carlo* (Rich and Cowan, 1951) with the kind permission of Ian McCorquodale. The same story borrows from the publishers' blurbs for *Naught for your Comfort* by Trevor Huddleston (HarperCollins) and *The Burning Man* by Sarah Gertrude Millin (Heinemann).

archipelago books

is a not-for-profit literary press devoted to
promoting cross-cultural exchange through innovative
classic and contemporary international literature
www.archipelagobooks.org